Mercer touched the goblet and shook his head. "Crazy, isn't it, what some people will kill for?"

It took a long moment for his words to sink in.

"Kill for?" Amanda straightened up slowly, her hands gripping the edge of the counter. "You think someone killed Derek for this?"

"Someone might have." He gazed down at her, his expression unreadable. "Let's start with you, Ms. Crosby."

"Me?"

"You have to admit, you make a really good suspect." His dark eyes studied her carefully.

"Mr. England just spent your cash cushion on a piece of stolen pottery that you're going to have to send back, which puts you out a great deal of money."

"That's absurd."

"And then there's this little matter. . . ."

From his pocket he withdrew a cell phone. Amanda recognized it as Derek's. Mercer scrolled down the screen, then pushed a button. He needn't have bothered. Amanda knew full well what the message was.

"Derek, you are so dead. If you have any sense at all, you'll stay in Italy, because the minute I see you, I am going to kill you."

Mercer turned off the phone. "Do I need to play it again?"

Also by Mariah Stewart:

DEAD WRONG
UNTIL DARK
THE PRESIDENT'S DAUGHTER

MARIAH STEWART

DEAD CERTAIN

BALLANTINE BOOKS • NEW YORK

This is a work of fiction. Names, characters, places, and incidents are the products of the author's imagination or are used fictitiously. Any resemblance to actual events, locales, or persons, living or dead, is entirely coincidental.

A Ballantine Book
Published by The Random House Publishing Group
Copyright © 2004 by Marti Robb
Excerpt from *Dead Wrong* copyright © 2004 by Marti Robb

This book contains an excerpt from the forthcoming book *Dead Wrong* by Mariah Stewart. This excerpt has been set for this edition only and may not reflect the final content of the forthcoming edition.

www.ballantinebooks.com

ISBN 0-345-46393-5

Manufactured in the United States of America

First Edition: July 2004

OPM 10 9 8 7 6 5 4 3 2 1

*For Saint Loretta the Divine—
with love and thanks.*

"Judgment for an evil thing is many times delayed some day or two, some century or two, but it is sure as life, sure as death."
—THOMAS CARLYLE

PROLOGUE

February 2004

JEEZ, BUT HE HATED THIS WEATHER. HATED THE WAY the sleet hissed against the window like a big old nasty snake. Hated the way the wind blew, sharp-edged and cold, across the courtyard behind the large stone building where the prison van had stopped to let its passengers out. They'd dropped awkwardly from the side door of the van as custody passed from the deputy sheriffs who'd ridden in with them to the ones who'd drawn courthouse duty that day, and the wind had bitten right through his jacket as if it had fangs.

Three other inmates had made the trip into court with him. A rangy kid who was all arms and legs, acne scars and attitude, a tall quiet man with long fingers and a steady stare, and the whackjob from the next cell block who called himself Dillinger, even though everyone in the prison knew his name was Waldo Scott. A rumor had floated through clandestine channels out at High Meadow, the county prison, that Waldo was going to try to escape this morning.

Vince Giordano was hoping the rumor was true, if for no other reason than to see how he did it and if he'd be successful. Life held so few true amusements these days.

Besides, the guys in his cell block had a pool going.

Giordano had put his money on the law, which was not necessarily a true assessment of his faith in the abilities of the local sheriff's department. He'd been in and out of the courthouse for more days than he could count between hearings and pretrials, and then finally during the trial itself, followed by a round of appeals. All in all, he figured he'd spent, on average, almost one day in court for every five days he'd spent in High Meadow. He'd gotten to know most of the deputy sheriffs pretty well and hadn't been much impressed with any of them. Barney Fifes, they called them back at the prison. Barney Fifes in dull olive green uniforms, and about as effective as the hapless television deputy.

But still, Giordano figured, Waldo didn't stand a prayer of escaping for good. There just weren't enough places to hide in the old building. The best Waldo could hope for, as Giordano had bet the guy in the next cell earlier that morning, was a few hours of sport while local law enforcement agencies hunted him down.

Giordano shifted in his seat in the small anteroom off courtroom number seven and awaited the arrival of his attorney. Harry Matusek had been expensive, but he'd lived up to his reputation as one of the county's best criminal defense attorneys. Personally, Vince thought he'd been worth every penny and hadn't regretted for a minute that he'd sold his house to finance his defense.

What did he need a house for, anyway? He had no

family to speak of. He'd personally seen to that on one hot day in July going on three years now.

"Giordano?" The young deputy sheriff poked his head in the door.

Vince shifted only his eyes to look up. He'd seen someone do that in a movie once, and it had made a big impression on him, because it had made the actor appear sinister and cool. He mimicked the move as often as he could.

"There's going to be a little delay this morning," the deputy began, then turned his head as someone spoke to him from beyond the door, someone Vince could not see. "Ah, I'll be right back. . . ." The door closed with a sharp click.

Vince leaned back against the hard chair, wondering what was going on out there in the hallway. There seemed to be a great deal of activity for so early in the morning. He strained to sit up as tall as his shackles would permit, trying to see what was happening.

Shouts. Running feet slapped the tile floor as they shot past the room. More shouts. More running feet.

Vince smiled. Old Waldo must have made his break. He wondered how long it would be before they'd catch him. He made a mental bet with himself that Waldo would be back in leg irons before noon. What that would do to Vince's business in court that morning remained to be seen. On the one hand, he resented that Waldo's little escapade was eating into his personal time. On the other, he applauded the defiance and initiative shown by the old man—Waldo was in his sixties—and thought that any chase he'd lead the locals on was bound to be a merry one. He decided he wouldn't begrudge Waldo his bit of fun.

Vince was wondering idly if the deputies would shoot Waldo when they found him, when the door opened and a young man in irons much like Vince's own was shown into the room by the deputy sheriff Vince always thought of as Deputy Dawg, due to his long face that reminded Vince of a basset hound.

"A little company for you this morning," Deputy Dawg announced as he pointed to a chair along the wall, and the newcomer took it without a word. The guard promptly snapped the handcuffs to the metal arm.

"Don't remember asking for company." Vince did the eye thing again because he knew it always rattled Dawg a bit.

"Don't remember asking if you cared." Dawg closed the door behind him.

"What do you think is going on out there?" the young man whom Vince recognized from the trip in from the prison asked excitedly.

"What *is* going on out there?"

"Lots of cops. *Lots* of cops. A coupla different departments and some state troopers. People running every which way."

"My guess is that someone might have escaped from custody." Vince stroked his chin thoughtfully, thinking it made him look wise.

"Really? You think someone's on the run? Someone from High Meadow?" The young man's eyes widened even more.

"You were in the van this morning."

The young man nodded.

"Me, too," Vince told him. "Me and Waldo—the guy who, I suspect, is on the run out there—we were in max together. There was a rumor that he might decide to fly."

Vince smiled. Not to make the boy—who couldn't have been twenty years old—feel at ease, but to make him understand that he was in the presence of a *bad dude*. It gave Vince the only pleasure he'd had in days.

"You think he'll get away with it?"

Vince pretended to ponder the question, but before he could speak, the door opened and another prisoner was ushered into the room.

"Here you go, boys," another deputy sheriff said. "Got another roommate for you."

The seated men watched as the prisoner shuffled in. Tall and slender, he looked to be in his mid-thirties. He wore his brown hair in a crew cut and had the air of one who was vastly amused. He'd been the fourth prisoner in the van earlier that morning. Vince recalled that he'd sat all the way in the back of the van and had not bothered to make eye contact with any of the others.

The deputy secured the new man's cuffs to his chair before admonishing the prisoners to behave and reminding them as he left the room that a guard would be right outside the door. "He's armed and he won't hesitate for one second to bring you down if you so much as move."

"A bit heavy-handed, wouldn't you say?" the newcomer remarked lightly after the door shut.

"He's just trying to scare us." Giordano shrugged, then added his take on the marksmanship of the local sheriff's department: "They ain't that good."

"Been here before?" the new man asked.

Giordano admitted that he'd spent a fair amount of time here.

The young man was beginning to get restless, squirming in his seat. "What d'ya suppose they're doing out there?"

"I told you, they're playing Where's Waldo?" Giordano turned to the man seated near the windows. "Waldo Scott. He rode in the prison van with us this morning. He got himself free somehow and took off." Giordano looked back at the younger guy. "Get it? Where's Waldo?"

"No." The young prisoner shook his head, and the two older men tried to explain about the guy in the books with the red-and-white-striped shirt or hat— neither seemed to remember quite which—who you had to follow from page to page and find in each picture.

The trio determined that the courthouse was now on lockdown while all available law enforcement personnel searched for the escapee. Which would explain why the three of them had been placed in a room together rather than in separate rooms with a guard at each door. All deputies would be needed to join in the search, and someone apparently felt that the three prisoners could safely share temporary quarters. None of the three had exhibited violent tendencies while incarcerated, and shackled as they were, none were likely to attempt to follow Waldo's lead and make a break for it.

"What're you in for?" Giordano asked, nodding toward the latest to join them.

"I was stopped for going through a stop sign—"

"Now there's a manly crime," Giordano scoffed, and made some crack about the need for the leg irons.

"—and it turns out there was an outstanding warrant for a guy with the same name. You?" the man asked.

"I'm in here pending appeal of a conviction," Giordano told them.

The youngest of the three finally spoke up. "For what?"

"A domestic dispute," Giordano said dryly.

The kid took the opportunity to whine about how he was supposed to have a trial today and how Waldo might be screwing things up for him. He was beginning to get on Giordano's nerves.

"What are the charges?" the man with the crew cut asked the boy.

"Well, see, they're saying that I stalked this girl. But I didn't stalk nobody," he protested. To Giordano's ears, it was nothing but more whine, whine, whine. "She was my girl, you know? They got the whole thing wrong."

"She must have complained about something for them to charge you with stalking," the third man noted. "What did she tell the police?"

"She was confused. The cops made her lie." The kid was protesting and rambling on about how the whole thing was a misunderstanding and growing more and more agitated all the time.

"What's your name, son?"

Giordano could have gagged. Was this guy for real? Who gave a shit what the kid's name was? Both of his "roommates" were starting to annoy him big-time, and he found himself grateful that by some stroke of luck, he'd never come in contact with either one of them before.

"Archer Lowell," the kid was saying.

What the hell kind of name was Archer? Giordano mentally sneered. In his neighborhood, the guys were Vic and Frankie and Tony—maybe an occasional Vito or Ralphie—but Archer?

Please.

"I'm Curtis Channing," the third man introduced himself.

"Well, Archie—" Giordano began.

"Don't call me Archie," the kid snapped. "Do not ever call me Archie."

"Whoa, buddy. Chill." Giordano tried to keep from grinning, understanding the need to keep the kid from bringing a potentially wary guard to the door. The shouts outside the door had continued, and it was clear that the search was ongoing. Some deputies' nerves might be getting frayed about now, and Vince saw no reason to invite trouble. Better to placate the kid—as much as he hated to—if for no other reason than to keep him quiet. "No offense. No need to get all upset."

"I hate the name Archie," the kid grumbled.

Giordano wanted to laugh. *Smartest thing you've said since you came in here. . . .*

Instead, he said, "Okay, then. You're Archer, and I'm Vince Giordano. I was named for my uncle, Vincenzo, but I'm Vince, since Vincenzo and me don't speak no more. Bastard testified against me in court. So much for blood being thicker than water."

Bastard, indeed. Uncle Vinnie had taken the stand and sat right there, fifteen feet away from him, and wept as he told the judge and jury that he'd seen with his own eyes how his nephew Vincent had smacked his wife around, had smacked his kids around, and that he, Vincenzo, had taken no steps to stop him. A regret he'd take to his grave, he'd said. *Bastard.*

Giordano looked up and realized that the kid, Archer, was staring at him.

"I know who you are," the kid said in a hushed voice. "I saw you on all the news channels. I saw when you were arrested."

"Yeah, well, I got a lot of press," Giordano acknowledged, secretly pleased to have been recognized. He was, after all, a local celebrity of sorts. "The trial got a lot of airtime."

Giordano could tell that Channing wanted to ask about that, but didn't. Instead, they talked quietly about the lockdown and the amount of press that was outside to cover the day's events. Channing, being closest to the window, could monitor the media activity on the courthouse lawn.

"I don't think it's fair that I should miss my trial just because they lost someone and can't find him." Lowell was whining again, and for two cents, Giordano would have taken him out, right then and there, had he been able to.

Giordano expressed his annoyance with a look that sent the kid shivering, and then told them, "I ain't too happy about the delay, myself. We had a big day planned here. My attorney thinks he can get my conviction overturned."

"What were you convicted of?" Channing asked.

"Shooting my wife, among other things." Giordano

watched Channing's face for a reaction. There was none.

"Did you?" Channing raised one eyebrow only slightly.

Giordano smirked.

Channing appeared to take that for a silent admission.

"Why would they overturn your conviction?" Channing asked curiously.

"Because the cop who testified against me—the cop who provided all the evidence against me—lied, and everyone connected with the investigation knows that the cop lied." *Smug little bastard. Thought he'd put a noose around my neck? He did me the biggest favor of my life, and the stupid shit will have to live with that the rest of his life—that his lies set me free.*

"They can let you off for that? If somebody lies?" The kid was all ears now, his personal whine-fest over for the time being.

"Yup."

"But don't they just try you all over again?" Lowell asked.

"Nope. My lawyer says they don't have enough untainted evidence to make a jaywalking conviction stick. First time around, the D.A. loaded the charges against me. Tried me for everything he could think of. All those charges were based on the testimony of this one cop. And he lied. Everything he said, all the shit he said at the trial, he made up. My attorney later proved it was all lies, and then the cop had to admit that he'd made it all up. They're gonna have to let me out. My lawyer says any day now."

Giordano closed his eyes and recalled with sheer

joy the look on the D.A.'s face when Matusek had stood up in court at the sentencing hearing and announced that he had proof that Police Officer Bill Caruso had planted evidence and lied through his teeth and that he, Matusek, had a witness who would testify under oath that Caruso had admitted doing so to make sure that Giordano got the maximum sentence allowable by law for having murdered his wife and his two sons in cold blood.

Who's sorry now, Billy boy?

"What's the first thing you're gonna do when you get out, Vince?" the kid was asking.

"Depends on whether or not I'd get caught." Giordano laughed.

"What if you wouldn't?"

"What, wouldn't get caught?"

"Yeah. What if you could do anything—anything at all—and not get caught." Lowell watched him intently.

"Gotta think on that a minute."

"Think of three." Lowell egged him on. "Let's each think of three we'd do if we knew we wouldn't get caught."

Three? And if he knew he would never get caught? Jeez, there were so many. . . .

Ha. There was Uncle Vinnie, but he was on his last leg anyway with lung cancer, which couldn't do its job fast enough as far as Vince was concerned. And then there were all the members of his family who had turned away from him after he'd been arrested. His mother—his own mother—had disowned him, but he couldn't very well whack his mother. What kind of a man would do a thing like that?

"If I could get away with it, I'd put a bullet through the head of my former mother-in-law. And then I'd do that woman—the advocate—who worked for the courts and told the judge to take my kids away from me. And then the judge who said I couldn't see my kids no more."

Giordano hadn't been aware that he'd spoken aloud. For the briefest of moments, he'd been revisited by those choking black emotions that had all but swallowed him whole that day he'd walked into the house he'd shared with Diane—that ungrateful little bitch—and done what any real man would have done under the circumstances.

No one takes what's mine. No one. Not my wife, not the court. And no judge—no one—can tell me I can't see my kids.

The words he'd shouted across the courtroom at the custody hearing rang in his ears. They'd earned him forty-eight hours in the county prison and a protection from abuse order for Diane. Like a piece of paper could stop Vince Giordano from doing what had to be done.

Giordano squeezed his eyes tightly shut for a moment, pushed his words back into one of those deep holes inside. Pushed it all away. Brought himself back to this place, this time.

"Where are your kids now?" Channing was asking in a way that hinted that he might have already guessed.

"They're with their mother." Giordano met Channing's eyes and dared him to comment.

Channing wisely declined.

"How 'bout you, Archer? What would you do, if you

could do anything and not get caught doing it?" Giordano asked calmly. "You get three, too, remember."

"I don't know," the kid said. He appeared to be giving the question a great deal of thought. "Maybe . . . I don't know, maybe that guy, that guy who kept bothering my girl. Maybe him, if he's still around. And maybe that neighbor of hers, that nosy bitch."

Archer's anger was building. Giordano wondered what would happen if it peaked.

"What about your girl?" Giordano asked to see how far the kid's anger could be stoked. "Seems like she's the real problem here. She's the one who called the cops on you. Seems like you'd want to be calling on her. I know I would."

"Oh, I'm gonna call on her, all right. I'm gonna call on her first thing I get out of here." Archer's rage had him tottering on the edge, and Giordano—no stranger to rage himself—sensed that it would take little to push him over.

Rather than push the kid—though it could be fun watching him lose control while chained to a chair—Giordano turned to the room's other occupant.

"What 'bout you, Channing? Three you'd go see?"

"Don't know, Vince." Channing shrugged.

"Oh, that's right." Giordano nodded. "You're in here because of mistaken identity. After being picked up for a traffic violation. Guess the first guy you'd be going to see is that *other* Curtis Channing. Then maybe the cop who arrested you—"

Channing laughed out loud.

"Hey, Curtis, we're just bullshittin' here. There has to be someone, some place, who you'd like to show a thing or two." Giordano watched Channing's face, knew instinctively that this man had seen dark places, too. There was no mistaking what he was beginning to recognize behind the eyes of Curtis Channing.

"Hmm, three people from my past . . . Well, I guess I'd make a stop at my stepfather's. He wasn't really my stepfather—he and my mother never were married. But him, yeah. I'd want to see him."

"That can't be all." Giordano urged him on.

"There's a writer I wouldn't mind having a chat with." Channing was nodding almost imperceptibly.

Strange, Giordano thought, wondering what kind of writer would draw the attention of a man such as Channing. He'd love to find out.

"That's only two," Archer noted. "You got one more."

"Well, there's a cute little FBI agent who I'd like to see again." Channing smiled enigmatically. "Just to see if the chemistry is still the same."

FBI? Giordano was even further intrigued. For a man who'd only broken a minor traffic law, Channing certainly had an interesting agenda.

"Course, if we really did these things, if we really ever did go see 'em and . . . well, you know, *did* 'em . . . it isn't like the cops wouldn't know who to look for, you know?" Archer whispered. "Like, Vince, they find your mother-in-law with a bullet in her head after you get out? The cops'll be like, *Duh. Wonder who did her?*"

"Well, it was just talk. Didn't mean nothing," Giordano assured him. Christ, what was he thinking, talking like that in front of two strangers? How did he know that one—or both of them—weren't plants from the D.A.'s office to trip him up? Wouldn't that be just swell?

"Unless we, like, you know, switch our people," Archer said.

"What d'ya mean, switch our people?" Giordano studied the younger man. What was this kid *talking* about?

"You know, like that movie. The one on the train, where these two guys meet and they each agree to whack someone that the other one wants dead—"

"Whoa, buddy. This was just idle talk. That's all. Just idle talk. No one said nothing about whacking anyone for real." Even as he protested, Giordano knew that Archer wasn't a plant from anywhere. He was every bit as dumb as he looked—Vince would bet his life on it.

He wondered if perhaps he just had.

"Sure, it's just talk. I know that. But it doesn't hurt to pretend. We got nothing else to do in here right now." Archer Lowell's face was as blank as a clean sheet of paper.

"How old are you, Lowell?" Giordano just had to know if the kid was young and stupid, or just stupid.

"I'm nineteen."

"That explains it."

"Explains what?"

"Your loose mouth, that's what." Giordano felt his anger start to rise.

"No, come on. It's just a game. A game, that's all." Lowell sought to placate him.

"You ever kill anyone, Lowell?" Giordano lowered his voice to ask.

The kid shook his head.

"You, Channing?" Giordano turned to face him and was stunned by what he saw in Channing's eyes. At that moment, he recognized Channing for exactly what he was, and a chill sped up Giordano's spine.

Lowell hadn't even noticed. "If we were going to play the game, then we would each have a list, and we would each promise to do the other's list when we got out, right?"

Relaxed now—there was no plant here; he was positive of that—Giordano laughed. "Boy, you don't give up, do you?"

"First, we'd have to decide how to figure out who would, you know, do whose people." Lowell paused to ponder this for a minute, then perked up. "I know. We could each pick a number between one and thirty and guess which number the other guy is thinking of."

Giordano laughed again. The kid was so earnestly getting into this. It was silly and immature, and he was wondering just what Mr. Cool Curtis Channing was thinking.

"Okay, you, Channing, you go first." Lowell grinned. "Think of a number between one and thirty, and me and Vince will see if we can guess. Whoever comes closest to your number gets your list."

To Giordano's surprise, Channing merely smiled and nodded. "Let's keep it simple. Archer takes my list, I'll take yours, Giordano, and you'll take Archer's."

"Cool." Archer Lowell nodded with such vigor that Giordano felt it necessary to remind the kid—and anyone who could be listening in—that this was not real.

"It's just a game, Archer. Just a game," Giordano said carefully. What if the room *was* wired? "Just a game."

"I know that." Lowell brushed him off happily and, grinning, turned to Curtis Channing. "Okay, tell us about your list, Channing. Tell me about who I'd be going to see."

"I think we should lower our voices. Just in case someone is listening. Even though it's just a game . . . and none of this is ever going to happen." Giordano leaned forward as far as he could.

The kid's eyes were glowing like a child's on Christmas morning. "Right, right. Sure. None of this is ever going to really happen. . . ."

Channing took the lead and began to speak softly.

The game had begun.

CHAPTER ONE

"I'm going to kill him. I swear, the minute his plane lands, I will kill him."

Amanda Crosby glared at the screen of the laptop that sat open on the cluttered counter near the door of Crosby & England, the antiques shop she co-owned with Derek England, the subject of her wrath.

"Is she sure? Is your sister positive it's the same piece?" Amanda closed her eyes and silently begged, *Please, please, let it not be the same piece. . . .* "Isn't there any chance she's mistaken?"

"Daria is positive the goblet in the photos we emailed to her yesterday is the same one that's on the list of items stolen from an Iranian museum some years ago. You read her reply yourself." Iona McGowan, Amanda's longtime friend and onetime college roommate, hit the print command and watched as the color image emerged through the printer accompanied by the email from Iona's sister.

Amanda read the email out loud glumly. " 'The goblet is in the stylized design of the finely painted pottery found at the Tell i Bakun site in southern Iran. Probably dates from 5 B.C. The mouflon horns are pretty typical of the time period and the culture. This piece would be especially prized and noteworthy because of its near-pristine condition, the vividness of the colors, the quality of the painted design work. I'm sorry, but there is absolutely no question that this piece could only have been bought on the black market.' " Amanda shook her head. "And I guess your sister would know."

"Daria is an internationally recognized expert in the field. Which is why you wanted to consult with her in the first place," Iona reminded her. She started to close out the window on the screen, but paused to ask, "Are we finished here?"

Amanda nodded in disgust and turned away from the counter. "Damn Derek anyway. *Damn* him. I told him not to buy anything on this trip, and to cover his eyes and ears if anyone offered to show him anything that couldn't be completely and thoroughly documented. I told him to run like hell the minute someone whispered, 'American, I have something special for you.' " Amanda continued to steam. "The business just can't afford to absorb this hit. I don't know how we're going to make up this loss."

"Look, Daria said there's a reward—"

"Which would just barely pay to send the damned thing to her, by the time we have it securely packed and insured and hire a courier to hand deliver it so that Derek doesn't get arrested for dealing in stolen antiquities." She blew out a hot, angry breath. "He has no idea how lucky he is that she's willing to help him out on this. I'm sorely tempted to let Interpol arrest him and be done with it."

"You know as well as I do that Interpol is hardly likely to waste its time and limited resources pursuing this one item. Especially since it's being returned to its rightful owner through a reputable archaeologist, which never would have happened if it had fallen into someone else's hands. Besides, you'd never do anything like that—turn your own partner in—no matter how angry you are, and we both know it."

"I don't think we'd want to test that right now."

"Manda, I'm sorry. I really am."

"Not as sorry as Derek is going to be when I get my hands on him."

"I'm sure there's a reasonable explanation. What exactly did he tell you when he called, anyway?"

"Just that he bought what he believed was an important piece, that he already had a buyer for it, and that he was having it shipped home and to watch for it because it was going to knock my socks off. Well, it did that, all right." Amanda slapped a hand on the top of a nearby oak farm table. "God, I could just *kill* him."

"I'm sorry I couldn't have given you better news."

"I appreciate everything you've done. I wouldn't have known what to do with this"—she waved her hand in the vague direction of the goblet—"without Daria's guidance."

"Glad I could help." Iona patted Amanda on the back. "I've got to get back to my shop. I told Carly she could leave early today. Give me a call next weekend. There's going to be an auction up near Pipersville in a few weeks. Maybe we can go together, pick up some goodies."

"Sure. Thanks."

Amanda walked Iona to the door and stepped outside onto the narrow cobbled walk that snaked around the well-manicured greens to tie together tidy shops, restaurants, and parking lots.

"I'll talk to you soon," Iona called over her shoulder before she disappeared around the corner.

Still sick to her stomach after having had her worst fears confirmed, Amanda stood for a few minutes in the doorway, barely noticing the shoppers who walked by. Even on this hot August afternoon, St. Mark's Village had attracted a lively crowd. Springing from a cornfield via the imagination of its founder, Mark Hollender, St. Mark's Village was a popular and pricey assemblage of antiques and specialty shops in Bucks County, Pennsylvania. On weekends such as this, it wasn't unusual to see busloads of visitors from New York, Washington, D.C., or Boston already lined up in the parking lot by nine A.M. for an all-day shopping experience. Not for shoppers faint of heart nor those with light balances in their checking accounts—or credit limits on their plastic—the Shoppes at St. Mark's Village were a tourist attraction for the discriminating.

Amanda Crosby had been one of the original dealers to sign on seven years ago when Mark Hollender had first proposed the idea of a cluster of high-end shops. She'd immediately recognized the advantage of being associated with a group that would be collectively marketed as upscale and high profile. And since most of the dealers specialized in one type of merchandise or another, there was little competition among the ever-growing number of merchants in the ever-enlarging complex. In addition to selling to the private shoppers drawn to the village, there was the profitable secondary market of selling to dealers from other parts of the country who often came east seeking items for their own shops or for special customers. The shop owners at St. Mark's had solid reputations and had networked nicely with their counterparts in other states.

Sighing heavily, Amanda walked back into her shop, pausing to wipe a speck of dust from a piece of art deco pottery on a stand to the left of the door.

"Oh, the hell with it," she muttered, tears stinging her eyes.

All of her hard work down the drain with one stupid purchase on Derek's part.

"Correction," she muttered aloud as she began to repack the pottery goblet as Daria McGowan had instructed. "One *more* stupid purchase on Derek's part."

Over the years, Derek's get-rich-quick schemes had cost him and the shop a tidy penny. This, however, was the worst. The sixty-five thousand dollars Derek had paid for the goblet—the now known to be *hot* goblet—had wiped them out. And if not for Daria's assistance, Derek could very well be a candidate for a nice long chat with Interpol or UNESCO.

Amanda gritted her teeth.

"But, Manda, I have a buyer," he'd assured her. "Don't worry about it, okay? To get his hands on this piece, he'll pay many times what I paid, trust me. I know what I'm doing here."

"No, Derek, you do not know what you're doing. Whatever it is, just let it go. Don't make any deals, don't buy— Derek?"

The line had gone dead, and he'd not called back.

Several days later, the goblet had arrived, and as soon as she unwrapped it, Amanda suspected they were in deep trouble. She'd immediately called Iona,

whose father and sister were well-connected archae-
ologists and who would know how best to deal with
an item one suspected might be stolen *without* getting
arrested in the process.

But, in spite of everything, Amanda did love Derek.
They'd been the best of friends since that day, junior
year in college, they'd discovered they shared a passion for American primitive furniture and art deco
pottery, and a desire to own a high-end antiques shop
someday.

Someday had come three years after they'd graduated from the University of Delaware. With heavy backing from Derek's parents and an equally heavy reliance
on Amanda's antiques training, Crosby & England had
done relatively well—well enough to support themselves, and a little more. They'd finally accumulated
a healthy bank account, thanks to Amanda's shrewd
eye. At a country auction just months earlier, she'd
spotted a set of four cottage chairs that she strongly
suspected might be the work of Samuel Campbell, an
early eighteenth–century furniture maker from west-
ern Pennsylvania who was just coming into vogue.
She'd bought the painted chairs for an astounding
eighty dollars—she'd expected the bidding to start at
ten times that figure—and held on to them for six
months, during which time she was able to confirm
their origin. Then, as Campbell's popularity hit its
stride, she resold the chairs for a tidy eight thousand
dollars each. Thirty-two thousand lovely dollars.
Money she planned to use to move the shop from its
present location at the upper edges of the original village to a more central location closer to Main Street.
Money to purchase more high-end stock . . .

Amanda punched in Derek's number on her cell phone.

"Derek, you are so dead," she hissed through clenched teeth at the *Record Message* prompt. "If you have any sense at all, you'll stay in Italy, because the minute I see you, I am going to kill you."

"Excuse me?" a startled voice from behind her asked.

"Oh." Amanda turned, equally startled. She hit the End Call button and slipped her phone into her pocket. "I'm sorry. I didn't hear you come in."

The well-dressed middle-aged blond woman smiled absently, her eyes scanning the shop's offerings.

"Was there something in particular you were looking for?" Amanda moved the wooden box holding the goblet to a shelf under the counter.

"I was wondering if you had any Weller pottery," the woman said. "My friend bought a vase here a week or so ago and she said you might have some others."

"A tall green vase? Raised dogwood blossoms?"

"Yes."

"Justine Rhodes?"

"Yes, Justine." The woman nodded. "She was showing me just yesterday what she'd bought from you."

"This is such a coincidence." Amanda forced a bright note in her voice. "I was planning on calling Justine in the morning, because I know she has the beginnings of a lovely collection, and I have some new items that just came in. I haven't even unwrapped them yet, and I thought I'd give her first look. But since you're already here, perhaps you'd like to see . . . ?"

The woman beamed.

It was a sure sale, Amanda knew. She'd sized up her customer well. There was no way this woman would leave the shop without purchasing most—if not all—of the new lot, if for no other reason than to be able to tell Justine about her fabulous find.

Amanda opened the first of the boxes she'd brought in from her car just hours earlier and began unwrapping the pottery. While not the most expensive of the potteries she carried, the Weller would bring a good price—maybe even a great price. American art pottery had become increasingly popular over the years, and the pieces she'd managed to get her hands on were far from run-of-the-mill. But there'd still be a long way to go to make up for what Derek's latest lapse of judgment had cost them.

Well, she sighed as she carefully sat a tall pale green vase on the counter, she'd deal with Derek later. Right now she was going to do her best to start making up the deficit. One sale at a time.

"This vase is really spectacular." She slid her glasses on as she slipped into her best sales mode. "It's signed by J. Green, one of Weller's most sought after artists. Now, note the lovely details . . ."

___ CHAPTER ___
TWO

THE ROAD WOUND THROUGH THE NIGHT, FOLLOW-ing the curve of the river. Headlights illuminated no farther than the next slow twist. Amanda hated this dark stretch of road between her home in Broeder, the town that just skirted St. Mark's Village, and the local college, where she had given a lecture that night: How a Stalker Changed My Life—and How to Make Certain It Doesn't Happen to You.

She could never drive this road without remembering those nights more than a year ago when head-lights would appear out of nowhere to blind her in the rearview mirror, making the drive home a night-marish ride into hell.

Her eyes flickered from one mirror to the other, checking behind her. Always checking behind her, even though she knew for a fact that the man who had stalked her for those six terrible weeks last year was safely behind bars. She'd been there on the first day of his trial, fully prepared to testify against him in open court, but at the last minute, his attorney had con-vinced him to accept the deal being offered by the D.A. Eight months in the county prison, three years' probation, and no contact of any kind with his vic-tim. Ever. After what he'd done to Amanda, a jury

would give him way more time behind bars, his attorney had insisted. Her stalker had finally agreed.

But Archer Lowell had gone to prison still not understanding just what exactly he'd done wrong. Amanda
had seen it in his eyes. He had really believed that
they'd shared a special relationship. That his infatua-
tion with her was mutual. That they belonged together, would be together. And God help anyone who
failed to understand that. Including Amanda herself.

She turned into her drive, eyes still drifting to the
dark road that now lay behind her. Of course she
knew she was safe, knew that no one was after her
anymore, but she just couldn't seem to help herself.

In the months since Lowell's trial, Amanda had all
but reinvented herself. The once-timid woman who
had for years made her partner bid for her at auctions
now spoke to women's groups and high school health
classes and the local civic association about how to
recognize when you're being stalked and what to do
about it. She resumed the martial arts classes she'd
taken years ago. She bought herself a gun and learned
how to use it. She met monthly with a group of other
stalking victims and wrote an occasional column called
Warning Signs for a county newspaper. In spite of all
she'd done to make herself strong and confident—
all she'd done to take charge of her life—she just
couldn't seem to break that one habit. She was constantly looking over her shoulder.

She parked her car next to the well-lit walk and
hurried across the cobblestones to the front steps of
her narrow three-story Victorian that had once housed
mill workers.

At her approach, sensors on either side of the porch

activated, and beams of light flooded the entire front of the house. No shadows where someone could hide. No dark places that could conceal someone bent on mischief.

She scooped the mail from the box near the front door, then unlocked the door and stepped into an already brightly lit entrance, glancing at the alarm system that had blown out the fuses in the old house each time she'd attempted to activate it. Timers had turned on lights in the foyer, the living room and the small hall that led back to the kitchen. Her thoughts were still with the group she'd addressed earlier that evening. It was clear to her that at least one—possibly two—of the women in attendance were dealing with unwanted attention. Amanda had made note of their names and would give them a call before the end of the week to see if she could offer some more personal advice.

The flashing red light on the answering machine caught her eye, and she absently hit the play button while she sorted through the mail. The first call was a hang-up, nothing too out of the ordinary. She glanced at the caller ID window. *Unknown number.*

One of those telemarketing thingies that dial your number by computer, most likely. She waited for the second message to begin. More of the same. She really needed to get on the National Do Not Call Registry.

The third began to play. Not an immediate hang-up—heavy breathing this time.

Her hands began to shake.

She placed the mail in a neat stack on the table next to the machine and backed slowly to the stairs, where she sat on the bottom step and forced herself to take a long deep breath.

Of course it's a telemarketer. Or a prankster. A kid's idea of a stupid joke. Not funny. Definitely not funny. But it's not what it had been before. Archer Lowell is in prison and does not have this number. He knows that if he tries to contact me in any way, additional charges will be brought against him, his sentence extended. He agreed to that. This isn't him.

Don't blow this out of proportion, she cautioned herself. *It could be nothing more than a mistake. A misdial. Someone's probably annoyed as hell that he— or she—has gotten the same wrong number three times in a row.*

Amanda stood and started for the kitchen, nearly jumping out of her skin when the phone began to ring again. She leaned against the doorway, holding her breath, waiting for the machine to pick up the call.

"Manda, it's me, Der—"

She grabbed the phone. "Where are you?" she barked into the receiver.

"I'm home. I told you I'd be home on—"

"We need to talk, Derek."

"I know, I know. How about breakfast in the morning? We could meet at that little B and B you love out on the river road, and we could—"

"*Now,* Derek."

"Manda, it's almost eleven, I just got in from an ungodly flight, and—"

"I don't care if you swam home. We have a serious problem. I've had it with this crap, Derek. It's no way to run a respectable business. It's irresponsible, it's—"

His sigh whispered against her ear. "Okay. You're right. Let's get it over with tonight so that we can move on tomorrow." Derek's voice was cheerless and held more than a trace of resignation. "I'll be there in thirty minutes."

"I'll be waiting." Her nerves already on edge from the hang-up calls, Amanda resisted the urge to slam the receiver onto its base.

She went into the kitchen and turned on the light, eyes darting around the room. Nothing amiss.

Tea would soothe, she told herself, and went about the process of filling the teakettle and hunting for the box of Morning Thunder that Derek preferred. Setting out two cups. Slicing lemon. Anything to avoid thinking about what she was going to say to Derek and how she was going to say it.

She still wasn't certain that she wasn't going to tell him it was time to dissolve the partnership. That maybe they both needed to move on. A last resort, to be sure, but exactly what she'd threatened the last time he'd done something stupid that had cost them a lot of money and cast a shadow on their reputation.

The kettle whistled and she turned it off, then looked out the window on the driveway side of the house, expecting Derek's Lexus to pull in at any minute. She glanced at the clock.

11:27. He'd called at 10:42.

She went back to the foyer and separated the junk mail from the bills, read through two department store circulars, and thumbed through a magazine. Gathering the junk pile, she returned to the kitchen and looked up at the clock.

11:43. It had been an hour since Derek called. For Derek, a mere hour late was early.

Regardless of how good his intentions might be, Derek never seemed to manage to get anywhere on time. He was distracted so easily. On the way to his front door, he would pause to rearrange the flowers in a vase on the sideboard as he passed through the dining room. He would turn on a light in the living room and straighten the pillows on the sofa. He might check the mantel for dust, then call up the steps to his long-time companion, Clark Lehmann, to announce that the mantel needed dusting and engage in a discussion over whether the cleaning woman should come two days a week instead of one. He would check the messages on the answering machine and fuss with a pile of magazines.

It drove Amanda insane.

"He could have walked here by now," Amanda grumbled as she reached for the phone on the wall and dialed his cell phone. When there was no answer, she called his home number.

"Clark? Would you please put Derek on the phone?"

Clark paused briefly before asking, "Isn't he there with you?"

"No. Look, I understand why he would rather deal with this in the morning, and at this point we might as well. So just tell him never mind. We'll meet for breakfast, as he'd suggested."

"Amanda, Derek left here right after he spoke with you. Not more than five minutes after he hung up." Clark's voice clouded with uncertainty. "He should have been there a long time ago."

"Well, he's not here. Where could he have stopped between there and here?"

"At this hour on a Monday night? I can't think of any place that's even open around here past ten."

"There's that bar out near Denton Road."

"We haven't gone there in months. He would never go into a place like that alone, and he wouldn't have gone there tonight. He's exhausted from the trip and he wants to get this over."

"Well, maybe he stopped at someone's house."

Clark fell silent, then said, "I guess there's a chance that he could have stopped at David and Robbie's. That's on the way to your place. Though it's unlikely. I mean, it's a weeknight, for crying out loud. You just don't pop in to see someone at eleven-thirty on a weeknight. Of course, there's always the chance that he stopped in the center of town to watch the fountain."

"The fountain?" Amanda frowned.

"Oh, haven't you seen the new fountain in the park? We drove past it today. It's lovely. And Derek did so love the fountains in Italy. . . ." Clark sighed. "I know, I know. He's so damned flighty sometimes. I know it makes you as crazy as it makes me, but he just doesn't seem able to help himself."

"This was important, Clark."

"I know, sweetie. And I know that you just want to kill him sometimes." Clark's voice softened. "Amanda, he's really, really upset over this pottery business."

"As upset as he was last year when he bought that samurai sword?"

"Oh, worse. Much worse. He knows he blew it."

"Big-time. He wiped us out and then some."

"He can make up the cash. You know I'll cover it."

"That's very generous of you, Clark, but you just can't keep bailing him out."

"Of course I can. And I will. Besides, I feel responsible. I'm the one who told Ahmed—"

"Ahmed? Ahmed who?"

"I didn't get his last name."

Amanda rolled her eyes. How stupid do you have to be to buy something in Italy—where so much black-market activity takes place—from a guy who identifies himself only as Ahmed?

"Anyway," Clark continued, "Ahmed had this goblet to sell. I told him Derek was an antiques dealer. I mean, Ahmed was telling me about his business, how he had so many high-end pieces, so of course, I told him about Derek. And, well, one thing just led to another . . ."

"Right. I can see how this happened." This was a lie, and Clark recognized it as such. Amanda would never purchase something without the proper paperwork.

"Just be gentle with him," Clark pleaded. "He knows he's a screwup."

"I'm not making any promises this time. Didn't it occur to him that something like this—buying an unknown piece with no provenance from an unknown source in a foreign country—could land his ass in prison?"

"Oh, God, don't say that."

"Don't either of you realize that dealing in stolen antiquities is a crime?" She ran her fingers through her closely cropped dark hair. "This isn't a matter of

Derek simply being flighty. It's about buying and selling something that was stolen. It's about—"

"We didn't know it was stolen, Manda."

"The authorities may find that very difficult to believe. The piece has absolutely no documentation. No chain of ownership, no record of its excavation."

There was a long silence. Finally, Clark asked in a shaky voice, "Do you really think he—we—could get arrested?"

"I'm doing everything I can to avoid having that happen. I did manage to make contact with someone who is going to do her best to help us. I'm having the piece picked up tomorrow afternoon by courier and delivered to a friend who is in the Middle East right now. She'll return it to the museum she believes it was stolen from."

"Who is this friend? Someone you can trust?"

Swell time to start thinking about who you can trust, she was tempted to say. Biting her tongue, she replied, "Iona McGowan's sister."

"The archaeologist. Yes. Excellent move, Amanda." Clark's mood brightened. "There. See? It's all going to work out."

"With any luck. But there's still the potential damage to our reputation if this ever gets out—after all, this wouldn't be the first black mark on our business—and we're still out sixty-five grand."

"No one is going to know, and I told you, I'll make up the loss. I made a killing in gold futures during last year's boom. It's going to be fine." Clark paused, then added softly, "Just don't hurt him, Manda."

"I'm not making any promises."

"Wait! I have a call waiting coming in. I'll bet it's Derek. Hold on, Amanda."

Amanda paced the length of the small kitchen until Clark came back on the line.

"Was it Derek?" she asked.

"I'm not sure." He sounded confused. "The number came up as Derek's cell, but there was no one on the line. I could hear something, like . . . some sound. Rustling. Weird. I couldn't place it. I said his name over and over, but he didn't answer."

"Look, let's hang up. Maybe he's trying to call you. Maybe his phone battery is low. Maybe he's had a flat or some kind of car trouble, and he's trying to call home. You know how unmechanical Derek is."

"Wouldn't know a chain saw from a jigsaw," Clark agreed. "I'll tell him to come home, that you said tomorrow is soon enough. And thanks, Manda. I love you."

"I love you, too, Clark. I love you both." Amanda added softly, "Welcome home."

An uneasy feeling swept over Amanda as she walked to the front door and peered out. Nothing but darkness all around. The lights on the neighbors' homes had long gone out. Not unusual. Broeder pretty much closed down by ten every night. She opened the front door, stepped onto the small porch, looked out into the pitch-black midnight sky, and thought about what she'd say to Derek over breakfast the next day.

CHAPTER THREE

"MANDA? YOU HAVE TO COME. . . . OH, MY GOD. Please," Clark sobbed into the phone at eight the next morning.

"Clark, what is it? What's happened?" A chill ran up Amanda's spine. "Have you heard from Derek?"

His reply was unintelligible.

"Clark? What's happened?"

"He's dead, Manda. Someone shot him," Clark whispered hoarsely. "Oh, God, someone's killed Derek."

"What?!" She dropped into one of the kitchen chairs.

"Derek is dead. He's been shot. The police found him in his car—"

"Dear God."

"He's dead. Just like that. He's gone."

"Clark, is anyone with you?"

"The police . . . the police . . ." He hiccupped. "Please come. Please."

"I'll be right there."

I don't believe this. I don't believe this. It can't be real. . . .

This can't be happening. How could Derek be dead?

She tried to stand on shaking legs, but finding she could not, sat back down and began to weep great wracking sobs of disbelief. Then, without realizing she was doing so, she gathered her keys and walked out the door, got into her car, and drove. A half-hour later, she was almost startled to find herself parked outside of the house Derek and Clark had shared for several years. She had no recollection of driving.

Still crying, she got out of the car and ran to the front door, barely noticing the police cars that were parked nearby.

"Clark," she called as she let herself in.

"Manda, thank God you're here!" Clark fairly flew from the living room to embrace her, then dissolved into tears all over again. "What am I going to do? What am I going to do . . . ?"

"You're the business partner?" A tall, dark-haired police officer stood as she entered the living room, her shaking arm draped over Clark's shoulder.

"Yes." She sat on the edge of the sofa and guided Clark onto the cushion beside her. "Amanda Crosby."

"Chief Mercer. Broeder Police."

"Of course." She nodded. She'd thought he looked familiar. She'd seen him around town, but she'd had no dealings with him. He'd only been in the job for several months. "Will you tell me what happened?"

"Mr. Lehmann called early this morning to report that Mr. England had gone out last night around eleven. He was on his way to your home, is that correct?"

"Yes."

Clark picked up a needlepoint pillow and crushed it to his narrow chest, seemingly oblivious to the conversation around him.

"Was he in the habit of visiting you at that hour, Ms. Crosby?"

"Generally, no. But he and Clark had been away—"

"Vacationing in Europe."

"Yes, and they just returned yesterday."

"I expect he'd have been tired after that long flight home. Jet lag, and all that. Why would he have wanted to pay a visit so late at night, after such a long, tiring trip? What was so important that it couldn't have waited until this morning?"

"We had some business to discuss."

"Business that couldn't have waited until this morning?"

"He'd been gone for two weeks. We had a lot to catch up on." Amanda searched her pockets for a tissue. Finding one, she wiped the tears from her face.

"So he left here around eleven, but he never arrived at your place?"

"No. He did not."

"Weren't you worried?"

"No, but I was a little pissed off. I thought he'd gotten distracted by something on his way over and just lost track of the time."

"Is this something he did often?"

"Get distracted?" Tears filled her eyes. "At least once a day."

Clark began to sob again, his head in his hands. Amanda rubbed his back to comfort him.

"What sort of things distracted Mr. England?"

"Anything that caught his fancy, really. It's just the way he is. He sees something that interests him, he stops to take a closer look." She wasn't aware that she was speaking of him in the present tense. "He loses track of time. Is late for work. For appointments. For the most part, people forgive him because he's charming."

"So when he didn't show up, you didn't think anything of it."

"Not really. Not at the time, anyway. We—Clark and I—thought maybe he'd stopped off at the home of some friends and maybe they were standing around talking. I told Clark that if he spoke with Derek before I did, to tell him to just go home, that I'd see him in the morning. And I went to bed."

"When did you first become aware that Mr. England did not come home last night?"

"Clark called at one this morning, then again at three and then around five. At that point, I advised him to call the police. He called later to let me know that he'd done just that and that you were looking for Derek's car."

"Was your partner in the habit of picking up hitchhikers?"

"Derek?" She shook her head. "He always said he read too many murder mysteries. He'd never stop for a stranger. Why do you ask?"

"Someone was with him in his car last night."

"How can you be sure?"

"He was shot through the head, Ms. Crosby. From behind. Whoever shot him was in the backseat."

Clark collapsed on the sofa.

"Ms. Crosby?"

Amanda emerged from the back of the shop to find Chief Mercer standing near the door. It was close to two-thirty in the afternoon. When Clark's brother arrived at Clark and Derek's house to provide support, Amanda had taken the opportunity to leave, suddenly needing some time to sort things out and to grieve alone. That apparently wasn't going to happen anytime soon.

"Oh. Hello." She closed the door to her work space behind her. "Do you have any news?"

"Not really." He looked around the shop as if assessing it. "I stopped at your house. I'd assumed you'd be closed for business today. I mean, after your partner being murdered like that . . ."

"I am closed for business," she said stiffly, resenting his assumption. "I just stopped in because I . . . I had to pick up something."

"Got a few minutes? I have a few questions."

"Sure."

"Did your partner have any enemies that you know of?"

"None that I know of."

"Anyone he'd argued with recently?"

"No. Again, though, not that I know of."

"Other than yourself."

"Derek and I were not enemies." She stared up at him. "We've been friends for years, business partners—"

"But I do understand there'd been an argument last night."

Damn Clark.

"Yes, we argued on the phone over a business matter." She kept her voice calm. "It wasn't the first time, and it wouldn't have been the last."

"Mr. Lehmann says your telephone conversation

was quite heated. That Mr. England was quite upset when he left the house."

"I imagine he was." She folded her arms across her chest. "I'd just reamed him out but good. He wasn't looking forward to facing me."

He smiled. Obviously, he knew all about that.

"Look, Derek has—had—a bad habit of making poor decisions. While he was on this trip abroad, he"—she checked herself—"made another one of his poor decisions. He bought something we couldn't afford. It hurt the business. I'm sending the item back. As a matter of fact, the courier should be here any minute. I'm surprised he hasn't been by already."

"Courier?" His eyebrows raised appreciably. "FedEx won't do? Must be something of great value."

She could have kicked herself.

"What's it cost to send something by courier these days, Ms. Crosby? And just where are you sending it back to?"

"What does this have to do with Derek?"

"Who else might have known that Derek brought valuable items home with him from this trip? I'm assuming these items were valuable, if they have to be shipped by courier."

"You mean, could someone have followed him to rob him?" Amanda shook her head. "I don't think he'd have told anyone else. And he didn't buy anything else on this trip that I'm aware of. Just the . . . the one thing. And he had that shipped back. It wasn't with him."

Mercer leaned one hip against the counter. "What was that one thing, by the way?"

"It was a pottery goblet."

"Where is it now?"

"It's in the safe, in the back room."

"May I see it?"

"It's already wrapped and ready for the courier," she protested.

"Well, if you're real careful when you unwrap it, you won't have a problem wrapping it up again."

She glared at him.

"The package, Ms. Crosby."

"Fine. I'll be right back."

"I'll wait."

Damn Derek. Damn Clark. Damn Mercer.

Damn damn damn.

She unlocked the safe and withdrew the crate. Grabbing a screwdriver from a drawer, she went back into the shop. Chief Mercer was staring at a bronze statue of the goddess Diana that was locked inside a glass case.

"Nice." He nodded toward the piece.

"Art deco." She placed the wooden crate on the counter. "It's an original Zelt. Quite exceptional. She did very few pieces in bronze. Seventeen thousand dollars. For you, maybe we could knock off a few bucks."

"I'll get back to you on that." He was all business again. "Now, let's take a look at this piece of pottery that needs such special handling. . . ."

He helped her to painstakingly remove the crate. Inside, another wooden box held yet another. When she finally got to the goblet itself, he stepped back as if to appraise it.

"That's it?" he asked skeptically. "That's the vase you fought with your partner over?"

"Goblet," she corrected. "It's from a site in southern Iran called the Tell i Bakun. Part of an old civilization that—"

"Sorry, but all that means nothing to me."

"Think very, very old and very, very rare." She fought hard against the urge to be sarcastic. "Think civilizations that are no more."

"I'm getting the picture. What's its value?"

"Whatever someone is willing to pay for it."

"What was Derek England willing to pay for it?"

"Sixty-five thousand dollars."

Mercer whistled. "But he must have thought he'd be able to sell it for more than that, though, right?"

"He said he had a buyer who'd pay many times that amount."

"Who was the buyer?"

"I didn't ask."

"Any particular reason why not?"

"Because it didn't matter. It had to go back."

"You'll have to forgive me for being dense, but why would you argue with your partner over buying an object that you could sell for such a large profit?"

Amanda hesitated. She had hoped to be able to somehow just get past the goblet without going into detail about its origins and Derek's involvement—however inadvertent—with the black market.

"Because its origins were . . . questionable."

"You mean it could be a fraud? A fake?"

"I almost wish it were." She sighed. "Unfortunately, it's very, very authentic."

"Then what's the problem?"

"The problem is that it was stolen some years ago from a museum in Iran."

"I see." Clark apparently hadn't filled him in on that little detail.

"Then you see how this is not only bad for business, but more important, that my partner could have been arrested for dealing in stolen artifacts."

He stared at her for a long time.

"I guess that's one thing you won't have to worry about now." He leaned against the counter. "The damage to your business's reputation, or bailing him out. So what's the hurry in sending this . . . Where were you sending this, anyway?"

"Back to its owner."

"Now how were you going to go about doing that? I mean, how would you know *how* to do that?" He paused, then added, "And with your partner dead, who would even know that you have this in your possession?"

It was her turn to stare at him.

"I mean, if it's so valuable, and no one knows that you have it, why would you send it back? Why not just sell it yourself, pocket that big profit?"

"I don't deal in stolen merchandise, and I don't support sales of antiquities on the black market," she snapped.

"But your partner did."

"Derek was clueless," she all but exploded. "He was smart enough to know that what was being offered to him was the real deal, but not smart enough to demand its documentation."

"Now I'm really curious. Why would you, someone so seemingly savvy about these things, be in business with someone who is, by your account, not very smart."

"Don't put words in my mouth." Her jaw tightened. "I didn't say he wasn't smart in general. He knows his American primitives—art and furniture—inside and out. That's his specialty. He just isn't all that familiar with items like this." She nodded in the direction of the goblet.

"And you are?"

"I know someone who is. Look, Officer Mercer—"

"Chief Mercer."

"Right. Sorry. *Chief* Mercer. Derek was not a crook. He was offered an opportunity to buy something very valuable, and since he's a dealer and knew he could make a tidy profit on it, he bought it. Once he found out what it was, he was in total agreement that it be returned to its rightful owner. And that's exactly what I'm going to do, as soon as the courier gets here."

"Ah, I see. Very righteous of you." He tapped two fingers on the counter. "But wasn't there a situation about two years ago . . . ? Seems to me I heard something about a Civil War–era uniform."

Amanda rolled her eyes. "That wasn't really what the papers made it out to be. Derek had a client—"

"And wasn't there a samurai sword some time back . . . ?"

"Derek—"

"Derek again? Not you?"

"No, of course, not me." She was becoming exasperated.

"So you're in business with a man who isn't really all that concerned with where he acquires his merchandise."

"That's not fair. Derek's just . . . well, sometimes he's just too trusting. Too naive about people."

"How so?"

"He takes everyone at face value. I'm sure that the man he bought this piece from looked totally on the level. That would have been good enough for Derek."

"And what would you have done under the same circumstances?"

"I would have asked to see some documentation on the piece. In archaeological terms, I'd have questioned its provenance. Its pedigree, if you will."

"Isn't that sometimes difficult to obtain?"

"When you're dealing with important pieces, there should be some kind of paper trail. A record of its excavation, for example, or a record of its chain of ownership."

"Generally speaking, would a sixty-five-thousand-dollar piece be considered important?"

"Not necessarily," she conceded. "At least, not on the international market, where artifacts can command hundreds of thousands of dollars."

"Then what should he have done differently?"

"He should have passed on the offer to buy."

"Because you suspected the piece was stolen."

"I know the piece was stolen. It's been confirmed."

"By?"

"By a noted expert in the field."

"When did you receive the piece?"

"Four days ago."

"And you've already confirmed its origins? My, that was fast."

"I have a friend whose sister is in the Middle East. She's an archaeologist, part of the international team currently evaluating the losses in Iraq. We emailed some photos of the goblet to her. She confirmed my suspicions."

"When did this take place?"

"On Sunday."

"The day before yesterday," he noted. "The day before Mr. England returned from his trip."

"Yes."

Mercer touched the goblet and shook his head. "Crazy, isn't it, what some people will kill for?"

It took a long moment for his words to sink in.

"Kill for?" She straightened up slowly, her hands gripping the edge of the counter. "You think someone killed Derek for this?"

"Someone might have." He gazed down at her, his expression unreadable. "Let's start with you, Ms. Crosby."

"Me?"

"You have to admit, you make a really good suspect." His dark eyes studied her carefully. "Mr. England had just spent your cash cushion on a piece of stolen pottery that you're going to have to send back, which puts you out a great deal of money."

"That's absurd."

"And then there's this little matter. . . ."

From his pocket he withdrew a cell phone. Amanda recognized it as Derek's. Mercer scrolled down the screen, then pushed a button. He needn't have bothered. Amanda knew full well what the message was.

"Derek, you are so dead. If you have any sense at all, you'll stay in Italy, because the minute I see you, I am going to kill you."

Mercer turned off the phone. "Do I need to play it again?"

She shook her head.

"And that is your voice?"

"Yes, of course it's my voice," she said, exasperated. "I was infuriated with him. Yes, I said that I would kill him, but that doesn't mean I was really planning on *killing* him. And I did not. I wouldn't have."

"I have only your word for that. You had motive; you had opportunity. We only have your word that he didn't arrive at your house last night. For all we know, he was there, or you met him someplace."

"That's preposterous."

"Let the evidence prove that. Ms. Crosby, I'm going to need you to come down to the station to give me a statement. I'd also like to stop at your house and pick up the clothes you were wearing last night."

"Looking for gunshot residue, right?" She began to seethe. "Want to test my hands with a metal detection reagent to see if I've fired a gun?"

"If you'll let us, sure." He hadn't expected this. "Watch a lot of *CSI*, do you?"

She ignored the question. "The sooner you eliminate me, the sooner you'll start to really investigate Derek's murder and make a legitimate effort to find his killer. Of course, then you'll have to do some real work."

"Well, then, point me in another direction, Ms. Crosby. Who else would want to see Derek England dead? Who else stood to profit from his death? I see you now as sole owner of the business with a very valuable piece of pottery in your hands."

"Why would I be sending it back, if I intended to sell it?"

"What proof do we have that you are sending it back?"

"Hang around for a while," she snapped. "The courier should be here any time now."

"Well, it's easy enough to confirm through the company," Mercer conceded, "though of course if he shows up now, it will be a wasted trip from his standpoint."

"What do you mean?"

"Evidence," he said as he began to secure the goblet in its wrappings. "The only place this is going is down to the station."

She stood and stared while he placed the goblet into the smallest of the wooden boxes.

He looked up at her. "Am I doing this the right way?"

"No." She pushed him aside and took over the task, fighting an urge to do him bodily harm.

She reminded herself that an assault on a police officer would get her jail time. She knew this for a fact, because her brother was a detective in a Philadelphia suburb and had recently testified against a woman who had attacked his partner with a baseball bat. His partner hadn't been badly injured, but the woman still got time.

"Hello?" a voice called from the door. "Amanda?"

Marian O'Connor, the owner of the shop next door and a very good friend, poked her head in. "Oh. You're busy. I . . . I can stop back. . . ." The woman backed up slightly at the sight of the police officer. "I can see you're . . . well, I just wanted to say how terrible I feel about Derek. I just saw it on the news. . . ."

She began to cry. Amanda went to her. "Marian, thank you. I know that you and Derek were such good friends. I know you'll miss him, too." Amanda attempted to comfort her.

"I just don't know how anyone could do such a thing. I truly don't. Derek was such a good soul. . . ." Marian wiped the tears away with tissues she pulled from the pocket of her sweater. "I just wanted you to know that I'll be at the funeral. We all will be. Everyone's going to close their shops whenever the services are held so that we can attend."

"Oh, that's so good of you. All of you." Amanda fought back the lump in her throat. "I know that Derek would have loved that you, well, that you all thought so highly of him."

"We certainly did. We all did. . . ." Marian dabbed at her face again, then turned to Chief Mercer. "Do you know who . . . ?"

"Nothing to talk about yet," he told her.

Marian nodded her head and backed toward the door. "I'm sure you have things to do here, Amanda. I won't take any more of your time. I'll see you later."

"Thank you, Marian." Amanda walked her to the door.

"Ms. Crosby, are you certain that no one else knew about the goblet?" Mercer asked as she returned to the counter and resumed wrapping the pottery.

"No, I am not certain. I do not know who Derek might have told. I assumed that he told no one, but I can't be sure. I hadn't seen him since he left for Europe. I never got to ask if he'd discussed it with anyone. You might ask Clark."

"I already did. He wasn't aware of anyone, either."

"If you're thinking someone killed Derek because they wanted the goblet, that makes no sense. For one thing, he didn't have it. *I* had it. Why didn't someone come after me?"

"Would anyone know that you had it? Maybe Derek bragged about it, and someone overheard and followed him home, not realizing that he didn't have it in his possession. Maybe someone tried to get him to give up its whereabouts, and when he refused, that someone killed him."

She looked at him skeptically. "Do you really believe it happened that way?"

"Actually, I'm surprised you didn't suggest it yourself. All things considered . . ."

She smiled wearily. It didn't take a genius to figure out what *things* he was considering. Or who his prime suspect was.

She reached for her phone and hit number three on her speed dial.

"Calling your lawyer, Ms. Crosby?"

"Calling my brother, Chief Mercer." She counted the rings until someone picked up. "I'd like to speak with Detective Crosby. This is his sister. Yes, I'll hold. . . ."

CHAPTER
FOUR

DEREK ENGLAND'S MEMORIAL SERVICE TOOK PLACE on a high bank overlooking the Delaware River one week and two days after his death. There were prayers led by a nondenominational minister and gospel music provided by a choir from a nearby church to whom Clark had offered a hefty donation to sing "Swing Low, Sweet Chariot" while he and Derek's family and friends scattered handfuls of his ashes on the river below. White orchids, tossed down to float upon the surface of the water, followed the ashes as the mourners then passed into the bar set up under a striped tent to toast Derek and drink to his memory.

"This is more like a cocktail party than a funeral." Amanda's brother, Evan, sidled up to her.

"Exactly what Derek would have wanted," she replied. "Oh, he would have wanted all the weeping and wailing. God knows he loved a good drama. But at the end of the day, he'd have wanted a party. Good champagne and some good hors d'oeuvres served by good-looking young men in tuxes. That was Derek's idea of a great party."

Evan's eyes scanned the crowd. "I see your local police chief is here. Mercer."

Amanda leaned a little closer to Evan. "He thinks I did it, you know."

Evan knew. He'd paid a visit to the police department on his way through town last night. He hadn't been very happy when he left.

"Well, you know that murders are usually committed by someone known to the victim. It is true that, statistically, the closer you are to the deceased, the more likely it is that you're involved." He tried to remain calm, but every time he thought about the absurdity of his sister as a murder suspect his blood pressure spiked.

"Do you think I need a lawyer?" she asked.

He hesitated. He'd seen the statement she'd voluntarily given to the police. He'd heard the voice mail she'd left on Derek's phone. He had to admit that, even to him, it had sounded pretty bad. He wished she'd spoken to him before she'd talked to Mercer, but the damage was done. Evan hadn't been in when she called, and so she had done what she thought was right. He knew that on paper, Amanda looked like a damned good suspect. Worse, he knew that if he was on the investigating team, he'd be doing everything he could to build the case against her.

"I think it's a good idea. I know a few good criminal defense lawyers at home, but none up here. Unless you have someone specific in mind, I'll check around, find out who has a good rep."

"I'd appreciate it. I hate that anyone would think I was capable of killing Derek—or anyone else, for that matter—but I understand why they need to consider the possibility." She looked grim. Then, seeing one of Derek's sisters in the crowd, she patted her brother on the arm. "There's Jessica. I didn't have time to speak with her earlier. . . ."

Evan watched his sister walk away, wondering if she realized how serious the situation really was.

The fact was, on paper, she just looked too damned good to ignore.

Then there was the matter of her clothing she'd voluntarily given up, and the fact that she'd submitted to a GSR swabbing at the hands of the local CSI team. He'd almost hit the ceiling when he'd found out about that, though it would definitely act in Amanda's favor when the tests confirmed that no fragments of unburned gun powder were found on her hands or clothing.

Evan sighed deeply. He knew that Amanda was incapable of killing anyone. It was unthinkable.

They'll railroad her over my dead body, Evan vowed as he accepted a glass of champagne from one of the waiters.

"So. Detective Crosby, was it?"

Evan turned to meet the eyes of the police chief.

"Chief Mercer." Evan acknowledged him with a nod.

"Call me Sean," he offered. "Evan, isn't it?"

"Actually, it's Detective."

"Professional courtesy?" Mercer asked dryly.

"Sure," Evan responded in kind. "So, you're here lining up your suspects?"

"Looking over the crowd," Mercer conceded.

"Got anyone in particular in mind?"

Mercer's eyes drifted to Amanda, who was holding the hand of Derek's older sister.

"Oh, come on, Mercer. You know she didn't do it," Evan told him tersely.

"You're her brother. I would expect nothing less from you."

"You don't understand. Amanda just isn't capable of doing something like that."

"You've been in law enforcement how many years now?" Mercer asked.

"Fifteen."

"How many times, over the course of those fifteen years, have you heard someone say those words? Be honest, Crosby. How many times?"

Evan stared at him hard. Of course, he'd heard those words a thousand times. He'd been in Mercer's shoes a thousand times himself.

"She didn't do it," Evan repeated.

"I hope you're right. I really do." Mercer paused to watch Amanda console the grieving family. "But I have to consider her a suspect until the evidence rules her out."

"Well, I expect you'll be able to do that real soon. We both know the GSR tests will confirm that she hasn't fired a gun recently." Evan nodded confidently. "And of course, you're keeping an open mind. . . ."

"Of course." Mercer's eyes scanned the crowd in the same manner Evan's had. "There's way too much we don't know yet. And there's the matter of that pottery vase. Goblet. I still like the theft angle. And frankly, I don't see your sister there. She told me she'd arranged to send it back, and that all checked out. The courier she hired confirmed that it was to go back to Dr. McGowan. So yes, we're keeping the investigation totally open, following up every lead. Besides, it just seems . . ." Mercer shook his head the slightest bit.

"Seems what?"

"Oh, a little too . . ." He appeared unwilling to complete the thought.

"Too easy?" Evan replied.

"Yeah. Maybe. Your sister's too easy a suspect. And that does bother me a bit. Things rarely turn out to be that pat." Mercer watched Clark Lehmann throw back yet another martini. His third, by Mercer's count. "Though Lehmann there stands to inherit financially. The house here in town as well as a summer place. The boat. And I understand that England carried a hefty life insurance policy."

"Clark doesn't need the money. There's a lot of money behind him."

"Where'd it come from, do you know?"

"Lehmann's Candy. He's a grandson of the founder, owns a big chunk of stock. And he's done well—very well—with his investments." Evan drained his glass. "But I'm sure you'll find that all out for yourself when you scrutinize his financials."

"You seem to know a lot about him," Mercer noted.

"Derek England and my sister were friends long before they were business partners. I knew him—and Clark Lehmann—pretty well."

"So I guess your sister knows Lehmann well, too. Would you say they're pretty close, the two of them?"

Evan stared at Mercer for a long time before he burst out laughing. "Right. Clark and Amanda conspired to kill Derek." He shook his head and deposited his empty glass on a silver tray as a waiter passed by. "You will have no more contact with my sister unless she's accompanied by her attorney, or by me."

Evan turned and walked away before he acted on his inclination to land a fist in the middle of Mercer's face.

"That went well," the chief muttered to himself.

He stepped back to the edge of the tent to watch the interaction of the crowd from the sidelines. It was a real mixed bag. Several same-sex couples gathered with Lehmann near the bar, while a group of older professional types stood off to one corner. The deceased's fellow antiques dealers, he supposed, recognizing Marian O'Connor in their midst. His eyes settled on Amanda Crosby from across a space of thirty or so feet. As if she were aware of his gaze, her eyes met his briefly before turning back to her companion, an older man in a dark suit with a red carnation in his lapel.

Mercer continued to study the faces of the mourners, returning to Amanda's several times before he realized he'd unconsciously been seeking her out as she moved around, stopping to chat with a young woman here, a small quiet group there. Her face was softened with sorrow, her eyes red, the circles under them deeper, darker than they'd been all week. Guilt or grief? he wondered.

At one point he'd caught the gaze of her brother again. Mercer had looked away abruptly, though he'd not totally understood why he'd felt compelled to do so. He'd be as protective of his own sister, wouldn't he?

Hard to tell, since they didn't have much of a history together, he reminded himself. Evan Crosby might know his sister well enough to state with total conviction that she was not capable of murder, but could he, Mercer, make that same declaration? How well did he really know Greer, anyway?

Not all that well, he sighed. They were trying to change that, but too many miles had separated them for too many years. They were still just getting to know each other, still learning to measure each other's character. It was a hard admission for him to make, but if Greer Kennedy was a suspect in a murder, her own brother wouldn't be able to swear that she was innocent.

The Crosby siblings looked like they were close, the way they leaned toward each other to chat under the conversation level of the crowd. They even looked a bit alike, both dark-haired and green-eyed and a little edgy. The angles of the brother's face were softened on the sister, her mouth fuller, her cheeks pinker. Evan's eyes saw more, his expression had a harder edge, and his movements were sharper, as one might expect given his profession. Brother and sister seemed to share a wariness, though it was more pronounced in him than in her, another concession to the job. There was a gentleness in her that surfaced every time she took someone's hands and offered a hug to a mourner who needed one. There was no such softness apparent in the brother, who was constantly scanning the faces, looking for the odd man, the one who didn't seem to belong, committing as many of those faces to memory as he could, much as was Mercer himself, silently questioning whether this face, or that, might be the face of a killer.

Mercer's eyes drifted back to Amanda Crosby once more. In spite of all the evidence, in spite of all he'd said, he found himself hoping that, in the end, that face wouldn't prove to be hers.

CHAPTER FIVE

Whistling, Vince Giordano unpacked the bags from the local market and put away his purchases. He was filled with a sense of self-satisfaction. Here he was, in the first living space he had ever had all to himself—his prison cell aside, of course. Sure, it was small, but he didn't need much beyond the few pieces of furniture that had come with the room. All he'd really wanted was a bedroom with a bath. The tiny kitchenette was a bonus. Besides, it wasn't like this was going to be his permanent home. All he needed right now was a place to hang his hat for a while. Just till he'd done what he had to do. Then he'd be free to go wherever the road took him.

There were things he'd have to take care of before he could complete his assignment, as he liked to think of it. For one thing, he'd have to get rid of his red hair. People always remembered a redhead. So he'd driven all the way out on Route 413 to an out-of-the-way drugstore to pick up some brown hair coloring. Right now, first thing before he did anything else, he'd color his hair. He rolled up his shirtsleeves and studied the hair on his arms. Should he do them, too? Was it possible to do that and not get the dye all over his skin?

Fuck it. He'd do the hair on his head and that was

it. Besides, if anyone saw his arms, they'd be more likely to remember all the freckles than what color the hair was. He'd just have to stick with long sleeves for now and pray that the month of September would be cooler than August.

He slid two six-packs of beer into the empty refrigerator, then added the hoagie he'd picked up at a deli on his way into Carleton that afternoon. A small blue-collar community, Carleton would serve his needs quite nicely. For one thing, it was only nine miles southwest of Broeder. Close enough for him to keep an eye on his quarry, far enough away from his old life in Lyndon that he wasn't likely to be recognized. The red hair, though, still had to go.

Right at one end of the block he now lived on was a food market, and at the other, a bar that laid claim to the best burgers in town. The bar looked like every neighborhood tavern he'd ever been in, and that was just fine with him. He could blend in there with no trouble at all. He knew the routine. By the end of the week, he'd be a regular.

As for his keep, well, he had enough money in his secret stash to last him for a long, long time, though he didn't plan on being around Carleton for more than a few weeks. Once his assignment was done, he'd retrieve the rest of his money and head for someplace warm. Arizona, or maybe New Mexico. He'd heard there was a housing boom out there. He could start up a new construction company with the money he'd stolen from the last one and start life all over again. The irony just about killed him.

He debated whether to eat first, then decided against it. He'd take care of the hair first, just like he'd planned, then maybe he'd eat. Pausing to glance out the window at the street below, he noticed several women walking into the bar. It had been a while since he'd had any female companionship. Well, perhaps tonight might be the night.

Whistling again, he tossed the box of hair coloring up and down in his right hand and headed off to the bathroom. Tonight could be the night, indeed.

Less than two hours later, Vince Giordano sauntered into the Dew Drop Inn and slid onto a stool just three down from where a couple of ladies were deep in conversation over their beers.

"And I told him, look, I don't need this shit. I have too much going for me—"

"Damn right, you do."

"—to be putting up with this kind of shit. I mean, do I look like I need the hassle?"

"You know you don't." The woman shook her head vigorously. "You got it all going on, Dolores. You got a job—shit, you got your own salon. Half of it, anyway. You got a car, you got your own house. . . . You don't need nobody leeching offa you."

"That's what I told him." Dolores tossed her bleached blond hair over her shoulders and took a long and righteous drag off her cigarette. "So that is that. I have washed my hands of Mr. Doherty. Done." She slid the palm of one hand over the other to show she was, in fact, done.

"Frankie, give Dolores another beer on me," her companion called to the bartender.

"You got it, Connie," Frankie acknowledged as he poured Vince's beer from the tap and set it before him.

Vince sipped at his beer and pretended to watch the

football game on the TV to his right at the end of the bar. The first Thursday night game of the new season had just begun. The ladies swung on their stools to watch the kickoff.

"Don't it seem like football starts earlier every year?" Connie asked no one in particular.

"That's a fact." Vince nodded without turning around.

"I like football," Dolores was saying. "Used to watch it with my dad and my brother when I was a kid. God rest their souls."

"To be sure." Connie nodded solemnly and made the sign of the cross in concert with her companion.

"Who do you like this year?" Vince asked the bartender, still careful not to pay too much attention to the ladies.

"Dunno. Too early to tell." Frankie stared at the screen for a moment, then turned to Vince. " 'Nother beer?"

"Sure. And one for the ladies, too."

"Aw, you don't have to. . . ." Dolores protested.

"Aw, thanks, that's so nice."

"Hey, we're gonna watch the game together, we have to toast the start of the new season, right?" He turned to them now for the first time and smiled his easiest smile.

"Right. To the new season." Connie lifted her glass and leaned forward just slightly to get a better look at Vince.

"To the season." Dolores did likewise. "To the NFL."

"Long may she wave," Connie giggled. "And long live those spandex pants."

"Shhhh," Dolores whispered to her.

"Hey . . . hey, what's your name?" Connie called down to Vince.

"Vinnie. Vinnie Daniels."

"Hey, Vinnie, you think those guys' pants are made from spandex?"

"Not sure what they're made from." Vince pretended to be amused.

"You hush, Connie. He's gonna get the wrong idea about you."

"What, that I'm interested in those big thighs and those big butts and those big—"

"Connie!" Dolores slapped a hand over her friend's mouth. "That's enough."

Red-faced, Dolores turned to him. "You have to excuse her, Vinnie. She gets a little mouthy when she drinks beer on an empty stomach."

"Then let's get some sandwiches out here." Vince signaled the bartender. "Your sign out front says you got the best burgers in town. Let's have a few of them while we watch the game."

He turned back to the two women. "My treat, ladies. To celebrate my first day in Carleton."

"Oh, you're new in town?" Dolores asked.

"Just arrived this afternoon."

"Where you from?"

He paused. Where was he from?

"Delaware." He had no idea where that came from but it sounded okay.

"Oh, where? My sister lives in Delaware. At the air force base in Dover," Connie said.

He avoided the question. "She in the air force?"

"No, her husband is. They been there for two years

now. I should get down there one of these days for a visit."

"Hey, look at that! A touchdown already." Vince raised his glass. "Here's to the first touchdown of the season."

"Amen."

"Cheers."

Before the first quarter had ended, their burgers had been served. By the time his burger had been eaten, he knew everything he needed to know about Dolores Hall.

She lived alone.

She had no family in town.

She was a hairdresser who, along with Connie, owned a salon.

She had just broken up with her boyfriend.

She wasn't too bright.

She was relatively passive, for all her mouthing off, and she was emotionally needy. He could tell just by the way she was looking at him that she had him pegged as a possible replacement for the now-scorned Mr. Doherty.

She was just the woman he was looking for.

All in good time, of course. For tonight, he'd buy her and her friend beers, watch the game, and make small talk. He wouldn't come on to her—nah, he'd wait maybe even a whole week before he even asked her out, and then he'd take her to dinner. Someplace other than here. Someplace where he'd have to pick her up at her house and take her home, where he could come in and get the lay of the land. By then he'd be a new regular at the Dew Drop. He'd have a pattern established, an identity that no one would have reason to question. He'd no longer be a stranger, a loner. He'd give them information about himself, and they'd believe him. He'd belong.

It would prove an amusing interlude while he went about his business. Who knew how long it would take to do the job right? He sure as hell wasn't going to rush into anything and blow his setup. For the past ten days the papers had been full of the story about the antiques dealer from Broeder who'd been found murdered in his car. Vince had bought every newspaper he could find and read them with fascination. He'd forgotten what a rush it was to read about your deeds in print. To be the only one who really knew what had happened; the only one who knew just how it really went down.

Vince had found England's house after its owners had departed for Europe, as was announced in big red letters across the calendar that hung on a wall in the kitchen. Knowing that the house would be vacant for a few days gave Vince some time to relax in the comfortable home of his intended victim, time to plan how best to accomplish his goal. He'd left on the morning the pair was due back, and had returned later that night, at which time he'd planned to shoot both men. But then there had been England in the doorway, obviously going someplace. He'd turned to say something to the man behind him in the house, and Giordano had taken advantage of the opportunity to pop into the backseat of England's car, where he'd stayed until they were almost to town, stopped at a light.

He could still see Derek England's eyes as they widened at first with surprise, then with fear, when he saw Giordano's face in the rearview mirror. The confusion when Vince told him to drive to the park. Felt the rush when he put the muzzle of the gun up close to England's head and pulled the trigger, just like that.

Well, that was then.

This is now. And now he was sitting here in this bar, taking the first steps into this new life he was creating for himself with the new friends he'd share it with until his job was done and it was time to move on.

In the meanwhile, he'd have this fun little world, this new identity. He could be anyone he wanted to be. After all the time he'd spent in prison, a social life—and hot damn, if he played his cards right, maybe even a love life!—sounded pretty damned good.

And no one would ever connect the dark-haired Vinnie Daniels with the redheaded Vince Giordano.

Even his own mother wouldn't put it together.

CHAPTER SIX

SEAN MERCER LEANED CLOSER TO THE WINDOW IN AN attempt to cut the glare so that he could see inside the neat three-story white clapboard Victorian house that Amanda Crosby called home, but the sun was behind him at precisely the wrong angle and he couldn't see a damned thing.

He rang the doorbell for the third time, though he suspected that she'd have answered the door if she were there. She didn't seem to be the type who would hide. Then again, she didn't seem to be the type to put a gun to the head of an old friend and pull the trigger, either. It remained to be seen whether she'd done just that.

Curious, though, that her car was in the drive.

Maybe he'd just take this opportunity to look around the property. One never knew what one might find.

The front lawn was neat and newly trimmed, the flower bed mulched. Baskets of purple and white flowers—tired blossoms at summer's end, in need of a watering—hung from the porch railing. Out back, black-eyed Susans grew in an unwieldy clump near the base of an apple tree that was long past due for a pruning, and daylilies with withered blooms grew in a patch along one side of the one-car garage. The lawn mower stood abandoned near the back porch, and the yard looked half-mowed, as if the person doing the job had been called away in the middle of it. He wondered what it was that had called Amanda from her yard work on this Sunday morning.

Peering through the glass panes in the back door gave him a view of the unlit back hall. As tall as he was, he could lean up to a high, small window to the right of the door and see into half the kitchen. It was a small square-shaped room, with a short row of cabinets and counters along the inside wall. The sink, stove, and refrigerator were just along the outside wall, the sink under the single window from which a wooden box of herbs had been hung. He reached up and grabbed a leaf, and crushing it between his fingers, held it to his nose. Spearmint.

It was an evocative scent. Mint had grown in the scrappy little garden his grandmother had tried to grow in the minuscule yard behind the Philadelphia row house they'd lived in when he was a kid. Nowadays, in some parts of the city, they called them town houses. He suspected that in his old neighborhood, they were still called rows. He couldn't imagine that gentrification had arrived in that part of town. If it had, it could only have come kicking and screaming bloody murder.

For years, he'd avoided thoughts of that house, that neighborhood, that time in his life. Lately, he'd thought of little else. That's what happened when the past unexpectedly collided with the present. He had a feeling that the rest of his day would provide ample proof of that.

He glanced at his watch. Almost noon. His stomach clenched. Only another hour . . .

He forced his attention back to Amanda Crosby and the results of the forensic testing that he'd found in an envelope on his desk when he stopped by the station last night. He still couldn't figure out whether he was surprised by the findings. He just didn't have a clear read on her yet.

The backyard was narrow but deep, with a koi pond complete with a lightly bubbling fountain and a stone bench near the rear boundary. At least, he assumed the post and rail fence marked the rear of the Crosby property. He wondered if Amanda spent much time back here. It was peaceful, serene, the sort of place one might seek out when the world got to be too much. He wondered idly what she might have on her mind those times when she sought some little bit of sanctuary.

For a moment, he was sorely tempted to sit on the bench and listen to the fountain and watch the koi for a while. But he had somewhere to go, someone to see. He walked straight down the drive and to his car. Later, maybe, after he'd done what he needed to do, he'd stop back to see Ms. Crosby. He couldn't help but wonder just what frame of mind he'd be in by then.

". . . and I just can't help it, Manda. I know it's silly, but I just can't stay in that house right now." Clark rubbed his forehead with his fingers.

"I don't think it's silly at all." Amanda leaned over and patted his arm. "You've lost the most important person in your life. Of course you're going to grieve.

If you feel you will deal with this loss better some-place else, then for heaven's sake, Clark, go. You don't owe me any explanations."

"Oh, I feel as if I do. I know that you and Derek were like sister and brother. I know how much he loved you." He wiped his eyes with his napkin and tried to smile. "You know, there was a time, early on, when I was so jealous of you. I knew how close you two were, and I was always afraid . . . well, that someday, maybe . . ."

"You know it was never like that between us. Derek never had any real love in his life before he met you."

"Thank you, Amanda." Clark did smile at this. "You have such a generous spirit. I know it's one of the things that Derek admired about you. He could be so . . . bitchy . . . at times."

"It was part of his charm." She reached over and took his hand and squeezed it.

She looked up just in time to see Chief Mercer slide into a booth on the opposite side of the aisle and up about four tables just as the brunch crowd at the Sawmill Inn had started to thin. She had to look twice to make certain that it was in fact the chief of police at the table near the window. For one thing, she'd never seen him out of uniform, and today he was wear-ing khaki Dockers, a blue-and-white-striped shirt with the sleeves rolled to the elbows, and shoes without socks. For another, it was unusual to see any of the lo-cals here on Sunday afternoon. The Inn was generally more popular with people passing through than with the residents who, if they were having breakfast out, tended to go early to the small café in the center of town or the diner just off Center Street. She wondered idly what brought him all the way out here on a Sunday afternoon.

Wonder if the results of any of the tests have come back. Wonder if he'd tell me if they had.

She'd just decided to excuse herself to the ladies' room so that she could stop by his table and see what she could find out, when the door opened and a woman walked in.

Amanda noticed her the second she stepped into the room. Everyone noticed. She was impossible to miss.

In her late twenties, with pretty features on a soft, round face and rich auburn hair that cascaded halfway down her back in thick waves, the woman wore a plaid sleeveless shirt over a tank top that left little to the imagination and black capri pants. Her biceps and what Amanda could see of her calves bore tattoos of thin branches with thorns interwoven with roses that wound around, front to back, to form a complete circle. Her nail polish was deep red and she carried a large tote bag. Mercer stood at her approach and she embraced him, holding him tightly and closing her eyes. Amanda couldn't see his face, but saw one of his big hands patting her somewhat awkwardly on the back.

When the woman sat across from him, there were tears in her eyes. She spoke softly, reaching out every once in a while to touch his hand. Feeling too much the voyeur, Amanda turned her attention back to Clark. There was something about witnessing such tender moments between others that made her uncomfortable. And just for a moment, there was a prickle of something that felt a lot like disappointment to find he was in a relationship. Not that she should care. After all, wasn't this the man who wanted to put her behind bars?

". . . so you won't be upset if I stay with Chris and Tammy for a while? Maybe a few weeks, maybe longer. I just don't know."

"Oh. No." Amanda tuned back in. "No, of course not. You just go ahead and do what you need to do. I understand perfectly."

"I was hoping you would. I mean, if it bothered you, I wouldn't go. I know you've gone through a lot, too." He leaned forward just slightly. "I know those pesky police have been asking you a lot of questions." He pretended to shiver. "Neanderthals, all of them."

"Well, you don't want to say that too loudly"—she lowered her voice to a stage whisper—"since the head Neanderthal just seated himself a few minutes ago four tables behind you."

He swiveled his head around, then wide-eyed, turned back to Amanda.

"Is that him there with the tattooed lady?"

Amanda nodded.

"Oh, where are the fashion police when you need them?" He rolled his eyes. "Gorgeous eyes and hair to dye for—get it, hair to dye for?—but those tattoos . . . those clothes." He groaned. "Everything about her just screams biker chick."

Amanda giggled and sipped her iced tea. "Enough, Clark . . ."

"Oh, not by a long shot. I haven't had this much fun in days."

"Forget it. She's with the chief of police and she's—"

"He should charge her with assault on the sensibilities. Dressing with intent to offend."

"Enough. You are wicked." She laughed.

"Derek was wickeder. He'd be unmerciful if he were here." His smile faded as he picked up the check the waitress had left on the table. He barely glanced at it. "Ready?"

"Yes, I'm ready." They stood in unison. Clark took her arm as they walked to the cash register by the door.

"Did you want to stop by and say hey to the chief?" he asked as he paid the bill.

"No." She shook her head and opened the door, held it for him while he put his wallet away. "I have the feeling I'll be seeing him soon enough as it is."

She couldn't have imagined just how soon that would be.

The sun was out in full when she arrived home. Feeling sluggish from having eaten an unusually full meal in the middle of the day, Amanda decided the best remedy would be physical activity. She'd left the backyard half-mowed the previous evening when she'd turned off the mower and gone into the house for a bottle of water and stopped to check the answering machine. The two hang-up calls had spooked her. While she was debating what to do about them, she'd gotten a call from Iona, and spent the best part of an hour sitting on the back porch, chatting on the phone. By the time they'd hung up, it was dark, and the last thing she wanted was to be outside in the dark, alone, armed with nothing more than an old lawn mower.

On her way home from the shop tomorrow, she'd

stop at the gun club and head out to the firing range for some practice. It had been two weeks since she'd dug out her .38 and shot off a few rounds. She liked to keep in practice, needed to feel sharp when it came to her handgun. She needed to know that if she had to use it, she could hit her mark. She hadn't come this far to do anything but.

Thinking about the gun club seemed to nag at her. . . .

She rolled up the sleeves of her cotton shirt and started the lawn mower. By the time she finished the back section of grass she was in a serious sweat. She shed the shirt and tossed it onto the stone bench, then set out to finish the job in her tank top.

The feeling that she was being watched began to creep over her as she started on the strip of grass on the side of the house that linked the front and back yards, and the sensation grew stronger as she returned to the back and turned off the mower. The slamming of a car door out near the street drew her attention and she walked to the end of the drive in time to see Chief Mercer standing near the mailbox and studying the house.

Never one to wait for trouble, she walked down to meet him. She wondered how he'd managed to slip the tattooed wonder as quickly as he had.

"Hi," he called when he saw her.

"I'm not supposed to talk to you." She stopped at the sidewalk and folded her arms over her chest.

"That the advice of your lawyer, or your brother?"

"My brother." She didn't have a lawyer yet, but he didn't need to know that.

He appeared to be debating with himself. Finally, he asked her, "Do you own a gun, Ms. Crosby?"

"Yes." She nodded. It was no secret. Half the people in town knew she had taken lessons at the firing range on the outskirts of town. She'd written about the experience in one of her newspaper columns several months ago.

"When was the last time you fired it?"

She paused, and it came back to her. The gun club . . .

Uh-oh.

Her eyes met his, and before she could remind herself not to answer the question, he said, "I was just wondering, because the GSR results are back."

"And?" She went cold inside. Her stomach flipped, then sank. She knew exactly what he was going to say and why he was there.

"You want to tell me the last time you fired that gun, or are you going to wait until I tell you what I found on the sleeves of the sweatshirt you gave us?"

Amanda sighed. She'd forgotten. Completely forgotten . . .

"I was at the range two Mondays ago. You can check with the gun club. They'll confirm that. You have to sign in—"

"What kind of a gun do you have?"

"A .38. Everyone in the county knows about it. I'm surprised you don't." Her hands were on her hips now, defiant. Derek had been killed with a bullet fired from a .38. Everyone in the county knew that, too. "I wrote all about learning to shoot the damned thing for the *County Express* back in March."

"Where's your gun now?"

"It's in the drawer in the table next to my bed."

"I'm afraid I'm going to have to ask you for it."

Amanda sighed. "I can make you get a warrant, can't I?"

"Sure. But what would that do besides delay the investigation? If the bullet that killed your partner wasn't fired from that gun, we'll be able to confirm that right away. Like you said before, the sooner we eliminate you, the sooner the investigation can move ahead. I'd think you'd want to clear that up as soon as possible. I mean, with the finding of the GSR on your sweatshirt . . ."

"I wore the shirt to the range two weeks ago. I didn't happen to wash it between wearings, so I imagine there would be residue on the sleeves."

"Why didn't you mention this to me before?"

"Because I wasn't thinking . . . I wasn't thinking about having shot off my handgun at the range as having to have anything to do, however remote, with Derek being killed."

"You knew though that he'd been shot with a .38?"

"Of course I did. It was on the news. But he wasn't shot with my .38."

"Let's prove it."

They stared at each other. She was the first to blink.

"All right. Evan will scream bloody murder when I tell him I did this, but you're right. You can prove that Derek wasn't killed by my gun." She started toward the front steps.

She was almost to the front door when she saw it.

She stopped abruptly and uttered a quiet little, "Oh."

Mercer followed her gaze to the porch. On the

decking, just outside the door, lay a long-stemmed red rose.

"Looks like someone left a token of their sympathy," he said.

Amanda's face had drained of color and her eyes had grown wary.

"Ms. Crosby? Are you all right?" He touched her arm, and she recoiled as if she'd been burned.

He went up to the door and picked up the rose. "There's no card."

"There never is." She remained on the step.

"There have been others?"

She nodded.

"Any idea who they're from?"

She shook her head.

He held the rose out to her, but knew she'd decline to take it.

She shook her head a second time, then walked past him and unlocked the front door with a key she'd withdrawn from her back pocket.

"Nice house," he said as she closed the door behind them.

"You've seen it before. You were here before."

"Yes, but things were a little hectic then. We'd just found your partner that morning, we were trying to get statements—"

"So what you're saying is that in all the confusion, you failed to notice how nice my house is." Before he could respond, she added, "So maybe you can understand how, in the midst of that same confusion—and considering that it was *my* partner and best friend who had been murdered—I forgot to mention that I do own a gun, and that I'd fired it the day before. It just never occurred to me, since it wasn't used to kill Derek."

"Ruling out your gun as the murder weapon will certainly go a long way to prove that, since there is that matter of gunshot residue on the sweatshirt you were—by your own admission—wearing on the night Mr. England was killed."

"Because I'd worn it to the firing range." Her jaw was clenched. "And I can prove that. There's a video camera set up on the range. Check it out and you'll see exactly what I was wearing."

"Thanks. I'll do just that."

Muttering under her breath, she turned and marched up the stairs to the second floor. She stopped midway up and looked down at him over one shoulder.

"You tested my hands and arms as well. What were the results of those tests?"

"They were clean. No residue."

"I could have told you that." She made no effort to hide the touch of smugness as she continued up the steps.

She held the gun out to him handle first, as she came back down a moment later.

"Here. It's not loaded. But you were taking quite a chance, weren't you? I mean, how did you know I wouldn't come back down, gun blazing?"

"My very obvious error." She would have expected him to look a bit embarrassed by this oversight, but he did not.

"I'll get you a plastic bag from the kitchen so that you don't even have to get your prints on it"—she waved for him to follow her toward the back of the house—"since you obviously didn't expect to gather any evidence this afternoon."

He walked behind her down the short hall and into the kitchen.

She opened a drawer and pulled out a plastic bag into which she unceremoniously deposited the gun. Handing the bag to him, she said, "There you go. In a few days, you'll know for certain that I am absolutely, positively telling you the truth. I did not kill Derek."

He accepted the bag and folded over the top. "Thanks," he told her. "I hope it proves you didn't."

"Why, Chief Mercer, I believe you—"

The air between them was split unexpectedly by the harsh ringing of the phone.

She glanced at the wall unit.

"You going to answer that?" he asked.

Amanda hesitated.

The answering machine in the front hall picked up. Even from the kitchen, the sound of heavy breathing was clear and distinct. Her face drained of color as she walked quietly into the hall, listening. Finally, Sean followed, then lifted the receiver and said, "Hello? Who is this?"

The phone immediately went dead.

The caller ID displayed two words. *Unknown number.*

He hit the buttons for the return call feature.

"The number of your last incoming call is unknown," the recording announced.

"You get a lot of those?" Mercer asked.

She nodded, not trusting her voice.

"When did they start?"

"A few days before Derek was killed."

"Any thoughts on who the caller could be?"

"No. I called the phone company and they said they couldn't trace the calls. That they were most likely being made from a cell phone using a phone card."

"Did it occur to you to report this to the police?"

"No, frankly, it did not."

"Why not?"

"Because you've made it clear that I'm your number one suspect in Derek's death. How seriously would you take me? Besides, the last time—" She stopped in midsentence.

"The last time?" He raised an eyebrow.

"Oh, come on, Chief." She ran an agitated hand through her short spiky dark hair. "You've been here long enough to have heard the story about how I was stalked and attacked. An attack which was followed by your predecessor's being fired, as I'm sure you know."

She turned on her heel and went back into the kitchen, where she ran water in the sink and filled a glass, which she drank down.

"I did know that you had been attacked, but I wasn't familiar with all the details. Since it was a closed case, I didn't look at the file. This is how it started, with heavy-breathing hang-ups?"

"Yes."

He leaned back against the counter. "The man who attacked you went to prison."

"He's still there."

"Do you think it's him making the calls?"

"Not a chance. He's been ordered to have no contact with me. Ever. Even a phone call to me will cost him more time."

"That's no guarantee that he isn't making the calls."

"No, but the timing is wrong. The calls come at all hours of the day and night. Inmates don't have such free access to phones. I admit that I've been thinking about calling the district attorney about it, but I just haven't gotten to it, with all . . . everything . . . Derek . . ." She shook her head.

"I'll look into it tomorrow."

"I said I'd do it."

"A phone call from you will not have the same effect as me showing up in the warden's office first thing in the morning."

"You don't have to do that."

"Of course I do. It's part of the investigation."

She looked at him quizzically.

"Someone killed your partner. Now someone appears to be harassing you. Coincidence?"

Amanda frowned. "That wouldn't make any sense." She shook her head. "There isn't any reason."

"No reason that you can see. Maybe someone sees something you don't."

"Are you still thinking there could be some connection to the goblet?"

"There could be. Maybe someone's figured out that it went directly to you." He picked up the gun that he'd earlier placed on the counter. "Anything else you want to tell me?"

She shook her head.

He nodded at the rose he'd left on the table. "Most women love to get roses. You went white when you saw that on the porch. Any particular reason why?"

"Archer Lowell—the man in prison for stalking me

last year—used to leave red roses in that same spot near my front door."

"And now someone else is doing the same thing? And you didn't think it was important enough to report?"

"I found the first one the day after Derek was killed. One every day since. At first I thought that maybe a neighbor had left them. As you said, an expression of sympathy."

"Where are the others?"

"I stuffed them down the garbage disposal."

"Even though you thought they were innocent gifts from a neighbor?"

"Since . . . since before, I can't stand to see or smell them. Regardless of where they come from, or from whom, or the sentiment intended."

He looked around the room, then, locating the roll of paper towels that hung from the end of the counter, tore off a sheet and wet it at the faucet before wrapping the stem in the damp paper. "I'll take this with me, since you don't want it."

"Fine." She shrugged her indifference.

"Well, anything else I should know? Anything else you didn't bother to report?"

"No. Just the calls and the roses."

"I'll get back to you when the tests on the gun are complete. In the meantime, I want you to tell me if you get any more calls or roses, or if anything else happens that might seem out of the ordinary. Anything that doesn't feel right, anything that makes you the least bit uncomfortable, no matter how small or insignificant it might seem at the time. Deal?"

"All right."

He nodded and walked toward the front of the house.

Amanda saw him out. She stood on the top step, watching his long form move down the walk. He paused midway, turned, and said, "I almost forgot. Earlier, when I asked you why you didn't report the calls, you started to say something about the last time, but never finished. What were you going to say about the last time?"

"The last time, I did report the calls." She crossed her arms. "I was told everyone got hang-up calls, that it was probably nothing more than someone dialing the wrong number."

"And the roses? You reported those?"

"Of course. But Chief Anderson told me that I was a lucky girl. That most women would love to have a secret admirer sending her flowers every day."

He visibly winced. He'd made a similar remark earlier.

"I'm sorry. That I wasn't any more . . ." He appeared to be searching for the right word.

"Sensitive?" she offered sarcastically. "Informed?"

"Both. I'm sorry," he repeated, and without waiting for her reply, proceeded down the path to his car.

As he drove away from Amanda Crosby's house, Mercer's eyes kept returning to his side view mirror, in which he could see that she still remained on the steps, even as he reached the stop sign at the end of her street. He wondered, after he'd made his turn, how long she stayed there.

He made two stops on his way home. One was at

the station, where he immediately tagged and bagged the gun. The second was at the neighborhood convenience store, where he ordered a take-out sandwich. While the young man behind the deli counter made his ham and cheese, Sean strolled around the store, picking up a bag of chips and a plastic container of iced tea. On his way back to the counter, he passed a circular bin filled with flowers.

3 FOR $5, a handwritten sign announced.

"You sell a lot of those?" he asked the woman at the register.

"Sure."

"You ever have roses?"

"Sometimes we get a few in. It depends on what the distributor has on his truck that day." She began to ring up his purchases. "But you want roses, the supermarkets usually have those."

"Which supermarkets?"

"All of them. They sell them by the stem or by the dozen. Nice to be able to stop and pick up something for dinner, grab a pretty something for the table at the same time." She smiled at him. "The regular flowers are nice, but a rose really makes a statement, you know?"

He nodded and handed her a ten. While he waited for his change, he wondered what kind of a statement was being sent to Amanda. He was pretty certain it couldn't be anything good.

It was almost ten when Sean closed Amanda Crosby's file. He'd known that the mishandling of her case had led to the removal of the previous chief of police nearly a year ago, but he'd been unaware of all the facts, as had been painfully apparent earlier that day. He'd not known that the stalking had continued for a full six weeks before culminating in an attack that had left Amanda facially scarred. He'd noted the L-shaped mark on the upper part of her cheek near her left eye. According to the report, the cut had been made by a ring worn by her attacker. After witnessing her reaction to the hang-up calls, Sean was well aware that she'd been left with more than a physical scar.

He tried hard to push the image of her from his mind. Sweaty in shorts and that little top, her tanned, muscled arms and legs, her feet in bright yellow flip-flops.

She had pretty feet, he'd thought at the time. Long and slender, the toenails painted a deep burgundy red . . .

Don't go there. She's a suspect in a homicide investigation. Doesn't get much more taboo than that. Don't even think about it.

Work. Focus on the work.

Right.

Focus on the work . . .

He couldn't believe that the reports she'd given to the police back then had been dismissed so easily. The stalker's pattern had all the signs of classic erotomania.

According to the file, Archer Lowell, age nineteen, was a truck driver for a nearby auction house and had delivered purchases to Amanda's shop on several occasions. Over the course of a year, he'd come under the delusion that Amanda was in love with him, though she'd testified in her sworn statement that she'd never given him any reason to believe that the kindness she'd shown to him was anything other than that. Simple kindness. She'd given water to him—and to the others on the truck—on hot days when they'd dropped off those items she or Derek had bought at auction the night before. Yes, she always greeted him—and the others—by name. No, she never treated him any differently than she treated any of the deliverymen. No, she never knowingly encouraged him.

Yet Lowell believed she was in love with him. That they were meant to be together, always, through all time. That she was the single most important thing in his life. That he was the most important thing in hers.

It was a case right out of a textbook. How could the signs have been missed by anyone who'd been paying attention?

Sean stood up and stretched, then went into the kitchen for a snack. He scanned the top shelf of his refrigerator. Half a tomato, half a six-pack of Coors, half an orange. He grabbed a beer and made a mental note to try to find time to hit the grocery store tomorrow. Well, he'd been planning on checking out the selection of roses. Maybe he'd do a quick shop while he was at it, save a few steps. He slammed the refrigerator door and went back to the living room.

He eased back into his chair, an old dark brown leather number he'd bought at a secondhand store for his first apartment, and put his feet up on the ottoman. They were the only pieces of furniture he'd brought with him when he moved to Broeder. Leaning his head back, he closed his eyes, rejoicing in the silence. No television, no radio. Just—silence. He wanted it to settle around him and linger for a moment or two while he cleared his mind of everything that clamored for his attention. Just for a few minutes, he wanted to be a blank slate. That's how he'd taught himself to picture his mind anytime he felt headed for an information overload. The skill had come in handy over the years.

He took a few deep breaths and opened his eyes, ready to go back into the Crosby file, when the phone rang.

"Mercer," he answered.

"Did you see her? Did you meet with her?"

"Yes."

"What did you think?"

"I don't know what to think," Sean said truthfully.

"Did she show you the photos?"

"Yes."

"Well?"

"Well, what?"

"Didn't you recognize anyone?"

"I don't know."

"How about the surroundings, then? Didn't any of it look familiar?"

"I don't know." His voice was taking on more of an edge.

"Of course you do." A pause, then, "Why are you being so difficult about this?"

"I need to think this through. . . ."

"What's to think about?"

"There's no proof."

"You saw the birth certificate. How much more proof do you need?"

"How do you know it wasn't a fake?"

"Oh, come on, Sean." His sister, Greer, burst out laughing. "Why would anyone claim to be related to us if they were not? For a share in the vast Mercer fortune? Please."

"I don't know what motivates people, Greer."

A heavy sigh whispered through the phone line. "I'm going to tell Ramona that you need time to digest all this. That it's all been a bit of a shock, coming out of the blue as it has. But that you're going to think things over for a while."

"All right."

"I just want you to think about it."

"I said I would." His nerves were beginning to fray. He was all but out of patience.

"That's all I'm asking, Sean. Please just keep an open mind."

He replaced the phone gently into its cradle, then rubbed his temples. He didn't want to think about Ramona anymore tonight.

After the death of her only child the previous year, Greer's longing for roots had driven her to search for family until she had found Sean. Greer had traced her brother through the foster system—the records of which were often missing—tricked him into a reunion he hadn't wanted, then through the sheer force of her will had made him believe they could be a family. Maybe they could still be. He wanted that, or at least thought he did, for her sake if not for his own. He'd been alone for so long that he wasn't sure he understood what the word *family* really meant. He wasn't sure either if what he felt for Greer could be called love, but he wasn't about to let anyone use her big heart to hurt her. Now she was elated to have found what she believed was another of her long lost siblings. She couldn't understand why he wasn't as thrilled as she was. As far as he was concerned, Ramona might or might not be the real deal.

He rubbed his temples, then forced himself to put it aside. He had work to do.

He reopened the file at the spot he'd marked earlier and resumed reading the witness statements.

"Well, shit," he said aloud.

Barely a week before the attack on Amanda, Derek England had called the Broeder police department to report that Archer Lowell had, on three separate occasions, threatened his life.

> *Complainant alleges that Archer Lowell told him that he had "a bullet with your name on it." See Incident Report 1497-02, and companion file 1554-02.*

Sean stared into space for several minutes, pondering the possibilities, before closing the file and turning out the light.

At dawn tomorrow, he'd be at his desk, looking over the cross-referenced file on the incident involving Derek England. When the warden pulled into his parking space at the prison in the morning, Sean Mercer would be waiting for him, and by then he'd know all there was to know about Archer Lowell.

CHAPTER
SEVEN

" 'BOUT TIME YOU SHOWED UP." IONA MCGOWAN poked Amanda in the middle of her back.

"Oh, hey." Amanda turned, smiling. "I had trouble finding a place to park. I thought you said this sale was supposed to be a small one."

"The auctioneer running it said he didn't expect a lot of traffic, since the estate insisted on holding the sale on the last day of the month, which just happened to fall on a Monday, which, as you know, is not the most popular day of the week for sales like this. However, there's reputed to be some Chippendale furniture that's top-of-the-line. That's expected to draw the most interest."

"If the big guns are here for the furniture, maybe there won't be much competition on the items we're here for."

"I wish. In my first hour here, I ran into no fewer than seven other jewelry dealers. Including your friend, Marian."

"Marian is here?" Surprised, Amanda looked around the large tented area where the offerings were displayed on long tables, with certain items housed in glass cases. Anyone wishing a closer look at an individual piece had to request a special showing from one of the auctioneer's assistants.

"She was an hour ago. She mentioned there were some miniatures she was interested in as well, and I think I heard someone say that all of the artwork was in the house. She might have gone inside."

"Well, there are some interesting pieces here, don't you think?" Amanda scanned the jewelry displayed on the long table.

"Most of this will go intact for resale. There are a lot of nice estate pieces. Lots of excellent silver—lots of art deco pins. Lots of high-end platinum and diamond pieces in that case over there, the one where the guard is posted. But, so far, not a lot of what I'm looking for."

"I think I saw a large brooch with some stones missing a few tables down. Amethysts." Amanda frowned, trying to recall exactly where she'd seen the piece.

"Oh? Maybe I should take a look. I have amethysts in mind for a ring I sketched out just last week." As a jewelry designer, Iona often scoured auctions and estate sales for quality gems that she could reset in her own designs. Her goal was to find pieces from which a stone or two had been lost and would be difficult to match and could therefore be picked up for a song. "I'll catch up with you for coffee in, say, a half hour?"

"Perfect. I heard there's a small offering of Hull pottery someplace. I want to check that out."

Amanda wandered off to the opposite side of the tent, where a vast quantity of art pottery sat on several sturdy wooden tables. There was a fabulous selection of Roseville, which explained the presence of several of the dealers from New York she'd worked with on many occasions. She knew there'd be no point in wasting her time on the Roseville, which was certain to fetch top prices. Though she often bought at smaller sales like this for the express purpose of reselling, the reputation of this particular collection had drawn many out-of-state buyers. She had a good idea of who would be bidding on what and had no desire to get in the middle. Especially since her own working capital was now so limited. This time around, she was out of the running for the prime pieces.

Like so many of the other dealers there, Amanda often shopped the sales with specific clients in mind, but today nothing really caught her eye until she found the table displaying the Hull. The small white bank in the shape of an owl could bring a nice price if she could get it inexpensively. The frog bank would bring even more. There were several jardinieres from the early 1920s that could be profitable. Her eyes continued to scan the selection, coming to rest on the grouping of vases in what she recognized as the Tropicana pattern. Though not representative of the earliest works, this design, popular in the 1950s, had become increasingly collectible. Amanda had a customer who'd pay dearly for the vases. She hoped that with the heavy emphasis on the Roseville, the Hull would be overlooked by the other dealers. She glanced at her watch. The sale would begin in less than forty minutes. She hoped they'd start on time and that the Hull would go early. She wanted to get back to St. Mark's Village by two. Not having anyone to watch the shop, she'd had to leave it closed in order to come to the sale, but had hoped to open for at least part of the afternoon.

It was just another reminder of how much she missed Derek. They'd shared the duties of both buying and selling. If one attended a daytime sale, the other tended the shop. Very often they'd both attend evening sales or auctions together. Back in the days when she was still easily intimidated, he'd bid for her. Within the past year, she'd become determined to be more assertive, and under Derek's tutelage she had become a shrewd bidder.

"Want to grab some coffee and a Danish or something before the auction starts?" Iona was at her elbow. "Unless you still want to browse . . ."

"No, I've seen what I need to see."

"Anything of interest?"

"Some vases one of my customers will love," Amanda said as she wove her way through the ever-growing crowd and headed toward the concession area. "If I can get them cheaply enough, I can make a tidy profit. How about you? Did you find the amethysts?"

"They are so perfect in size and color for the ring I have in mind that I'm pinching myself." Iona's dark eyes shone with anticipation. "And there's also a bracelet with some lovely peridot stones, about a quarter of which are missing. The green would be gorgeous with the purple. There are enough of each for maybe a pin or a pendant as well as the ring. I'm in heaven."

"Well, then, maybe we should go find seats before all the chairs are gone." Amanda glanced at the tent where the actual sale would be held. "It looks like it's filling up pretty quickly."

"Not to worry. I was here early and left my jacket over two near the front."

"Let's hope it's still there."

"It will be. People are generally pretty good about respecting a reserved seat at sales like this. But just to be on the safe side, let's get our coffee now and get ourselves seated."

They did so, with ten minutes to spare.

"Daria called last night," Iona said as she fiddled with the lid to her coffee in an attempt to lift the flap up so that she could drink without spilling it all over herself. "She was concerned about your email."

"Oh, you mean the email telling her that the goblet was not on its way back after all and that I didn't know when it would be since it's currently being treated as evidence in a murder investigation but could she please not turn me in to Interpol?" Amanda said dryly. "You mean that email?"

"Yes, that one." Iona sipped her coffee. "She was upset for you—and sends her condolences on Derek's death—but she said that as long as the piece is safe, she's okay with the situation."

"She's okay with it? I promised her it would be in her hands within a week, and now it's sitting in the evidence room at the Broeder P.D. and will be for God knows how long. How could she be okay with that?"

"Because she knows where it is and that it's intact and in safe hands. Keep in mind that most of the antiquities that disappear do not resurface, and very, very few of those that do are returned voluntarily. She knows she'll get this goblet back eventually, and that's more than she knows about ninety-nine percent of what's been sold on the black market over the past hundred or so years."

"You know, it just occurred to me. . . ." Amanda lowered her voice to a near whisper. "What if . . . ?"

"What if what? What are you thinking?"

"What if Chief Mercer is right and there is a connection between the pottery and Derek's murder?"

"You think there could be?"

"I don't know. Maybe. I dismissed the possibility at first, but at this point, I'm starting to wonder. It makes about as much sense as anything else, though I think it's a real stretch. I honestly can't think of one reason why anyone would want him dead."

"Then turning the goblet over to the police was probably the smartest thing you could have done." Iona patted Amanda on the arm. "If someone was after the vase, we don't need him coming after you to look for it."

It was almost four o'clock by the time Amanda unlocked the door to her shop, and after five by the time she'd brought in the boxes of carefully wrapped Hull vases and called her customer, who promised she'd be there first thing in the morning to pick them up. Relieved to know that she'd have certain income that week, Amanda cleaned up the pottery pieces in the sink in the back room, dried them, and looked for a place to display them. Deciding on a shelf near but not quite in the front window, she set about the task of moving a row of cut-glass bowls. They were dusty, so she washed them off as well, then arranged them inside the glass counter near the cash register.

Derek was so good at this, she thought as she looked

around for a place to stand the onyx bookends she'd removed from the counter to make room for the cut glass. He just always seemed to know exactly where to display things. He had such a great eye.

She wasn't even aware she was crying until she saw the fat drops begin to puddle on the countertop. She'd shed many tears over the past two weeks, but until now, his death had barely seemed real. Now, after having spent most of the day at a sale without him and returning to the silent shop, she knew the loss of Derek was undeniable. The rituals of death now over, she would have to deal, day to day, with the reality of Derek being gone. Gone from the business—gone from her life.

Numb for most of the days since the murder, she was just beginning to thaw. It hurt terribly, and would, she knew, for a long time.

She was still sniffling when she heard the sound of something dropping outside her door. She peered through the window and saw Marian O'Connor struggling to lift a box that was obviously too much for her. Unlocking her door, Amanda stepped outside and all but tripped over Marian's purse where it lay on the walk between the two shops.

"Marian, here, let me help you with that." Amanda, the stronger of the two, grabbed the box and took it. "You pick up your purse there, get your keys out, and unlock the door. I'll hold this."

"Oh, Amanda, thank you. I was having a devil of a time with that. It's not that it's so heavy, it's just bulky, and I was having a hard time getting my arms around it." Marian picked up the dropped purse, then dug in her pockets for her keys, speaking the whole time.

"Here we go. . . . There, just bring it in here and you can set it down anywhere."

"Are you just getting back from the auction?" Amanda asked.

"Yes. I'd hoped to be out of there earlier. I hate to keep the shop closed all day. Such a silly way to lose business. My neighbor's daughter, who worked for me all summer, left for college on Saturday. But I really wanted this clock." Marian cut through the packing tape and sorted through the newspaper in the box. Marian always came to sales prepared to buy and prepared to carefully wrap her purchases to protect them on the ride home. She was the most organized person Amanda had ever met. "Look here, isn't it wonderful?"

"It's lovely, yes." Amanda leaned forward for a closer look. "Russian?"

"Yes." Marian was positively beaming. "I'm so excited. I can't believe my good fortune. Everyone was knocking themselves out, bidding on the early American works—and they were admittedly fabulous; did you stay for those? The Russian pieces were all but overlooked. Look here—look at what else I got."

Marian lifted a tissue-shrouded package from the bottom of the box. "One of the last miniatures to be put on the block today. It's Alexander the First." She handed the small portrait gingerly to Amanda, turning it over as she did so. "See the signature?" Marian was all but crowing as she announced, "Argunov."

Amanda whistled. "Wow. The court portrait painter. This is quite a find, Marian."

"You're telling me. I have a customer who will faint when I tell him about this. He'll give me just about anything I want for it. Well, within reason, of course." She dipped back into the box and pulled out a very small package. "And this . . . do you know what this is?"

Amanda unfolded the wrappings to find a small silver box. "A salt box?"

"An open salt, yes. It was an old Russian custom to give one of these to your guests for good luck." Marian pointed out the details. "Enamel on filigree. Turn it over."

Amanda did as she was told.

"See the initials there? G.K. Gustav Klingert." Marian was all but singing now. "So collectible. He worked for Fabergé in Moscow in the late 1870s. Cloisonné with enamel. This one is marked 1888."

"It's remarkable. You really had quite a day, didn't you?"

"I had a wonderful day. One hell of a day. I also managed to pick up a few choice pieces of jewelry—a pendant, some earrings. All quite fine." Marian set the salt box next to the portrait on the glass counter. "I can barely wait to call my customer. He'll be so excited. Oh, and I have a dealer friend in D.C. who will just jump through hoops to get this Klingert piece."

"Well, then, what are you waiting for?" Amanda laughed. "There's the phone."

"I am going to call my customer right now. I just can't wait to see his face when he sees the miniature." Marian reached behind the counter for the phone and lifted it, placed it next to her prizes. "You know, finds like this are what keep you in this business. You just never know what the next day is going to bring."

Still beaming broadly, Marian dialed the number.

"Lock this behind me," Amanda called to her as she left the shop.

"I will. . . . oh, hello? Mr. Peterson?"

Back in her shop, Amanda made calls of her own. To Iona, thanking her again for telling her about the sale and for dragging her to it. To Evan, apologizing for not having been able to meet him for lunch today. She'd had to leave messages for both of them.

She locked the shop behind her, then walked the cobblestone path to the parking lot where she discovered that she had a flat.

"Damn," she said aloud, her fisted hands on her hips, before kicking the tire a time or two.

"That was mature," she muttered, and went to the rear of the car. Opening the trunk, she checked for her spare tire. "Great. A doughnut. My tire goes flat and all I have to replace it with is a doughnut. . . ."

Rooting around, she found the tool kit that came with the car. She removed the spare tire and rolled it to the front of the car. "Might as well get this over with . . ."

"Do you need a hand there?" The voice seemed to come from nowhere.

Amanda jumped, her fingers tightening around the tire iron. "No, thank you. I can take care of this."

"Hey, I don't mind." The man stepped from around the side of the pickup parked next to her car. "Pretty girl like you shouldn't have to change her own tire. Chivalry ain't exactly dead, you know."

"Thanks anyway, but I really can do this for myself." She turned away and returned to the task at hand.

"Okay. Just trying to be friendly here."

"I appreciate the offer," she said, barely looking at him, "but really, I don't need help. But thank you. It was nice of you to offer."

"Hey, anytime," he said somewhat sourly, as if he felt he'd been rudely rebuffed.

A minute later, Amanda heard the pickup roll off, and she slid the jack under her car, her would-be Samaritan already forgotten.

___ CHAPTER ___
EIGHT

VINCE LAY BACK ON THE BED IN HIS RENTED ROOM and tried to organize his thoughts. He had a lot on his mind tonight and needed to make sure he had it all straight. He'd had a busy day.

He'd made his first contact with both of his intended victims. He'd only meant to check up on that Marian O'Connor, the one Archer had called the "antiques lady with the big mouth." She'd been the one who'd called the police that night when Archer had had to teach Amanda who wore the pants in their relationship.

Vince snickered out loud.

Like anyone in their right mind would believe that a woman like Amanda Crosby would be in a relationship with Archer Lowell. Vince had seen her up close and had known right away that she was classy and smart. How deluded would you have to be to really think that a quality broad like her would look twice at a moron like Lowell? Well, that pretty much said it all about Archer, didn't it?

However, a deal was still a deal, no matter how stupid one of the parties might be. Vince wasn't about to go back on his word just because he was beginning to realize just how nuts Lowell really was. That would

hardly be fair. If nothing else, he owed it to Curt
Channing—a real stand-up guy, in Vince's book—to
keep the game going. Vince never lost sight of the fact
that if he took care of his piece, then Archer, once out
of prison, would be obligated to take care of Channing's. That was the way it was going to be. A new
twist on the old *eye for an eye* thing.

Marian O'Connor would be easy to take out. She
was alone in her shop all day, every day, from nine or
earlier in the morning till she opened at ten, then later,
from when she closed at six to maybe seven, when
she actually left. And she wasn't physically strong.
He'd watched her struggle with a box that the smaller
Amanda had carried effortlessly. Easy enough to set
this up, once he decided on a method.

A glance at the clock reminded him that he had just
an hour or so to shower, dress, and pick up Dolores
at her apartment. Over the past week, they'd become
friends over beers and conversation down at the Dew
Drop, just as he'd planned. Tonight would be their
first real date. Dinner and a movie. And he had even
bigger plans for Miss Dolores. Oh, yes, he certainly
did.

Grinning to himself, he went into the bathroom
and turned on the shower. He had those plans already
mapped out. Dinner tonight would be just the beginning. He had to let her see that he was a class guy, a
gentleman. He had her figured out, all right. He'd had
from the minute he first laid eyes on her. He might not
be a genius, but he could read women better than
most.

Dolores was what Montel or Oprah would call
needy. Late thirties, single, a dull mouse of a woman.

Went to church every Sunday. Owned her own business—well, half of one, anyway. But for all her talk of independence, for all she managed to do for herself, she was one of those women who, deep down inside, believed that her life wasn't complete until there was a man in it. And she was still idealistic enough to believe that, late though he might be, her prince could still come. In fact, she was counting on it.

Prince Vinnie, that's me, Vince chuckled as he got into the shower. *Oh, yeah. I'm a real prince of a guy. . . .*

The way he saw it, soon enough he'd be moving in with Dolores and setting up house for a while. He liked having a home, being part of a domestic scene. He hated this rented room thing. He wanted a nice hot home-cooked meal every night, wanted a woman in his bed, wanted . . . well, wanted all of the comforts of home.

However temporary that might be.

Dolores, being Dolores, would never ask him where he'd been or where he was going. If he told her he had a meeting for work at night, she'd believe him. If he told her he'd been working a sixteen-hour day, she'd believe him—a virtue under these circumstances. If he told her the truth, of course, he'd have to kill her. And he'd hate to do that. She really was a nice lady.

Of course, if it ever came down to her or him, he would have to be the one to survive. There was no question about that. But it wasn't likely to happen. He was going to play this one really, really smart. No one would ever be able to connect the killer of a couple of antiques dealers with Vince Giordano—er, Vinnie Daniels, that is. He'd changed his look, he'd changed his name. He'd even gotten a new social security number, thanks to the real Vincent Daniels, who'd died at age two and who was buried in the cemetery behind the old Methodist church three streets down. He watched all the cop shows. He knew how to change his identity.

And when his victims were found, why, he'd sit right there at the bar in the Dew Drop and shake his head, just like everyone else would be doing, and wonder aloud who could do such horrible things and talk about being worried that there was so much crime in a town just miles from here.

Whistling, he turned off the water and stepped out of the shower. He felt better than he had in a long time. Focused. Powerful. He had the cops totally stumped, and he loved it. They had no clue as to who had put the bullet in Derek England's brain. He'd committed cold-blooded murder and gotten away with it. Again.

One down, two to go.

He turned on the small radio and hummed along as he shaved before the small mirror above the sink, thinking back on how easy it had been to kill Derek. Just one *bam!* and it was done. He'd felt oddly disappointed. There'd been no challenge and therefore no real sense of satisfaction. Of course, he had experience with using a handgun to kill. But those deaths, well, they had been different. There had been passion. Purpose. Those deaths had meant something to him on a deeply personal level. Maybe that was what was missing now. That personal touch . . .

He pushed the past aside as easily as he pushed the newspaper from the chair to the floor.

It occurred to him then to wonder if he should shoot Marian, too. But then there would be a quick connect-the-dots, and then it would be murder—he chuckled aloud at the pun—to get close enough to Amanda for him to TCB.

Perhaps the victim should determine the method.

He liked the sound of that.

Meanwhile, he could think about Amanda and the chaos he'd set loose in her life. He'd felt a thrill just getting close to her earlier in the day. Just hearing her voice had excited him. He had been more than just a little pissed off that she'd blown him off the way she had. After all, he'd only been trying to help. Who did she think she was, anyway, to dismiss him like that?

He'd show her, soon enough, who was who.

Marian first, of course. Maybe he'd go into her shop one day soon, maybe even buy a little something for Dolores. Maybe even flirt a bit with middle-aged Marian, make her day before he killed her. Let her die with a smile on her face.

As if, he thought with a smirk, his good mood returning.

He dressed quickly and ran down the steps. Dolores was waiting.

──── CHAPTER ────
NINE

SEAN STUDIED THE REPORT THAT HAD BEEN FAXED TO him from the county detectives and left on his desk by Eddie Shanahan, the night duty officer. There was no longer any question that Amanda Crosby's gun was not the gun that had killed Derek England. Somehow he wasn't the least bit surprised. What did surprise him was that he felt a flash of relief while reading the report. In his typical fashion, he managed to ignore it.

The victim's companion, Clark Lehmann, would have made a perfect suspect, too, but his phone records proved that he'd been at home, calling around, looking for Derek, on the night of the murder, just as he'd said. There were hardly more than forty minutes unaccounted for the entire night. Of course, conceivably, he could have killed Derek before he'd left the house, driven the car to the park where it was found the next morning . . .

Nah. There just wasn't enough time for him to have done that. When Lehmann had said he'd called everyone he knew that night, he wasn't kidding. His phone records bore that out. He'd made several long distance calls that accounted for most of the evening. He wouldn't have had time to have driven the car to the park, positioned Derek behind the wheel, shot him, then walked back home.

Unless someone was working with him. Someone who met him at the crime scene, drove him home . . .

Maybe that's how it had gone down. Maybe Lehmann and someone else—maybe Amanda—had planned it down to the minute. Maybe Lehmann had gone with Derek to Amanda's, had somehow gotten Derek to stop at the park, where . . .

Where what? Where Lehmann jumped into the backseat, put a bullet through Derek's head, then jumped into Amanda's car, she drove him home, then rushed home to place the first phone call to Lehmann . . . ?

"It didn't happen that way," he said softly. "There was only one set of tire tracks at the park. . . ."

Besides, this was a simple murder. Somehow the murderer had gotten into the backseat of Derek's car, put the gun to his head, pulled the trigger. Got back out of the car and calmly left the scene. There was no sign of gravel being kicked up by a car racing away. No sign of panic. Nothing to suggest this hadn't simply been a cold-blooded murder.

He didn't think Lehmann or Crosby was capable of that.

He glanced at the clock. Barely six in the morning. Too early to call Clark Lehmann to ask if he'd been able to come up with any reason why someone would have wanted Derek dead.

He'd already spoken with all of Derek's friends, and every single one of them could account for their time that night. Most had been contacted by Clark at some point over the course of the evening. All of them said that they couldn't imagine Derek stopping to pick up a stranger.

Well, somewhere between his house and the park he must have picked up someone. Someone who'd been very, very careful to leave no prints, no trace of any kind. He must have gone over the backseat of the car with one of those sticky-tape rollers, because the preliminary tests had come up with no hairs, no fibers that they couldn't identify.

What kind of person would be that thorough?

Sean reviewed what he knew about Clark Lehmann. Members of Lehmann's family and many of his friends had already been interviewed. All had agreed that there was no question that Derek and Clark had been devoted to each other. No one knew of any friction between them, nor was there any talk of any problems in their relationship. They'd just returned from a vacation they'd planned together, and by all accounts the two men had had a wonderful time. And while they'd had reciprocal wills, there was no question that of the two, Clark Lehmann—heir to a sizable fortune— was far better off financially than Derek was. All Clark stood to inherit was Derek's half of the house and a vacation property. Maybe half a million dollars, all told. A lot to someone like Sean. Peanuts to someone in Lehmann's position.

Amanda, on the other hand, inherited Derek's half of the business. Admittedly, it wasn't worth a whole lot, especially since Derek had just spent most of their nest egg on one item that was going to be returned to its rightful owner with no reimbursement to the business. Nothing there worth killing for, as far as Sean could see, but the two witnesses he'd be interviewing that afternoon might shed a little more light on the relationship between Crosby and England.

Maybe it had been a robbery—random or otherwise—after all.

And there was still the possibility that the killer was someone who knew about Derek's purchase of the goblet on the black market. Someone who had followed Derek from Italy, or someone he'd told about his find.

Sean began to make a list of all the questions he'd need answered about that goblet, starting with its authenticity. He had only Amanda's word for what the item actually was. Well, her word, and the emails from this Daria McGowan. He'd have to check her out, too, make sure she was who Amanda claimed. He made a note to call Dr. Abraham at the University of Pennsylvania Museum of Archaeology and Anthropology. Perhaps he could corroborate Amanda's version of what the goblet was and its potential value to a collector.

And he'd need a list of collectors of this sort of object. Maybe have Amanda go through her list of customers and see if she could figure out who the intended buyer might have been. And wasn't there a possibility that the intended buyer was another dealer? Guess he'd have to stop by her shop this morning and ask.

Of course, he'd planned on stopping at Crosby & England anyway on his way back from the prison after he'd had a little chat with Archer Lowell. Which reminded him that he needed to leave now if he was going to arrive by eight.

He'd intended to make this trip on Monday, like he'd told Amanda he'd do. But a major accident out on

River Road involving several cars and a tractor trailer had resulted in three fatalities, and the investigation—not to mention the paperwork—had consumed much of the past two days.

Well, no harm, no foul, he told himself. Archer Lowell wasn't going anyplace any time soon.

The Avon County prison—also known as High Meadow—sat on 265 acres in the middle of what had at one time been a cow pasture. Now housing developments encroached from every side. Though why in the world anyone would pay big dollars to live in the shadow of a prison, Sean could not fathom. The developers could build their berms and plant their trees and erect their stone walls, but they couldn't change the fact that just beyond those flimsy little barriers lived some of the most hardened men—and women—in the state.

Nice place to raise your kids, he thought dryly as he turned off the main road and stopped at the guard post. He reached for his identification, but was waved through by the guard, who called, "Go on up, Chief." He drove to the visitors' lot, which lay just beyond the row of reserved parking for prison VIPs. The warden's spot was still empty. Sean rolled down his windows and leaned back against the seat. He could wait.

He mentally ran through the questions he planned to ask Archer Lowell. He'd read the file through twice over the weekend and was probably more current with the story than Lowell himself was at this point. Though Sean doubted anything would change, as far as Lowell was concerned. It was obvious from the file that Lowell believed that he and Amanda were star-crossed lovers; obvious too that he'd believed Derek was his rival for Amanda's affections. He apparently hadn't known that Derek was gay, hadn't realized that the two were best of friends, hadn't realized that Derek was in the shop all the time because he was half owner of the business. According to the interview, Lowell believed that Derek was in love with Amanda, that he was trying to wrest her away. It was textbook classic. The court-appointed psychiatrist who examined Lowell had been fully prepared to testify that Lowell suffered from delusions as well as erotomania. While Amanda was an acquaintance of Lowell's, he could hardly be called her peer. Which was, of course, typical in a case like this, where the victim was often of higher social standing.

And Lowell's pattern of stalking had also been lifted right out of a textbook. He wrote notes to Amanda, called her home and shop at all hours of the day and night, left gifts for her. He'd become angry when she asked him—then told him—to stop contacting her. He'd later told police that he and Amanda loved each other and would be with each other if Derek didn't stand in the way. Derek was trying to come between him and Amanda. That was why he'd threatened Derek.

A black Impala pulled into the lot and parked in the spot Sean had been watching. He got out of the car and walked over to the sidewalk to wait for the warden to turn off his engine.

"Hey, Mercer. Whatcha doing out here?" Warden Fred McCabe rolled his large self out from behind the wheel of the car. Newly promoted from assistant warden to warden, he took his time getting from one place to another.

"Wanted to have a few words with one of your boys."

"Inmate or employee?"

"Inmate." Sean extended his hand when McCabe drew close enough to shake it.

"Who do you need?" They headed for the prison entrance.

"Archer Lowell."

"Lowell?" McCabe frowned. "What would you want with him?"

"Need to ask him some questions about his stalking techniques."

McCabe stopped in midstride. "He hasn't been in contact with her, has he? Because if he has, I'll have his sentence doubled. The district attorney himself warned that little shit that he was to have no contact with his victim. I guess it didn't hurt that her brother was a detective down there in Lyndon, you know? Heard he's working for the county now."

"I heard." Sean paused. "Do you know him personally? The brother, I mean . . ."

"Evan? Sure. He's a good cop. Maybe the best they had." McCabe held the door open for Sean. "Man, he was incensed when he heard about how she'd reported everything and how old chief Anderson blew her off."

"I know the story."

"Well, suffice it to say that Evan raised so much hell with the D.A. that there was no choice but to fire the poor bastard. There were some who thought Crosby went a little too far with that." McCabe waved to the receptionist and started down the hall to his office, Sean right behind him. "Course, that bastard Lowell had tried to kill his sister. Guess it would tend to piss off just about anyone, you know. I mean, if it had been your sister . . ." He opened his office door and stood aside for Sean to enter. "So why the sudden interest in Lowell?"

"Amanda Crosby's business partner was murdered last week in Broeder." Sean took a seat on a chair that was every bit as uncomfortable as it looked.

"That gay guy? The one who was shot through the head?" McCabe took off his jacket and hung it on a shiny brass coatrack that looked out of place in the dull surroundings. "I heard about that. Didn't realize he was the same guy, though."

"The same guy who'd been threatened by Lowell, the same guy Lowell thought was out to steal his girl . . ."

"Yeah, right. Like a woman like that Crosby girl was gonna give the time of day to a punk like Archer Lowell." McCabe looked disgusted. "He beat her up, you know? Broke a few of her ribs, broke a couple of her fingers. Messed up her face, too, I heard."

Sean held up a hand to stop him. "I read the reports." He didn't want to discuss Amanda's beating at the hands of Archer Lowell. He'd seen the pictures, and they'd made him not only ill, but angry.

"Other than the fact that this guy was threatened by Lowell over a year ago, what's the connection?"

"I don't know that there is one. I just want to talk to him." Sean wasn't ready to share with anyone the possibility that Amanda may have drawn the attention of someone who appeared to be following in Lowell's footsteps.

"I'll have him brought up." McCabe grabbed the

phone and gave the order to bring Archer Lowell to interview room twelve as soon as possible. "You remember the way?"

The first thing that occurred to Sean when Archer Lowell shuffled into the room was that he looked way too young to be harbored here with so many hardened criminals. The second thing was that there appeared to be little or no life in his eyes.

No sign of *intelligent* life, Sean amended.

"Who are you?" Lowell asked as he sat down in the plastic chair.

"Chief Mercer, Broeder police."

"Yeah, I heard they fired Anderson's ass." Lowell nodded. "What do you want?"

"I want to talk about the crime that got you in here."

"Wasn't no crime," he muttered.

"It wasn't?"

"No, man. Me and Amanda . . . she and I were . . . well, you know."

"Lovers?"

"We would have been," Lowell said sullenly.

"What happened?"

"You're the chief of police, you got the file, you can read. Figure it out."

"I read about how you were obsessed with Amanda."

"Hey, man, she loved me. Maybe she still does, all I know."

"Do you still love her?"

"No, man, I got no use for her now. It's all confusing, you know?" He scratched his elbow. "I mean, we were going to be together. Should have been together, but it all got mixed up. First that old biddy next door got involved. . . ."

"You mean her next-door neighbor?"

"Nah, I mean the old lady with the shop across from hers. Bigmouthed bitch."

"Marian O'Connor?"

"Yeah, somethin' like that. Anyway, she told the cops I was bothering Amanda, told them she'd seen me around the shop at night. And then that guy got involved. He was hanging around her all the time. Every day, man, he was right there, in her face."

"You're referring to her business partner?"

"Huh?"

"Derek England was her business partner."

"Whatever." Lowell shrugged.

"He was murdered a week ago." Sean leaned forward to watch Lowell's face.

"What?" His brows drew together slowly. "The dude is dead?"

Sean nodded.

"Ha. What do you know about that?" Lowell sat back in his chair. "Someone took the dude out."

"You wouldn't happen to know who, would you?"

"Me? You crazy?" Lowell scoffed. "I didn't even know about it till just now. Why would you even think that?"

"Because right before England was killed, someone started sending Ms. Crosby the same kind of messages that you had."

"Someone's sending . . ." He looked puzzled. "I don't know nothing about that, man. How could I? I been in here all this time. The judge, he told me not to have any contact with her, not ever. I can't talk to her, call her. . . . Shit, when I get out, I won't even be able to drive down her street without getting arrested."

Sean continued to watch the young man's face. "Maybe you have a friend—"

"I got no friends, man."

"Who comes to see you?"

"My mother, once in a while. My sister, she came a time or two back in the beginning, but she hasn't been around in a long time. You can check that out easy enough with the warden, though. I ain't telling you anything you can't find out on your own."

"It's odd, don't you think, that whoever is doing this is following exactly the pattern you set?"

"I don't understand what you mean."

"I mean the person who is calling her and hanging up the phone is also leaving red roses on her front doorstep."

"Huh. Really?"

"Really. And since the police never released the information about the roses to the public, I got to thinking that maybe you told someone about it."

Sean's eyes never left Lowell's face.

"No, I never told . . ."

A faint light began to dawn ever so slowly in Lowell's pale blue eyes. Sean could see it.

"I never told no one." Lowell shook his head vehemently, his gaze suddenly fixated on a spot on the wall somewhere behind Sean's head.

"Then I guess that means that someone else is in love with Amanda Crosby and bringing her roses."

"I . . . I don't know. I mean, I guess maybe. Yeah. Her luck, huh?" Lowell stood up and nodded to the guard. "I want to go back now."

"So you have no thoughts at all about who could be copying you?"

"I told you, man." His parting smile was faintly smug. "No. I don't know nothing about it."

The guard unlocked the door, and Archer Lowell disappeared through it.

Sean remained in the chair, rubbing his chin. He'd bet everything he had that when Archer Lowell first entered the room, he'd had no idea that someone had been mimicking his actions. Yet when he walked out, there'd been the briefest hint of . . . something. As if Sean had tipped him off to something so secret even Sean wasn't aware of it.

What, Sean wondered, had he said that had sparked that dim little faraway light in Archer Lowell's dull eyes?

——— CHAPTER ———
TEN

SEAN SETTLED INTO THE BACK ROW OF THE SMALL lecture hall at the Avon County Community Center, where Amanda Crosby was speaking, glad that he'd taken the time to change from his uniform to street clothes even though the stop at home had made him late by several minutes. As one of the few men in the crowd of roughly fifty people, he stood out enough as it was.

At the front of the narrow room, Amanda was already speaking, leaning back against a wooden table. He appreciated the opportunity to observe her without those green eyes boring into him, to look at her as something other than a suspect.

Her short dark hair spiked a little higher than he'd ever seen it, she wore trim black pants and a white shirt, shiny round silver earrings, a thin band on the middle finger of her right hand, and a silver watch with a narrow black leather strap on her left wrist. Though he couldn't see them from this distance, he knew her eyes were flecked with gold and outlined by dark lashes. She looked relaxed and casual, almost elegant. And totally in charge.

". . . on the handout to see the statistics. One out of every twelve women—one out of forty-five men—will be the victim of a stalker at some time in their life. If you are a woman, there is a seventy-seven percent chance that you will know your stalker—sixty-four percent if you are a man. Ladies, if you are a victim, you have a sixty percent chance of being stalked by an intimate partner. Men, almost the opposite is true. Thirty percent of men who are stalked, are stalked by an intimate partner."

Her hands slid into the pockets of her pants as she paced slowly, walking the distance between one end of the table and the other with measured steps.

"How will a stalker most likely try to get your attention? He'll place unwanted calls to your house, to your place of business. Sometimes he'll breathe into the phone. Sometimes he'll just hang up when you answer, or he'll leave messages on your answering machine. If you have email, he might send you cryptic messages or e-cards. Maybe he'll vandalize your property—scratch your car or break a window in your house. Maybe he'll threaten harm to you or someone you love, maybe your pet. He might leave you gifts, anonymously or not. He will watch you at all hours of the day or night. He'll know where you go, and he'll go there, too. He'll show up at your home, your work, your favorite restaurant, your friends' homes. Sometimes you won't even know he's been there. Until he calls you later to describe what you were wearing."

Amanda leaned against the table again and planted both feet in front of her.

"Why does he do these things?"

Sean glanced around the room. The crowd was hanging on her every word. Some were taking notes.

"He does these things because he doesn't seem to

be able to *not* do them. There are different degrees of behavior, of course, and different types of stalkers. But they all share certain characteristics." She cleared her throat.

"As a general rule, all stalkers suffer from some mental or personality disorder. They may be obsessive-compulsive, schizophrenic, paranoid, delusional, socially maladjusted with low self-esteem—or a combination of some one or several. Sometimes they will fixate on a famous person—a celebrity or an athlete—and will fantasize about a relationship that doesn't exist except in the mind of the stalker. Sometimes he or she will imagine a personal relationship with a stranger or an acquaintance. Or maybe the stalker will have had a past relationship with the victim. Some stalkers are violent; some are not. Some are likely to come no closer to their victim than the telephone. Others are capable of the most vicious attacks. Some are even capable of murder. Over the course of the next hour and a half, we'll talk about what steps you can take to protect yourself and what to do if you think you are being stalked."

She walked behind the table, took a sip of water from a bottle, then searched through a pile of papers until she found what she was looking for. She handed a stack to one of the women in the front row and asked her to distribute them to the others.

"Let's talk about how to recognize if you're being stalked. . . ."

Sean's attention began to drift. He knew this part. He'd given a similar lecture himself to the women's club in Normandy, West Virginia, where he'd last worked. There had been times since moving here to

Broeder that he'd questioned the wisdom of leaving Normandy, but all in all, he suspected, it was for the best. Greer had been so insistent.

"Come on, Sean. This is fate. It just can't be a co-incidence that we're in need of a new police chief at exactly the same time I finally found you again. Say yes, Sean, please?" When he hadn't responded, she'd pleaded, "At least come and interview for the job. Maybe you won't like it here. Maybe they won't like you. But at least say you'll apply?"

He'd applied. And he had liked the town, liked the feel of it, liked the pace, just as much as he'd liked Normandy. And the committee appointed by the president of the borough council to select the new po-lice chief had liked him, Greer assured him after his first interview. What she hadn't told him was that Steve, her husband, was the president of the council, and that she'd made sure that he understood how im-portant it was to her to have her younger brother back in her life again after all these years of being separated.

Sean couldn't help but smile to himself. Greer had always been a bossy thing. He remembered that much about her.

And it wasn't as if he wasn't happy here. He liked the job. He had a force of men and women he was proud of, good cops, each of them professional and caring. He was paid well and sensed that the towns-people both liked and respected him and the job he'd done so far. He had a little house—Greer had found it for him and was forever nagging him about its lack of furnishing and general warmth, but he suspected she'd been watching too many decorating shows on

TV. Lately she'd been threatening to just take over and "create an environment" for him. Whatever that meant.

". . . document every single incident," Amanda was saying. "Take photographs if you can. Videos can be even better. Get statements from anyone who witnessed the incident and save every one of the answering machine tapes . . ."

He wondered how Amanda's story might have been different had she done those things right from the start. From the file, it was obvious that she'd reacted too late to the situation. Things had escalated to a point of no return before she'd begun to build her case against Archer Lowell. Because she'd thrown away the early notes that Lowell had left for her and because she'd taken no photos and erased all the messages on her answering machine, she had nothing to show the police when she went to them.

He wondered what her detective brother had had to say about her lack of forethought. He wondered how long it had progressed before she even told him. Sean had read her statement several times. He understood why she had thought she could handle the young man herself, why she thought a simple, *Sorry, Archer, I'm not interested in you that way, but I would like to be your friend,* would be sufficient. Most women would think that way.

He guessed that might be why she'd taken it upon herself to volunteer to give these lectures.

She may have been naive as far as Archer's intentions were, but she sure as hell projected self-confidence now. Ms. Crosby was, without question, large and in charge these days.

Not so large, though, he thought, watching her slender body pace as he leaned forward to hear a question someone had asked. Amanda's response was crisp and to the point. Watching her, one would never suspect that anyone had intimidated her, broken her down, least of all some slimy little wienie like Archer Lowell.

Then again, the woman standing at the front of the room seemed harder, stronger, than the woman whose step had faltered when she'd found the rose that someone had left for her, or whose hands had begun to shake when she'd gotten that hang-up call.

Which was the real Amanda Crosby? he wondered.

And was either of them capable of murder?

Sean had been asking himself that all afternoon, ever since he'd interviewed Marian O'Connor and Iona McGowan, both of whom Amanda had spoken with about her partner's black market purchase. Both had admitted that Amanda had been furious with Derek. And both, after he'd worn them down, had admitted that Amanda had made some pretty damning remarks.

"Ms. McGowan, what did Ms. Crosby say about Mr. England's buying this vase?" he'd asked.

"It was a goblet," Iona had replied.

"Right. Goblet. I know she discussed this with you. She had you get in touch with your sister—she told me that. So she must have said something to you about her partner buying it, and I'd like to know what that something was."

Iona had stared at him for a long minute, then said, "Amanda was not happy that Derek had bought the goblet."

"Not happy. Is that what she said? 'Iona, I'm not happy that Derek bought this goblet'?" He had leaned forward just slightly. "Or did she say something a little stronger than 'I'm not happy . . .'?"

His witness appeared restless then, and he knew his instincts had been right. They both knew what Amanda had said. He just wanted to hear Iona say it.

"Ms. McGowan?" He tilted his head to place himself in her line of vision, since she'd turned away from him just slightly, as if unable to meet his eyes. "Did Ms. Crosby say she was going to welcome Mr. England home with open arms?"

"She said . . . something about not being sure she wanted to continue the business partnership."

"That's all? 'I'm not sure I want to be his partner anymore'?" He had stroked his chin thoughtfully. "Well, I guess I can understand that. The guy spent all their money on a black market purchase. I can see where she'd be really pissed. And she was really pissed off, wasn't she?"

Iona had nodded stiffly.

"And she said . . . What else did she say?" he persisted.

"I don't remember everything she said."

"Oh, I'll bet you do. I'll bet she said something along the lines of 'I could just smack him.' Or 'I could just shoot him.' Or 'I could just—' "

"Yes."

"Yes, what?"

"Yes, she said something along those lines."

" 'I could just kill him.' " Sean had watched Iona's face. "That's what she said, isn't it?"

"She didn't mean she'd actually kill him."

"I'm sure she didn't. But that is what she said, isn't it?"

"Well, yes, but how many times have you been so angry at someone that you said that? Or something like that? I've done it."

"We've all done it."

"It doesn't mean she killed him. She would never . . ." Iona had struggled for words. "She would never hurt anyone. Especially someone she loved. And for all their differences, all the ups and downs they've had over the years, she and Derek loved each other. They were like brother and sister. That's how it was between them. She'd get angry with him, and at times he'd get angry with her. But she would never have hurt him, nor him, her."

"Thank you, Ms. McGowan. You're free to go."

Even now, hours later, Sean wasn't sure he didn't regret having goaded Iona into the admission. It smacked of dirty pool, of the type of police interrogation he'd always tried to avoid. Of course he had thought that Amanda might have made a statement like that in anger. And Iona was right. He had said things like that himself over the years. The difference was, he had never gone and done it. It remained to be seen whether Amanda Crosby had.

"Certainly, if the stalker is someone you know, you need to tell him—or her—that they need to stop. Tell them you will go to the police—and then do it." She seemed to be addressing a woman several rows back. Had they moved into Q and A already?

And then there was Marian O'Connor, the woman who owned the shop directly across from Amanda's. She, too, had heard Amanda make damning statements, but she, too, had insisted that it had been nothing more than a reaction, words tossed off in the heat of the moment.

People often committed murder in the heat of the moment, he could have reminded her.

So here he had a prime suspect. She had motive. She had opportunity. After all, he had only her word that Derek had not arrived at her house that night.

He heard his name and snapped out of the zone he'd drifted into.

"Chief Mercer, since you're here, perhaps you'd like to add something to what I've said?" She stood with her hands on her hips, her voice just slightly mocking, as if confident that she knew as much—maybe more—about this particular crime as he did.

"No, I think you've about covered it all." He nodded. "I can't think of a thing to add."

"Perhaps you could run through the process by which a victim might obtain a protection from abuse order?"

"Oh. Well, sure . . ."

She gestured for him to join her at the front of the room. He cursed her silently as he made his way up the aisle. He really hadn't been prepared for this, had wanted to attend tonight only to watch her, see what he could learn about her. He didn't appreciate being pulled into the spotlight.

"Are you sure there's nothing you can add to what we've already discussed about what you should do if you suspect you're being stalked?" She smiled sweetly. "After all, you are the expert."

Ignoring her sarcasm, he shrugged nonchalantly.

"Well, I think the advice you gave—document the incidents—is really important."

"And if one were interested in obtaining a protection from abuse order, how would one go about doing that?"

"You come right on down to the station, bringing everything—tapes, photos, whatever you have—and I'll get in touch with the district attorney's office. We'll help you put the wheels in motion."

"But what if you don't have any documentation? What if there are no answering machine tapes, for example?"

"You can always record the dates and times you received the calls. Use the return call feature on your phone to see if the number can be traced. Make a note of it. In some areas you can report the call directly to the police by dialing a specific number. And if you haven't done any of those things, just bring yourself in and tell me what's been going on. We'll do our best to help you. Of course, it's easier if we know who the stalker is." He looked directly at Amanda. "Things get a bit dicier if we're starting from scratch, trying to figure out who an anonymous caller is, for example."

"Questions for the chief?" Amanda moved right past that last remark.

Q and A ran out the rest of the clock. Some were starting to get a little antsy to leave, and Amanda had announced they'd run past time by twenty minutes. She closed by reminding them that if they suspected that someone's attention was becoming a bit more than they could deal with, they should talk to someone.

"If there's no one else, you can always talk to me," she assured them. "My phone number is right there at the top of the first sheet."

Several of the women in attendance stopped on their way to the door to tell Amanda how informative her talk had been, or to relate a story, or just to thank her for giving them a way to fight back through the legal system. When the last of the group had filed out, Amanda turned to Sean and said, "I'm assuming that you didn't hang around because you wanted some tips on what to do if someone starts leaving unwanted gifts in your mailbox."

He opened his mouth to respond, but before he could get a word out, she said, "I know that you talked with my friends today. With Iona and with Marian. I know what they told you. I'm not going to deny it, so leave them both out of it, okay? I mean, Iona is so upset. She's positive I'm going to be arrested for Derek's murder because of what she said."

Her hands shook slightly with barely repressed anger. "I understand why you spoke with them. I understand why you felt it was necessary to lean on them. My brother's a cop, remember? I know the drill."

She didn't wait for an answer. "But don't upset them anymore, all right? You have the voice mail I left for Derek. You know what I said." She slammed her leather binder that held her notes and extra copies of her handouts on the table and glared at him. "I did say it. But I didn't do it. I didn't even see Derek that night."

"We only have your word of that."

Color flushed her cheeks. "I'm not used to being

called a liar." She gathered her things to leave. "I don't like it."

"I'm not calling you a liar, Ms. Crosby, but the truth is, I don't know what happened that night."

"Neither do I. But it seems to me that you're spending an awful lot of time trying to fit me into the scenario when you could be looking for the real killer."

"We have every available officer working on this case, looking for leads. Actually, that's why I'm here tonight."

She stopped near the door and turned. He was closer behind her than she'd expected him to be. Somehow he looked bigger, more formidable, in jeans and a shirt than he did in his uniform. She took a short step back without realizing she'd done so.

"You mentioned that Derek told you he had a buyer for the goblet. Have you given any thought who that might have been?"

"Yes, and I haven't been able to come up with anyone. You'd think that if someone was waiting for it, they'd call and ask me about it. Unfortunately, I don't know who all his clients were."

"His clients? I thought you co-owned the business."

"We are—were—equal partners. But we each had some of our own clients, people for whom we shopped for specific items. For example, I have several customers who like certain kinds of art pottery. When I go to sales, I'll look for pieces I know they don't have and would want. I know they'll buy what I bring them. Derek was the same. There are some who deal directly with him."

"But you don't have a list of his customers."

"No. I know he kept an address book. And I can go

through the Rolodex. Maybe he made some comments on some of the cards. You know, *Has no conscience, is willing to buy black market*—that sort of thing. I can make a list for you."

"Call me when you get it together. I'm going to want to talk to everyone on that list as soon as possible."

"Or maybe . . ." She hesitated. "Maybe Derek kept some of the information on the computer."

"Mr. Lehmann said Derek didn't own a computer."

"He didn't. He used my laptop when he came into the shop. He kept his sales records on disks."

"Where's your laptop now?"

"In my car. But the disks are at the shop."

"Can I stop by and pick them up tomorrow? I have a few appointments in the morning, but I'll be free around four."

"Just in time for tea." She smiled weakly. "I'll look over the names and see if any of them stand out for any reason."

"Great. I guess we're done here, then?" He paused in the doorway.

"Yes. If you'd just snap off the light . . . thanks."

They walked down the dimly lit hall together, their shoes making tiny squeaky sounds on the tile floor.

"I stopped in to see your old friend Lowell this morning."

"You did?" She frowned. "When were you going to tell me that?"

"I just did."

They had reached the front entrance. Sean waved to the guard as he held the door open for Amanda. He followed her through it.

"And . . . ?"

"I'll tell you the truth, there was an odd vibe there. At first, he seemed genuinely shocked when I told him that it was starting to look like someone was stalking you."

"Maybe he was acting."

"You've met Archer Lowell. You think he's that good an actor?"

"You have a point. Where does the odd vibe come in?"

"All of a sudden, it was like he had a little light go on someplace."

"You're kidding."

"No. And as slow as he is . . ."

"Any little bit of light looks like a beacon."

"Exactly."

"Well, what was it you said that might have set that off?"

"I'm not sure." Sean stopped at the back of her car while she unlocked it. "We were talking about the roses and how the public had not been informed that he'd left roses at your house. He says he never told anyone that he'd done that."

"You believe him?"

"Not really."

"Then again, maybe he just got a thrill thinking about me again," she said dryly.

"Not to disappoint you, but he doesn't seem all that interested in you anymore."

"Shucks. Ya think there's another woman in his life now?"

"Well, you know, there are a lot of women who are attracted to men who wear a uniform."

"Personal experience, Chief?"

"Nah. I wish," he laughed self-consciously.

She opened the driver's side door and leaned in to drop her things onto the passenger's seat.

"Oh, I'm sure you're not wanting for female companionship." She smiled. *Like that hot-looking redhead with all those tattoos.*

"I haven't had a whole lot of time lately for female companionship."

She slid behind the wheel of the car without comment. She knew better. "Well, Chief, I guess I'll see you tomorrow afternoon."

He nodded and slammed her car door for her. She rolled down the window and put the car in gear.

"Chief Mercer," she said just as he turned to walk to his own car two rows down. "Do you think I did it? Do you think I killed Derek?"

"It doesn't matter what I think," he told her. "The only thing that matters is what the evidence shows."

"Thanks. Always good to know where you stand."

"Be careful driving home, Ms. Crosby."

"Thanks."

She was halfway home when she realized he was following her. When she pulled into her drive, he parked across the street in the shadow of a long hedge. Going into the house, she ignored his presence and the blinking light on her answering machine and went into the kitchen to rummage for something to replace the dinner she hadn't had time to eat that night, thinking that while the woman she was today was far better equipped to deal with a possible stalker situation than she'd been a year ago, it still gave her some measure of comfort to know that someone was watching her back.

There was something coolly reassuring about Chief Sean Mercer, with his deep dark eyes and soft voice and his way of looking at you that could stop you cold. If she were a bad guy and he turned that gaze on her, she'd abandon any plans to break the law.

Of course, she reminded herself ruefully, he had turned that gaze on her. On several occasions. But she'd been able to meet him head-on. She was innocent. She should have nothing to fear.

Oh, but the thought that she might be a suspect in Derek's death was unbearably painful. That Sean Mercer could believe she might be a murderer somehow made the cut that much deeper. Well, she'd just have to do whatever she had to to prove her innocence and, at the same time, turn over every stone in search of Derek's killer.

Maybe Mercer was right. Maybe there was a connection to the goblet. Maybe she'd been wrong to dismiss the possibility so quickly. Tomorrow she'd find Derek's client list. If she had to call everyone in his address book, everyone on his Rolodex, everyone he'd ever made a sale to, she'd track down the person he had in mind to sell the goblet to. Then she'd do whatever it took to find out just how badly he—or she—wanted it.

CHAPTER ELEVEN

FOR THE FIRST TIME IN ALL THE YEARS SHE'D BEEN IN business, Amanda was happy to have no customers in the shop to distract her. She'd awakened a little before five that morning, eager to begin going through the lists of Derek's customers in the hope of identifying a possible buyer for the goblet. She showered, then breakfasted on an English muffin and some chocolate yogurt, planning on stopping at the convenience store at the end of her street for coffee on her way to St. Mark's. Dressed in a denim skirt and a yellow cotton twin set, she slipped into flat leather sandals and out the door.

The sun was barely up and the grass still wet and slick with dew. Her feet kicked up dots of water that tossed themselves onto the backs of her legs as she walked to the end of the driveway to pick up her morning newspaper. The air was rich with the scent of apples from the trees on her neighbor's property and the sweet autumn clematis that covered one side of her garage and had just started to bloom. It was still warm, but there was no question that summer, however reluctantly, was slipping away.

Amanda pulled into the parking lot at St. Mark's,

expecting to be the first of the shopkeepers to arrive, and was surprised to see Marian's car already there.

She must have gotten in touch with her out-of-town buyer for the miniature, Amanda supposed as she walked to the front of her own shop, keys in one hand, coffee in the other. Before sliding the key into the lock, she tried Marian's door, but it was locked. She peeked through the front window but couldn't see anyone inside. There was a light on in Marian's office in the back of the shop, however, and Amanda assumed she was there, perhaps doing paperwork or preparing a new display. Amanda returned to her own door, thinking she'd work for a while and then give Marian a call later on in the morning to share some break time, as they often did.

Derek's disks were in the top desk drawer, stacked in no particular order. Amanda booted up her laptop, popped in a disk, and, one by one, scanned the files wherein her late partner had recorded all his sales transactions. Not finding anything that rang a bell, she went on to the next disk, then the third, which contained a list of all of Derek's customers. Thinking this list might be more useful, she sat down at the desk and sipped at the last of her coffee while she scrolled through the names. Next to each, Derek had typed in the customer's preferences. She went from *J. Adams, early American stoneware,* to *H. Zelinski, Mission Oak.* The nearest she'd come to a notation of anything even remotely akin to the goblet was *K. Minnette, Turkish bronzes.*

A search through the remaining disks didn't seem to be any more useful. Maybe Derek's intended customer was another dealer, she theorized. Maybe one of his contacts in New York or Chicago or Boston . . .

Amanda raised the coffee cup to her lips and realized it was empty. Frowning, she decided now was as good a time as any to take a break. She'd been working since six-thirty, and it was now closing in on eleven. She walked to the front of the shop and opened the door to take in a bit of the morning. It was then that she noticed that the CLOSED sign was still hanging on Marian's door.

She tapped on the window. When there was no response, Amanda rang the bell, which she'd been hesitant to do, because Marian said the sound of it always startled her. When the bell went unanswered, Amanda went back to her own shop and dialed Marian's number. When there was no answer, she searched the top drawer of her desk for the spare key Marian had asked her to keep on hand for the inevitable day when Marian forgot her own. Amanda returned to Marian's shop and unlocked the door.

"Marian?" Amanda called from the doorway.

She'd gone but three steps into the shop when she realized that something was wrong. Something *smelled* wrong.

Tiny inner alarms began to clang with increasing intensity as she made her way toward the back of the shop. The door to Marian's office was partially closed, but she could see a sliver of light spilling out under it. Light deepened in spots by something else. Something dark.

Even as she pushed against the door, the hairs on the back of her neck, on her arms, began to rise.

"Marian?"

She pushed again and fell forward, landing partly on what was left of Marian O'Connor.

"Marian . . . Oh my God, no . . . oh my God . . ."

Her hands covering her mouth, Amanda scrambled away from the body. She rose on shaking legs and backed into the main room, oblivious to the blood that clung to her face, her hands, her clothes.

Gagging, knees about to give out on her, Amanda stumbled toward the counter, searching for the phone. She found it on the shelf behind the cash register, where it usually sat, but couldn't make her fingers punch in the three numbers that would bring the police. Over and over she tried, until she finally was able to hit 911. When the dispatcher picked up, Amanda was barely coherent. By the time Sean Mercer arrived, she'd already been sick twice and was barely able to string two words together to make a sentence.

"Try to tell me what happened." Mercer had taken her outside, away from the gore, away from the bloodied body of the woman who had been her friend. He sat with her on the bench outside Marian's shop, waiting for the medical examiner to arrive. "Take your time, Amanda. You've had a terrible shock. Take a deep breath, and tell me what you saw."

"She didn't answer the door. So I used my key—she'd given me a key. I went in and I called her but she didn't answer and I saw the light from her office and I went back there but there was something on the floor and I couldn't get the door open. . . ." She wished she could stop rambling but didn't seem able to focus. "I pushed on the door. I pushed and I fell. She was on the floor and I fell on her."

"Take another deep breath. Go on. Okay, let's start again," Sean said softly. "What time did you get to your shop this morning?"

"Around six-thirty."

"Any idea what time Marian O'Connor arrived?"

"No. She was here. Her car was already in the lot. . . ."

"So she arrived before six-thirty."

"Yes."

"Is that unusual?"

"Yes. She doesn't open till ten. But she bought some things at a sale the other day and was eager to turn them over. She was excited. She said she had clients who'd want certain of the pieces. She'd make a great profit, and she was so pleased with herself."

"These pieces—were they similar in any way to the goblet?"

"Derek's goblet? Oh, no. Not at all. Marian's were all Russian antiques. It was a specialty of hers."

"Do you know if she had contacted these customers, if she had a sale pending?"

"I wouldn't know. And no, I have no idea who her customers were. She did mention something about someone in D.C.—she might have even said a name— but I don't remember."

"So go back. You were going over lists . . ."

"Yes, I'd gone through several disks of private customers and decided to start going through the list of dealers Derek sometimes had business with, when I thought I'd take a break. I went over to chat with Marian but the shop was locked and she didn't answer the bell."

"You said you have a key. . . ."

"Yes. She left a spare key with me, just in case." She licked dry lips with a dry tongue. "Can I get some water?"

Sean got the attention of someone in uniform, and within minutes a bottle of water appeared. Amanda took long draughts, then leaned back against the bench.

"I knew when I opened the door that something wasn't right. Something didn't smell right. Didn't feel right."

"Try to think. Did you hear anything?"

"Nothing. That was another thing. Marian always had music in the shop. She had a CD player, played music all day long. But it was so quiet in there this morning. All I could hear were the clocks. She had a good eye for clocks."

He reached out and took her carefully by the wrist, raising one of her hands. She looked down slowly, then pulled her hand away, recoiling.

"Oh, my God. My hands . . . the blood . . ." She stood and started toward her shop. "I have to wash my hands. Oh, God, it's on my shirt. . . ."

She took off the yellow cardigan and held it in front of her, staring at the bloody smears across the front and the sleeves.

"You can wash your hands after we swab them for blood type," Sean told her.

"I can tell you whose blood it is." She looked at him as if puzzled. "It's Marian's. Whose else could it be? I fell over her when I opened the door."

"Let's get it swabbed, and then we'll know for sure," he said calmly.

"You have got to be kidding." Her voice began to rise with the first touches of hysteria. "You think that

I . . . that this is mine . . . I would never . . . How could you even think . . . ?" Indignation rose steadily.

"This isn't about what I think. This is about looking for blood other than the victim's. You're covered in it, and there are bloody fingerprints, footprints. Let's find out whose it is."

Mercer stood and nodded to the young policewoman who'd been keeping guard at the front of Marian's shop. "Take Ms. Crosby down to the station. Swab her, get her clothes. Keep her company, and keep her comfortable. I'll be along in a while."

Amanda's jaw dropped. Did he think she had something to do with Marian's death?

He turned his back and walked into Marian's shop, stopping to speak with one of the county's crime scene investigators who had just arrived.

"Ms. Crosby?" The young officer touched her arm gently. "If you'd come with me . . ."

Numbly, Amanda followed, wondering what horrible nightmare she'd stumbled into, and how she could find her way out before someone else she loved died.

Vince lay in the dark, balancing the glass ashtray on his abdomen, thinking about Marian and how she'd tried to scream. Not that it would have done her any good. Weak broad like her didn't have a chance. He shook his head. Why did women let themselves go like that? She didn't have the strength to fight off a ten-year-old. She really should have been in some exercise program. Gone to the Y, joined a gym. She looked like she could afford to join a gym. Lifting would have been good for her.

And for me. He smiled in the darkness and flicked the ash from his cigarette.

He thought about Amanda Crosby. That one would fight. And she didn't look like the type to scare so easy, either. He wasn't in a hurry, though. He wasn't finished playing with her yet.

He grinned. Shit, he'd only just begun to play with her. He had plans for Miss Crosby. Oh, yes, he surely did. If she wasn't scared now, she would be. Before it was over, she'd be on her knees begging for mercy.

Savoring the image, he took one last drag from the cigarette before stubbing it out. He placed the ashtray on the end of the table next to the bed and turned toward the window where a nice breeze was starting to blow in. He was grateful that the heat of summer seemed to have passed. It had been too hot in this little room without air-conditioning, hot enough that he'd had to break down and buy himself a window fan. Well, if he played his cards right, he'd be out of this cheap little room soon enough and into that nice place that Dolores had a couple of blocks down. And he had just the key to that nice little place of hers right over there in that little black velvet box.

It had been nice of Marian to give him the box for the pretty necklace. He'd heard Dolores say that emerald was her birthstone, and when he'd stopped in Marian's shop, For Old Time's Sake, picking out a present for Dolores had not been his goal. But once inside, old Marian had started chatting away and he'd had to express interest in something. The emerald pendant cost way more than he'd ever spent on any present for anyone in his whole entire life, and the fact that he'd even consider giving Dolores something that valuable, well, that just showed what he thought of her, didn't it?

"It's an estate piece," Marian had told him. "I just picked it up yesterday."

She said it like it was supposed to mean something to him. Like she assumed he'd know. Not that he'd actually considered buying it, but still, he watched Marian take it from the glass case in which it had been locked and lay it out on the counter before him like he was some mogul looking at jewels in some fancy jewelry store. It gave him a kick to think that anyone would look at him and think he could afford to buy something like that emerald pendant. So of course, he had to act the part. He picked the pendant up by the chain. Marian had said she'd throw that in for him, if he thought his lady friend might not have one, and he was thinking for what she was asking for the pendant she could throw in a blow job, too, but he didn't say that.

He'd flirted with her a little—nothing crude, of course; Marian was a lady, anyone could see that— and mentioned that the recipient would be his sister, not a lady friend. When she offered to set it aside and hold it for him for a few days, he'd pretended to think it over, then said, "You know, I think that's a good idea. I'll give it some thought and stop back tomorrow night if I decide to take it. Is eight too late?"

"I'm sorry, I close at six on weeknights. Perhaps Thursday morning?" Marian had suggested.

"My sister's birthday is Friday, and I'm taking her to visit our mother for a few days."

"Oh? How thoughtful of you. Won't your mother be thrilled. Where does she live?"

"Akron." It was the first place that came to mind, even though he'd never been there.

"Well, I'm sure you'll have a lovely visit. And I know she'll love the pendant. What girl doesn't love emeralds?"

"I'm hoping she likes it. She's had a bad year. She lost her husband. . . ."

"Oh, I'm so sorry to hear that." Marian's face had just oozed sympathy. "Look, here's my card. If you decide you want the pendant, you call me. I'll open the shop tomorrow night for you."

"Why, you'd do that for me?"

"Of course. Why not?"

"Well, then, maybe . . . Nah, you wouldn't want to . . ."

"Want to what?"

"Well, I was just thinking . . . not to put you on the spot or anything . . ."

"What?" She leaned on the counter and smiled.

"Well, maybe . . . since it might be a little late by the time I get here . . . maybe I could take you out for a bite after we conclude our business." He lowered his eyes, thinking it made him look shy, unassuming.

"Oh, you don't have to do that." And she actually blushed!

"But I'd like to. Unless, of course, there's some-one . . ."

"No, no." The blush deepened.

"Then that's what we'll do. I'll give you a call either way, let you know what I decide about the pendant, and then we'll go . . . well, why don't you decide where we'll go? Someplace nice."

"All right. I'll do it." Marian had looked very pleased with herself.

"I'll talk to you tomorrow. And if I decide against the pendant . . ."

"Yes?"

"Maybe you can show me something else that I might like."

Vince laughed out loud in the dark room. There was just nothing in the world like a single, middle-aged woman. He could wrap any one of them around his little finger, just like that.

He figured she'd be waiting all day for his call, so he'd put it off until almost five. Using a phone card, he'd called the shop from his mobile phone and told Marian he'd be there by eight-thirty. She said she'd probably close at the regular time and come back later to meet him.

And she had. It had been all just as he'd pictured it. She was wearing a simple dress, a knit in a subtle shade of green. She'd looked nice, happily expectant. He'd wished he'd had time to play it out a little more with her, maybe have a few dates, just to see how far he could go with her, but he didn't want to risk having anything go wrong. For one thing, she'd have time to start talking about him to her friends and family. A woman like that would be talking if she thought she had a live one, and that just wouldn't do. This way, he was in, he was out, the deed would be done, and no one could connect him to her.

He patted himself on the back for passing on the gun. He'd really felt little satisfaction plugging the queer. It had been over just like that. Of course, having had experience with a gun in the past, he'd expected that. This last time was different, though. There'd been no burning anger, no blind rage, no real emotion to speak of as he pulled the trigger. It had just been *bam!* and done. Where was the fun in that? Not much fun at all.

At least Marian had been a bit more lively. His arms were stretched over his head, and he flexed his hands. The Band-Aid he'd wrapped around his right thumb pulled a little, and he loosened it. He'd somehow cut himself, wasn't sure how. Maybe they'd ID his blood type as being different from Marian's, maybe they wouldn't. Not that it mattered. They'd never be able to connect him, Vinnie Daniels—or Vince Giordano, either—with this. No one had seen him going in or coming out, just like he planned. He'd been smart, all right. It had all gone so smoothly. Just right. Right down to bringing a towel and a clean change of clothes with him, and a brown paper bag to carry away the dirty ones. Somehow, he'd just known he was going to make a mess.

Oh, yeah, this had been much better than offing someone with one shot to the head.

Of course, stabbing Marian had been so much harder than shooting Derek. He rubbed his sore right shoulder. He'd had no idea of how much strength— the amount of *pressure*—it took to stab through to someone's heart. You really had to push down hard on that knife. One handed, no less, since the left hand was covering her mouth when she started to scream. Somehow after he'd stabbed her, she'd broken away from him, running for the back door. Like she really would have had a chance to get away from him.

He'd caught up with her in the office, thought about

looping his belt around her neck to strangle her from behind, then thought, *What the hell, let's go for broke here,* and he'd slit her throat. One nice slick slice and it was over. Sprayed blood like a son of a bitch, though. He was glad he'd thought to bring a change of clothing. She bled out so fast, it had almost been a disappointment to him to have it over so quickly. He had toyed with the idea of cutting off her head, but with his hands so sticky and the handle of the knife so slippery, it was just too much work. Why should he exert himself, when she was already dead, maybe from the chest wound? Why strain himself?

He wondered idly if perhaps he shouldn't think of a different, even more exciting means of dispatch for Ms. Crosby. He smiled, contemplating the possibilities, and drifted off to sleep.

_____ CHAPTER _____
TWELVE

"CHIEF, A DETECTIVE CROSBY HAS BEEN CALLING you. Called twice in the past twenty minutes."

Officer Dana Burke had slipped into the hallway to make the call to Mercer, who was still at the crime scene. Her boss hadn't said whether Amanda Crosby was to be treated like a witness or a suspect, but either way, Burke didn't think Amanda should be privy to the chief's calls. Even if the caller said he was Amanda's brother.

"What did he say?"

"He said if he didn't hear from you within the next ten, he'd have the county D.A. up your ass before noon."

"Did he leave a number?" Sean stole a look at his watch. He had one minute.

"Yeah, it's right here." She read it off to him. "She called him. I let her. You didn't say that she couldn't make any calls, so when she asked, I said okay. I hope that was all right."

"It was fine, Dana. Keep her company for a while longer. I'll be here for another hour or two."

"Well, I'll try. I mean, I'll keep her here as long as I can, but unless she's a suspect, if she wants to leave . . ."

"She's not a suspect. If she leaves, you leave with her. Just don't let her out of your sight."

"Chief?" Dana stopped him before he could disconnect. "She's been swabbed and all. Can I take her home and let her shower and all? I'll bring the clothes back to the station, but it doesn't seem right to make her sit there, covered in her friend's blood."

Sean cursed softly. "Jesus. I'd forgotten . . . yes, of course. Take her home. Take someone else with you to watch the house while you and she are inside. Help her clean up if she needs it. See if she wants anything to eat. I'll meet you at the station in about an hour."

Shaking his head and embarrassed at his own thoughtlessness, he hung up, then dialed the number she'd given him.

"Crosby."

"Mercer here. I understand you wanted to—"

"Mercer, I don't know what kind of game you're playing with my sister, but I want it stopped," Evan Crosby exploded. "You had damn well better have a good reason to be holding her."

"I'm trying to keep her alive."

"What?"

"I said, I'm trying to keep her alive," Sean repeated calmly. "I'm sure she's told you about what happened to Marian O'Connor, so you've got to be feeling at least as nervous as I am when you start thinking about the fact that both her business partner and her close friend have been murdered within the past two weeks. Right now Amanda's in the company of two officers, which is where she will remain until we figure out what the hell is going on and if there's any danger to her."

He paused. "Good enough reason, Crosby, or will the D.A. still be looking for a way up my ass by . . . what was it, noon?"

"I'll be there in an hour or so. I'm going to want to hear the whole thing." Evan didn't bother to say good-bye.

"Nice talking to you, too, Detective."

Sean closed his mobile phone and slid it back into his pocket, then stepped around the tape that ran from Marian's shop to Amanda's.

"You almost done in there?" he asked one of the crime scene techs.

"Another few minutes, I guess. We're just finishing up a sketch of the scene, then we should be able to wrap it up." The tech stood in the doorway and looked back into the shop. "Think this was a robbery gone bad?"

Sean shook his head. "I'll be surprised if anything is missing. Oh, maybe he took a little something to remember her by, but most B and E men are pretty careful to make sure there's no one home before they make their hit. They want to grab and run, quick and clean. No confrontations, no witnesses. Just in and out. Whoever did this knew exactly what he was about. There's nothing accidental about this crime scene. I'd say our boy came here expressly to kill his victim."

"He? I thought you already took her"—the tech nodded in the direction of Amanda's shop—"into custody."

"Whoever killed Marian O'Connor was tall enough to stand behind her and slash her throat in one clean motion, left to right. Jugular to carotid. The victim was considerably taller than Amanda Crosby. It wouldn't have been possible." Sean shook his head, thinking that the killer was also strong enough to have plunged a fairly large knife into the victim's sternum hard enough that a piece had broken off and remained in the wound, but since the tech had twice come close to losing his breakfast, Sean thought it best not to remind him of the details. "So no, Amanda Crosby is not a suspect. But she is a witness, and right now we're just trying to keep her out of harm's way until I can question her a little more thoroughly."

"Gotcha." The tech nodded, took a deep breath, and disappeared back inside, stepping aside to let the medical examiner pass.

"You done?" Sean asked as the doctor came through the door.

"Jesus, what a mess." Bill Westcott stripped off his plastic gloves and tossed them into the bag he held under his arm. "I can't remember ever seeing a worse crime scene." He shook his head, his expression grim as he bent over to remove the covers from his shoes and toss them into the bag with the gloves. "Whoever did this was one mean SOB."

"Can you estimate how long she's been dead, or do you need to complete the autopsy to establish that?"

"I'll know better after I've been able to take a closer look, but I'd say she's been dead for roughly fourteen, fifteen hours."

"You sure?"

"Yeah. I got fixed lividity, I got full body rigor. Corneas are cloudy. I'd say time of death is going to come in between nine and midnight last night." He nodded as he unwrapped a stick of gum and folded it into his mouth. "If that changes, I'll let you know, but it won't change by much."

"Thanks."

"Man, between the stab wound to the chest and the wound to the throat, the poor woman bled to death." The young doctor shook his head as he walked away. "Hell of a way for anyone to die. *Hell* of a way . . ."

When Sean entered his office, the first thing he noticed was that Amanda Crosby was seated on a hard chair in the far corner of the room—alone. Her hair was wet and brushed straight back from her face, which looked colorless and thin. He'd started to call Officer Burke to explain why the witness had been left alone in the room when the officer walked in behind him.

"She wanted water," the young woman explained before he could ask. "It's the first she's asked for anything."

"I didn't want her left alone."

"I only went across the hall," she replied. She twisted the top off the water bottle and handed it to Amanda.

"Thank you." Amanda nodded.

"You're welcome." Dana turned to her boss. "You'll take it from here?"

"Yes. Thanks."

"Her statement's on your desk. I've already sent her clothes to the lab."

Sean nodded his thanks, then closed the door after the departing officer and sat on the edge of his desk, fingering the file holding Amanda's written statement.

Before he could speak, Amanda looked up at him with sad, weary eyes and said, "I did not kill Marian."

"I know that."

"You do?"

"For one thing, you're not tall enough to have—" He hesitated. "To have done what was done to her."

She appeared to waver between asking and not asking.

"Someone slit her throat from behind," he said as gently as he could. Better she hear it from him, here and now, than later, on the evening news.

"She had blood . . ." Amanda's hands patted her chest.

"Yes. He did that, too."

Her eyes filled with tears. "Why would anyone . . . ? She was such a sweet and gentle woman. Why would . . . ?" She looked bewildered, lost.

"We're going to do our best to find that out."

"Why are you holding me if you know I didn't kill her?"

"You're not being held. You can leave whenever you want. I'd rather you didn't, for two reasons."

"They are . . . ?"

"One, because I might still have some questions I need you to answer about what happened. What you saw. What you heard."

"I've already told Dana—Officer Burke—what I know, but if you have other questions, okay."

"Chief, Detective Crosby is here and he's asking for you." Joyce barely got the words out through the intercom before Evan Crosby opened the office door after little more than a cursory knock.

"So I see." Sean waved Evan in as if he hadn't already entered the room.

Evan pulled a chair next to his sister's and sat on the edge, taking her hands in his. "How are you feeling, sweetheart?"

"I'm okay," she said, though tears were forming in her eyes all over again.

Her brother continued to hold her hands even as he looked at Sean. "Want to fill me in, Mercer?"

Sean quickly did so.

Evan blew out a breath. "Jesus. First Derek, now Marian. Any idea of what is going on around here?"

"We were just about to get into that."

"Chief Mercer was just telling me why I'm not a suspect," Amanda said.

"Well, isn't that nice of him." Evan turned to Sean. "I think I'd like to hear that myself."

"Marian O'Connor's throat was slit. From behind. By someone taller and stronger than she was. Now, I don't know how strong she was physically, but I know she was close to five foot ten. Amanda, you're what, five foot five?"

Amanda nodded.

"But you still think she had something to do with Derek's death?" Evan pressed.

"I think she had something to do with it, but not in the way you mean." The two lawmen stared at each other for a long moment. "I'm thinking there's a connection between Derek England's murder and Marian O'Connor's."

Evan nodded slowly. "You think the same person committed both."

"Yes, I do. But I don't think that person is your sister."

"Why would someone want to kill Derek and Marian? What do they have in common?" Amanda stood, her arms wrapped around her middle. "Other than the fact that they're both shop owners dealing in antiques, what do they have in common?"

"You," Sean told her. "They both had you in common."

"But that's silly. That makes no sense to me." She shook her head. "I mean, why?"

"If I knew that, I'd probably be able to figure out who, but right now, I don't have a clue," he admitted. "Now, I have to think that the phone calls, the flowers, were probably from the same person who—"

"What?" Evan grabbed Amanda's arm. "You didn't tell me that you were getting calls again."

"They just started right before Derek's death, and it had happened only a few times. I didn't want to jump to conclusions. I mean, it could have been legitimate wrong numbers. As for the flowers, I found the first one the day of Derek's memorial service. I thought it might have been left there by a friend, or a neighbor," she explained.

"Don't sit there and tell me that it didn't occur to you that you'd been down that road before, Manda." Evan's gaze was stony.

"Well, it did, but I didn't want my imagination to run away with me. I didn't want to make it something other than what it was. It took me a long time to get myself together after Archer Lowell, Evan. I did not want to crumble the first time someone hung up my phone when I answered."

Evan turned to Sean. "She told you about this?"

"Yes."

"And what did you do about it?"

"I tracked the rose to a grocery store out on Route Thirteen, but there's no way to trace the buyer. The store manager told me they sell dozens every week."

"Store surveillance tapes?"

"Destroyed after ten days. But even so, we don't know who we're looking for."

"Anyone walking out of the store with a rose would be a good place to start."

"Most of the flowers leave the store in a bag. The cameras don't come equipped with an X-ray function."

"So that's it?"

"Pretty much."

"What are you doing to catch him? He's been at her house—"

"But he's never gone in," Amanda pointed out.

"You don't know that when you're gone, he hasn't been sneaking in and out," Evan pointed out. "Did you ever get your security system straightened out?"

Amanda looked sheepish. "The electrician said the entire house would have to be rewired and the service upgraded before the alarm system could be activated again. It kept blowing fuses and going off at all odd hours, so I just left it inactive."

"Amanda . . ." Evan pulled a hand through his hair.

"I thought it would be okay, Evan. The only person who ever bothered me is in prison. I didn't expect to have to worry about anyone else."

"Famous last words," her brother muttered.

"We've been watching her house," Sean said matter-of-factly. "No one's been going in and out except Amanda."

"You've been watching my house?" she asked.

He nodded. "Twenty-four/seven."

"You were outside last night. Across the street."

"All night," he admitted.

"So you know that I didn't leave my house all night."

"That's right."

"Does this mean that she's no longer a suspect in Derek's murder?" Evan asked.

"The county forensic team found a black hair on the floor of Derek England's car. Dyed black. Amanda's hair is dark, but it's not dyed black. Nor is Clark Lehmann's. And according to him, the only thing the backseat of that car was used for was transporting bags and such from the store. No one ever sat back there."

"Except for Derek's killer," Evan said.

"That's how I see it."

Evan nodded. "I'm assuming that you're sending that hair out for a DNA analysis, and that you're going to run the results through CODIS."

"Well, hey, if that's what you county detectives do, then I guess we should do that, too, huh?" Sean scowled and folded his arms over his chest. "Maybe you could walk me through the process so that I know how to do it."

"Will you two please stop?" Amanda said wearily.

"Just because we're a small town with a small force doesn't mean that we don't understand and utilize the national databases."

"Sorry." Evan backed down. "That was the big brother thinking out loud. Though you might be surprised at how many police departments still balk at anything outside their own little realm. I'm sorry if it sounded as if I was giving you instructions. I didn't mean it that way."

"Apology accepted."

"Now, what about this Archer Lowell, this guy who stalked Amanda last year? I know he's still in prison, but do you think he might be behind all this? Maybe got someone to harass her?" Evan asked.

"I visited him yesterday. He swears he didn't know anything about it. Says that he understands what it will mean if he contacts her in any way, shape, or form. That he hasn't even had any visitors other than his mother and his sister."

"And you believe him?"

"It checked out at the prison. No visitors except for Mom and one sister, and that's been really sporadic. No outgoing mail. Only calls are to his mother's house, so I don't know how he could be pulling it off. And he seemed genuinely surprised when I asked him about it." Sean shook his head. "On the other hand, there seemed to be something there, under the surface. Nothing I could put my finger on, but a sort of awareness of something."

"Maybe I'll pay him a little visit before I go—" Evan stopped midsentence.

"Before you go where?" Amanda asked.

"Before I go back to Lyndon." He averted his eyes.

"That's not what you were going to say." Amanda poked her brother in the chest. "Where are you going?"

"You know how I left the Lyndon P.D. to work with the county?"

"Yeah, so you're a big-time detective with the county CID now." She nodded. "So?"

"So there was an opportunity to send someone down to Quantico for some intensive training, and—"

"You're going to the FBI Academy?" Her eyes lit up. "Evan, you've been wanting to do that forever. This is wonderful news! When were you going to tell me?"

"Actually, it's for the National Academy, not to be an FBI agent. And I just found out yesterday. The guy who'd been asked to go had a family emergency and had to back out, so they asked me if I wanted to take his place." He smiled at his sister. "But I can go some other time. It doesn't have to be now."

"Are you crazy?"

"No, but you are if you think I'm going to leave for eleven weeks when someone is stalking you. Someone who may very well have just murdered two of your best friends for reasons we haven't even begun to explore." His mouth settled into a grim line, Evan added, "You're coming back to Lyndon with me."

"No, I am not. I have to be here for Marian. She only has one niece in Wisconsin, and someone is going to have to be here to walk her through things, to help her out, if she needs or wants it. She's only nineteen."

"If she had a niece, she had a sister or a brother."

"Brother. Died three years ago." Amanda shook her head. "Marian had only the one niece. Oh, maybe an odd cousin or two, but the niece is her heir, and she's very young to have to do this alone. I'm sorry, Evan. I appreciate your concern, but I'm not leaving Broeder."

"Then I'll come here."

"And miss your shot at some big-time training? Come on, Evan . . ."

"I'm not leaving you alone here."

"I have a business to run," Amanda reminded him.

"Your life is more important than your business," Evan countered.

"If I could make a suggestion . . ." Sean offered. "Maybe Amanda could stay at my sister's house. That way, she wouldn't be alone, she'd be here for the funeral, and she'd be able to keep her business open. And we could keep a close eye on her. Besides, I need Amanda to go through the deceased's shop and see if she can tell if anything is missing. This investigation is just beginning, Detective. Amanda may have information that she doesn't even realize she has."

"I'll be fine in my house. You've just admitted that you've been watching it for the past few days, and there haven't been any problems. I don't see any reason to move out. Why can't you just keep up the surveillance?" Amanda asked. Still, she was somewhat intrigued. She couldn't help but wonder what any sister of Sean Mercer could be like. He was all business all the time, and had been since the minute she met him.

"That was before I had two murders on my hands."

"I'd feel better if I were the one watching her back anyway," Evan noted.

"Well, since she's a witness in a murder in my jurisdiction, I think that responsibility is mine." Sean held the phone in one hand, the fingers of the other hand poised to dial. "Besides, if we're wrong about this, and these two murders are just some fluky coincidence—"

"Which neither of us is inclined to believe," Evan muttered.

"—and have nothing to do with your sister, you'll have missed a hell of an opportunity."

"How big a town is Broeder, Chief?" Evan asked.

"We have about seven thousand people."

"Incidence of violent crime?"

"Very little, actually."

"And the last murder in Broeder was . . . when, Chief? Before Derek England, that is."

"About six years ago," Sean conceded.

"Well, if none of this is connected, you have one stalker and two killers on the loose at the same time. How likely is that, Chief Mercer?"

"Not very. I agree. But we have to keep an open mind and see what the investigation concludes." He held up the phone. "Do I make the call?"

Amanda folded her arms. "I don't need a baby-sitter."

"Amanda, this is not negotiable. You stay with someone here in Broeder, or you come back to Lyndon with me now. Simple as that," Evan told her.

"I'm staying, and you're going." She sighed and turned to Sean. "You win. If it's all right with your sister, that is. Just make certain that she understands that I may have a bull's-eye painted on my back."

"I just hope we don't have cause to regret this later," Evan said, resigned to leaving Amanda in Broeder.

"Evan, I owe it to Derek and to Marian to do whatever I have to do. I couldn't live with myself if I walked away now. I still have some of Derek's records to go through. If there's anything I can do to help with the investigation, I need to do that."

"You'll keep me in the loop?" Evan asked Sean.

Sean nodded. "Leave your card with your numbers on it—one for me, one for my secretary."

Evan peeled two cards from his wallet and handed them over. "At the first sign of something not being right—the first time something doesn't feel right—she's out of here, agreed?"

He stuck out his hand. This was more than an agreement between two law enforcement agents and they both knew it.

"Agreed." Sean shook Evan's hand.

"Go on then." Amanda pointed at the phone reluctantly. "Make the call."

Sean finished dialing the call, and after a brief conversation, hung up the receiver. "Greer said she'd love to have you stay. She's happy to have the company, since her husband is going to be out of town at a sales meeting for most of the week and she doesn't like to stay alone in the house."

"Great," Amanda said with more enthusiasm than she felt.

"All right, but you call me if you need me," Evan insisted. "Don't do anything stupid. Don't go anyplace alone, don't—"

"I'm going to be fine, and I'm not going to do anything stupid." She hugged him. "Go on now. Get back to Lyndon and get yourself packed to leave for

Virginia tomorrow. Don't worry about me. Just go and do your training thing."

"Right." He kissed her on the cheek, then nodded to Sean on his way out of the room, pausing for one moment in the doorway. "Anything at all . . ."

"You'll be the first to know," Sean assured him.

"I'll need to go to my house to get some things. Clothes, my toothbrush, you know," Amanda said after Evan left.

"I'll drive you."

"I'll need to get my car. It's still out at St. Mark's."

"We'll leave it there for the time being. You're not going to be going anyplace alone, and if it's parked anywhere else, it will be a clear sign to anyone who's looking for you. Oh, before I forget, wait just a minute. . . ."

He walked into the hall, and Amanda could hear his footsteps fade slightly. Minutes later, he returned, her gun in his hand.

"I really have no reason to keep this." He handed it over to her. "I'm sorry, Amanda. I should have returned it to you sooner."

"You just did it again. That makes twice today."

He tilted his head to one side, puzzled.

"You called me Amanda. You've always been so careful to address me as Ms. Crosby."

"Oh. Well, you're not a murder suspect anymore."

"Good to know." She tucked the gun into her purse. "If I'm not a suspect anymore, do I get to call you Sean?"

"Sure."

"You're very serious about your job, aren't you?"

"It's the most important thing in my life."

"More important than your family?" The words were out of her mouth before she could stop them.

"I have no family, other than my sister." He held the door for her and gestured for her to walk through it, adding, "And I really don't even know her."

CHAPTER
THIRTEEN

IF AMANDA HAD BEEN PUT IN A ROOM WITH A HUN-
dred other women and told to pick out Sean Mercer's
blood relative, Greer Kennedy would have been guess
number one hundred. Where Sean was tall and dark,
Greer was petite and blond. Where more often than
not his facial expression was somewhere between
scowl and skepticism, Greer's was cheery and open,
and she exuded a generally happy nature that her
brother seemed to lack.

"I'm so sorry about your friend." Greer met Amanda
in the driveway outside her home with a hug that was
both welcoming and sympathetic. "What a terrible
thing. Now, you come right on in here and, Sean, you
bring her bag. Don't make her carry that. . . ."

"Oh, it's okay, I can—" Amanda reached for the
bag she'd dropped when Greer had first embraced
her.

But Greer had already taken her arm, and Sean had
picked up her bag, so Amanda permitted herself to be
led inside of the little house that was every bit as
cheerful as Greer herself.

"Your home is so lovely." Amanda stood in the
entry, from where she could see the dining and living
rooms, both of which were painted in rich jewel col-

ors, the furniture polished and pampered, the hard-
wood floors draped in oriental rugs. Homey touches
abounded, from the plump pillows on the sofa to the
bowl of phlox and black-eyed Susans that sat in the
middle of the dining room table. "It's so generous of
you to let me stay. I mean, a stranger, no notice . . ."

"Don't be silly. Any friend of Sean's, and all that."
Greer dismissed her compliment with a wave of one
hand.

"You're very kind." Amanda smiled, wondering
when she and Sean had become friends.

"Now, don't mention it again. Sean, you just take
that bag of Amanda's up to the guest room—she'll be
in the room you stayed in when you first got to
Broeder—then come back down to the kitchen."
Greer turned to Amanda. "Unless you feel you need
to rest. I can only imagine how terrible this day must
have been for you. . . ."

Amanda shut her eyes, trying to avoid the memory
of Marian's body on the floor. The blood. All that
blood.

"I'm all right. Thank you." *I will be all right. I will
be. . . .*

"Then let me get you something to drink. Perhaps
some soothing herb tea. Or something stronger
maybe? A glass of wine?" Greer was all motion, all
energy. She talked fast, and her footsteps seemed to
keep pace with her mouth. Amanda had trouble keeping up.

"Actually, I think a glass of wine would be wonderful, if it isn't too much trouble. Thank you."

"Oh, no trouble. Now, would you like to sit out on

the patio? We just had it screened in. West Nile, you know."

"What?"

"West Nile virus. Spread by mosquitoes. We screened in the patio so that we could sit outside and enjoy the nice summer evenings without slapping ourselves silly." Greer continued to talk even after she disappeared through the dining room door. "Those mosquitoes were brutal this year. Damned things were everywhere. And of course, the summer is nearly over now. Won't be but another month we'll be able to sit out there without bundling up."

She bustled back into the room, two crystal wineglasses in hand.

"We'll use the good stuff today. Just because I feel like it." She smiled at Amanda as she pulled a bottle of white wine from the refrigerator. "Not every day that Sean brings a girl home." She searched a nearby drawer, pausing to say, "Actually, Sean has never brought a girl home. . . . Ha, here it is."

She held up a corkscrew, then turned her attention to using it.

"Oh, Mrs. Kennedy, Sean and I aren't—"

"Greer. Please call me Greer. Mrs. Kennedy was my mother-in-law, God rest her soul. What a character she was. Sean tell you about her?"

Pop. The cork was out.

"Jesus, Greer, what the hell was that?" Sean appeared in the doorway, his eyes scanning the room.

"It was a cork. What do you think it was? You think someone was shooting at us?" She laughed, then looked at the expression on her brother's face. "Shit, you did think someone was shooting at us."

Sean sighed.

"Sean, why would you think—"

"Got any coffee left from lunch?"

"I'll make a pot. That's been sitting there for hours. And while I do that, you can tell me why you thought someone might be shooting at this house."

"It's not the house, it's me," Amanda told her. "Sean, didn't you tell Greer about Derek? Don't you think she deserves to know what she's getting into?"

"I started to tell her," Sean began to explain, "but sometimes, when you're trying to talk to Greer . . ."

"Who's Derek?" Ignoring Sean, Greer turned the spigot on and began to fill a glass carafe with water.

"See what I mean?" He turned to Amanda.

"Derek England was my partner. We owned an antiques shop together out at St. Mark's." To Sean, she said, "You could have tried a little harder."

"Oh, which one? I shop out there all the time. Why, that little clock out there on the hall table came from St. Mark's." Greer poured water into the coffeemaker, set the carafe, and hit the on button.

"Our shop is Crosby and England. And Derek—"

"Derek England is the man who was found shot in his car two weeks ago, Greer," Sean filled in when he saw Amanda falter.

"Oh, my God. Of course. I read about it." She turned to Amanda. "Oh, honey, that was your partner? You've really had a time of it, haven't you? I'm so sorry. What you must be going through . . ."

"Thank you, Greer." Amanda swallowed back the lump that was forming in her throat.

"Didn't I hear that the police—" Greer stopped midsentence and turned to Sean. "Sometimes I still forget that's you. You have no leads, right? I heard it on the news."

"Right. And then this morning we found another shop owner from St. Mark's dead—another friend of Amanda's, as I explained to you when I called earlier."

Greer stared at Sean for a long moment. "So you're saying that someone is killing off shop owners at St. Mark's?"

"You could say that."

"Should I expect the rest of them sometime between this afternoon and this evening?" Greer asked.

"The rest of who?"

"The other shopkeepers." Greer fixed her brother with a stare. "Or is there some reason why Amanda might be a target whereas the others are not?"

"We don't know. Right now, she looks like the only obvious common thread between the two. The only one I know of who was close to both victims."

"They're not just victims, Sean, they're her friends," Greer admonished him as if Amanda wasn't sitting at the kitchen table.

"You're right. They were friends. Sorry." This to Amanda.

She nodded and reached for the glass of wine Greer had poured for her.

"Did you eat anything today?" Greer asked.

Amanda shook her head.

"I thought Dana picked up lunch for you." Sean frowned.

"She offered. I couldn't have eaten anything." Amanda sipped at the wine. It was cool and slightly fruity and just what she needed at that moment.

"Then go easy on that and I'll see what I can find for you," Greer said.

"Please don't go to any trouble . . ."

Greer waved off her protests. "Not a problem. I was in the mood for an early dinner, actually, and just about to have some of this wonderful tomato and cheddar cheese pie I made yesterday. Oven's already heated." Greer turned back to the refrigerator and pulled out a light green pie plate covered with aluminum foil. "What do you think? Want to try it? It really is delicious."

"Sure. Thank you."

"How 'bout you, Sean?"

"I'll pass, Greer, but thanks." He grabbed an apple from a bowl on the counter. "I'll pick up something later on. Right now, I need to get back to the station."

"Oh, sure. Of course. You go on back to work and find the person who killed Amanda's friend." She filled a plastic travel mug with the freshly made coffee and handed it to her brother. "Her friends. The same person, right? The same person killed them both?"

Sean nodded. "It looks that way."

"Then go catch him. I'll save you some dinner."

"What can I do to help?" Amanda asked, watching Sean cross the grass on his way to his Jeep, then wave to someone on the opposite side of the street. She leaned a little closer to the window, saw a parked police cruiser. Someone to watch the house, she thought, while Sean was at the station.

"Not a damned thing. You just sit right there, and I'll heat this up. We can go outside for a bit and put our feet up and drink our wine. And after you eat, you can go lie down for a bit, if you like, or you can sit outside by yourself, if you need to be alone. I'll understand."

"Thank you. I appreciate how kind you're being."

"Well, this has to be just a terrible time for you." Greer took a baking sheet from a cupboard and a knife from a rack that stood on the counter. She sliced off two pieces of pie and deposited them on the baking sheet, then popped the tray into the oven. Everything the woman did was quick and smooth.

"Now, shall we sit out on the patio while our dinner heats up?" Greer asked.

Not waiting for an answer, Greer picked up her wineglass and motioned for Amanda to follow her out the back door. The patio was a snug enclosure, with a white wicker love seat and two chairs grouped around a matching table with a glass top. Greer sat on the love seat, and Amanda chose the rocking chair.

"I love a rocker, don't you?" Greer asked as she set her glass on the table. "So soothing."

Amanda smiled and sipped her wine. It was cool and silky going down, and she leaned back against the thick chair cushion, grateful for its comfort.

"Now, Sean said your brother was here?"

"He was. He went back to Lyndon, where he lives. He's got a chance to train down in Virginia at the National Academy." Amanda heard the trace of pride in her voice. "I didn't want him to miss the opportunity."

"Of course not," Greer agreed readily, though she wasn't sure what the National Academy was, or why it was important that Amanda's brother go *now*, but she let it pass. "So, you don't have other family in the area?"

"No. Our parents divorced years ago. Mother and second family in California, Dad and second—and third—family in Minnesota."

"Oh." Greer appeared momentarily surprised. "You have half siblings? Stepsiblings?"

"Both, but they're all much younger. We hardly know them."

"A pity." Greer sipped thoughtfully at her wine. "Why?"

"If something's more important than family—however far extended—I do not know what it is."

"Are you and Sean from a large family?"

Something settled over Greer's face. "Sean didn't tell you?"

Amanda shook her head.

"Why am I not surprised?" Greer rolled her eyes skyward. "We lived with our grandmother until she died, then we were put up for adoption. Separately. I was placed with a wonderful couple. Just the loveliest people. I had the best upbringing possible. They're retired now, living in Arizona and living life to the hilt."

"And Sean?"

"He . . . had a harder time of things." Her voice was level, matter-of-fact. "He was a tough cookie, even as a little kid. Too much of a handful, they all said. The county would send him out with a family, he'd last maybe a couple of months before they sent him back. Eventually, they just put him into foster care, and he bounced around for a while, until he was eighteen and could join the army."

"Poor Sean." Amanda frowned. She'd had no idea. "How did your parents die?"

"What?"

"Your parents. I'm assuming, since you said you were living with your grandmother and later adopted, that your parents had died?"

"I don't know how our father died, or if he did, for that matter. He could still be alive, for all I know. I have no memory of him at all, nor does Sean. He was never in our lives, and apparently in our mother's only from time to time, and then just long enough to get her pregnant before he took off again."

"I'm so sorry. I had no idea. I wouldn't have asked . . . Please, don't feel as if you have to talk about it."

Greer waved away Amanda's protests. "And our mother . . . well, we're still not certain what happened to her." Her jaw settled into a hard line even as her voice softened.

"I don't know what to say." Amanda flushed with embarrassment, but Greer didn't appear to notice. "I'm sorry."

"It wasn't your fault," Greer stage-whispered, and forced a smile. "On the one hand, I figured you knew, if you were close to Sean, but on the other, knowing Sean, I should have known that he wouldn't have talked about it."

"Greer, Sean and I are . . . not close. He's brought me here because he thinks I'm at risk at home alone."

"I see. Oh, there's the timer. Shall we eat out here? No, don't get up, I'll bring it. You just sit and relax."

"Are you sure I can't—"

"No, no. You just stay put."

Amanda took another small sip of wine, mindful that it would take little more than a thimbleful to make her head spin, given the day's events and the lack of food. She put the glass down on the table and looked around the room. On the table next to her chair was a small photo album. She picked it up and began idly thumbing through it.

"Oh, that's our Kevin," Greer said as she returned carrying a tray laden with two salad bowls and two plates, each holding a generous wedge of tomato pie.

"Your son?"

"Yes." Greer set the tray on the wicker coffee table. "He was the joy of my life. I miss him like crazy, every day."

Amanda was afraid to ask.

"Yes." Greer recognized the look on the younger woman's face. "We lost him last year."

"He was sick?"

"Kevin had Down's syndrome. He also had spina bifida. Poor baby had so many problems . . ."

"Greer, I don't know what to say."

"You don't have to say anything." She shook her head. "He was a challenge in every way, that boy of ours was, because he faced so many challenges developmentally, physically. But God, how I—we—loved him. He brought us such joy. It was hard sometimes, but he brought us the greatest joy. . . ."

"I'm so sorry," Amanda apologized for what seemed like the fifth time that afternoon.

"Thank you. So are we." Greer fussed with her plate. "He just picked up one infection after another. Colds so often turned into pneumonia. That last infection, well, we caught it early, but it was just determined to do him in. It all went so fast. . . ."

Amanda reached out her hand and Greer took it.

"I haven't really known what to do with myself

since he died. Kevin had needed so much care, and I was so happy to be with him, in spite of the fact that it was pretty much continuous. I was lucky that Steven's job was such that I didn't have to work, so that I could be with Kevin every day. We always knew he was just here on loan to us, that we wouldn't be keeping him." She brushed away a tear. "Well, we just figured we'd have had him a little longer than we did. It's been hard to . . . adjust . . . to it just being the two of us. In a way, I think it's easier on Steve, because he travels with his job, and that keeps him busy."

"Have you thought about looking for a job?"

"I don't feel ready to commit to something all day, every day. But I've been doing some volunteer work at the local hospital, and some over at the library. That's where I started reading up on ways to use the Internet to look for lost people—you know, people from your past?" She smiled. "That's how I found Sean. I searched the Internet. Of course, he was easy to find. Well, I keep telling myself how lucky I am. I lost my son, but I did find my brother. I can't tell you how much it meant to me to see Sean again. And here's the icing on the cake. I just recently found—"

"Hey, girls." A tall, thin, balding man with an easy smile poked his head into the room.

"Steve, honey, this is our guest for a few days. She's a friend of Sean's. Sort of . . ." Greer made the introductions and gave Steve a quick rundown on Amanda's situation.

"I'm grateful to you for staying here with Greer while I'm away," Steve said as he shook Amanda's hand. "I always hate to leave her alone."

"I've always been fine." Greer wagged the fingers

of one hand at him. "But I think it will be fun to have Amanda here. Now, honey, are you all packed?"

"I think so. I just stopped home to pick up my suitcase. I was hoping to take along my blue shirt, though. I can't seem to find it."

"I know just where it is." Greer put her plate down and excused herself to Amanda.

"Oh, no, please. Do whatever it is you need to do. I hate feeling that I'm holding you up."

Greer and Steve left the room in a flurry, and Amanda continued to nibble at her lunch. She flipped through the photo album again, one picture to the next. Kevin with Greer, Kevin with Steve. The three of them together in the backyard. At a lake. In front of a large building that could have been a museum, Kevin in a wheelchair, wearing a New York Giants cap and a crooked smile, Greer and Steve standing proudly on either side. So sad that they'd lost the son they'd both clearly loved so much.

"I lost a son, but I did find my brother. I can't tell you how much it meant to me to see Sean again. And here's the icing on the cake. I just recently found—" Greer had been saying when Steve had entered the room.

Amanda couldn't help but wonder who else Greer had found. Whoever it was, she hoped it was someone who would bring a little of the lost joy back into Greer's heart. And maybe, just maybe, a little of that might rub off on Sean.

Later, when Sean showed up after ten—and several hours after Amanda, citing exhaustion, had excused herself and gone off to bed—Greer tried pumping

Sean for information. As far as she was concerned, if he was involved with Amanda—or wanted to be— she wanted to know about it. If he wasn't, he needed his head examined.

"So, how long have you been seeing Amanda?" She tried the soft approach.

"Since her partner turned up dead." Sean speared a couple of green beans with his fork.

"You didn't know her before that?"

"Greer, I've been in Broeder for a little more than six months. In that time, I've put in sixteen-, eighteen-hour days, seven days a week." He took a long drink from the bottle of water he'd brought in with him. "So you figure out when I would have gotten around to romancing Ms. Crosby—or anyone else, for that matter—which you obviously think I am doing."

"I was just wondering if you'd been seeing her, that's all."

"Oh, I've been seeing her, all right." He snorted. "Of course, until this morning, I figured that from here on out, I'd be seeing her through the bars of one of my cells. At least until they gave her one of those nifty orange jumpsuits and hauled her off to the county prison."

"I just thought that maybe you'd been going out with her, Sean. You don't have to be such a smartass about it." Greer frowned. "I get it. You're not dating. Though I don't understand why not. Such a pretty girl, and she seems like she's real smart. Owns her own business—"

"Don't you get it? Amanda has been a suspect in a murder I'm investigating. You don't get chummy with suspects, Greer. You don't see them as anything other than that, and you don't ask them if they're free on Saturday night. At least if you have more than half a brain, you don't."

Greer gave him her iciest stare. "You can't possibly be serious. You could not have thought that sweet woman could have killed anyone."

"Greer, I'm a cop. I can't make assumptions. I can only evaluate the facts, not appearances. And until the facts are in—until the evidence points one way or the other—it has to be played strictly by the book. Cross the t's, dot the i's." He paused to chew and swallow a piece of steak. "Look at Ted Bundy. Lot of people had a hard time believing he could be guilty of the things he did."

He cut another piece of meat. "The steak is great, by the way. Thanks for fixing it for me."

"You're welcome."

"Oh, don't look at me that way, Greer."

"I cannot believe you just compared Amanda to Ted Bundy."

"I did not. But in the beginning—after the first murder—things didn't look too good for Amanda. She had motive, she owned a gun the same caliber as the murder weapon, the sweatshirt she'd admitted to wearing on the night her partner was killed had gun-shot residue on it. Christ, she'd even left a message on the victim's voice mail saying she was going to kill him."

"She isn't the killer type, Sean. Anyone can see that."

"Sorry to shatter your illusions, but there is no one killer type. Christ, Greer. Derek England's murder was my first homicide here in Broeder. Everyone's watching to see what I do. I know that. Especially since my brother-in-law is the one who brought me in here, got me the job." He took another sip of water. "How would it look for Steve if I did a lousy job? And you tell me what the hell kind of cop would I be if I ignored evidence just because the suspect is beautiful and smart and owns her own business?"

Greer smiled with satisfaction. *So he had noticed. . . .*

"What?" Sean asked.

"You said beautiful." She picked up his empty plate and took it to the sink to rinse off. "I only said she was pretty."

Muttering curses under his breath, Sean thanked his sister for dinner and headed out the door.

Amanda lay beneath the covers in the darkened room at the end of the hall and turned over yet one more time, wishing she could close her eyes and not see the blood. She'd taken two showers already that day, the first in her house, when Dana Burke had so kindly taken her home and let her take off the clothes that were heavy with Marian's blood. Dana had bagged and tagged each item of clothing as Amanda had removed it, then turned on the shower for Amanda and told her she'd wait downstairs, for Amanda to take her time. She must have known how long it would take to wash away the blood. Amanda had stood beneath the steaming stream of water, mindlessly scrubbing her skin raw, trying to remove every last trace of the morning's tragedy, every bit of pain, knowing she never really would.

She squashed the pillow under the right side of her head and allowed her body to sink down into the too-soft mattress, listening to the dull hum of voices somewhere far away. Greer and Sean. She knew instinctively that they were talking about her. If she hadn't been so damned tired, she'd have been tempted to sneak to the top of the stairs to try to listen.

Now, that's something I haven't done in a long, long time, she mused. *Not since we were all together— Mom and Dad and Evan and I—living in the same house. We'd never given the voices a second thought, Evan and I hadn't. We thought everyone's parents argued at night after the kids had been tucked in. Thought all kids fell asleep to the sound of those hushed accusations, those angry voices touched with a quiet civility.* There'd been a familiar comfort in the consistency of the hum of voices from the floor below. It wasn't until after her father left that she began to understand the price of that comfort.

The voices below weren't raised in anger, but there was a steady flow, a certain rhythm, to the conversation between sister and brother. There'd been questions she'd have asked of Greer earlier if they'd been more than mere acquaintances.

Amanda rolled onto her left side, thinking about her brother. She couldn't imagine having grown up without Evan, couldn't imagine having had suffered through her parents' divorce without his calm, steady influence. He'd always been there for her. Still was. She smiled to herself, recalling his indignation at her being suspected in Derek's death. Even knowing the admittedly damning facts against her, Evan had been infuriated that Sean Mercer—or anyone else—considered her capable of killing.

She sat up and dangled her legs over the side of the bed. Overtired now, she was unable to sleep, and yet lacked the strength to get up, dress herself, and go back downstairs. Not that she wanted to engage either Sean or Greer in conversation. She'd been living alone far too long to enjoy such intimate contact in the middle of the night. If the truth were to be told, she'd been mildly uncomfortable since the minute she stepped into this house.

For one thing, she wasn't accustomed to sharing living space with anyone else. Sharing it with a stranger was that much more disconcerting. But she recognized that stubbornly insisting on staying alone, in her house, until questions were answered about the killings of two so close to her would have been folly. She understood that there was safety in numbers, and she was safer—theoretically—here, under the same roof with the sister of the chief of police, but even that knowledge didn't make her much more comfortable with the situation.

For another, over the past year, she'd learned to rely upon herself for her strength and her safety. Allowing someone else to keep her safe smacked of a cop-out. But there was that little matter of a killer who'd already struck too close to home not once, but twice. In the end, she'd endure the discomfort of living under someone else's roof, depending on the efforts of someone else to watch her back. She may not like the arrangement, but she wasn't stupid.

She lay back down, flat on her back this time, and stared at the ceiling, wondering how long she could keep her eyes open. Closing them merely served as an invitation for the nightmare images to return, and she'd seen enough that day to last a lifetime. Marian on the floor, blood smearing her clothes and her chest and her throat and puddling under her head.

Marian, just a few days earlier, bringing Amanda tomatoes from her garden and gleefully confiding that her beefsteaks were a full twelve ounces heavier than the best her next-door neighbor had grown that summer. Marian, proudly showing off the treasures she'd bought at the house sale earlier in the week . . .

It just wasn't fair, Amanda's weary brain protested. It just wasn't fair that good people like Derek and Marian died so terribly when the person who killed them was out there somewhere.

She got out of bed and raised the shade on the window that overlooked Greer's backyard. Now, at half past ten, the yard lay in semidarkness, the lamp from the patio casting just enough light to throw shadows across the flat expanse of lawn. Somewhere out there was someone with blood on his hands. If Sean was right, this someone was watching for her, waiting for her. Maybe right now, at this minute, this someone was cutting the glass in one of the panes in her back door, sliding the glass out carefully and quietly, then lifting the latch. Was he already inside, treading carefully across her kitchen floor, maybe in bare feet, pausing every few steps to listen for sounds of her stirring on the second floor? In his pocket did he carry the same knife he'd used to butcher Marian, or the gun he'd used to put a bullet through Derek's head?

And what, she wondered as she chewed on a fingernail in the dark, was the point? What had he, this faceless, nameless someone, wanted from Derek, from Marian, that he might now want from her?

Hard as she tried, though she lay awake several more hours thinking about it, Amanda could not come up with one good reason why anyone would want her—and Derek, and Marian—dead.

CHAPTER
FOURTEEN

HUMMING ALONG WITH THE RADIO, HIS FINGERS TAP-
ping out the beat on the steering wheel of his car,
Vince Giordano sat in the cool shade of a sweet gum
tree, watching the cars that buzzed by, waiting for
Dolores to arrive home from work and hoping she
wouldn't be too late. He had a surprise for her. Oh,
did he ever.

The white compact slowed, then pulled into the
drive and disappeared around the back of the house.
Still humming, thinking how it was a shame that
some car company had started using that particular
song in their commercials, because now every time he
heard it, he thought about pickup trucks, he craned
his neck, hoping she'd come back around the front.
And just as he thought it, there she was. He got out of
the car and started across the small patch of grass
that had gone too long without water in the late summer sun.

"Hey," he called amicably.

"Vinnie." Dolores's face brightened. "What are
you doing here?"

"I was passing along the street, and I looked at the
clock and said, 'Hey, Dolores should be just about
getting home right about now.' And you know what?"

He took one of her hands in his own and watched her blush. "Just as I was thinking it, didn't you pull right into the driveway?"

"No way."

"Oh, yeah. So I'm taking that as a sign that you don't have plans for dinner tonight, and that you'd come out for dinner with me."

"Well, I . . . I just got home." She blushed again, brushing off her dark pants. "And I'm not really dressed up. . . ."

"You look great, Dolores. Better than great." He lowered his voice and leaned forward to touch her forehead with his own. Richard Gere had done that in some movie, and Vince had been hoping that someday he'd have occasion to use that move in real life.

"If you could give me a minute, maybe to fix my makeup, feed my cat . . ."

"Sure. Whatever time you need."

"Okay, then. Yes. I'd love to have dinner with you tonight." She backed toward the sidewalk, still beaming, the faint blush still tingeing her cheeks. "Would you like to come in, just while I . . ."

"Sure. Sure. That would be nice." Vince smiled gently, as if he were a simple man being invited into the home of a friend.

The small twin house had a porch with an old-fashioned swing at one end. A row of geraniums in plastic pots that were supposed to look like clay were set along the perimeter of the porch, where a railing had once been. There was a rusty black mailbox attached to the front wall and a wreath of bright plastic flowers on the door.

"The previous owner took the rails off," she explained as if she needed to. "I want to put them back on someday. But I had to put money into the kitchen—"

"Hey, don't feel like you have to make excuses to me. Please." He held up one hand as if to halt her words in their tracks. "I think it's wonderful that you own your own home. I'm really impressed. I mean, how many thirty-year-old women can say that they bought their own house?"

"Vinnie, I'm thirty-seven," she laughed.

"Get outta town," he scoffed. "Thirty-seven. Right. What do I look like, huh?"

"No, really, I am." She unlocked the door, and he took note of the type of lock. Just in case he needed to know at some future date. "I was thirty-seven last month."

"Now you're telling me that I missed your birthday." He put on a sad face as he followed her inside. "Well, I'll make it up to you. I know just the way."

"Oh, Vinnie, you don't have to do anything. Just"— she smiled, her entire face lighting up—"just . . . well, just dinner out tonight, that will be enough. More than enough."

"I can do better, but we'll let that go for now. You go on and do what you have to do, and I'll just wait for you."

"I'll hurry, I promise." She paused on the bottom step and called, "Cujo, where are you?"

"Cujo?"

"Cujo's my— There's my baby."

A large gray cat ambled out from the dining room, pausing on his way to Dolores to give Vince the once-over. He did not appear to like what he saw.

"That's my baby," Dolores cooed, and bent down to scoop up the cat. "Say hello to my friend Vinnie."

Cujo glared imperiously in the general direction of the intruder.

"What a nice cat," Vince said, thinking he was expected to say something. He didn't like cats, never had, but figured that wouldn't be the appropriate thing to tell her. "He's . . . big, isn't he?"

"Huge. Weighs almost forty pounds. But he's a sweetie. Oh, I should feed him before I run upstairs."

"Oh, hey, I can do that. Just tell me what to do."

"You wouldn't mind? I'm just thinking that it's already so late, since I got home so late and everything . . ."

"I wouldn't mind at all."

"Well, then, there's a can of cat food on the counter in the kitchen—that's straight through here, straight ahead through the dining room—and the can opener's mounted under the cupboard closest to the sink."

"I'm sure I can find it. You run along." Vince thought momentarily about giving her backside a tap as she turned to the steps, but decided that might be a bit premature, all things considered. He was going to do a little something a little later to speed up the progress of their relationship as it was. *One thing at a time,* he cautioned himself as he went to the kitchen.

Dolores's house was a lot like Dolores. Nothing fancy, but sturdy, practical, functional. Few flourishes, but tidy, with the occasional attempt at decor. A few pots of plants here, a crystal bowl there, colorful candles in assorted holders on the sideboard in the dining room. A nice enough package—as was Dolores—but nothing to get too excited about.

"Come on in here, cat," he muttered as he turned on the overhead light, and failed to notice that the cat had declined to follow him into the near-dark room.

He found the can, located the cat food, then dumped it unceremoniously into a ceramic dish with raised purple fishes on the bottom and around the rim.

"Hey, cat. Dinner." He went to the doorway and looked down at the cat, who glared up coolly, calmly whipping his tale snakelike on the hooked rug. "Okay, have it your way. Personally I don't give a shit if you ever eat again."

He rinsed the can out in the sink the way his mother used to do, then looked for the trash can, which he found near the back door, which gave him an opportunity to look around. Scope out the yard, check out the back door, the basement door. You just never knew.

He took a minute to play with the lock, listening to the little cylinders tumble, thinking how easy it would be to break in.

"Vinnie?"

"Oh. Hey, that was fast."

"What are you doing?"

"Oh, I was just checking the lock on your back door. Making sure it was tight, you know."

"It should be fine. I had them changed after I moved in last year."

"Never hurts to keep track," he told her with a comforting smile. "You gotta make sure your home is secure. Jeez, don't it seem that every night you hear about another home invasion? It's on the TV just about every night."

"I don't watch the news." She shook her head,

her permed blond curls barely moving. "It's too depressing. Rapes. Murders. Robberies. Little kids being abused. Little sick kids selling lemonade to help pay their medical bills."

Dolores's mascara-darkened eyes brimmed with sympathetic tears. "I know all those things happen every day. So I don't watch. And between you and me, Connie drives me nuts some days. Noon news, news at four. News at six. I tune it out. I just don't want to know."

"Yeah, well, you know what they say about ignorance being bliss. Not that I think you're ignorant," he hastened to add. "I mean, you're smart, Dolores. Maybe the smartest woman I know. And you're right. There's so much bad stuff going on in the world that we just don't have any control over. It hurts to watch that stuff."

"Exactly. That's exactly my point." She peered behind him to see if he'd fed the cat. "Cujo. Come on in here, now. Vinnie's got dinner for you. Isn't he a nice man?"

Cujo continued to stare from the safety of the dining room.

"Maybe he's not hungry right now," Vince offered, hoping that he wasn't going to be expected to stand here and wait for the cat to eat. "Cujo might not be hungry, but I sure am."

"Oh, of course you are. It's almost eight o'clock. We can go. We don't have to wait."

Like I was gonna . . .

"Now, you like the Pepper Pot or the Oak Tree Inn?" Vince asked while Dolores pulled on the front door to close it tightly.

"Oh, they're both wonderful." Her eyes lit up. "But they're both so expensive, Vinnie. Are you sure you don't want to have a burger down at the Dew Drop?"

"Dolores, we have had burgers together at the Dew Drop Inn for the past two weeks. Now I want to have a nice dinner out with you, just you and me, at someplace nice. Someplace special." He slid into his smooth role, donning sincerity like a pair of gloves. "Because you are special, Dolores. The most special lady I ever knew. And I want you to have the best."

"Oh, Vinnie." She stopped dead in her tracks on the top steps. The blush was back, her face scarlet with pleasure even in the dim porch light. "That's so . . . so sweet."

"It's true, Dolores. You're . . . well, you're one of a kind."

"And you're one of a kind, too, Vinnie."

"Well, then, shall we go?" He offered his arm and she took it, smiling.

"We can go in my car," he told her when she paused at the sidewalk.

"It's a beautiful car," she told him. "I don't think I've ever ridden in a Lincoln town car before."

"Well, it's not new, you know." He opened the door for her and held it until she had slid past him onto the seat.

"Oh, the leather is so nice. It looks almost new."

"Well, I got a good deal on it," he said. For a car that was eight years old and had more than a hundred thousand miles on it, he'd gotten a damned good deal, since he'd paid cash.

"I don't think I ever even saw your car before."

"That's 'cause I always walk to the Dew."

"Well, if I lived half a block away, I'd walk, too."

"I'm only there until I can find something more permanent," he told her as they pulled away from the curb. "I took the room because it was the only thing immediately available. Plus, when I first came to town, I wasn't sure how long I'd be staying. But now . . ."

"Now . . . ?"

"Now I'm thinking I might want to stay around for a while." He winked at her.

"Oh," she said under her breath.

Oh, indeed. He smiled at her across the front seat.

Dinner went exceptionally well. By the time the last bit of red wine had been sipped and coffee and dessert had been served, Dolores was starry-eyed and Vince Giordano—Vinnie Daniels, that is—was feeling about as confident as a man could be. There was only one more thing to do.

He'd baited the hook. Now all he had to do was reel her in.

He stopped the car in front of her house and reached for her face, caressing it gently, touching her lips with his fingers. Then he sighed, got out of the car, and went around to her side to open her door.

"You're such a gentleman, Vinnie," she said as she got out of the car.

"You're a lady." He shrugged, as if it went without saying. "You deserve to be treated with respect."

She took his hand and led him up the narrow walk to her front door. At the top of the steps she paused and asked, "Would you like to come in for a night-cap?"

"Oh, I . . . oh, yes, thank you." He grinned his boyish best. "If you're sure . . ."

"I'm sure. I think I have a little brandy. My ex . . . that is, an old friend used to drink brandy on holidays." She unlocked the door and pushed it open.

"Well, this is a holiday of sorts," he said as he stepped inside. "Since we are celebrating your birthday."

She went directly into the kitchen. "Cujo?" she called.

Fucking cat. It had better not screw this up. He needed to get this show on the road. He was tired of sleeping in a cold lumpy bed—alone—and eating out every fucking night. He figured he had a good shot tonight if he played this right, and no damned cat was going to mess it up for him.

"There you are. Did you eat your din-din? No?"

Oh, brother.

"Vinnie, the brandy is in the sideboard. Middle door."

"Okay." He opened the door, thinking he could just about down the whole bottle himself. Or use it to drown the fucking cat. He found the bottle and shook it. Not enough for the cat. They might as well drink it.

"Here we go." Dolores came into the room holding a chunky water glass in each hand. "Not exactly brandy glasses . . . what do you call them?"

"I call them brandy glasses." He smiled and took both from her and placed them on the table. With a flourish, he poured the brandy and handed a glass to her.

"To us," he said. "To many, many, many more nights just like this one."

A blushing Dolores tipped her glass to his, touching rims.

"You did have a good time, didn't you?" Sincere Vinnie. Concerned Vinnie. Gentleman Vinnie.

"Oh, I had a wonderful time, Vinnie. It was a perfect night."

"I thought so, too. And that's why . . . well, come into the living room. I have something to say to you." He grabbed the bottle of brandy in one hand and his glass in the other, and shepherded a curious Dolores to the sofa.

"What, Vinnie?" She took a slug of brandy, as if she felt she needed to fortify herself.

"Well, Dolores . . . Oh, give me a minute. I'm not good at stuff like this." He rolled his eyes upward, as if seeking guidance, closed his eyes, then turned to her and took both of her hands in his. "Dolores, I know we haven't known each other for very long. Just a few weeks, I know—you don't have to say it. But from the first minute I saw you—the first time I looked at your face—I just felt something. Something . . . special. Something that I never felt before with no one else."

"Oh, Vinnie," she cooed, much as she had earlier cooed to the cat. "That's so sweet."

"Now, I think you felt it, too, didn't you, Dolores?" He drew his brows together thoughtfully. "But you can tell me if you didn't. It would be better if you did. Tell me, I mean. Now. Before I make a fool out of myself."

"Oh, Vinnie, you could never do that." She squeezed his hands. "And you're right. I did feel something that night. And every night. Every night when I go down there to the Dew, I'm hoping that you'll be there at the bar. Just like that first night."

"And I have been, haven't I? Waiting for you, every

night." He swallowed hard, as if making this little speech was impromptu, even though he'd spent most of the afternoon practicing it. He could barely keep from laughing in her face.

"Yes, you've been there."

He reached into his pocket and pulled out the small blue box that he'd taken from Marian O'Connor's shop just the night before.

"Go ahead. Open it," he told her as he pressed the box into her hands.

"What in the world . . . ?"

"Open it."

Her hands were shaking just the tiniest bit with excitement as she pulled the lid off.

"Oh, Vinnie. It's beautiful." She looked up at him, wide-eyed. "But this can't be for me. Those look like real emeralds."

"They not only look like real emeralds," he told her as he lifted the pendant and chain from the box, "they are real emeralds. And they're only what you deserve, Dolores."

"But I couldn't . . . I mean, why—"

"This belonged to my grandmother, Dolores. She told me to hold on to it until I found a woman worthy to wear it. Until now, I never have. Will you wear it, Dolores? Will you wear my grandmother's necklace?"

"Oh, but, Vinnie . . ." Her eyes went back to the pendant, to the little swirls of forest green colored stones that wound around and around. "I don't know what to say."

"Say yes. Say you'll wear it."

"If you want me to . . ."

"Oh, I do. I want you to wear it. It would mean the world to me."

"Then in that case, I will."

She leaned forward so that he could fasten it around her neck.

"Grandmother would approve," he told her as he kissed her lips.

"Oh, Vinnie," she sighed, and dropped back onto the sofa, one hand around the back of his neck to draw him down with her, the other fingering the most expensive piece of jewelry she'd ever owned. "Oh, Vinnie . . ."

CHAPTER FIFTEEN

"ARE YOU A COFFEE DRINKER?" GREER LOOKED UP from her breakfast when she heard Amanda's footsteps nearing the kitchen.

"Oh. Yes. Thank you." Amanda stood awkwardly in the doorway, not quite certain what to do next. Both seats at the small table were already occupied.

"I know I can't start a day without it," Greer told her cheerfully. "Now, Steve, he's a tea drinker. Loves the smell of coffee, but can't stand the taste of it."

"Morning, Amanda." Sean looked up from the newspaper he'd been reading.

"Good morning." Did the chief of police really feel she needed an armed guard at breakfast?

"Now you sit right here . . ." Greer moved her own plate over and added a third to the table. In the same motion, she produced a stool seemingly out of thin air.

Amanda's head was spinning by the time she sat down, her protests falling on totally deaf ears.

"You just sit yourself there on that chair. I'll take the stool." Greer waved a hand in the general direction of the table where Sean sat, an amused look on his face. Apparently, he was well accustomed to his sister's take-charge ways. "Now, are you eggs and bacon, cereal, fruit and yogurt—"

"Oh, please don't go to any trouble." Amanda frowned as she reached for the coffee cup Greer was passing to her.

"Well, I've already made eggs for Sean and myself. I like to start the day with some protein, you know." Greer handed a small pitcher of half and half to her guest. "I've been thinking about one of those low carb diets. You know anyone who's been on one of those?"

"Not that I can think of." Amanda took a sip of coffee. It was hot enough to burn the roof of her mouth, and it did just that. She blinked against the pain as she set the cup back onto its saucer.

"Now, I have tried just about every diet"—Greer cracked two eggs into a bowl and began to whip them furiously—"but I just can't seem to lose those last twenty pounds. So much easier ten years ago. Hell, it was easier five years ago."

"Eggs will be fine," Amanda offered as if Greer was actually paying attention.

"Oh, damn that phone." She carried the bowl of eggs along with her to answer the phone. "Oh, hi, sweetheart. No, just having breakfast with Sean and Amanda. How's Houston?" Greer set the bowl on the counter and took the phone into the dining room, chatting merrily the entire time.

Sean smiled at Amanda from across the table and folded his paper. Without a word, he rose, took the bowl of eggs, and poured them into the pan, where butter had already melted.

"I can do that," Amanda said, feeling slightly embarrassed though not quite knowing why. Sharing early morning time with anyone was something she wasn't accustomed to. Sharing that time with Sean Mercer seemed too intimate a thing for so casual a relationship.

Casual. She could have laughed out loud. Up until yesterday, the man had been ready to put her away for life.

"I've got it," Sean said easily, as if making breakfast for former murder suspects in his sister's kitchen was an everyday event. "Toast?"

"I'll do it." She got up and walked to the stove, needing to move, to do something besides sit there. "Really. I can make my own breakfast. I've been doing it for years."

"Me, too." He popped two slices of bread into the toaster and slid several long strips of well-cooked bacon onto her plate. "Relax, Amanda. Pour yourself some orange juice if you like."

She did so silently, still uncomfortable here. Sean's presence only added to her discomfort.

"Here you go." He handed her the plate with eggs and bacon. "Toast will be up in a minute."

Having skipped dinner the night before in an attempt to get some sleep, Amanda felt her salivary glands go into overdrive as the aroma from the plate began to drift upward.

"It smells wonderful. Thank you."

"You're welcome," he said, one eye on the clock.

The toast popped and he piled it onto a small plate that he delivered to the table.

"There's butter here and some strawberry jam that Greer claims to have made. It's pretty good." He stood with his hands in the pockets of his jeans, watching her eat for a long moment before refilling his coffee cup from the pot that was still plugged in on the counter. Greer waved a thank-you to him as she passed back through the kitchen on her way to the patio, the phone still attached to her ear as she chatted away.

"That's Steve on the phone," Sean told her.

"I figured."

"I didn't want you to think she was being rude by being on the phone while you were here."

"I doubt Greer has a rude bone in her body, and since I'm the oddball out here, you don't need to apologize to me on her behalf." She pushed her eggs around on her plate after having taken several bites, her appetite waning.

"I just meant that she normally wouldn't take a call while she had company."

"I'm not really company." She nibbled at a strip of salty bacon.

He sighed heavily as he sat back down at the table and, before she could comment, asked, "How are you?"

"I'm okay." She put her fork down on the side of her plate and thought about it for a minute, her eyes stinging. "I want to be okay."

"Were you able to get any sleep at all last night?"

"The bags under the eyes give me away?" She grimaced. "If you want to know the truth, I don't feel much at all. Numb, more than anything. Dizzy in the pit of my stomach. I still can't believe all of this has happened. Derek, now Marian. I can't believe she's dead now, too."

"It's hard to lose someone you love under the best of circumstances. Harder still to lose two in so short a time. Especially like this . . ."

"I guess you have no clues yet. About who did this, I mean." She swallowed back the lump that had lodged itself in her throat and refused to budge.

"Nothing yet. We're looking at the antiques angle, of course. I understand that you've signed off on the inventory of your shop? Nothing was missing—is that correct?"

"Right. Nothing out of place that I could see."

"So we have the pottery that Derek bought in Italy, which, by the way, I've made arrangements for a professor at the University of Pennsylvania down in Philly to take a look at. Just to authenticate it."

"I told you that Dr. McGowan already did that." There was an unmistakable touch of starch to her voice. "Daria is extremely well known in the field and highly respected."

"I understand that. And the professor at Penn is familiar with her work and speaks very highly of her. But I want someone with expertise to look at the piece— not a photo—and inspect it carefully to confirm that it's not a fake."

She digested this for a moment, then nodded. "Okay, right. Make sure that we do have the original. If it turned out to be a fake, it would alert the authorities to counterfeit objects being sold on the black market as new. Not that *that's* a new concept, but I understand the need to keep track of where the bogus stuff is coming from and how many pieces are entering the market. And someone would have to be very familiar with the originals in order to duplicate them in a credible manner, which would narrow the field of possible forgers considerably. Plus, if it is counterfeit, that could maybe tie into the motive for killing Derek somehow."

"Very good." Sean nodded, obviously impressed.

"But that wouldn't explain Marian, would it?"

"I can't see how it would."

"God, I hate this." She covered her face with both hands as if to block out all of it.

Sean reached toward her, hesitated as if unsure of what to do next, then gently touched her shoulder.

"I'm sorry," he told her, drawing his hand back as if the gesture had been a foreign one. His face bore the expression of one who knew that something should come after *I'm sorry,* but didn't know what that something was.

"So where do we go from here?" she asked, her voice like gravel, her hands dropping into her lap.

"You mean, as far as the investigation is concerned?"

"Yes."

"Well, we'll need to determine if anything was stolen from Marian's shop. See if we can determine if robbery was the motive." He paused before asking, "Would you be up to going through the shop, taking a look around, seeing if anything is missing?"

"I don't know her entire inventory, but yes, of course I'll do it. It's the very least I can do for her. I may be able to tell you if something obvious is missing. She did have some valuable pieces in there. Paintings and old silver were special interests of hers, and she had some lovely jewelry as well. And I can probably find her shop inventory lists. Her record keeping was meticulous. We should be able to find hard copies of the lists in her desk, and I'm sure she kept copies on disk."

"When do you think you'll feel up to it?"

"Now. This morning. Let's get it done," she said, her jaw set, hardened, emotions shoved into the background. "If it will help your investigation in any way, play even a tiny part in finding her killer, then let's do it now."

"You sure you're all right?" Sean's body blocked Amanda's entrance into the shop.

She nodded and pushed past him, then stopped near the counter and looked around.

Shadows stretched long in the pale morning light. Dust motes drifted aimlessly in the front window, and the air lay still around them, but the remains of the crime scene investigation were harsh reminders of what had happened just a little more than twenty-four hours earlier in the back room of For Old Time's Sake.

Amanda stepped over the limp strand of police tape that snaked from the front door to the back room. She turned her back on the office, on the wooden floor with its brown stain and nightmare images.

Focus.

Amanda had been in this shop at least once every day for the past several years. She should be able to pick out empty spots on the shelves where certain pieces had stood, perhaps even recall what was missing. *Focus on that,* she reminded herself. *On helping Marian. Forget about how she looked the last time you saw her, there on the floor . . .*

"Anything seem out of place?" Sean watched her carefully from the front of the shop. At the first sign that she might begin to crack, he was prepared to take her right out the front door. He'd carry her if he had to. She'd been through so much, and she was trying so hard to keep on going.

"Nothing . . . no." She shook her head, her eyes moving shelf to shelf, cabinet to cabinet. "Nothing so far . . ."

She walked the perimeter of the shop, carefully noting the placement of furniture and artwork, shaking her head. "As I told you earlier, I wasn't familiar with all of Marian's stock. I don't see anything obviously out of place, but . . ."

She paused near the counter. "She did buy some Russian antiques earlier in the week. I don't see any of them here. She mentioned she had potential buyers, though, so she could have mailed them out before . . . before yesterday." She looked over her shoulder. "Maybe in the office . . ."

"I'll go in." Sean walked toward the back of the shop. "You just tell me what I'm looking for."

Amanda described the items for Sean.

"There's something here all packed up for the post," he called from the office a moment later. "It was under the desk. And here are a couple of receipts from one of those express delivery services. Picked up some stuff on Wednesday afternoon, it looks like." He brought the box and the papers with him to the front of the shop and placed them on the counter.

"Let me see those," she said. "They should note what was in the packages and give an approximate value . . . yes, here, see?"

She held up one of the slips.

"It says salt box." Sean frowned. "She mailed a box of salt?"

"A box used to keep salt in," Amanda explained. "She insured it, see here?"

Sean whistled at the amount the piece had been insured for. "That must have been some box."

"It was. Rare and beautiful. Silver and enamel." She waved a second receipt. "And this is for the clock. Can we open the box to see what's in it?"

Sean nodded and pulled out a pocketknife.

"This might be the miniature she bought," Amanda offered.

"Miniature what?"

"Portrait. Of Alexander the First." She waded through the packing. "Here it is."

She held up the small painting. Sean leaned closer for a better look.

"That's Alexander the First? The Russian who was assassinated with his family? Anastasia, and all that?"

"That was Nicholas."

"Oh, right. And she was going to trust this to the mail?"

"No, this was going by courier, see? She was paying a premium to have this handled with kid gloves."

"You familiar with this service?"

"Yes. I've used it myself. We all have. They're reliable, fast, and relatively inexpensive, compared to the competition."

Sean folded the wrapping back over the package within a package and prepared to take it with him.

"We'll want to speak with the service, see if their man made it down here yesterday before you did."

"They would have called the police right away and volunteered the information, if they'd been here. They're very reliable." She added, "And for the record, the company is owned by a woman. Several of her drivers are women."

"Sorry," he said absently. "So, everything else is intact, you think?"

"I think so. I wish I'd been able to be of some help."

"Oh, but you have. If nothing else, we've been able to pretty much rule out robbery as our primary motive."

"Then what was the primary motive?" She frowned.

He'd been afraid she'd ask. "I think he came here with the express purpose of murdering Marian."

"But why?" she whispered hoarsely.

He hesitated a little too long. She caught it.

"What?" she asked, her eyes narrowing.

"Well, as we discussed, I do believe that the same person killed Derek and Marian—"

"But why? Why would anyone want them dead?"

"Well, as I said before, the only strong link between the two of them—besides their profession—is you."

"That doesn't make any sense to me."

"It makes sense to the killer. We just have to be smart enough to figure it out."

"Do you have any ideas on this?" She folded her arms across her chest as if suddenly cold.

"Well, there's the pottery. . . ."

"But Marian had nothing to do with that. She never even saw the piece."

"How about this?" Sean leaned his elbows on the

glass counter. "How about if someone was here, going through your shop on Wednesday night, after you closed, looking for the goblet. Maybe Marian saw something—a light, a figure, whatever—and came over to investigate. Maybe at first she thought it was you working late, just as she had been. Maybe she tried the door and found it open, came in. He forces her back over to her place, where he kills her."

"Maybe. Maybe. She would have come over, if she'd seen something." Amanda nodded thoughtfully. "Just like I went to her shop when something seemed wrong."

"Or . . ."

"Or . . . ?"

"I mentioned, I think, that I'd read through your file. The one from last year."

"The case against Archer Lowell, you mean."

"Yes."

"Okay, and you found that Lowell had threatened Derek. We knew that."

"Did you know that he had threatened Marian as well?"

"What?"

"When Lowell was arrested, he made the statement to the arresting officers that if it was the last thing he did, he'd get back at that bitch who'd called the cops on him." He leaned back against the counter. "Marian was the one who called 911 the day that Archer attacked you outside your shop."

"Yes." She nodded, her face grave. "Yes, she did. And she was going to testify against him in court."

"But then he pled out, and there was no trial."

"You think somehow this is all connected to him?"

"It's worth following up on. At one time, he'd threatened both Derek and Marian. And now they're both dead."

"But you said the prison officials confirmed that he's had no other visitors, no contact with anyone other than his mother and his sister."

"We're going to have to look a little closer at Mr. Lowell. Maybe there's a former cell mate, someone he came in contact with—"

Her hands started to shake and her legs went weak. "I don't want that to be it. I don't want it to be because of me. I don't want them to be dead because of me."

Without thinking, he put his arms around her and let her cry, held her until she stopped shaking.

"Bastard," she growled. "I thought this was all behind me—that *he* was behind me. *Bastard*. If he had anything to do with this . . ."

"We'll figure it out. If it's him, if he's involved somehow, we'll find out. If he's behind this, we'll find out."

"It's so hard to believe. For one thing, I would never figure him being smart enough to plan something like this. I mean, wouldn't you have to be pretty smart to pull off something like this from behind bars?"

"Maybe he has a smart friend."

"He'd have to." She disengaged herself and dug into her purse for a tissue. Not finding one, she went behind the counter and pulled one from the box that sat on the shelf. She wiped her eyes and blew her nose and turned back to him. "Let's find him. Let's find Archer's friend, if he has one."

"Let's do that." *Before Archer's friend finds you . . .*

Her eyes returned to the glass case that stood between them. "Marian bought several pieces of jewelry at the sale." She leaned down to peer at the items on display. "There are the earrings . . . and there, there's the bracelet."

She frowned.

"Something wrong?"

"There was a pendant on a nice gold chain. Emeralds set in concentric circles, quite lovely. She had that in here."

"Maybe she sold it."

"If she did, it would have had to have been sometime on Wednesday. I can't believe she wouldn't have mentioned it, though. Let me check her receipts for this week."

She took a few steps in the direction of the office, then stopped.

"Tell me where it is. I'll get it," Sean said.

She shook her head. "No, I'll do it."

She pushed open the door and went into the small room, which still held the smell of blood and fear. She steeled herself against it and walked around the stain, refusing to let the images in.

In the top desk drawer was the black folder in which Marian recorded her purchases. Amanda grabbed it and returned to the front room.

"You might want this," she told Sean. "Though there doesn't seem to be too much sales activity this week . . ."

She scanned through the folder once, then a second time.

"It's not here. If she sold it, she would have noted it. She was a stickler for keeping track of her sales."

Amanda went back to the glass case to take another look. "Not here."

"When had you last seen the necklace there?"

"Late on Wednesday afternoon."

"And it was in that case?"

"Right there on that black velvet stand. Unless she moved it to another case . . ." Amanda made her way around the shop, studying the contents of each glass case. "It isn't here, Sean."

"Then she must have sold it after you saw it on Wednesday."

"There'd be paper on it."

"Maybe she planned on taking care of that when she got in yesterday. Maybe it was late in the afternoon . . ."

"No. She would have done it there and then. There was no mañana to Marian. She would have written a receipt at the time of the sale."

"Did you happen to notice any customers going in or out of her shop on Wednesday?"

"Only earlier in the day. There was a busload of shoppers from Maryland who came in around ten and left around three."

"But you saw the necklace after that. Later in the day."

"Closer to four."

"So if the necklace was in the shop on late Wednesday afternoon, where is it now?" Sean rubbed his chin. "A souvenir, maybe . . ."

"I'm sorry?"

"He could have taken it as a souvenir. Do you remember what it looked like?"

"Yes."

"Enough to make a drawing?"

"I can try, but I'm afraid I'm not much of an artist. And I may not remember all of the details. I only saw it once close up."

"Maybe you can sketch out what you remember, then we'll pass it on to Dana and maybe she can work something up. She's a pretty fair artist. Would you have time to sit with her for a while today?"

"Sure. I have all the time in the world."

She looked across the cobblestone walk to where her own shop sat, locked up and dark. She had no desire to so much as unlock the door.

"Ready, then?" Sean stood near the door.

"Sure," she sighed. "Why not?"

Her two best friends were gone, her business— once her sanctuary—now a sad and silent reminder of all she'd lost over the past few weeks.

She might as well spend the rest of the day at the police station. She had nowhere else to go.

Now, where was the bitch? Honest to God, you turn your back on a woman for twenty-four hours and she disappears.

Vince had tramped through the woods that bordered the open field behind Amanda's house, climbed a tree he'd used for this exact purpose several times before, and, binoculars in hand, studied the house for the past three hours. There'd been no movement. No lights on at dawn, no music, no TV chatter, as was her usual routine.

Maybe she's in mourning, he thought wryly, then glanced at his watch.

Till nine-thirty in the morning? Not likely. Not her. She was the original early to bed, early to rise girl.

He should know.

So far this morning, he'd watched the neighbors on either side of the little Victorian house leave for work. Amanda should have followed them by now.

"Oh, what the hell . . ."

He swung his legs over the branch below and dropped effortlessly to the ground. Cautious, just in case someone in the neighborhood was still at home, he approached the house along the shrub line, bent over at an angle so that his head never rose above the shortest of the shrubs. When he got to the back of her garage, he straightened up and stealthily inched along the wooden structure until he had an unobstructed view of the driveway.

Her car wasn't there.

Well, well, well. Wonder where Missy Amanda slept last night?

He crept along the drive, then made a dash for the back of the house. Once near the porch, he knew he was safe. The steps blocked off the view from the neighbors on the left, even if anyone had been home at that hour. He dropped to his knees and ever so carefully pushed out a pane of glass in one of the basement windows. He placed it on the grass, out of harm's way, and pushed in the sash. He lowered himself through the opening and dropped quietly into the basement, as he'd done so many times before.

"Let's see what Miss Amanda has been up to," he muttered.

He went directly to the far end of the basement and into the small room where a washer and dryer stood on a raised pedestal of concrete. He opened the washer and looked in. Empty. He peeked in the dryer. Empty as well. No laundry yet this week, Amanda?

Disappointed, he went up the stairs. Last time he'd lifted a pretty thong made out of a pale pink fabric and stuck it in his pocket. No such prize today.

He wondered if she'd even noticed it was gone.

Maybe she thought she'd left it someplace else, he snorted as he used a credit card to unlock the basement door.

The house lay still. Even the air seemed to be undisturbed until he made his way through it. He looked through the refrigerator and helped himself to a handful of strawberries, which he munched while he rifled through her mail and selected a magazine. He popped the tab on a beer and took it with him up the steps to her bedroom. Pausing in the doorway, he looked around the room.

Nothing had changed since his last visit a few days earlier.

He placed the beer bottle on the magazine on the bedside table, then lay down on the bed and stretched out. Catching her scent, he followed his nose, then buried his face in the pillow. It smelled clean, slightly lemony. It turned him on. He'd have to check her dresser and see if he could figure out which of those bottles held this perfume. He'd buy some for Dolores and make her wear it when they went to bed.

He wondered when he'd gone from wanting to kill Amanda, to wanting her.

He wondered if it mattered. His plan hadn't changed.

He'd still kill her. But if he could have her for a while first, if he could indulge himself in her for a time, why shouldn't he have that pleasure?

He closed his eyes and thought about having spent the night in Dolores's bed. He felt himself start to grow hard, remembering the enthusiasm with which Dolores had thanked him for his gift. He slid the zipper down on his jeans and freed himself, stroked himself, an image filling his mind's eye.

Dolores's body, Amanda's face.

Amanda's face. Amanda's body.

Everything he wanted to do to her. Everything he *would* do to her.

God, he couldn't wait.

CHAPTER
SIXTEEN

"Was it more rounded like this, do you think, or was it more oval-shaped?" Dana slid the sketch pad across the table to Amanda.

Amanda studied Dana's efforts. "I'm not sure," she said, and shook her head slowly. "I'm sorry, but I just don't remember. I really didn't study the pendant all that closely. Marian had bought several pieces at the same sale and was showing them off all at once. I do remember that the general shape was round, that there were concentric circles in the middle there, just like you've done, but I don't remember what kind of bale was at the top and whether or not it had stones in it, and I don't remember if there was some sort of gold fretwork around the outside. I seem to think there was, but I can't swear to it."

She looked up at Dana and exhaled slowly, one long tired breath. "I'm so sorry. That's the best I can do."

"Hey, don't apologize. You did just fine. We have a fairly good description of the pendant, enough that should alert the dealers throughout the county that we're looking for a similar piece." She stood, smiling. "I'll run this past the chief, then maybe we'll put it out to the press and the pawnshops throughout the county."

Dana bit her lip, examining her work. "Maybe we should send it out a little farther. Down to Philly. No, all of Pennsylvania. North Jersey, New York." She looked up at Amanda as if just remembering that she was there. "Though I'm betting we don't find it. I'm thinking he's going to keep it. A pretty souvenir. Which would be good for us, you know?"

"Because when you find the pendant, you'll know you've found the killer."

"And then"—Dana scooped up her drawing and headed to the door—"we'll hang him with it."

"Nice work." Sean looked over Dana's sketch. "Very nice. I'll get someone to send out the faxes right now." He glanced at the clock. "And if I hurry, I can get a press conference in before the early news begins, show it off. Get the local papers to run the sketch."

"You don't believe he's pawned it, do you?"

"Not a chance." He shook his head. "He's holding on to this or keeping it someplace close to him, where he can see it."

"That's what I thought, too."

"But there's always that one-in-a-million chance that he's decided to dump it. We'd be foolish to operate only on assumption here. There's too much at stake."

"Maybe we'll get real lucky. Maybe he's shown it to someone." Dana glanced at her watch. "It's well past noon. I'd like to leave for lunch. Do I take Amanda with me?"

"If you don't mind."

"I don't mind, but I know that my spending time with her takes an officer away from the investigation." She leaned against the doorjamb. "Last time I looked, we only had five other officers in the department."

"Nothing we can do about that. We can't take the chance that he'll move in on her if she's alone."

"Have you thought about asking for help from the FBI?"

"For all of about thirty seconds," he snapped.

"Sorry." She took a few steps back, surprised by the sharp tone of his voice. "I just thought . . . It's just that we have such a small department. Maybe we could use a little help, that's all."

"We have some fine officers. We'll do just fine."

"Sean, I didn't mean . . ." Dana sighed. "I'm sorry."

"Take Amanda to lunch. The department will reimburse you."

"Chief, your sister is on line two," Joyce announced through the speaker.

"Thanks." He hit the button and waved to Dana as she turned her back and left the room. "What's up, Greer?"

"Did you really sleep in your patrol car out here in front of my house last night?"

"And top of the morning to you, too."

"Did you? Kay across the street mentioned it when I went out to my fitness class this morning. Wondered what was going on."

"Actually, I slept on the sofa in your den last night." He shuffled through some papers on his desk, looking for the reports on an armed robbery suspect they'd transferred to the county prison two days earlier. "And you're just figuring that out? Hell of a detective you'd have made."

"And here I thought you just showed up early for breakfast." Greer paused. "You plan on doing that again tonight?"

"Most likely." Where the hell was that ballistics report?

"I'll leave you some proper bedding then. Honestly, Sean, why didn't you say something?"

"Didn't think about it. Got tired of sitting outside, started thinking about that sofa, figured, hell, what difference did it make if I was outside or inside, as long as I was there."

"True enough, though why you thought you should be sleeping outside is beyond me. By the way, did I think to tell you this morning that I have the Karmas monthly pot luck dinner tonight? It's at Mary Beth's."

The Karmas was the official name of the group Steve referred to as Greer and the Do-Gooders. Each month they met to discuss who in town was going through a hard time and what they could do to help out in a small, anonymous way. The ladies had chosen Karma as the name because they believed that you got back what you gave out, and by giving out a little kindness into the world, the world would give them kindness in return.

"No. You hadn't mentioned that."

"I'll be home by ten or so, but you might want to make other plans for Amanda, if you think she still needs watching. Unless you think she might want to come along."

"I'll let you know. Thanks, Greer." He wasn't sure Amanda was ready for the Karmas.

He hung up the phone and walked down the hall to the reception area.

"Dana go through here yet?"

"She and what's 'er name—the Crosby woman—just left," Joyce said without looking up from her keyboard. "You can probably catch them in the parking lot."

He caught up with them just as Dana was backing out of her parking place. Sean walked toward the car, motioning for her to roll the window down.

"Dana, what time do you go off today?"

"My shift is up at four, why?"

"Got plans for the evening?"

"Preview night at school for Courtney. She starts kindergarten next week, and tonight's the night when the parents bring the kids in to check out the classroom and the teacher. Get them familiar with the whole deal. Why, what's up?"

"Well, I'd thought Amanda would be having dinner with Greer tonight, but she just informed me that she has a previous commitment. It's the Karmas' night to have dinner." He leaned into the window just slightly. "Amanda, looks like you're stuck with me for a while tonight."

"Who are the Karmas?" Amanda frowned.

"Group of friends Greer gets together with to do good deeds and spread positive vibes through the cosmos. I'm sure she'd be more than happy to tell you about it."

He heard someone call his name and turned to see

Joyce waving from the doorway, indicating that he had a phone call.

"Look, I could probably—"

"No, you probably could not." He smacked the palm of his hand against the side of the car. "Dana, you'll bring her back to the station after lunch."

"Why can't we go to my shop for a while?" Amanda asked. "I want to try to get in touch with Marian's niece, and the only place I have her phone number is on the Rolodex in my office."

He thought it over for a moment, then said, "I guess it doesn't matter where you are, as long as you're not alone. Just keep in touch, though. Let me know your plans."

"Will do." Dana rolled up her window and put the car in drive.

Sean jogged back to the building, his mind on making the phone call to the D.A. to discuss a possible press conference. He wanted that sketch of the pendant out today. Someone might have seen it. Maybe they'd be willing to tell him where.

"Do you mind stopping at my house for just a minute?" Amanda asked as the police cruiser pulled out of the parking lot of Broeder's one and only fast-food restaurant. "I wasn't prepared to spend more than one night at Greer's. It looks as if I might be there for a few more days."

"Not a problem. It's down Jackson, if I remember correctly."

"Right."

"This is a nice neighborhood," Dana noted. "I like how you have such big lots, and those fields and woods behind. It feels like you're out in the country, but you still have sidewalks and other houses along the street. When Kyle and I first moved to Broeder, this was the neighborhood we wanted, but there was nothing on the market at the time. I love these old houses. They all look so trim and homey. Like a neighborhood in a magazine."

"I was lucky, I admit. Derek's aunt had owned the house, and she had decided to sell it right about the time I'd decided to look for one." Amanda pointed to their right as a reminder to Dana that they were almost to her house. "There, it's three down from here."

The car came to a stop, and Amanda opened the door. "I'll be right back. This won't take but a minute."

"Uh-uh." Dana shook her head. "I'm with you. White on rice and all that." Dana followed Amanda up the drive. "Front or back?"

"We'll go in the front." She turned up the cobbled walk. "And I'll just grab the mail while I'm here."

Amanda reached into the box and pulled out a stack several inches thick. "Magazines, junk mail, and bills. And a new Publishers Clearing House thing. There's something to look forward to. . . ."

She unlocked the front door and stepped into a silent house. Setting the mail down on the small oak hall table, Amanda paused, her head tilting slightly to one side.

"What?" Dana asked softly, straining as if listening to the house sounds.

"Nothing, I guess." Amanda still stood in the same place near the table.

"Something off?"

"Something . . ." She laughed self-consciously. "You'll think this is strange, but something smells off. Must be something in the trash." She walked down the hall toward the kitchen. "Though I could have sworn I'd emptied it before I left the other day. . . ."

Dana's hand was on her gun as she checked the first floor, room by room, on the way to the back of the house.

"Well, I'm not crazy. I did empty the trash." Amanda opened the refrigerator and scanned its contents. "Nothing going bad in here. . . ."

"What exactly do you think you smell?"

"Can't put my finger on it. Just something that shouldn't be here. Cologne or something."

Dana sniffed the air. "I don't smell it."

"I don't either, not in here." Amanda nodded. "Just there in the front hall. Maybe it's my imagination."

"Maybe not. Maybe someone was here." Dana drew her gun. "Let's go on upstairs. Stay behind me."

They crept up the stairs and into each room, each closet. Behind the shower curtain, through the small attic, back down to the second floor.

"Anything look out of place?" Dana asked.

Amanda shook her head. "Not that I can tell. Let's get my stuff and get out of here. I'm feeling spooked."

She grabbed an overnight bag from a peg on the back of the guest room closet and went into her bedroom, pausing in the doorway to look around.

"Anything?"

"I guess not. Let's just get out of here." She laid the bag open on the end of the bed and proceeded to go through a few drawers, pulling out some underwear here, a few shirts there, another pair of jeans, tucking all into the oversized bag. Another pair of shoes from her closet, a small leather case holding her few good pieces of jewelry from a shelf under her bedside table.

She hesitated, frowning.

"What?"

"I must really be losing it. I don't remember bringing this magazine up here." She gestured toward the bedside table. "I guess I'm just letting my imagination get the best of me. Let's just go."

Amanda noticed that the light was blinking on the answering machine in the hallway when they came back down the stairs. She hesitated, then pushed play. Her dentist's office, reminding her to call to make an appointment for a checkup. One of her young stepsisters calling to see if she wanted to be involved in plans for a sixtieth birthday party for their father. A hang-up call. Several colleagues who'd heard the news about Marian. Another hang-up. She hit the speaker and dialed the number for last incoming call.

"The number of your last incoming call is unknown."

"Thanks," she muttered, then gestured to Dana to go on out the front.

Dana paused at the door. "You going to set that alarm?"

"I can't, not until I have the entire house rewired, which I haven't been able to afford to do," she said, thinking that now would be a good time to have it working. "It sure would come in handy, but unfortunately, the old wiring just sets it off. The alarm company started charging me for false alarms, so I disconnected it."

Amanda locked the door and started across the porch, then stopped. "I meant to pick up a book while we're here," she told Dana. "I'll just be a minute."

"Well, here, give me that and I'll put it in the car." Dana reached up for the bag and caught Amanda's easy toss.

Unlocking the door, Amanda stepped back inside. The house was still as a tomb. The unfamiliar scent lingered in the air. Was it more pronounced now? Stronger? Amanda shook her head. Impossible. She and Dana had just been all through the house. There was no one there.

She ran up the stairs and quickened her pace as she went into her bedroom. She went straight to the chair near the window and picked up the book she'd been reading before all of this started. Maybe she'd have time to read a little tonight while Greer was out. Maybe it would take her mind off—

Without warning, an arm snaked around her throat and tightened, abruptly cutting off her air. A rough hand covered her mouth and she bit down hard on a finger. Something hissed in her ear, and the hand that she'd bitten punched the side of her head once, twice.

Gasping for breath, blinking against the bright lights that exploded inside her head, she gathered all her strength and bucked forward, far enough to create space between her body and that of her assailant. One elbow sent sharply to his midsection surprised him, caused his grip to slacken enough that she could throw him off. He bounced backward and she spun on one foot, her weight and force centered in the leg and heel that landed a direct shot in his jaw. He howled, shoving her hard, and spun backward through the door, then took the stairs two at a time. She heard him hit the landing on both feet just as her head struck the side of the dresser.

"Son of a bitch," she growled from between clenched teeth, and struggled to the top of the stairs. "Son of a bitch . . ."

She made it to the front door and all but fell down the steps.

"Jesus!" Dana yelled and dashed from the car. "What the hell . . ."

"He was inside . . . in the house . . ." Amanda gasped and slumped to the ground halfway across the lawn. "He was in there the whole time."

Drawing her gun, Dana dashed into the house. Within minutes, she was running back down the driveway.

"He went out the back door, probably through the field and into the woods." She reached into the car for her radio. "Are you all right? Did he hurt you? Do you need an ambulance?"

"No. He roughed me up, that's all. Surprised me, mostly." She rubbed her throat. "Neck's going to be sore. Head's sore. Not as sore as he's going to be, though."

"You land a shot?"

"Right to the jaw." She looked up and smiled. "With any real luck, I might have even broken it."

"He'll need it set, if that's the case." Dana nodded and turned her attention to the dispatcher as she called for backup.

Within minutes, the street was alive with activity, the woods swarming with officers searching for signs of Amanda's assailant.

"Tell me again why you went into the house alone?" Sean stood next to the passenger side of the patrol car in which Amanda now sat.

"I went in for a book—"

"And Officer Burke was where?"

"She was on her way back to the car. She was taking my bag. We'd just come out and I'd locked the door and I remembered that I'd left the book—"

"So instead of having Officer Burke accompany you back inside—"

"Stop right there. Dana did nothing wrong. We'd just both come out of the house. There was no one there . . . no one that we'd seen, anyway. He must have been hiding someplace—"

"Well, gosh, who'd have suspected he'd have hidden himself when he heard you two come in? How clever of him."

She lowered her voice. "Stop it, Sean."

"He could have killed you, Amanda." His eyes narrowed, darkened. "Do you understand? This is the man who killed Derek. He killed Marian. He wants to kill you."

"Yeah, well, he didn't, did he?" She got out of the car, her jaw set squarely, her eyes flashing like lightning. "I fought back this time, Sean. I was ready to fight back. He's the one who left here hurting, not me. I fought back. . . ."

He watched the fury gather in her face, watched it explode as she shoved him away and walked off down the drive toward the back of her property. He gave her a minute, then followed.

He found her sitting on the bench near the koi pond.

"That's what this is all about to you, isn't it?" He sat on the end of the bench. "Fighting back."

"Everything I've done since Archer Lowell has been about fighting back." She looked him directly in the eyes.

"Didn't it occur to you that he might have had a knife? Or a gun?" He tried to avoid looking at the reddened area near her temple that had already begun to swell. Since she'd denied being hurt, he chose not to mention it.

"Do you know what it's like to be a victim, Sean? To be totally helpless, to be at the mercy of someone bigger and stronger and have no way to fight back? To be afraid all the time, and everywhere you go?" She wiped away a few escaping tears, not waiting for a reply. "After the attack last year, I promised myself I would never be anyone's victim again. Lowell took every bit of security, every small bit of confidence I'd ever had. He made me afraid to be in my own home and afraid to leave it. Afraid to go to work. Afraid to run early in the morning or go to the grocery store alone."

She drew her knees up to her chest.

"Before all that last year, I was very shy. Timid. Didn't even have the nerve to open my mouth to bid at auctions for things I wanted for the shop." She smiled ruefully. "Derek even had to negotiate prices for me. I wasn't assertive enough to argue with any-one over money."

She looked up and saw the look of skepticism on Sean's face.

"Archer Lowell changed all that. That woman—the one he had terrorized—no longer exists."

Sean leaned forward and with one finger traced the L-shaped scar on her face.

"Yeah, that's the mark of my liberation," she laughed darkly. "The doctors suggested that a little plastic surgery would take that right away, but I wouldn't let them. I think they thought if they removed the physical evidence, I'd be able to put it all behind me."

"That's only the scar that shows on the outside," he said softly.

"Right, Chief. Though I must say, I've done a damned good job of healing the inner ones all by myself." Her chin thrust forward just slightly. "I've driven away my demons and I'm a stronger person for it. I can take care of myself for the first time in my life. I wasn't afraid in there, Sean. I wasn't scared."

"You should have been."

She shook her head. "I knew I could take him. I knew he wouldn't expect me to fight back. Especially not with the level of expertise that I did."

"Black belt?" he asked.

"You betcha."

"How'd you manage to do that in sixteen months?"

"Well, I was hardly starting from scratch. I'd taken tae kwon do in high school and in college. Evan insisted on it. But after Archer, I started back to class three, sometimes four nights every week. It didn't take long to get back in the swing of things." She made a meek attempt at smiling. "No pun intended."

He sat beside her quietly for a long moment, as if trying to decide what to do next. He took both her hands in his and just held them. After a minute or two, Amanda rested her head on his shoulder and closed her eyes. He put one arm around her and drew her against his chest.

"I was lying," she said softly.

"What?"

"Before. When I said I wasn't afraid. That was a lie." She opened her eyes and stared up at the sky. "I was afraid."

"Well, it's only normal to—"

"Not of him. I was afraid I wouldn't be able to fight. That I'd panic and not fight back. And if I couldn't fight, it would mean that everything I thought I'd learned about myself, everything I thought I'd become, was a myth. That after all I'd done and all that I'd been through, I'd find out that deep inside, I was still that meek, helpless woman Archer Lowell had preyed on. And that the past sixteen months of my life hadn't meant a damned thing."

Sean tried hard to think of something to say that would make her understand that it was neither her strength nor her weakness that determined whether her life had meaning. But while he was searching for the words, she looked up at him and said, "But I did all right, didn't I? I fought back. I beat this bastard, ran him off. This time, I won."

"Yeah." He nodded, one hand stroking her arm in reassurance. "You won this round."

They sat close together on the bench for another ten minutes or so, until the last of his officers came back through the field shaking their heads.

"Nothing, Chief," Dana told him. "Ground's too hard and there's too much underbrush to get a trail through the woods. It's like he disappeared into thin air."

"He couldn't have gone too far, if he was hurt as badly as Amanda thinks he was."

"I only landed one kick to his jaw," she noted. "He must have been stunned, and he probably hurts like hell. But he'd have had no trouble getting through those woods by the time your other officers arrived."

"Kicked him in the face, did you?" Dana asked.

"With every ounce of strength I had." She smiled. "Kicked like a mule . . ."

CHAPTER SEVENTEEN

BITCH KICKED LIKE A FUCKING MULE.

Vince lay back against the pillow, the plastic bag filled with ice numbing the left side of his face. There'd be no partying down at Dolores's apartment tonight, that's for sure. He'd have to leave a message on her answering machine—as soon as he could work his jaw to talk, that is. Didn't want her wondering where he was, coming to his room to look for him. Or worse, thinking he was dumping her, after last night. Damn, but that Dolores was one hot little tamale. Turned him inside out and all but ripped him to shreds. But that was fine. He liked it like that.

That little bauble he'd given her had been worth its weight in gold—he'd been right about that. It had turned her on like a Bunsen burner.

And here was a little bonus he hadn't counted on. Any time he wanted to see it, it would be there, hanging around her neck. And every time he looked at it, he'd be reminded of Marian and how she had tried to scream. He'd found the experience of killing her unexpectedly sweet in retrospect, had found it thrilling to think back on how he'd plunged the knife in and out. In and out. In and out. Just like he'd plunged himself into Dolores over and over the night before. It had been the absolute best sex he'd ever had, hands down.

Well, it was just like he'd figured. Dolores was one of those women who just crumbled when she thought a straight-up guy like him was into her for the long haul. And he would be, relatively speaking. He liked this little town, liked the way things were going for him here. He could see himself hanging around for a bit. And he would, since he did not intend to do anything stupid that would attract attention. Nope, as far as everyone around here was concerned, Vinnie Daniels was a stand-up guy. Salt of the earth, and all that.

That's what his mother used to say when she described someone she really admired. "He's the salt of the earth, Vince," she'd say, and nod her head, her mouth set in an approving line. It was her highest compliment.

Wonder what little words or phrases she was using to describe him these days, he thought idly. It sure as hell wasn't salt of the earth, or anything even near as nice.

The last time he'd seen her, she'd cursed him, then cursed herself for having given birth to him. That had been a little hard to take, having his own mother damn him to the fires of hell and mean it.

Yeah, okay, so he fucked up. He probably should have dealt with Diane some other way. He was ready to admit that now. Killing her and the boys had not been the best way to resolve the custody dispute. But she had just made him so goddamned mad with her bitching at him in court, right there in front of everyone, talking about how he lost his temper with her and the boys, about how he'd slapped her around now and then. Okay, so maybe sometimes it had been more than a few slaps. Didn't a man have the right to keep his woman in her place, remind her who she had to thank for the roof over her head and the clothes on her back? Not that he'd have allowed her to work. Uh-uh. Not his wife.

And then that damned advocate, that Douglas woman—the one appointed by the court to review everything and make recommendations about the boys—got involved. Stuck her two cents in. Next thing he knew, that bitch of a judge was yapping at him and telling him he couldn't so much as set foot in that house he'd worked and sweated his balls off to buy.

Yeah, right. Like that was gonna happen.

Well, she got hers, hadn't she? The judge? His buddy Curt Channing had seen to that. Curt had screwed up where the advocate had been concerned, but hey, he'd gone two for three, hadn't he? Besides, Vince was almost finished with his three. Then he'd take care of Mara Douglas on his own. Gotta be careful there, though. That one would be too easy to trace back to him. Everyone knew he hated her guts and would blow her away as soon as look at her.

She had been something to look at, though.

Well, he'd think of something where she was concerned. He'd heard she'd taken up with some slick FBI agent, though. And now that Vince thought about it, wasn't her sister some FBI type, too?

Better let that one go for a while. He'd have to wait. He could wait. He had all the time in the world now.

Besides, hadn't he read something in the prison li-

brary that someone had said something like revenge
was a dish best served cold? Vince took that to mean
that he'd be better off just letting it go for a while, letting things cool down, and then, someday, some long
time from now, he could do her and no one would
suspect him. That's what he thought it meant, anyway. It sounded like good advice to him.

He painfully turned his head to look at his watch.
It was almost seven. Dolores was going to be getting
home anytime now. Last night she'd said her last
client today would be a cut and color at six and she
probably wouldn't get home until seven-thirty or so,
and it would be closer to eight by the time she got to
the Dew. He was going to have to tell her he'd been
called out of town for a few days. On business.

*Yeah, business. The business of putting my jaw back
into alignment.*

Who'd have thought that little slip of a thing could
pack such a punch? He sure hadn't. Damn, she was
fast. And tough.

Yeah, well, she won that round, but next time—
and there would be a next time—he'd be ready for
her. She'd just caught him off guard, that was all.

In spite of the pain and the humiliation of having
had her get the best of him, he almost smiled.

Derek England had been all too easy. One quick
pop and he was history. One down, two to go.

Marian had been more lively, true, and much more
rewarding, all things considered. But there'd been no
real sense of sport to it. The old *veni, vidi, vici* thing.
But Amanda, well, she was something else altogether.

And then there was the little matter of knowing
that her big brother, that hotshot detective, would

never know she'd gone down at the hands of Vincent Giordano.

Hot damn. This was going to be so sweet. The fact that he and Detective Crosby had a history, well, that made it sweeter still.

Two down, one to go.

CHAPTER
EIGHTEEN

"SEE ANYTHING ON THE MENU THAT APPEALS TO you?" Sean sat across the booth from Amanda in Broeder's one true diner and pretended to be considering the day's specials.

"I'm not really all that hungry."

He folded his menu and put it aside. "I realize that you've had a really, really bad day." The glint in his eyes told her he knew he was understating the situation. "But you ate hardly anything at breakfast, too."

"It was the bacon. Not a good idea. Bacon is not a good choice on an unsettled stomach." She continued to scan the menu.

"What did you have for lunch?"

"A salad."

"Yummy," he mumbled.

"You ready to order, Chief? You see our specials?" The cute little waitress whose name tag identified her as Linda set two fat glasses of ice water on the table. Under normal circumstances, she would have been flirting like crazy with Sean, but today she busied herself with inspecting Amanda from the corner of one eye.

"Yes, but I'll have the meat loaf." He handed her his menu.

"Mashed or baked?"

"Gotta have the mashed with meat loaf." He winked at her and she giggled.

"Miss?"

"Does the salmon special come with a sauce?" Amanda asked.

"Ah, it comes with lemon." The waitress screwed up her face as if it were an unnatural thing to ask. "What kind of sauce were you looking for?"

"Something herby."

"I can ask the cook," she offered but made no move toward the kitchen.

The look on Sean's face was pure amusement.

"What?" Amanda frowned.

"This is a diner," he stage-whispered. "Not a French restaurant."

"What would you suggest, then?"

"The meat loaf."

"Not a big favorite of mine."

"That's because you probably haven't had diner meat loaf."

"Fine." She looked up at the waitress. "I'll have what he's having. And an iced tea."

"Iced tea sounds good. Make it two, Linda."

"I'll be back in a flash."

"Can it be possible that you've never eaten at the Broeder Diner before?" Sean said.

"Guilty."

"How could you have lived here for so long and not have eaten here?"

"I don't know. I just never did."

"Just take a look around. We're talking classic American diner here," he told her. "White walls. Black-

and-white checkered tile floor. Red leather benches for the booths. American as apple pie."

"Well, that's not a favorite of mine, either."

"Let me guess. Chocolate mousse." He smiled up at Linda as she returned with two tall glasses of iced tea, lemon wedges riding on the rims.

"Yum. Although I do prefer a good pear tart. But nothing gets me going quite like bananas Foster."

"Whatever," he muttered, shaking his head, and she laughed for the first time that day.

"That's better," he said softly, wanting to reach across the table to her, but knowing that sort of intimate gesture would generate a little too much fodder for the small-town gossip mill. "How long do you suppose it's been since you laughed?"

"There hasn't been much to laugh about lately." She rested both arms on the table in front of her and looked solemn.

He started to say something, but her attention was drawn to the front of the diner. The door being directly in her line of vision, she could not avoid seeing every patron who came in or went out.

The redheaded woman walked slowly down the aisle as if counting heads or looking for someone. Amanda had a feeling she knew who that someone was.

"Sean?" The woman stopped next to their table.

"Ramona." He looked up and appeared to be trying to smile.

"Did you get my message?" The woman's voice was very soft and very sweet and almost apologetic. "I called you. . . ."

"I've been a little busy." He looked pained. "We've

had a few homicides here in Broeder. You might have read about them in the paper."

"I don't usually read the papers." She shook her head. "Too much bad news, you know?"

"Well, bad news is my business, Ramona."

She nodded and turned to Amanda as if seeing her for the first time.

"Are you Sean's girlfriend?" the woman asked.

"Ahhhh . . ." Amanda stuttered, taken aback by the question.

"This is Amanda. She's a friend." Sean's face was unreadable.

"It's nice to meet you," Ramona said to Amanda.

"It's nice to meet you, too, Ramona."

The waitress arrived with their meals. "Sorry, I forgot about your salads," she said as she put their plates down. "You eating, hon?" she asked Ramona.

"Oh. No. I . . . I'm not staying." She gave Sean a weak smile. "Will you call me? Please?"

"Sure." He nodded.

"Bye." She turned sad eyes to Amanda, then walked away.

The waitress returned with their salads. "Sorry. Things just got hectic all of a sudden in the kitchen." She looked over the table. "I forget anything else? More iced tea, Chief? Miss?"

They both shook their heads.

"Holler if you need me."

They ate in silence for several minutes.

"How's your meat loaf?" he asked.

"Fine."

More silence.

Finally, Amanda couldn't stand it any longer. "She seemed so *sad*. Ramona."

When Sean did not respond, she said, "Sorry. Didn't mean to pry."

Sean continued to chew.

"It's not what you think," he said after a time.

"I wasn't thinking anything."

"Yes, you were. You're thinking she's an old girlfriend"—he put his fork down—"and that I just rudely blew her off."

"None of my business."

The fingers of his right hand began to tap on the tabletop, and his eyes narrowed, as if he were in the midst of an inner debate.

"I hardly know her," he finally said.

"Sean, you don't need to feel that you—"

"She thinks she's my sister," he pretty much blurted out.

Amanda's jaw dropped noticeably. "She thinks she's . . ." Amanda repeated slowly, as if not quite understanding.

"She thinks she's my sister." He said it again, more deliberately.

"Why does she think that?"

"Because Greer told her she was."

"You'll forgive me if I appear to be having a little problem following all this."

"How do you think *I* feel?"

"How do you feel?"

"I don't know."

"Okay, Greer told Ramona that she is your sister." Amanda paused. "Half sister or whole sister?"

"Greer thinks maybe half, but no one's really sure. That part's apparently still up in the air."

"How did she find you?"

"Greer found her."

"How?"

"Same way she found me."

"Well, that turned out fine. I don't understand what the problem is."

"The problem is that Greer wants to embrace Ramona like—" He stopped in midsentence.

"Like a long lost sister?" She finished it for him.

"You've seen how Greer is. She is just too trusting. Too open. Before you know it, she'll have Ramona under her wing like the mother hen she is."

"And that would be wrong because . . . ?"

"What if it turns out not to be true? Greer's heart is going to be broken."

"I would think that for Greer to have contacted her, she'd have researched this pretty carefully," Amanda said gently.

"I have no reason to believe that my mother ever had any children other than Greer and me. And she didn't want either of us. Dumped us both on her mother and never looked back. Why would she have gone and had another child?"

"You were very young then. You wouldn't have known whether your mother had had another child. And what if it's the truth? What if Ramona really is your sister?"

"She's not."

"How do you know that?"

"Because." His jaw set squarely and he made a point to look away.

"Because you don't want her to be?"

"Bring you folks anything else? Coffee? Dessert?" The waitress paused in flight past the table.

"Amanda?"

She shook her head.

"Just the check, please, Linda."

Linda stopped long enough to total up the check and drop it onto the end of the table. "Thanks, Chief. See you tomorrow."

"You eat here every day?" Amanda asked on their way out, more to break the uncomfortable silence than because she was deeply interested.

"Pretty much."

A serious rattle of thunder greeted them as they started down the steps from the door to the parking lot. A crackle of lightning burst close by. They both looked skyward and mentally calculated the arrival time of the impending storm.

"Look, I guess I was out of line," she said when they'd gotten into the Jeep. "I said more than I should have. I'm sorry. It's none of my business."

"My fault for bringing it up."

He started the Jeep and headed off in the opposite direction from Greer's.

"I need to stop at my place for just a minute. I need to pick up a few things," he said.

"Okay."

They drove in silence for several blocks before making a right turn onto a narrow side street where the houses were small and for the most part nondescript. Sean pulled into a gravel driveway and turned off the engine.

"Since I'm not comfortable leaving you out here alone, I guess you're going to have to come on in."

"Okay." She unlocked her door and jumped out onto the stones and followed him to the front door. A soft rain had just begun to fall, and the sky continued to darken. Large fat clouds gathered overhead at a steady clip.

The house was small and brick with white shutters and no front porch. Three concrete steps led directly to the front door. There was no name on the black metal mailbox affixed to the front of the house, no shrubs or flowers, nothing to lend even a trace of warmth to the property. Scruffy grass ran right up to the foundation, and all of the wood trim—windows, shutters, door—looked like their next paint job was already several years overdue.

Sean unlocked the door and swung it open, stepped aside to let Amanda enter the narrow foyer.

"I'll just be a minute." He moved past her to turn on a lamp in the living room.

"I guess I'll just wait here. . . ." she said, even though he'd already left the room on his way to the stairwell.

She looked around the living room, marveling at the sparseness of the furnishings.

Sparse? She almost laughed out loud. This was beyond sparse. The living room held one dark brown leather chair and an ottoman, both of indeterminable age, and a table painted white upon which sat the lamp he'd turned on. There were stacks of books on the floor on either side of the chair, hardbacks and paperbacks in small haphazard towers, one of which had slumped over to spread out under the table.

There was nothing else in the room. No television. No pictures on the wall. Nothing. The walls were all stark white.

She stepped forward through what she assumed was intended to have been the dining room. What might have served as a dining table under other circumstances held an open laptop and piles of paper, files with their contents partly exposed, and stacks of newspaper articles. The lone wooden chair sat pushed up to the table.

Into the kitchen, where counters stood empty and the sink held nothing but a coffee mug. The one surprise was the color on the walls.

"Admiring the decor?" he asked dryly from the doorway.

"Sorry. I was just wandering. Sorry."

"Now you and Greer will have something else to talk about."

"What's that supposed to mean?" She frowned.

"She's always on my back about not having any furniture. She says I live like a hermit."

"Well, you have to admit that you have a lot of empty space just waiting to be filled here." She chose her words carefully, and it made him laugh.

"I'll have to remember that next time Greer starts in on me. She thinks it's cold as a tomb. I'll just tell her it's empty space waiting to be filled." He shrugged. "I don't know what she thinks I ought to do. I'm just renting here."

"Lots of people rent, but they still find ways to make the place their home."

When he didn't respond, she said, "I like the dark red walls in the kitchen."

"Greer did it. Said the place needed some color."

Actually, what Greer had said was that the dark red suited his moody personality, but he felt no need to go into that.

She followed him into the dining room. "You know what they say, there's no place like home."

"Well, maybe that's it then." He turned off the lights, giving her no choice but to head for the front door. "I've never really had one."

"I'm sorry," she said quietly.

"Yeah, well." He turned on the outside light, avoiding her eyes.

"Sean, I—"

"It's okay, Amanda." He locked the door. "Let's just forget about it, okay?"

"I'm sorry," she whispered to his back as she trudged across the uneven lawn to the Jeep, dodging the rain that had begun to fall in earnest. "I'm so sorry. . . ."

After a few long minutes of the windshield wipers' monotonous *swish slap, swish slap, swish slap,* Sean turned on the radio. Ten nonstop minutes of classic rock followed but neither sang along. It was a less than comfortable silence and lasted until Sean pulled into his sister's driveway and peered up toward the garage.

"Looks like Greer's not back yet." He frowned and sat tapping the wheel, as if debating with himself. Finally, he said, "Oh, hell. What's the difference? I'll move her car in the morning."

"Move her car?" Amanda looked behind them toward the end of the drive.

"Yeah, when I leave in the morning." He got out of the Jeep and opened the back door, took out his duffel bag.

"You're staying here?" She got out, too, and immediately hunched against the rain.

"Yeah. Come on, it's really starting to come down now." He ran ahead to the back of the house and paused at the edge of the walk, then opened the door to the screened porch for her, let her proceed in first.

She brushed against him and made the mistake of looking up into his eyes. As if having a mind of their own, his hands reached for her shoulders and turned her around so that she was in his arms. She smelled of lemons and late summer rain. He kissed her, because he couldn't not.

He'd expected her to move away, push him away, and when she didn't, when she raised her arms to wrap them around his neck, he kissed her again, mesmerized by the way she felt in his arms and the way her mouth felt against his. She seemed to melt into him, every bit of her.

"I've been wanting to do that since the first time I saw you there in your shop," he heard himself say.

"What stopped you?"

"Well, the thought that maybe you were capable of cold-blooded murder . . . I don't know, that kind of thing has always been a real turnoff for me."

She smiled in the darkness, and he bent his head to kiss her again, his tongue tracing the outline of her mouth.

"And I saw myself maybe having to slip handcuffs on these pretty wrists and dragging your admirable butt off to my jail. Now, I realize that some men like that whole bondage thing, but to tell you the truth, I've put too many women into cuffs to get off on it. And just thinking about you in one of those ugly orange jumpsuits . . ."

"Can't blame you there." She shook her head. "I can't think of anyone who looks good in orange."

"Well, there you go then." He leaned back against the doorway and pulled her with him. He was all set to kiss her again, when she asked, "Did you really believe, in your heart, that I'd killed Derek?"

"My heart has no place in a homicide investigation. The only thing that matters is the evidence." He rested his chin on the top of her head.

"Haven't you ever been tempted to say the hell with it and let your heart sneak in a comment or two?"

"No." He looked at her as if she were speaking an unfamiliar language. "No. That's not why you wear the badge."

"Why do you wear the badge?"

He looked surprised by the question. "Because it's the only thing I know how to do." He took her hand and led her to the door, which he unlocked and opened.

"You got out of school and set out immediately to become a cop?" Amanda dropped her purse onto the counter.

"I joined the army right out of high school and just went from there." He walked through the downstairs to the front door, where he checked to make sure that the lock was still set. On his way back to the kitchen, he turned on a lamp in the hallway.

"Why the army?"

"I got out of foster care a month before my eighteenth birthday. My foster parents had made it pretty clear they expected me out the door after I graduated from high school. So I enlisted. Two weeks after graduation, I left for basic."

"I'm sorry."

"Don't be. It all worked out for me. It's been okay. More than okay. I liked the army, liked the structure of it, liked that every man there started out on a level playing field. It didn't matter who you were or where you came from. The only thing that put you out ahead of the others—or behind them—was your own actions. It was all in your hands. For the first time in my life, I was on equal footing with everyone else. I could sink to the bottom, or I could rise to the top. And that's just what I did. I rose above. After I'd gone as far as I could go, I left."

"You went right into law enforcement?"

"I had a buddy who had gotten out a few months before me. He had gone home to the small West Virginia town he'd grown up in and became a cop. They had an opening for another rookie. I applied. My record in the service was good." He shrugged. "It all worked out."

"And then you came here."

"Greer tell you any of this?" He raised a suspicious eyebrow.

"Just that she'd found you and wanted you to come here when the chief's job opened up."

"Greer does not know how to tell half a story."

"She did tell me she'd been looking for you for years."

"Then she told you about how our mother dumped

us on our grandmother, and how when our grandmother died, social services sent us on our way through the system. Unfortunately, the system could only place pretty kids who were well mannered and who never caused trouble."

"She told me you two were separated, yes."

"Then you know the whole story."

"I doubt I do."

"Just as well. Not a very pretty one." His eyes went hollow.

"It must have been wonderful to be reunited with Greer again, though. After all those years."

"I didn't remember her. Not really. I remembered her absence more than her presence. Remembered what it felt like after we'd been sent to different places. Remembered waking up in the night and wondering if I'd dreamed her, because it had been so long since I'd seen her face."

"How old were you then?"

He shrugged. "I don't know, pretty young. Four, maybe five."

"When did they stop?"

"The dreams? About six months ago."

"That's when you—" The words *when you came here to Broeder* stuck in her throat.

"Yes."

"That's a long time to hurt," she said softly. "A long time to be sad."

"You're thinking of Ramona," he said flatly. "Well, don't. She didn't even know about us when she was a kid. So she never missed us."

He didn't want to talk about this anymore. He wanted to kiss Amanda.

"Are you afraid you'll get to know her—maybe even like her—and then she'll disappear?"

"I just don't have time right now for more people who will complicate my life."

"Oh. I see." She nodded slowly. "People that you care about, who care about you, complicate your life. Has Greer complicated your life?"

"You're kidding, right? Greer has done everything she can to take over my life."

"And another sister—if you had one—might try to do the same. Put her two cents in."

"Probably." His eyes narrowed. "Some women just can't help themselves."

"Ha ha. I'm going to pretend that you didn't say that. And I'm not going to let you bait me into walking away from you so that you don't have to deal with me. Nice try, though."

"Thank you."

"Don't mention it."

He laughed and reached for her.

"Well, I have to say that I like you a lot more when you're not trying to lock me up." She slid into his arms, her eyes and mouth inviting his kiss. "I like you a lot more just like this."

"Ummmm," he said, leaning down to meet her lips halfway.

The sound of the front door opening startled them both.

"Sean?" Greer called from the front of the house.

He sighed into Amanda's hair and reluctantly moved from her to the doorway. "In the kitchen."

"Is Amanda with you?"

"Yes."

"Are you sure?"

"I'm here, Greer." Amanda stepped into the hall.

Greer stopped, looking puzzled.

"What is it?" Sean asked.

"It must be my imagination." Greer shook her head as if to clear it, and took off her wet sweater. "Believe how fast this storm came up? It's teeming out there now. Terrible."

"What was your imagination?" Sean took a towel from the drawer and handed it to his sister.

"Oh, thank you, honey. I am soaked to the skin and chilled right through." She draped the towel around her neck as she went toward the patio, holding out the dripping sweater.

"What was your imagination, Greer?" Sean repeated.

"Amanda, honey, check and see if there is any water in that teakettle? I could use a nice hot cup of tea."

"Greer, I asked you—"

"Oh, I'm sure it was nothing." She waved her hand absently. "I mean, Amanda is here, so it couldn't have been."

"Greer." Sean closed his eyes and counted to ten.

"When I pulled up, it looked like someone—a woman—was running up the drive, but since Amanda is here and no one in their right mind would be out in this . . ." She draped the sweater over the back of a chair. "I'm sure it was just a shadow from all that lightning. I'm sure that was it."

Sean and Amanda exchanged a long look.

He pushed past Greer and opened the door leading out to the yard.

"Sean, where are you . . ." Greer shook her head and turned back to Amanda. "I shouldn't have said anything. Now he's going to run around the neighborhood in this storm, get soaking wet, and come down with pneumonia."

She went to the door and called out into the dark. "Sean? Come back in here." She stood at the door and scanned the yard each time lightning flashed.

Finally she came back inside, shaking her head. "Cops. He's not going to be satisfied until he's gone through every yard on the street."

The teakettle began to whistle.

"I know I need some nice hot tea right now, and I'm sure Sean will, too, by the time he's done scouting the neighborhood for prowlers." Greer dried her arms with the towel. "Amanda, would you get three mugs down?"

"Better make that four," Sean told her as he came back inside, ushering a shrouded figure. "We have company."

CHAPTER NINETEEN

"WANT TO TELL ME WHAT YOU WERE DOING HIDING in the garage?" Sean turned the wet shrouded figure around.

"In case you hadn't noticed, it was pouring buckets out there." Ramona pulled down the hood of her rain jacket and shook out a mass of wet red curls. Her gaze went from Sean to the two women, who stood speechless nearby.

"Ramona, honey, why didn't you just knock on the door?" Greer asked.

"There weren't any lights on when I got here, so I just assumed no one was at home."

"So you decided to break into the garage." Sean nodded. "Sure. That makes sense."

"I hadn't planned on . . . well, on anything. I just wanted to see . . . Oh, hi." She seemed to notice Amanda for the first time. "We met at the diner earlier."

"We did," Amanda said, then smiled weakly. "Nice to see you again."

Ramona laughed. "I'll bet."

"I want to know what you're doing here." Sean reached for the roll of paper towels and tore off a few sheets to dry his arms and face.

"I could use a few of those paper towels, too." Ramona put her hand out for the roll, which Sean passed to her. She dried her face, then rolled the paper towel into a tight ball. "Greer, I was in the area, and I wanted . . . I wanted to see the house, that's all."

"I don't think I belong here. I really shouldn't be part of this." Amanda backed toward the door. "So if you'll all excuse me, I'm going to turn in."

"I'll see you in the morning," Sean said as if nothing extraordinary was going on. "Try to get some sleep tonight."

"Look, I just wanted to see where you lived. And once I saw how cute the house was, I just wanted to see it a little closer. I parked the car and got out and was just going to walk up the drive a little, but then it started pouring buckets and I ran for the first cover I could find, which happened to be the garage. I thought the storm would blow over real fast the way they do sometimes when they come on all of a sudden like this one did. I figured I'd be here and gone and no one would even know. But then you all came home in the interim. Look, I didn't mean to upset anyone." She looked at Sean, then at Greer. "I'm so sorry."

"Well, honey, you don't have to apologize. You haven't done anything wrong." Greer turned on Sean. "You're making too much out of this, Sean. She has every right to stop here if she wants to. I don't understand what your problem is."

"I think you—we—need to take this just a little slower, that's all."

"Sean thinks I'm probably the daughter of some *other* Veronica Mercer who was born on the first of May in 1948 and who just happens to have the same social security number that your mother had," Ramona said.

"It's a possibility." Sean nodded. "We don't know anything about you—"

"And I didn't know anything about you, either, mister, when I pulled into that little town down there in West Virginia to look for you, did I?" Greer's temper was starting to flare. She turned to Ramona. "Tell him. Tell him what you told me. Show him the pictures."

Ramona opened her bag and slid open the zipper on an inside pocket. She took out a battered plastic sandwich bag in which several photographs lay trapped. She opened it and laid the first one on the table.

"This was my mother." She looked directly at Sean. "She look familiar to you?"

Sean studied the photo for a long time, then looked up at Greer questioningly.

"This is the same picture you showed me," Sean said. "Did you give her a copy?"

"No. That's hers. She brought it with her to show me, the first time we met." Greer smiled at Ramona. "I brought the same picture to show her."

"Couldn't she have found them . . . ?" Sean asked, his protest sounding silly and weak, even to himself.

Ramona demanded, "To what end, Mr. Chief of Police? What reason could I possibly have to pretend to be this woman's daughter?" She tapped an angry finger on the photo. "What would I have to gain? Speeding tickets fixed for life? There is nothing that you have that I want, okay? Nothing that you can do for me. Except maybe help me to understand who I am, and why she . . . why . . ."

"Why she gave you away?" Greer spoke the words Ramona wasn't able to say.

"I was barely five. She gave me these"—Ramona picked up the bag of photos—"and dressed me up and took me to someplace. . . . I don't remember much except that there was an elevator and it had mirrors in it. I remember thinking how pretty Mommy looked. She wore a new dress that day, and so did I. We got off the elevator and there were nice red carpets on the floor. We went into a room that had a long table in it. There was a man in there, he sat at the head of the table and he smiled when we came in."

Ramona squeezed her eyes tightly shut, wanting to remember every detail so she could tell the others, but not wanting to remember because it hurt so much to look back.

She opened her eyes, determined to see it through.

"He told me what a pretty little girl I was. How pretty my red hair was. My mother made me sit and color while she signed some papers, and then he gave her something that she put into her pocketbook. She stood up and I did, too. I thought it was time to leave. But she told me I had to stay. Then she told me I had to be a very, very good girl, and if I was, that good things would happen for me. But if I was bad, something very bad would happen."

"And she left you there," Greer whispered, ashen, as if reliving the scene with Ramona.

"Yes." Ramona nodded. "She left me there. And a few minutes later, a man and a woman came into the room. They were all smiling and made such a big fuss over me. . . ."

"Your new parents," Greer said softly.

"Yes. My new parents. They were so excited." Ramona swallowed hard. "The first thing they said to me was how they'd wanted a little girl just like me, one with red hair, for a long, long, time, and that they were so happy they'd waited for me."

"Were they . . . ?" Greer struggled with the words.

"Oh, they were wonderful," Ramona assured her. "I couldn't have had a nicer family. They gave me everything. But there was always that . . ."

"That hole inside you," Greer whispered. "That knowing that you weren't good enough to keep. That somehow you just weren't . . ."

"Yes."

Ramona slid another photo across the table. Greer picked it up and stared at it before passing it to Sean.

"My mother gave me that before she took me to the office that day. She said that was my big sister and brother." Ramona looked directly at Greer. "Only she called you Sasha, not Greer."

"My adoptive parents named me Greer. Before that, my name was Susan. Everyone called me Sasha."

"What do you think, Sean, should we do DNA testing?" Ramona's jaw set stonily. "Would that prove to you that I am your sister? Half sister, at the very least."

Sean appeared to be at a loss for words.

Ramona reached for the photos. Greer covered her hand with her own. "No, don't leave in anger."

"I'm sorry, Greer. I need to get home. I told the babysitter I'd be back before ten."

Sean found his voice. "You have children?"

"A boy and a girl."

"Where do you live?"

"In East Hilton."

"Are you married?"

"Divorced."

"Do you work? Do you—" Sean shook his head. "I don't even know where to start."

"Start by saying that you believe I could be who I say I am." Ramona's eyes pleaded. "We can go on from there."

Greer looked back at the photo. "I have this picture, too. It was taken on Grandma Michaels's front porch."

"That's what it says on the back." Ramona flipped the photo over and read the tidy handwriting. *"Sasha and Sean on Mom's front porch."*

"Makes you wonder about her, doesn't it?" Greer shook her head slowly. "Why she had the three of us, if she was going to give us away . . ."

"Yeah, well, all these years, I thought it was just me. That maybe she kept the two of you in some secret place, and just got rid of me because I was . . ."

Unable to finish the sentence, Ramona pulled the hood of her raincoat up around her face, preparing to go out into the storm again. "I need to go," she said in a shaky voice as she moved quickly toward the door.

"Don't you dare." Greer got up from the table. "Don't you even try to run away from us."

She wrapped her arms around the young woman and held her for just a minute as Ramona's shoulders began to shake and she wept silently.

"Now, you don't have to do that, hear? It's going to be all right. It will be. We will work this all out, the three of us, and everything will be fine."

Ramona nodded and whispered, "Thank you."

"Oh, thank you, darlin'." Greer gave her a hug. "Thank you."

Ramona nodded and opened the door. With a look back at Sean, she stepped through it.

"Now, you be real careful going home." Greer followed her outside. "And you call me in the morning, and we'll talk, okay, honey?"

When Ramona had disappeared down the driveway, Greer turned to Sean, her eyes wet, and said, "I understand that you are a skeptic by nature, Sean. But you could have been a little kinder."

"I didn't know if she was telling the truth." He shifted uncomfortably in his seat.

"Why would she make up a story like that, about going to that office and being handed over like that? It's not like we're the heirs to some big family fortune." Greer came behind him and put her arms around his shoulders. "I guess you were too young back then, but I remember like it was yesterday what it felt like to be taken away from that house— Grandma's house—and away from you, to be put in with strangers. Everything changed, Sean. Even my name. I kept waiting for them to bring you. I felt sure that if I was really good, that they'd let you come, too. I waited and waited. . . ."

Her tears rolled down the back of his neck, but he sat, still as a stone.

"I missed you every day. And every night, when I said my bedtime prayers, the only thing I ever prayed for was to be with my little brother again." She sniffed and searched her pockets for a tissue. "When I found you, it was the sweetest day of my life. So I know exactly what Ramona means when she says she has a hole inside her. I've had it all my life." She blew her nose and stuffed the tissue back into her pocket. "I suspect you do, too." She gave his shoulders a gentle squeeze. "Only difference between you and me is that I want that hole inside filled up. You seem to be content to let it stay empty."

She gave him one last pat on the back, then turned off the outside lights. "It doesn't have to be that way, Sean. But of course, it's your choice."

She tossed the tissue into the wastebasket on her way out of the room, leaving her brother alone in the quiet kitchen.

The room was nearly dark, the neon under-the-counter lights the only ones left on. Amanda stood in the doorway, studying the silhouette that sat motionless at the table.

"Are you all right?" she asked. "Sean?"

He nodded. "I'm fine."

"So fine that you're sitting here in the dark at two in the morning?" She ventured closer.

"Why aren't you asleep?" He ignored her question.

"I could ask you the same thing." She paused at the stove. "I thought I'd make a cup of tea, maybe it would help me sleep. Want one?"

"No, thanks."

"Yeah, me either." She came closer.

He watched her cross the room. When she got to

his chair, she moved his arm aside and sat on his lap.
He couldn't help but smile.

"So. Want to talk about it?" She poked him gently
in the chest.

"I wouldn't know where to start."

"Start with Ramona."

"I believe her." He leaned back away from her.

"And that bothers you because . . . ?" She gestured
for him to continue.

"I don't know."

Amanda ran her hand over his head, stroking him,
as one might a child who needed comforting. He
leaned back and closed his eyes, relaxing for the first
time in days.

"She was adopted, too. Given away by her—our—
mother."

The clock over the back door ticked softly.

"What would make a woman do that? Give away
her children like that?" His eyes were still closed.
"Ramona talked about being taken to an office. She
described what sounded like a conference room,
probably in a lawyers' office. She said the man there
gave her mother something in an envelope and then
her mother left."

"You think she got money from the adoptive parents."

"Yeah." His jaw tightened.

His arm drifted to her back and kneaded her shoulder gently.

"Greer said something about having a hole inside
and wanting it filled up. I've lived with that same
emptiness for as long as I can remember. I never knew
it could be filled," he said softly.

"It must have been so hard on you as a little boy. Being separated from Greer."

"When Ramona said that her mother called the girl in the photograph Sasha, I knew she was legit. Just hearing the name brought it all back. I'd forgotten it, but hearing her say it, I remembered. Remembered being there in my grandmother's house and being so scared the day they took her in the ambulance. And then people came—strangers—and took my sister and me away. I don't remember where we went or who was there; I only remember being afraid. And then my sister wasn't there anymore. And I don't really remember too much for a while after that. Just a lot of faces and confusion and not knowing what was going on. Nothing specific, you understand, just a feeling of confusion all the time, through that whole time in my life. I didn't have the words for it then."

"You were a very frightened little boy. All alone . . ."

"I'm afraid it didn't bring out the best in me. I wasn't a very pleasant child."

"I don't think anyone could blame you, Sean."

"But everyone did. And with good reason. I mean, I was a really obnoxious kid. No matter where they placed me, no matter how nice the people tried to be, I wanted no part of anyone. I broke things, got into fights, was overly aggressive, and as I recall, had quite the colorful vocabulary in those days. No one wanted to keep me for very long." He shook his head, remembering the child he had been. "I made sure of that."

"How did you manage to stay out of jail?" She continued to stroke his hair.

"God only knows. I wonder sometimes if things

might have been different for me if Greer and I had stayed together."

"She said she had wonderful parents."

"I'm sure they were. Look at Greer, at the person she is."

"You really love her, don't you?" Amanda smiled. "Whether you wanted to or not, you really love her."

"It's kind of hard not to. She just sort of wraps herself around you. You saw how she welcomed you here, how she was with Ramona."

"You're afraid you'll have to share Greer with Ramona."

"Am not."

Amanda laughed out loud and he laughed with her.

"I just don't know how to deal with . . ." He struggled for words.

"Having people in your life that you could care about."

"Yes."

"Because if you care about them, maybe they'll leave you."

"Something like that. Maybe."

"On the other hand, it could turn out to be very good. Just like knowing Greer has been a very good thing."

"After so many years of being alone, of not really having anyone I cared all that much about, my life is starting to feel a bit crowded right now."

"Is that a bad thing?"

"I don't know. It seems that the more people in your life, the more complicated your life becomes."

"Well, then, here's something else to think about. Things are about to become even more complicated."

She leaned down and kissed his mouth softly, first one side, then the other.

"Consider me part of that crowd who wants in," she whispered, then kissed him again, hungrily.

Sean pulled her against his chest, his mouth meeting hers, his tongue teasing the inside of her lips until she thought she was going to implode with the heat.

"This is a complication I can handle," he whispered into her ear.

"That's good, because I've decided to stick around for a while."

He slid his hands up and down her back, needing her warmth and her softness. Needing more of her mouth, more of her sighs, more of her hands on him. He shifted her so that she was facing him and drew her down and into him as closely as he could, caressing her until her head was swimming, her body adrift in sensation. His lips moved across her throat, a steady line of kisses that moved ever downward. She leaned her head back, exposing her neck, urging him to take more.

They barely heard his cell phone when it rang.

"Shit," he grumbled, then reached into his pocket, his mouth still on her skin.

"Yeah," Amanda sighed.

He leaned his head back against the chair and studied her face while he listened to the caller. "All right. I'm on my way." He turned off the phone. "I, ah, have to go."

"I figured as much." She pulled away and slowly stood up, her legs slightly numb.

"There's been an accident out on Harkins Road."

She nodded. "You're the chief of police. I understand."

"There's a cruiser parked outside. I'm not leaving you unguarded. The house is being watched."

"I know." She buttoned his shirt and straightened his collar. "You're a bit disheveled."

"Hold that thought . . ." He smiled and kissed her before heading out the door.

"I'll be here," she said as he went through it, then she moved to the window to watch him hurry down the drive to his car. "I'm not going anywhere."

CHAPTER TWENTY

"VINNIE, WHAT ARE YOU DOING HERE?" AN OBVIOUSLY pleased Dolores smiled at him in the mirror, then turned to touch his arm, her eyes alive with pleasure at his unexpected arrival at her shop.

"I missed seeing you yesterday," he said, returning the smile, "so I thought I'd stop in and check out this little business of yours."

His glance traveled the room, one end to the other, assessing his surroundings. There were six stations, each with a nice work counter, large wall mirror, and the obligatory swivel chair. All very standard, even to the black-and-white patterned linoleum on the floor. The walls were painted a pale pastel pink, the furniture in the dryer section black vinyl, and the receptionist area a high counter with a phone, appointment book, and small stack of business cards. Photos of pretty women with elaborate hairstyles and makeup lined the walls.

"Nice, babe. Very, very nice." He nodded his approval.

"Thanks. We're really proud of it, me and Connie." She beamed. "We worked real hard for a long time to get this place together. Right now it's just the two of us, but we're hoping to hire someone to do manicures part-time for the holidays. And eventually we'd like to have a receptionist. We're doing our own phone work and bookings for the time being. But we have big dreams, Vinnie."

"And there is no doubt in my mind that you'll make all those dreams come true." He patted her on the back affectionately, then winked at the woman upon whose head Dolores was applying some sort of goop. "Talented as you and Connie are, you know you're going to be a big success here."

"That's sweet of you to say." Dolores turned back to her client and resumed spreading the light-colored stuff on top of her head. "I can talk but I have to keep going here. We don't want Mrs. Olinski's hair to be two different colors now, do we?"

"Might be interesting." Mrs. Olinski shrugged good-naturedly.

"I won't keep you. I just thought I'd stop in and see if you would be free for lunch later."

"Oh, I'd love to, but I am booked straight through till seven again tonight." Dolores made an exaggerat-edly sad face.

"Well, then, how 'bout dinner?"

"It's my night to clean up. We take turns, me and Connie. She closed last night," Dolores explained.

"You need to leave early for something, Dolores?" Connie came into the shop, a plastic bag in one hand, a folded newspaper under her arm. Seeing Vince in the shop, she slowed her pace. "Oh, hi, Vinnie."

"Connie." He nodded, sensing something in her face, her manner, that brought all his senses to life. "How are you?"

"Good. I'm good." She walked past him and took a bottle of soda from the bag and deposited it on the counter next to where Dolores was working. "They didn't have Diet Pepsi. I had to get you Diet Dr Pepper."

"That's fine, Con. Thanks." Dolores continued to work, oblivious to the faint trace of tension. "Ellie Cohen called. She's running fifteen minutes late."

"That's okay. Gives me a minute to put my feet up." She went back to the reception area and sat down. She took the top off a bottle of water and downed a long drink before setting it on the counter and opening the newspaper.

She called back to Dolores. "Dee, what were you saying about closing?"

"Just that you closed last night so it's my turn to close tonight."

"I could close if you needed to do something." Connie opened the appointment book and studied the entries. "I'm going to be here late anyway. Your last is at seven, just a cut. My last is at seven-thirty, but it's a double process and a cut. You'll be done by seven-thirty. I'll be lucky to get out of here by nine-thirty." She turned to look back at Dolores. "No point in you hanging around until I'm finished."

"Are you sure? I could close for you tomorrow and the next night, then."

"That works." Connie nodded, toying thoughtfully with one corner of the newspaper.

"Looks like I'll be free for dinner after all," Dolores told Vince. "Want to pick me up at home?"

"Sure. Eight-fifteen good?" he asked.

"Perfect." She nodded. "See you then."

"See you then." With one more wink for the elderly Mrs. Olinski, Vince started toward the front of the shop.

He slowed his step as he reached the desk. At his approach, Connie folded the paper quickly and stuffed it into a nearby trash can.

"Have a nice day, Connie," he said as he passed by.

"You, too, Vinnie," she said without looking at him.

"So, Dolores, that's your new beau?" Mrs. Olinski asked after Vinnie left the shop.

"Yeah. Yeah." Dolores nodded. "He's my new guy."

"He seems very nice."

"Oh, he's wonderful. And a perfect gentleman." Dolores rolled her eyes in pleasure. "An absolute doll."

"Dee, you wearing that necklace Vinnie gave you?" Connie leaned over the back of the chair at the next station.

"Of course I'm wearing the necklace. I never take it off." Her fingers reached to touch it, then she recalled the plastic gloves covered with hair dye and stopped.

"Where'd he say he got that again?" Connie's eyes narrowed.

"It belonged to his grandmother."

"And he gave it to you. Just like that."

"Just like that." Dolores grinned. "He said he'd been waiting for the right girl to give it to. Am I lucky or what?"

"I guess."

"Your young man gave you a family heirloom?" A curious Mrs. Olinski looked up at Dolores.

"Yes." She raised her chin. "Can you see it?"

Mrs. Olinski leaned closer as Dolores leaned over to show off the V formed by the collar of her shirt.

"Oh, that pretty little circle there? Oh, my, are they real emeralds?"

"Real emeralds. Real diamonds." Dolores nodded, a trace of pride in her voice.

"Oh, that is lovely," Mrs. Olinski said. "You are a lucky girl. . . ."

Connie stood up and went back to the receptionist's desk. Slumping into the chair, she retrieved the newspaper, smoothed it out, and leaned over the counter to study the article spread out before her. When she was finished, she looked around for a place to put it where Dolores would eventually find it on her own.

Vince stopped at the newspaper box on the corner and dropped in two quarters, opened the door, and yanked out a paper, curious to see just what it was that Miss Connie had been hiding back there.

The paper under his arm, he walked a block to the one and only coffee shop in Carleton. He ordered a large special Hawaiian blend, cream and sugar, and took a seat nearest the window at the coffee bar. He opened the paper and began to scan each page, trying to figure out what it was that Connie had wanted to keep him from seeing.

"Town Council Votes on New Parking Meters"? Nah.

"Rabid Raccoons Found Near Carleton Park"? Not likely.

"Broeder Police Release Sketch of Stolen Pendant."

Uh-oh.

With a calm he did not feel, he hunched over the page, reading as rapidly as his eyes could move and his brain could absorb.

> *Broeder police chief Sean Mercer yesterday released a sketch of a pendant similar to one stolen from For Old Time's Sake, the antiques shop that was the scene of a grisly murder. Forty-seven-year-old Marian J. O'Connor was found murdered . . . yada yada . . . emerald pendant missing from the scene . . . yada yada . . .*
>
> *"We believe the killer may have grabbed the pendant on his way out of the shop as a souvenir," Chief Mercer said in a recent telephone interview with the* Broeder Herald. *"And the sketch we're releasing, while not exact, is similar enough to the one stolen that anyone seeing it would make the connection. Of course, there is the chance that the person who has the pendant in their possession could have purchased it from the shop before the killer came on the scene. In any event, we are most anxious to speak with anyone who, within the past week, has seen an emerald and gold pendant that in any way resembles this one."*

Yeah, I'll just bet you would. Vince drummed anxious fingers on the countertop. When he realized the girl behind the counter was staring at him, he smiled weakly, gathered the newspaper, and walked out of the shop.

Once out on the street, he walked in tune with his thoughts, which were at full throttle.

Connie. She saw the article. She saw the pendant. She put it together.

Yeah. She did. I saw it in her face. She knows.

The question now is, who has she told?

It was a source of concern for him all afternoon. Had she shared her suspicions with Dolores? Because—*let's keep calm now*—that's all Connie could have at this point, suspicions. He'd studied the picture in the paper, and while the general shape was accurate and they'd gotten the circles right, there was enough of a difference between the drawing and the real deal that a case—a very strong case—could be made for them not being the same. Sure. If Connie showed the article to Dolores and Dolores mentioned it to Vince, he'd just say, "Hey, how 'bout that? Must have been made around the same time. They're both old pieces, right?" And Dolores would believe him, of course, because she'd want to.

But Connie?

Connie could be a problem. Over the past few weeks, as he and Dolores spent more and more time together, Dolores was spending less and less time with Connie, a situation that Connie clearly resented. Wouldn't she be just pleased as shit to show him up? Even if she did nothing more than plant a seed of doubt in Dolores's mind, it could prove to be a problem for him.

These days, he had a zero tolerance policy when it came to problems.

CHAPTER
TWENTY·ONE

VINCE GNAWED ANXIOUSLY AT A FINGERNAIL, THE third one he'd chewed down to the quick that afternoon.

"Bitch is just too damned smart for her own good," he muttered. "Just too damned smart . . ."

He paced a bit in his room, then realized it was way too small for the amount of pacing he needed to do just then. Tucking the newspaper under his arm, he locked the door behind him, then took the steps two at a time. He drove the three blocks to the Cut N Curl and parked in the small lot behind the shop.

Don't do anything stupid, he cautioned himself. *What are the odds Connie's going to say something to Dolores?*

After all, what would she say? *Hey, Dee, that new boyfriend of yours is a real killer.* He chuckled a little.

Ah, always the cutup. Always the clown.

No, *she's not going to say anything. Not yet, anyway. She's going to think about it for a while. She's not going to want to hurt Dolores.*

Which would, of course, work to his advantage.

He tapped his fingers on the steering wheel, idly noting the other shops in the small shopping center. A dry cleaner was next to the Cut N Curl on the right, and a children's clothing store on the left. There was a card shop, a shoe repair shop, and a vitamin shop. A dentist's office stood at one end and an Italian restaurant at the other. Vince noted three streetlamps, one on each end of the parking lot, one in the middle. The back lot itself was narrow, just two rows deep with just enough space for the shop owners and their employees. Customer parking was provided around front.

It would be pretty dark back here at night, he was beginning to think. Very little action and very little light.

His fingers continued to tap against the wheel, while the wheels in his head began to turn a little faster.

It occurred to him that by the time the Cut N Curl closed up at night, there'd probably be no one else around except for that restaurant down at the end, as they'd be doing a night business. These other places, he noted, would have their traffic during the day. Bet they were all closed up nice and tight by nine P.M. at the latest.

Except for the restaurant.

Satisfied that he had it all under control again, he backed the car out of the lot and drove home. He had a few hours to kill between now and the time he'd pick Dolores up for dinner.

He hoped she liked Italian.

"So all this time you haven't even tried this place for dinner? Four stores down from your shop and you haven't even been in?" Vince rested his arms on the Formica table and gazed at his love, who sat opposite him in the booth.

"We've done takeout for lunch a coupla times, but we don't get a lot of time to eat, you know?" Dolores skimmed the menu.

"Guess that's how you two keep your girlish figures." He grinned.

"Oh, you." She rolled her eyes.

"See anything that looks good to you?" he asked.

"I see a lot that looks good. What are you going to have?"

"Well, I really want those mussels, but the last few times I ate them, I got so sick."

"If they make you sick, why do you keep eating them?"

" 'Cause I love them. And 'cause I keep thinking, 'This time, maybe they won't make me sick.' " He shrugged. "There's just nothing in the world like a big dish of mussels in red sauce and a bowl of pasta. A little salad, a little wine . . ."

He smiled.

"I just talked myself into it." He hailed the waiter and after a discussion of the specials, placed their orders.

"Vinnie, are you sure? What if they make you sick?" Dolores asked after the waiter hurried off to the kitchen.

"So I throw up a little—begging your pardon—and then I'll feel fine again." He gave her that boyish grin thing again.

Dolores shook her head. "You're crazy."

"Crazy about you." He reached across the table

and took her hand. "Hey, I see you're wearing the necklace I gave you."

She touched it with her fingers. "I haven't taken it off since you gave it to me, Vinnie."

"Aw, that's really sweet, Dolores. My grandma would be pleased."

"Everyone admires it," she said.

"You been showing it off?"

"Sure. Just to people in the shop who notice it, you know."

"Sure." *Shit. Shit. Shit.*

"I don't flaunt it, though."

"Oh, I wouldn't expect you to do that." He played with her fingers for a minute, then said, "You know, I just thought of something. I meant to get that insured for you. You know, in case it gets lost or stolen. It being a valuable piece and all."

"You think it's all right that I'm wearing it?"

"Well, maybe you shouldn't wear it out until I get in touch with the insurance guy. I called him last week but he was out of the office." He pretended to think it through. "Might not be a bad idea. Just until we get the insurance."

"I'll put it back in the box tonight and I'll keep the box in a safe place."

"That's probably a smart thing, Dolores. It should only be a few days till I can get in touch with him."

The waiter returned with their orders and a smile. "Lobster ravioli for the lady, and mussels in red sauce for the gentleman." He beamed. "Enjoy."

"Vinnie, I hope you know what you're doing," Dolores whispered after the waiter walked away.

"Hey, at least I'll die smiling."

"Don't even say that." She crossed herself, and he laughed out loud.

"So you're superstitious," he said.

"No, but I don't believe in courting trouble, like my mother always said." She took a sip of her wine. "God rest her soul."

He tipped his glass in her direction. "Here's to a great dinner and an even greater dessert." He winked.

He plowed through the mussels. They were excellent—he was going to hate even pretending that they made him sick, but hey, you do what you have to do. And right now, what he had to do was to get rid of Connie.

He glanced at his watch. It was twenty after nine. Her last client should be gone by now.

He'd give her another five minutes.

"Vince, you feeling all right?" Dolores tore off a piece of garlic bread and placed it on the edge of her plate.

"Actually, now that you mention it, I am feeling a bit queasy."

"Are you serious? Really? You really feeling sick?"

"Yeah." He tried to look sheepish. "I hate to admit it, but yeah, I'm not feeling so good right now. Would you excuse me?"

"Maybe we should tell the waiter . . ."

"No, no. I don't want the chef to feel badly, you know, like there was something wrong with the mussels. It's me, not them, you know?" He shook his head. "I think I'll just head on back to the men's room. Just give me a few minutes. I'll be okay. But don't say nothin' to the waiter. Don't want anyone feeling bad . . ."

"Vinnie, I think we should leave—"

"Nah, nah. I've had this before. Just a stomach thing. It might take a few minutes, but don't worry. I'll be fine."

He pushed away from the table, smiling stoically, and walked to the back of the restaurant. He went three steps past the men's room door and right out the rear door.

Keeping to the shadows, he ran past the back of the darkened shops to the one place that was still lit. He paused and looked around. There was no one in the parking lot. He pulled the thin rubber gloves from his pocket and slid them on, opened the back door of the Cut N Curl, and slipped inside. Connie had just turned off the outside lights and those that illuminated the front of the shop. She was walking toward the rear, a broom in one hand, her handbag in the other, when Vince stepped out of the back room.

"Dee isn't here," she said bluntly, making no attempt at hiding her feelings for him.

"I'm not here for Dee," he told her.

"What do you want, Vinnie?" She leaned the broom against the wall and one fist on her hip. "What is it you want?"

"I want to eliminate a potential problem, Connie. That's what I want."

She took a step back. "What problem is that?"

"Oh, come on. Don't play with me. I already know that you saw the newspaper article. That drawing. You made the connection. You know it's the same pendant." He took a step forward, careful not to walk into the light. "I know that you know, and now you know that I know. And you know what that means, don't you, Connie?"

"Vinnie, I didn't tell anyone. I swear. I didn't say a word to Dolores. I won't." She backed away, her eyes filled with terror.

"I know you won't." Before she could scream, he pulled the small handgun from his pocket and fired.

In the blink of an eye, she was bleeding out on the floor. Damn, but that had been fast.

He stepped over her and went to the cash register. The day's proceeds were missing. Of course. Her purse . . .

He went back to the body and opened the bag that had fallen onto the floor. There was a thick envelope containing cash and checks. *Might as well make it look like a robbery,* he figured. *Might as well take the cash along for my trouble.*

As he leaned down to scoop up the cash, the light caught on the ring on Connie's middle finger. He straightened out her hand, tugged the ring off, and gave it a quick look. It was gold, with five little round pink stones that formed a flower. He stuffed the ring and the cash in his pockets and scattered the checks around the floor. With Dolores waiting back at the restaurant, thinking he was in the men's room puking his guts out, he had to hurry. What if she asked the waiter to go in and check on him?

There was no time to spare—just take care of business and get the hell out. Well, he'd done that. He'd taken care of business, all right.

He clung to the dark as he hurried back to Luigi's, and less than ten minutes after he'd first mentioned that his stomach was upset, he was sliding back into the booth.

"Vinnie, are you all right?" Dolores placed a hand on his forehead. "You're all flushed and sweaty."

"Oh, you know, you get like that when you get sick sometimes." He took his napkin and wiped the sweat from his face. "But to tell you the truth, I'm starting to feel a little better."

"Look, we'll just get the check and leave."

"No, no. You finish your dinner. I'm serious, I'm starting to feel a little better. I'll just drink a little water here, and that'll help."

"Ginger ale," she said.

"Huh?"

"Ginger ale. My mother—"

Vince mentally crossed himself and added, *God rest her soul.*

"—she always gave us ginger ale when we were sick. It helps." She signaled for the waiter. "Could we have a ginger ale here? My boyfriend's a bit under the weather."

"Actually, I'm okay now." He eyed her plate and the leftover ravioli. "You gonna eat that? I'm starting to get my appetite back. . . ."

"Miss, I'm sorry, but the street is blocked from here down to Price Avenue." The young police officer held up his hand to stop Dolores from making the turn on the side street that would lead to the parking lot behind the Cut N Curl.

"But I need to get into the parking lot," she told him. "I need to get to work." She gestured in the general direction of the strip mall.

"Where do you work, ma'am?"

"The Cut N Curl."

"The beauty shop there?" He pointed toward the small shopping center.

"Yes. I'm the owner." *Well, one of the owners,* she added to herself.

"Ma'am, would you mind pulling over to the side here?"

"Is something wrong?"

"Just pull over to the side of the road, please."

What the hell? she thought, annoyed that she'd stopped. Should have come in the way she usually did, from Market Street. But she hadn't had time to make coffee that morning, and she and Vinnie had overslept. . . .

"Ma'am, your name?"

"Dolores Hall. Officer, what is this all about?"

"Ms. Hall, I need to ask you to come with me." The officer stepped aside to give her room to get out of the car.

"Why? I haven't done anything wrong." She frowned. "What's going on?"

"There's been a . . . a situation at your shop." He took her arm and led her around the back of the restaurant where she and Vinnie had eaten just the night before.

"A situation? What the hell does that mean? Is the place on fire?"

Once around the corner and into the parking lot, she stopped in her tracks. The lot, usually empty at this hour of the day except for the guy who arrived to open the dry cleaner at seven, was filled with police cars.

"What the hell is going on here?" she asked, a cold fear growing in the pit of her stomach.

"Chief?" the young officer called to a tall, thin, balding man in uniform. "This is Ms. Hall. She owns the shop—"

"Well, I own it with a partner. I have a partner. Connie Paschall." She looked from the chief to the officer and back again. "Is someone going to tell me what is going on here?"

"I'm afraid there's been a break-in at your shop," the chief told her. "Looks like a robbery."

"When?"

"Last night."

Something in his eyes told her there was something more. "And . . . ?" She motioned for him to get on with it.

"And I'm afraid that your partner—"

"Connie?" The fear clenched around her heart. "Connie? Is Connie all right?"

"I'm afraid not, Ms. Hall. I'm afraid—"

"No. She can't be. There has to be a mistake. . . ." Dolores bolted for the back door of the shop and was stopped by the arm of the police officer, holding her back.

"There's no mistake, Ms. Hall. I'm sorry. Could you come with us, please? We have a few questions."

CHAPTER
TWENTY-TWO

"I'M NOT SURE I LIKE THIS IDEA." SEAN LEANED BACK in his chair, frowning.

"Dana will be with me. I swear, Sean, I am not going to do anything stupid. Especially after Marian's service this morning." Amanda gave her head a quick shake.

The church service had been short and not especially sweet, and it had been apparent that Marian's niece was merely going through the expected motions. The graveside service had been closed to all but family—meaning the niece—leaving all of Marian's friends and colleagues in Broeder feeling slightly, well, *slighted*. So while the niece and the minister stood at the grave, old friends gathered in Marian's favorite restaurant for a long lunch during which they laughed and cried together while trading favorite memories of the deceased.

"It was just like an old-fashioned Irish wake," Amanda told Sean. "And after seeing everyone this morning, well, I just want to get back to work. I want to open my shop again. I need to do something besides sit around Greer's house, as I did all day yesterday, or have Dana trailing after me in the grocery store."

"She's going to be trailing after you, regardless."

"Yeah, well, she has a job to do, and so do I." She glanced at her watch. "I'd better get going. Dana is waiting for me outside. And yes, before you ask, she's right at the door."

"I guess I'll see you at dinner, then. I'm thinking we should maybe go out tonight, seeing as Steve will be home from his trip. He and Greer might like some time alone." He paused, considering. "Of course, they have been married for a long time. Maybe it's no big deal. . . ."

Amanda laughed. "Maybe it is. Dinner out sounds like a good idea. I'll just come back here with Dana, then, when I close up the shop for the day. I can't wait till this is over, though, and I can just hop in my car and go where I want without checking in with you. No offense."

"None taken."

She left his office, and he went to the door to watch her walk down the hall.

"Amanda," he called after her.

When she turned to him, he said, "Do I have to say, 'Let me know if anything seems out of place' or 'Call me if anyone's hanging around'?"

"No, you don't have to say any of those things."

"Didn't think so."

He heard the front door clang closed, then went to the window and watched the car until it was a speck at the end of the road, feeling just a little anxious. He'd never admit it, but he didn't believe that anyone would keep as close an eye on Amanda as he would. Thinking about there being someone out there who wanted to kill her unsettled him in ways that were beyond his experience. He'd cared about victims before—of course he had—but never on this level, never to this degree, and he wasn't sure how to deal with what he was feeling or what to do about it. He figured that maybe, at this point, just keeping her alive was a damned good start.

He walked back to his office thinking that it was a little frightening to realize that caring about someone gave her power over you. He wondered if Amanda had a clue as to just how powerful she was.

It was twenty after four when Sean's phone buzzed.

"Chief Benson from the Carleton P.D. is on line three for you, Sean," Joyce announced.

"Thanks." Sean hit the button for line three. "Bob, how are you?"

"Good, good, Sean. How are things in Broeder?"

"All right. No complaints."

"Glad to hear it." Benson paused for a moment, then said, "Sean, we had a shooting here Saturday night. Hairdresser closing up her shop apparently was surprised by a robber. Shot and killed her, clean as a whistle."

"I heard about that."

"Ran the bullet through Drugfire. There was a match." He paused. "You want to take a guess on what it matched up with?"

"I don't have a clue."

"Your antiques dealer who got shot a few weeks back? Same gun killed my hairdresser, Sean."

"Same gun . . ." Sean's mind raced. "You're sure, Bob? Positive?"

"It was a clear match. The striations on the bullets are identical."

"Son of a bitch," Sean muttered thoughtfully.

"You have any suspects?"

"None. We have nothing. The only thing we have is another homicide that we believe is connected." Sean filled him in on Marian's murder and explained the connection that Marian and Derek had with Amanda.

"So you've got two vics who were threatened by a guy who is serving time for stalking a woman who just happened to be a close friend of both victims." Benson seemed to be contemplating this. "And you've got a con who doesn't appear to have any contact with anyone except his mother."

"That's about all I've got."

"She a good shot, the mother?"

"My guess is the closest she ever comes to firearms is watching *Law and Order.*"

"Just thought I'd ask."

"Yeah, we looked into her and into the sister who visited him a few times, but there's just nothing there. I don't think the sister gives a damn about the brother. She made it real clear that she thought he was a creep and a sicko. Pretty sure those were the words she used."

"Sounds like a charming family," Bob Benson said dryly. "Your shooting victim, he was shot clean, right? No other wounds? No robbery?"

"Right. At one point early on I thought there might have been a connection to a piece of pottery the victim had bought on the black market in Europe recently. Thought maybe someone had trailed him to steal it, but that just seems like a dead end. And yeah, it was one clean hit through the head."

"Same with our hairdresser. One shot to the head. Anything missing from the scene?"

"Nothing that we know of. The victim's wallet was still in his pocket with a substantial amount of cash in it."

"Our hairdresser's cash register was cleaned out except for checks."

"Nothing personal stolen off the body?" Sean asked.

"A ring her business partner says she never took off is missing. Yours?"

"Nothing at all for the shooting victim, but there was a pendant stolen from the other victim. The woman dealer who was killed in her shop."

"That the woman who was stabbed?"

"Yes."

"Seems to me the MO for mine and your first are the same. But the MO for the woman there, there don't seem to be any similarity at the scene."

"Except the taking of the jewelry, apparently as souvenirs. Derek England was wearing a ring on each hand and an expensive watch, but they weren't touched. Why not?" Sean tapped his fingers on the desktop. "Can you fax over a copy of everything you have on this, let me take a look? Maybe something will occur to me."

"Whatever you need. In turn, maybe you can fax me a copy of your reports. Maybe between the two of us, we can catch this son of a bitch."

"Maybe we can. I'll get those reports over to you this afternoon."

"Mine is on its way. Should start coming through your machine any minute now."

"I'll watch for it. And thanks, Bob, for the heads-up."

Sean went immediately to the small reception area, where, as Benson had promised, the fax machine was already starting to hum. He waited patiently as page after page came through, then, when the signal flashed to indicate that the send was complete, he scooped them up and returned to his office.

Straightening the papers into a neat stack in the center of his desk, Sean began to read the Carleton police reports detailing the investigation into the murder of Connie Paschall.

"Oh, Vinnie, I feel like I'm going to die." Dolores sobbed into his shirt. "Connie was the best friend I ever had. How could anyone have done such a terrible thing to such a good, sweet person?"

Actually, it had been pretty easy. He suppressed a grin as he held her and patted her back in what he felt was a comforting gesture.

"She was the sweetest person I ever knew." Dolores hiccupped. "She never did a thing that hurt anyone."

Well, not yet maybe, but she had plans to hurt me big-time. Vince continued patting.

"The bastard even took the ring right off her finger. Can you imagine being so cold? So heartless?" Dolores wiped her face on his shirt and began to wail again.

Pat pat pat.

Finally, when he could not take one more second of weeping and could pat no longer, he took her gently by the shoulders and said, "Dolores, you're gonna make yourself sick. Now, I understand that you and Connie were close friends. But the last thing she would have wanted is for you to make yourself sick over her dying. It's time to get a grip, Dee. You gotta get a grip."

She nodded. Of course Vinnie was right. She rested her head against his shoulder. "You think they'll catch him?"

"Catch who?" He was looking over the wild mass of blond hair piled on top of her head to the TV where the highlights from last weekend's NFL games were being played.

"The bastard who shot Connie." She pushed him away. "Who the hell do you think I'm talking about?"

"Sorry," he mumbled, trying to catch the score of the Jets game.

"Oh, so am I. I shouldn't take it out on you." She sighed, then started to cry again. "But it's just so terrible. . . ."

Vince rolled his eyes to the heavens. "Well, Connie was a nice girl and all. And I know she was your best friend and your partner. But I'll tell you what I think would be really terrible." He lowered his voice, searching for his sincere tone. "What would've been really terrible is if it hadda been you. Think about it, Dolores. Remember how you were gonna close instead of Connie? You would have, too, if we hadn't gone out to dinner."

"Oh, my God, Vinnie, that's right. Oh, my God. It coulda been me." She looked up into his eyes and whispered solemnly, "She died for me. Connie, my best friend, died for me."

Vince flinched. *Let the wailing begin.* As the level of weeping rose louder and louder, he squeezed his eyes closed, wishing he could close his ears just as easily. Something told him this was going to be a long night.

Pat pat pat.

CHAPTER
TWENTY-THREE

SEAN'S CELL PHONE WAS RINGING IN THE POCKET OF his jacket, which at that moment was hanging on the back of his office door. By the time he got to it, the ringing had stopped, and the message *1 missed call* displayed a few seconds later. He viewed the number of the missed call, but did not recognize it, though it was a local area code. He hit the automatic dial button and waited to see who would answer.

"Mercer here," he said when the call was picked up but the voice was only vaguely familiar. "I'm returning a call to this number."

"Sean, it's Evan Crosby. I was just checking in to see how my sister is doing, see what's going on. She told me about the attack . . ." Evan paused. "How is she?"

"Amanda's fine. She's at her shop—and before you ask, yes, someone is with her. We've had a watch on her house, but no movement. And the investigation is pretty much at a standstill. No leads, no suspects. If anything, the water just keeps getting muddier."

"What do you mean?"

"I got a call earlier from the chief of police in a neighboring town. A hairdresser was shot and killed in her shop on Saturday night, the cash register emptied."

"So? Your two killings were not robberies."

"The hairdresser was killed with the same gun that killed Derek."

"Any connection to Derek or Marian? Or Amanda?"

"Nothing that we can find. The Carleton P.D. interviewed the woman's business partner and according to her, the murdered hairdresser not only did not buy antiques, she didn't like what she called 'old stuff.' The business partner didn't even recall her going in to Broeder for much of anything. No cause to, she says."

"And Amanda doesn't know her?"

"Never heard of her, and never had her hair done by either of these women."

"So maybe it was just a quick robbery. Maybe he's on the move and he needed some cash. Saw the shop . . . Was the woman in there alone?"

"Yes. It happened close to nine-thirty. She'd had a late appointment and was closing up the shop."

"So maybe he was passing by, saw the lights on, figured a quick in and out . . ."

"Maybe. Maybe. But it's the damnedest thing. We know it's the same guy, but there's no prints anywhere, nothing to tie them together, except the gun."

"Maybe he sold the gun—or tossed it—after the Broeder killing."

"I thought of that, but trust me, it's the same guy. Took a souvenir from each of the ladies—a piece of jewelry from Marian's shop, a ring from the hairdresser's finger—but nothing from Derek, even though he was wearing several good pieces."

When Evan failed to respond, Sean said, "Evan? You still there?"

"Yeah. Listen, we had a case not long ago down in Lyndon, the damnedest thing. Two killings with the same MO, one different. Two really violent rapes—these women were butchered with a knife—and one shooting, cool as ice. Couldn't find a motive until we realized that all three victims had a connection to a man down in High Meadow: Vince Giordano. All three of these victims had pissed off Giordano in a major way before he was locked up. At the time of the murders, he was still in prison. No visitors, no mail, no phone calls."

"Just like Archer Lowell. No apparent contact with the outside, but he sure enough has connections with the victims."

"It was the same thing in Lyndon. This guy Giordano was locked up tight, no contact with anyone—I mean anyone, except his lawyer—but people connected with him were dropping like flies."

There was silence on the phone as each man turned it over in his mind.

"Maybe Giordano and Lowell are somehow orchestrating this from prison," Sean thought aloud.

"Giordano has been out for about six, maybe seven weeks now," Evan said softly.

"About a month before Derek was murdered," Sean murmured.

"Trace him. See if you can find out where he's hanging his hat these days."

"Parole officer?"

"He wouldn't be on parole. His conviction was

overturned. One of those cases you wish you never heard about."

"What do you mean?"

"The son of a bitch was guilty as sin and everyone knew it. Unfortunately, the first cop on the scene turned out to be a guy who'd been real sweet on Giordano's wife back in school, so he planted some evidence, swore he saw Giordano leaving the house that day. The entire prosecution was built around his testimony and the evidence he says he gathered from the scene. But Giordano was miles away by the time that cop showed up at the house, and a crowd of people swore old Vince had been there all afternoon, and they couldn't tie him to anything the cop said he found at the scene. They had to let the sucker walk. And the sin of it was, he was guilty and everyone in that courtroom knew he was guilty. But every piece of evidence the prosecution presented had been tainted."

"What had he done?"

"He put a bullet through the back of the heads of his sleeping children, then turned the gun on his wife."

"Jesus . . ."

"Yeah." Evan sighed. "Yeah."

"And this was the guy who committed those other murders you mentioned, the ones in Lyndon?"

"No. They were killed by a man named Curtis Channing."

"I'm confused. I thought you said all three victims were connected to Giordano. What was the connection to Channing?"

"I was never able to figure that out. But this is all just as weird. Think about it. Three people connected to Lowell. Before that, three people connected to Giordano. Now, Giordano is out, Lowell is in."

"And Channing?"

"No longer in the picture."

"Can I get a copy of your file on Channing?"

"I'll call the department right now. I was the lead investigator on that case. I'm no longer with the Lyndon P.D., but my ex-partner is still there. I'll have someone call you when it's ready for pickup."

"I appreciate it."

"I appreciate your keeping my sister alive and well."

"Nothing is going to happen to Amanda," Sean assured him.

"I'm counting on that." Evan paused, then asked, "Have you thought about bringing in the FBI?"

"I've thought about it, yes."

"They have some pretty good agents in the area, Sean. Don't write off asking for help just because you're afraid they're going to take over your case. That hasn't been my experience."

"Good to know."

"Look, if you don't mind, since I'm already down here, I want to run this past one of their profilers."

"Evan . . ." Sean's voice tightened.

"No, no, it's not what you think. Really. She's extraordinary. Anne Marie McCall is her name—Dr. McCall. She's . . . she's quite amazing. Helped us out immensely when we were trying to get a handle on Channing. I saw her from a distance the other day, so I know she's down here. She's teaching a class on behavior." He sounded more than a little disappointed when he added, "Unfortunately, not the one I'm in."

"Unfortunately?"

"Like I said, she's . . . extraordinary."

"I see."

"Maybe you do. Anyway, I'd like to discuss this with her, see if she has any insights. Okay with you?"

"Okay. But don't pull in the FBI, Evan. I'm not ready to throw in the towel."

"Since only you can bring them on board, you don't need to worry. I'll make certain Anne Marie understands that. In the meantime, I'll give my old partner a call and get them moving on that Channing file. I think you'll find it interesting."

"No doubt I will. Thanks."

"Hey, when you see my sister, tell her to hang in there, okay?"

"Will do." Sean disconnected the call and sat at his desk for a long time, staring into space, wondering if he should be doing something else to move this investigation forward. Should he put in a call to the FBI? Should he be asking for help? Was he putting others in danger by not calling in the feds?

He glanced at the clock over the door. Greer had hung it the day he was named chief. It was a silly squirrel whose tail moved back and forth with every tick of the second hand. It drove him crazy so most times he refused to look at it, but today he couldn't seem to look away.

He'd review the file from Lyndon on this Curtis Channing, then he'd decide what his next move would be. If it seemed like the FBI was the right choice, that would be his next call. Whether he personally liked it or not.

* * *

Dolores Hall was a mess. Here she was, in the front row of chairs set up at the funeral home, and she just could not stop crying. And forget about approaching the coffin, which Connie's two sisters had wisely left closed. They'd come to bring the body back to Illinois to be buried with their parents in an old family plot, but agreed to have a viewing here in Carleton on Tuesday night for all of Connie's devoted following.

"It's only right," Nancy, the oldest sister, told Dolores. "She's been doing hair here in Carleton for sixteen years."

"Half the heads in town," Dolores had sniffed.

"Then we'll do a little something here at one of the local funeral parlors. Can you suggest one? Who do you think does the best job?"

"McCardle's," Dolores had said without hesitation. "They always call us in to do . . . you know . . . heads. We didn't especially like the work, but we thought of it as, you know, a public service. . . ."

McCardle's first floor was jammed with mourners on the night of Connie's viewing. Dolores stood side-by-side with the sisters, introducing them to the many who'd come to pay their respects to the deceased. Vince stood in the background and watched, amazed at the size of the crowd.

His gaze roamed the room, trying to pick out the undercover police, knowing that they would be in attendance. It was no secret that killers often attend the funerals of their victims, so it followed that the Carleton P.D. would be hanging around, looking for suspects. For this reason, Vince made a point of chatting with the mourners—a lone figure was much more likely to become the object of speculation—and went from time to time to stand by Dolores's side as if he were an important part of the proceedings.

Which in a way, he was.

He just couldn't wait until the sisters took the box away and Connie would be gone from his life forever. Then he could get on with things—move in with Dolores on a permanent basis, move out of that dinky little room he was in. He much preferred the comfort of Dee's bed to the lumpy little thing he'd been sleeping on. Of course, with Dee in such grief and shock these days, he'd barely left her side. Which was just fine with him. It was helping him to solidify his place in her life, move their relationship along.

"Vinnie, you're my rock," she'd cried the night before. "I don't know what I'd have done these past few days without you."

"I'm here for you, Dolores," he'd told her solemnly. "I'll always be here for you. . . ."

At least, for as long as you are useful to me. And after that, well, who knows . . . ?

CHAPTER TWENTY-FOUR

"ARE YOU SURE YOU WANT TO GO THROUGH WITH this?" Sean asked as he parked the car, still not certain he was doing the right thing.

"Absolutely," Amanda replied without hesitation.

"I don't know how Lowell is going to react to seeing you," he reminded her. "And you know I'm going to be showing him some photographs you might not want to see."

"I'm fine, Sean. If you think Lowell is somehow involved in these killings, I will do whatever I can to help flush him out. Maybe my being there when he's forced to look at the photos of Derek and Marian might rattle him a bit. I know it's a long shot, but it can't hurt."

"As long as it doesn't hurt you. And who knows, if you appeal to him to tell what he knows—if in fact he knows anything about this guy Giordano—it could pay off. At this point, I'll take whatever I can get."

"You're still thinking about my brother telling you that you should bring in the FBI."

"I'd be lying if I said it wasn't on my mind."

"You're afraid they'll take over your case." She smiled. "Would it help you to know that I remember my brother being afraid of just that same thing on more than one case?"

"I guess no one wants to relinquish the wheel, so to speak. And bringing another agency in feels like an admission that you can't do it alone."

"What's wrong with that? What's wrong with admitting that you need help?"

"I guess it's the same as admitting to failure."

"How do you figure?" She frowned. "Where is the failure in taking advantage of every available tool to get the job done? The FBI is just another tool, Sean. Evan learned that on his last big case."

"I'll keep that in mind." He took one of her hands in his and asked, "Ready to go in?"

"I'm not afraid to see him, Sean. He can't hurt me now. I'm the strong one now."

"Damn if you aren't. I'd put my money on you any day of the week."

"Then let's go see what Mr. Archer Lowell has to say." She squeezed his hand and opened the door.

While not quite as fearless as she'd made herself out to be, Amanda was relatively confident as she strode through the front door of High Meadow Prison. She'd never had a glimpse inside, never known anyone other than Lowell who was incarcerated.

The pungent scent of institutional cleaning fluids, antiseptic and acrid, filled the air inside the long, wide corridor that led from the front desk to the small anteroom off the warden's office, where they were to meet with Lowell.

"Last chance," Sean said, his hand on the door of Warden Fred McCabe's office.

"Lead on," Amanda told him.

"Come in, come in." Warden McCabe rose to greet his visitors with an outstretched hand. "Amanda Crosby, I know your brother. Fine man. Good detective. Sean, good to see you again."

"Thanks for setting this up for me." Sean held out the lone visitor's chair for Amanda.

"Sorry about that. All my chairs were commandeered and sent down to the conference room this afternoon. Some big meeting with the insurance people." He stole a peek at his watch. "Meeting should be starting soon. I need to make an appearance. Anything I can get you before I go on down?"

"Not a thing." Sean shook his head.

"Well, you go on in"—McCabe nodded toward the room next door—"and you let Corporal Leonard there know when you're ready for Lowell. He's at your disposal this morning."

"We really appreciate it."

"Anything I can do to help out . . ." Warden rose and gathered a folder, patted his pockets for his glasses, and searched the top of his desk until he found the pen he was looking for. "Anything else you need, the assistant warden is right down the hall. Anything you need . . ."

Smiling absently, his visitors already forgotten, he waved and left the room.

"You ready?" Sean asked.

"You betcha," Amanda assured him with a smile. Deep inside, however, the faintest thread of uncertainty began to quiver.

Corporal John Leonard was already in the small room next door, waiting for them, when Amanda and Sean stepped inside.

"He's on his way up," Leonard told them.

"Fine." Sean gestured for Amanda to sit facing the door.

He took the seat next to her. Leonard would be seated on her other side, and the guard who was accompanying Lowell would sit on his side. There would be no chance for him to so much as reach out to touch her.

A sharp rap at the door was followed quickly by the door being pushed open. Archer Lowell took one or two uncertain steps into the room, then, seeing Amanda, his eyes widened.

"Uh-uh. No way. No one said she was going to be here." He shook his head adamantly and tried to back out through the door. "I'm gonna be out of here in six weeks. The D.A. said if I so much as thought about her and he found out about it, he'd slap more time on me. Nope. Get me outta here. Take me back to my cell—"

Sean held up his hand. "Relax, Archer. I spoke with the D.A. this morning. He said we could have this meeting and it wouldn't count against you."

"I don't believe it." Archer refused to take another step closer, refused to even look in Amanda's direction.

"Give me the phone," Sean directed the guard, who passed it to him. "Do I need to dial a number to get an outside line?"

"Dial nine, then the number," Corporal Leonard replied.

"Kathy? Sean Mercer, Broeder. Yes, thanks, fine. She's fine, thank you. Is your boss in? Sure, thanks. I'll wait."

Sean stared at Lowell while he waited, stared until Lowell looked away. "Jack? I'm out at the prison with Archer Lowell. He needs your assurance that speaking with Ms. Crosby today will not be a violation of his sentence. . . . Yeah, here he is."

Sean passed the phone to the guard, who held it up to Lowell's ear, as Lowell's hands were secured behind him.

"Uh-huh. Uh-huh. Uh-huh . . . okay. But do I, like, get any time off for this? Hello?" Lowell made a face. "Dude hung up on me."

"That dude could hold your life in his hands one day. You might want to be a little more respectful." Sean took a file from his briefcase and placed it on the table. "Never know when you're going to be going head-to-head with him, Archer."

"Not me, man. Once I get out, I am never coming back."

"Sure, sure. You all say that."

"Yeah, well, I mean it. I've had enough of this place." Lowell looked at Sean, but avoided so much as a glance in Amanda's direction.

"So, Archer." Sean crossed his arms over his chest. "I know how you knew Derek England . . ."

"Who?" Archer frowned, then nodded as if a little light had gone on someplace deep in the recesses of his memory. "Oh. You mean the dead guy you talked about last time?"

"Yes."

"I didn't have nothing to do with him. I told you that. Shit, I been in here—"

"Yeah, we know where you've been." Sean nodded. "How about Marian O'Connor?"

"Who?"

"Marian O'Connor. You remember her, Archer. She owned an antiques shop across from Amanda's."

"The busybody. Yeah, I remember her. What about her?"

"She's been murdered."

"Yeah, well, that's got nothing to do with me." Lowell shook his head. "I don't know nothing about no murders."

"Derek was my business partner. He was one of my best friends." Amanda spoke for the first time since she'd entered the room. She'd had a few tremors when Lowell had first entered the room, but seeing his reaction to her—his fear at having her in the room—had somehow empowered her. It was a moment of great satisfaction when she realized that he was much more intimidated by her presence than she was by his. "Marian was a close friend, too. I loved them both."

"Yeah, well, you used to love me, too," Lowell sneered.

"You know that wasn't true, Archer." She forced a kind note into her voice, one she did not feel. It occurred to her then that she was grateful that his hands, the hands that had beaten her, were secured behind his back.

"I know that you betrayed me. You knew that I loved you. You let me think that you loved me—"

"Archer, that isn't the way it was. Please try to remember the way it really was." She pushed away the image of those hands and forced herself to sit up just a little straighter, to stare him in the eyes and not blink.

"I do remember how it was. He was always hanging around. And her, nosy old lady, she called the police on me."

"You threatened them both," Amanda said without flinching. "You wanted to hurt them both."

"But I couldn't have been the one who hurt them, could I?" He seemed to gloat. "Since I was safe and sound in here when they got whacked, wasn't I?"

"But maybe you had a friend on the outside, one who was happy to help you tend to that unfinished business," Sean interjected.

"I told you before, man, I ain't got no friends."

"Okay, Archer. So we know how you knew Derek England and Marian O'Connor. Tell me how you knew Connie Paschall."

"Who?" Archer tilted his head to one side.

"Connie Paschall. The hairdresser down in Carleton."

"I swear, I have no idea who you're talking about. I swear, I don't know a Connie whatever-her-name-is and I don't know no hairdressers in Carleton. I don't know nobody in Carleton." Archer looked from Sean to Amanda to Corporal Leonard. "What is this?"

Sean opened the file and slid several color photos across the table. They stopped, as intended, directly in front of Archer.

"Oh, man, what is that?" He drew back sharply.

"That is Connie Paschall, after someone put a bullet through her head."

"I swear, man, I do not know anything about this." He shook his head, his face pale. He pushed back in the seat and turned his body so that he wasn't even facing the photos. "Get them out of here. That's so gross, man. I never seen a dead person before."

"Vince Giordano." Sean threw the name out there as glibly as he'd tossed out the photographs.

"Wha-what?"

"Vince Giordano. What's he to you?" Sean leaned back in his chair.

"Nothin', man. Don't know him." Lowell shook his head a little too briskly.

Sean took another photo from the file and leaned across the table to slap it down on the Formica in front of Lowell.

"What can you tell me about this man?" He tapped the photo of Vince Giordano taken right before his trial.

"Nothing."

"Well, how about in this picture, then? You recognize him now?" Sean took out one of the photos that the Carleton police had faxed over that morning. "That photo was taken at Connie Paschall's viewing two nights ago."

Lowell shrugged and looked away.

"Take another look, Lowell."

Archer Lowell leaned forward obediently and did a double take at the picture that lay before him on the table. He stared at it for a long time, then shook his head.

"I don't know the man," he said calmly. "Never saw him before in my life. I already said, I don't know nobody named Giordano, and I don't know nothin' about these dead people."

He looked up at the guard. "I wanna go back to my cell now. I don't have nothin' else to say."

"So help me, God, Lowell, if I find out you had anything to do with this . . ." Sean's voice was taut with emotion.

"I don't know nothing." Lowell stood with the help of his guard and turned to the door.

But he just couldn't resist looking back over his shoulder and smirking, just a little, as he left the room.

"So, what do you think?" Amanda asked as she tried to keep up with Sean, who was all but racing to the assistant warden's office.

"I think he was lying through his teeth. Oh, I think he might have been telling the truth about Connie Paschall, but he definitely recognized Giordano. In both pictures. Did you see the way he studied the picture from Paschall's viewing? It took him a few seconds to catch on to the fact that Giordano had dyed his hair. That red would have been a dead giveaway, so Vince went to brown. The mustache, the glasses— it took Lowell a few seconds to see past those, but the minute the light went on, bingo. It was pretty obvious he recognized him." He stopped in a doorway and added, "I'll bet he's a lot of fun in a poker game."

"Can I help you?" The secretary at the desk nearest the door rose at their entry.

"I'm Chief Mercer, from Broeder. Warden McCabe said if I needed anything . . ."

"Yes, he said you might stop by. What can I get for you?"

"I'd like copies of your cell-block records. Who is housed next to who. More specifically, I want to know who has lived, slept, eaten, showered, exercised, or watched TV with Archer Lowell since the day he was incarcerated."

The secretary stared at him as if he had lost his mind.

"Have a seat." She pointed to a love seat and chair in one corner. "This is going to take a while."

Back in his cell, Archer Lowell marveled at the changes in his onetime victim. She was a different woman than the one he'd known. He'd liked the old Amanda far better. This one—this new one—just left him cold.

But hey now, how about that Vince! I hardly even recognized him. Dark hair, glasses, muzzie. And he has a lady friend. Way to go, Vince, you dog, you.

But as the implications of Mercer's visit slowly began to come together in Archer's mind, he began to pace back and forth in his cell on increasingly worried feet, and his fears began to gather and take shape, looming before him like a still shot on a big-screen TV.

Somehow, someone had figured out there was some connection between him and Vince Giordano.

There were dead people, people who were part of his past—except for the hairdresser—who were now being connected to Vince, and the dots were leading right back to Archer.

But unless those dots could be connected, there was no way they could bring any of it back on him. Unless Giordano named him, there was no way they could prove anything.

Would Giordano name him?

Jeez, he'd seemed like such a stand-up kind of guy. . . .

Denial took over and those feet began to pace a lot faster.

I don't really know what Vince has done. I ain't had no contact with him. It could be a coincidence, right? Sure, that's it. It's all a coincidence. And I ain't about to admit to knowing him. Six weeks left on my sentence. Uh-uh. I ain't done a damned thing to get into trouble since the day I was brought in here, and I ain't about to blow it now. I just want out. Besides, I didn't do nothin'. Whatever Vince has done, well, that's on Vince, isn't it? I don't know nothin' about it and I don't know him. I been in here and I ain't seen no one and I don't know why he did what he did.

Yeah, that's it. I don't even know him. No one can prove that I do. . . .

CHAPTER
TWENTY-FIVE

DOLORES LOLLED BENEATH THE SHEETS FOR A MOment or two before she realized that the bed was empty. Vinnie must have left for work hours ago.

She stretched and rolled over to look at the clock. It was almost three-thirty in the afternoon. She'd spent most of the day in bed, alternating between sleeping and weeping. She knew she had to get herself together, but it was so damned hard. Besides, it hadn't even been a full week since the murder. She missed Connie terribly. Every time she thought about never seeing her friend again, Dolores burst into tears.

She swung her legs over the side of the bed as soon as she felt her eyes begin to well up again. She knew Vinnie was getting tired of her weeping and moping, but jeez, she and Connie went way back. Back to the days when they were both newly divorced and working for that scumbag Richard who owned that shop down on Adams. Man, he had been one mean son of a bitch.

She shook her head, remembering. She and Connie had bonded over their bad hours and bad pay, and had become real close. Together they'd left Richard and gone with another shop, where they both did better, but still not well enough.

"Dee, we need our own place," Connie would say. "If you save, and I save, and we get enough socked away, we can get a loan to cover the rest of what we'll need to start our own business. All we need is the right place to come along at the right time. We gotta start now to save for it, so we'll be ready."

And eventually the right place did come along, and thanks to Connie's goading, they were ready. The Cut N Curl had been well established before either of the two women had moved to Carleton. While its clientele was aging, the facilities were still solid and the location was good. The fact that zoning had just given the green light to a new apartment village to be built right across the road had been the deciding factor. They'd inherit the clients from the retiring owner and would be conveniently located to attract the hip young singles targeted by the apartment complex.

"Opportunity is knocking loud and clear, Dolores," Connie had told her over Chinese takeout in her apartment after they'd gone to see the shop for the first time. "We gonna open up that door and let 'er in or not?"

"We'll do it!" Dolores had boldly thrown in with Connie and the two of them made an offer on the Cut N Curl the next morning.

It had been a hectic nine months, but they were doing just fine. Business was booming even before the apartments were completed.

"You believe how lucky we are?" Connie had said to Dee just the week before. "I mean, are we lucky or what?"

Yeah, Connie. Real lucky . . .

Dolores wandered downstairs, thinking that while Connie's luck may have run out, hers was holding strong. After all, she did have Vinnie to hold on to, Vinnie to help her through these dark days and nights. She couldn't even begin to think of how she would have made it without him.

She went into the kitchen, still in her nightgown, wondering what to do with her day. She still wasn't ready to face going into the shop. She went to the front door and looked out and saw the morning newspaper still out on the lawn.

Kid can never seem to get it past the first few squares of walkway. What is it with him?

She opened the door to go out for the paper, but a chilly gust of wind pulled her back. She grabbed the first thing she could find to wrap around her, the sport jacket that Vinnie had worn earlier in the week and had left over the back of the chair nearest the front door.

She slipped into the jacket and pulled it snug around her and walked outside. The sun was brighter than she'd expected, and she squinted as her bare feet crunched through the dry leaves that were already falling from the oak on her neighbor's lawn. She picked up the newspaper and tucked it under her arm, remembering how Connie had loved the change of the seasons.

And Halloween. Damn, how Connie loved Halloween. Every year they'd worked together, Connie would make up little goodie bags and bring them into the shop for the customers.

She jammed her hands into the pockets of the jacket as she turned back toward the house. The fingers of her right hand felt something in the lining, something small and round. Almost without thinking, she explored the tiny hole in the bottom of the pocket. She worked the object out of the hole, taking it out as she walked up the steps. She looked down at her hand and blinked several times, certain she was not seeing what she was seeing.

Connie's ring. There was no mistaking it.

With trembling hands she turned it toward the light, her eyes searching the inside of the ring. There it was. CNP. Connie Noelle Paschall.

But how could Connie's ring have gotten into—

Her legs began to shake and went out from under her as she sat down on the top step.

Connie's ring.

Connie's ring in Vinnie's jacket.

The chief of police had said that it was likely that whoever had killed Connie had taken her ring as a souvenir.

Dolores's mind raced back to the night Connie was killed, remembering how Vinnie had disappeared for ten or fifteen minutes and came back in a sweat that she'd excused as the result of the mussels.

It wasn't possible. Not Vinnie. Oh, not Vinnie.

Oh, please, God, not Vinnie . . .

Turning the ring over and over in her hand, she pulled herself up by the stair rail and went back into the house in a daze. She dropped the jacket onto the chair where she'd found it and went upstairs to change. Connie's ring on her finger, she pulled on a sweatshirt and a pair of jeans. When she could locate only one sneaker, she slipped on a pair of orange rubber flip-flops and grabbed her purse. Back downstairs, she paused at the chair where she'd draped Vinnie's jacket. Should she return the ring to the pocket or not?

She left it on her finger and tore out the back door, needing to be gone. Needing to find a place away from here where she could think. Without planning on it, she found herself parked behind the Cut N Curl.

Yellow crime scene tape still floated from the back door, and the light just inside still burned. Dolores unlocked the back door and stepped into the quiet of the shop.

There was the smallest spot of red-brown on the floor inside the outline that marked where Connie's body had lain. Dolores stood staring at it, unable to look away, rubbing the ring between her fingers as if trying to conjure up her lost friend. When her fingers were all but raw, she went to the receptionist desk and sat down, staring into space.

She spun around and around in the chair mindlessly, trying not to think. Trying to push it all away. Trying to pretend that it was all a bad dream. On one of her spins around she saw a newspaper folded up on the shelf near the hair care products, where Connie must have left it. Funny place to leave the paper . . .

Dolores got up and went to the display and pulled the paper out from between the rows of hair spray and gel and conditioners and took it back to the desk. She opened the paper and spread it out flat, skimmed the stories on the page.

In the lower left corner was a drawing of a necklace that looked an awful lot like hers. She sat down and read the accompanying article.

Stunned, she put a hand on her chest. Her heart

was pounding so badly she thought she was going to pass out.

Taking the paper, she grabbed her purse and left the shop.

As she locked the back doors, she could see their faces in her mind's eye.

Connie, her best friend.

Vinnie, her lover.

How could it be that one might have murdered the other?

And just what was she going to do about it?

Dolores drove around the block three times before pulling into her driveway, just to make sure that Vinnie's car was not parked out back or along the side yard. Convinced that he was not there, she parked as close to the back door as she could. Once inside, she ran up the steps to her room, threw open the closet door, and pulled out the suitcase. She tried not to pack haphazardly, but the thought that he might come through that door any minute now had her totally unnerved. The hell with it. She'd take just a few things, her jewelry, one pair of shoes, some underwear, and the box containing the pendant. She snapped the lid closed and dragged it down the steps and out the door. She opened the trunk and slid it inside, then went back into the house.

"Cujo?" she called as she ran down the basement steps, looking for the cat carrier.

Hearing his name, Cujo sauntered out from under the dining room table and rubbed up against her legs.

"No time, sugar," she whispered as if afraid to be overheard.

She picked up the cat, tucked him inside the crate and lugged it outside, where she slid it across the backseat. One more thing, and she'd be gone. Cat food, cat dish, cat toys, cat treats, all into a grocery bag.

"What the hell am I doing?" She laughed nervously. "Packing more for the cat than I did for myself . . ."

Back out to the car with the cat bag.

What else? she demanded of herself. *What else . . . ?*

Nothing else. You're fine. Leave. Get out of here.

She dug in her pocket for her keys, then realized she'd left them and her purse on the dining room table. She ran, tripping up the steps and over her own two feet.

Calm down, she laughed crazily. *Calm down. Done. It's done. Just go.*

Go . . .

She got her balance and went into the dining room. She had just swung her purse over her shoulder when she heard the back door close. She froze where she stood.

"Dolores?" Vinnie called from the kitchen. "Dee? You there?"

"In the dining room." She ran her dry tongue over her suddenly dry lips.

"Hey, you're up, you're dressed. You must be feeling a little better today." He dropped his keys into a dish on the sideboard, a habit he'd developed the first night he'd spent there.

"A little." She nodded her head. "Like you said, I have to move on."

He drew her into his arms, and it was all she could do not to scream when he kissed her. And she knew right then that if she was going to walk out of this house alive, Dolores Marie Muldowny Hall was going to have to pull off an Academy Award winning performance.

"Say, you going someplace?" he asked as he nuzzled her neck.

"I was going to pick up Chinese for dinner from that place you like over on Fourth Street."

"You order me the Three Phoenix?"

"Just like you like it." She nodded, molding her mouth into a smile. "Extra scallops."

I can do this. I can do this. . . .

"You call the order in?"

"Ten minutes ago. I figured I'd have enough time to get down there and back before you got home. I know you like surprises. I didn't think you'd be home this soon."

"I closed up a little early today. I was worried about you." He kissed her mouth, and she held her breath and hoped he didn't notice.

"Why don't you run upstairs and take a nice hot shower while I pick up dinner? And maybe after dinner, we can go out for a while. Maybe to the Dew, or someplace." She backed away from him slowly, trying to make it appear natural, not giving any sign, however small, of the revulsion she felt. She picked up her keys and headed for the door. It took every ounce of her willpower to not run.

"That's my girl. Gotta get back into the world again. Can't keep yourself locked up and crying for the rest of your life." Vinnie gave her a pat on the behind as she walked past him.

But with luck, that's where you'll be. Locked up for the rest of your life. You betcha, Vinnie.

You bastard.

She held her breath as she walked out the back door and down the steps slowly, as if she had all the time in the world, just in case he was watching. She opened the car door and slid behind the wheel, then locked the doors. She put the key in the ignition and turned it, forcing herself not to turn frantically to look behind her. With nonchalance and total cool, she put the car into reverse and backed leisurely out of the driveway, somehow resisting the urge to floor it.

"Yup," she said aloud as she rubbed the ring in her pocket between her fingers. "Locked up for the rest of your natural life. And me and Connie are gonna put you there."

___CHAPTER___
TWENTY-SIX

"You got company," Joyce told Sean when he and Amanda arrived back at the police station. "The small conference room."

"Who is it?" He frowned.

Joyce gestured at Amanda, who had continued toward his office, and whispered, "The brother. And he's not happy right now."

Sean leaned forward and whispered in return, "What's made him unhappy?"

"He wanted to know if I knew where his sister was." She shrugged. "How was I supposed to know he'd be pissed off about her going to the prison?"

Sean sorted through his phone messages as he walked to the small room across the hall from his office. Might as well get this over with.

He entered the room to find that Amanda had beaten him there. Evan was seated across the small round conference table from a very pretty, very feminine blonde.

Sean arrived just in time to hear Evan say, "Mrs. What's-er-name out there on the front desk is under the impression that you and Chief Mercer spent a good part of the afternoon out at the county prison, but since I know that you have better sense than that, I figured she just must have misunderstood."

"No misunderstanding." Amanda kissed her brother on the cheek. "I'm happy to see you, too."

"Her choice, Detective." Sean shrugged.

"A poor one. You have any idea what that guy did to her?"

"I do. Yes, I do." Sean nodded thoughtfully.

"And you still dragged her out there—"

"Enough, Evan," Amanda said. "I appreciate your love and concern. I do. But for crying out loud, give me a little credit, will you?"

Before he could answer, she leaned on the table next to the chair in which he sat. "No one dragged me, Evan. I wanted to go," she said with no small amount of pride. "And for the record, Archer Lowell was a lot more uncomfortable than I was."

"I wouldn't have taken her, if I'd thought otherwise," Sean assured him.

"By the way, I'm Amanda Crosby," Amanda introduced herself to the other woman in the room.

"Anne Marie McCall." The blonde smiled warmly and extended her hand.

"Annie is a profiler with the FBI," Evan told them. "We met a few months ago while working on a case. She's here as a friend."

Amanda took a seat next to her brother. "Speaking of the FBI, why aren't you down there in class or doing whatever it is you're supposed to be doing?"

"I ran into Annie down in Quantico where she was giving a lecture. I knew she had a little history with Vince Giordano and might be able to shed some insight into Sean's case."

"But when I heard the story, I wanted to come talk to you myself. Evan decided to take a few days off to come with me," Anne Marie told them.

"You know Vince Giordano?" Sean asked.

"We—Evan and I, as well as my boss at the Bureau—believe he's the man who set in motion several attempts on my sister's life."

"What was your sister's connection to Giordano?" Sean asked.

"You're familiar with the case down in Lyndon?" Anne Marie asked. When Sean nodded, she told him, "Mara, my sister, was the child advocate who recommended that the court terminate Giordano's parental rights."

"I did read through the file Evan had sent up, but I thought the Mary Douglas killer was a guy named Channing."

"Yes," Anne Marie said. "Curtis Channing."

"What was his connection to Giordano?"

"We were never able to figure that out," Evan admitted.

"Just like we can't figure out the connection between Giordano and Lowell," Sean noted.

The four of them sat in silence for a while.

Finally, Amanda said, "Okay. I'm the odd man out here. I don't know this case except that I remember that Evan was really involved with it. Tell me what this guy Channing did."

"Curtis Channing killed Giordano's mother-in-law," Evan said, "the judge who severed Giordano's parental rights, and several women named Mary Douglas. Anne Marie's sister, *Mara* Douglas—*Mara,* not *Mary*—was the advocate. Channing got the name wrong. He killed three innocent women trying to get her. All three targeted victims—Mara, the mother-in-law, and the judge—had in one way or another crossed Vince Giordano."

"Then they were friends," Amanda murmured, intrigued. "Giordano and Channing."

"We haven't been able to determine when—or if—they ever actually met," Anne Marie told her. "And now we have two people who crossed Archer Lowell dead—as well as one who may or may not have gotten in his way somehow—and one other potential victim who's been stalked and attacked. You."

"*Strangers on a Train,*" Evan said softly. "I can't believe it didn't occur to me before."

"What?" Anne Marie said, startled.

"*Strangers on a Train.* You ever see that movie, where two guys meet and decide to kill for each other?"

"You think the three of these men . . ." Anne Marie played with the idea.

"It makes as much sense as anything else at this point," Sean told her. "Evan, this may not be so far off the wall."

"When I was trying to get a handle on the Channing case, I found out that both these men were in High Meadow at the same time, but not in the same wing. Their paths did not appear to cross there. As far as we were able to determine, the only time they were in the same place at the same time was one day earlier this year, when they were transported to the courthouse in the same van. But we interviewed the driver and the guards, and they swear there was no conversation in the van. There never is, they told us. They said these guys didn't even sit near each other."

"There had to be something, some time when they talked," Amanda said.

"So we need to get to Lowell . . ." Anne Marie thought aloud.

"Oh, we just had a nice conversation with him. Let me tell you, he's really good at playing dumb. Swears he doesn't know Giordano. Never heard of him, never met him." Sean taps a pen on the table. "But here's something else to think about. Archer Lowell gets out of prison in a few weeks."

"Makes you wonder what's next, doesn't it?" Amanda glanced around the room at the others. "If there was some kind of secret agreement, what do you suppose he agreed to do? What's his part of the bargain?"

Sean left the room and came back with the file of photographs he'd earlier shown to Lowell. He separated several from the stack and handed them to Anne Marie.

"Take a look at these. These were taken at Connie Paschall's funeral earlier in the week. Anyone look familiar?"

She looked at each one carefully, then said, "This of course is Vince Giordano. He's darkened his hair and didn't wear glasses or a mustache when I met him, but it's clearly the same man."

Amanda leaned forward to stare at the Giordano photo. "You know, now that I look at this, I think he's the guy who offered to change my tire."

"What?" Sean all but exploded. "When?"

"A few weeks ago." She paused to think. "Actu-

ally, I think it might have been the week Marian was
killed. I was a little late coming out of the shop one
night—I think it might have been the night of the
house sale where Marian bought the Russian pieces.
I'd completely forgotten about it."

"What happened?" Sean asked.

"I came out of the shop and went out to the parking lot and found that I had a flat tire. I got out the
spare and was starting to put it on when this man
came along and offered to do it for me. He got a little
huffy when I told him I could do it myself. I remember that about him. He was almost insulted that I'd
refused his help."

"And you're sure it was this man." Evan pointed to
the photo.

"Pretty sure, yes."

"Has anyone spoken to the woman he's with in the
photos?" Anne Marie asked. "Do we know who she
is?"

Sean nodded. "Name is Dolores Hall. She co-owned
the shop with Connie Paschall. Chief Benson over in
Carleton did take a statement from her."

"Maybe she's involved in this. Maybe she and
Vince planned to kill her partner so that she could
have the business to herself," Amanda suggested, recalling that once upon a time, she'd been a suspect in
her business partner's death as well.

"I don't think that's his style." Anne Marie shook
her head. "He wouldn't have a partner, and if he did,
it certainly wouldn't be a woman. He doesn't trust
them, doesn't respect them. All of his crimes have
been against women. He holds women in very low es-
teem. He would never confide in one."

"I agree," Evan said. "I think this thing is his all the way."

"You have the girlfriend's statement, the one she gave to Benson?" Evan leaned back in his chair.

"Right here. I'll make a few copies." Sean stood. "And I'll ask Joyce to bring in a pot of coffee. Looks like we're going to be here for a while."

Evan stared at the photos of Dolores Hall. "I agree with Anne Marie. I'd be real surprised if Hall had anything to do with this. I think this is all his."

"Sean, have you considered bringing in the FBI?" Anne Marie asked. "Officially, I mean."

"I've been thinking about it," he acknowledged.

"I can arrange to bring in an agent who has had dealings with Giordano before."

"I've never heard of the FBI sending in only one agent," he noted skeptically.

"This is one very good agent." She smiled. "What do you say?"

Sean bit the inside of his lower lip. He didn't really feel that he had a choice. "Make your call," he told Anne Marie.

"Consider it done." She drained her coffee cup and turned to Evan. "Will you be driving back to your place in Lyndon for the night, or will you be staying here?"

"I'd planned on driving back to Lyndon," he replied.

"May I hitch a ride? I thought I'd stay at my sister's house, since I do have a key, and she's out of town for a while."

"This is your sister the advocate?" Amanda asked. "The one Channing tried to kill?"

"Yes."

"Is she on vacation?"

"Not exactly. She's on her way out West, tracking down a lead on her missing daughter." Anne Marie stood up and smoothed her black skirt. "Seven years ago, Mara's ex-husband disappeared and took their daughter with him. Mara's been searching for her ever since."

"Oh, my God. That's horrible." Amanda set her cup down. "That's just . . . horrible."

"It has been a nightmare," Anne Marie agreed. "But this new lead looks very, very promising. We've all got our fingers crossed."

"Can't the FBI help?"

"The FBI is on the case, trust me." Anne Marie turned to Evan. "If you're ready . . ."

"I'm ready. Amanda, you're still staying with Sean's sister?"

"Yes," she laughed ruefully. "I am never alone, Evan, never fear. I haven't been alone for five minutes since Marian died."

"Getting to you, is it?" Evan paused to study her face, his hand on her shoulder.

"A little." She smiled. "It's okay, though. I don't really mind. And it sure as hell beats the alternative."

The house was strangely dark and quiet when Vince came back downstairs, humming "Sweet Home Alabama" and dying to dig into the Chinese. He flipped on the lamp nearest the stairs and went in the direction of the kitchen.

"Dolores?" he called as he walked through the dining room and into the kitchen.

The basement door stood ajar. He leaned through it and yelled, "Dee! You down there?"

When there was no answer, he looked out through the back door window and realized that her car was not in the drive.

"Idiot. Can't find her way to the Chinese restaurant and back by herself," he muttered as he rustled through the stack of take-out menus on the counter.

He dialed the number for Ming Gardens. "Yeah, I'm calling to see if an order has been picked up yet. Called in about thirty minutes ago. Name is Hall."

He waited while the take-out bags were checked.

"No order for Hall."

"Oh. Well, maybe she put it under Daniels. Look and see if there's something there for Daniels."

More rustling in the background.

"No order for Hall, no order for Daniels. You want to place an order?"

"Maybe she just picked it up. Dolores, you know Dolores Hall. Blond lady . . . comes in a lot."

"Yes, yes. I know Miss Hall. She's not here."

"But has she been there?"

"No. You want to place an order?"

He hung up without responding.

She must be on her way back. Well, she'd better have a damned good reason why it took her so long to go a couple of blocks and back. He was *starving*.

He'd spent the day wasting time walking around the mall about thirty miles away. It had bored him near to death, but he had to maintain the pretext that his construction company was busy and that he had lots of work lined up. How else could he explain all the money he spent if he didn't work?

He had also made a quick stop to check out his stash of cash, as he did once every two weeks or so. You couldn't be too careful.

He made a pot of coffee and drank a cup as he paced back and forth. This was getting ridiculous. Where could the stupid cow be?

Soon the quiet was beginning to get to him. He went into the living room and turned on the TV, then hesitated before sitting down on the sofa. It never failed—the minute Vince got comfortable, the damned cat showed up and tried sitting on his lap. He tolerated it when Dolores was around, but wasn't above giving it a good kick when she wasn't.

Where was that damned cat, anyway?

"Cujo, you furry pain in the ass, where the hell are you?"

He went back into the kitchen, figuring if he dropped some cat treats into the bowl, the cat would come running, like it always did. Piggy cat.

He opened the pantry door.

No cat treats.

He looked down at the floor.

No cat bowl.

"What the fuck?" he muttered.

The unthinkable occurred to him. Vince raced back through the house and up the steps.

He flung open the closet door in the bedroom, but the suitcase that had stood there just a few days earlier was gone. He opened drawers to see if he could tell if anything was missing, but jeez, the woman had so many clothes.

He opened the top drawer and searched under her underwear for the box in which she kept the pendant. Nothing.

He slammed the drawer shut.

Son of a bitch. Dolores, you son of a bitch. He knocked a lamp off the end of the dresser.

He went back down the stairs, trying to put it all together. Had she been so crushed by Connie's death that she just had to run away? Could that be it? But she would have said something, wouldn't she?

Wouldn't she?

Or was there something else . . . some other reason why she might want to leave without him knowing she was going?

Vinnie took a deep breath and picked up the tweed jacket. He stuck his hand into first one pocket, then the other. Nothing.

In total disbelief, he lowered himself onto the sofa cushion.

The little bitch had outsmarted him.

She'd outsmarted *him.*

Who'da thought it. Dumb little Dolores. Dumb, dull little Dolores. Somehow she'd figured it all out.

Even as his anger grew, so did a perverse sort of admiration for her. She'd outsmarted him.

He went up the steps to get his things. With no time to waste, he shoved his clothes, his shaving things, his toothbrush into his travel bag.

For all he knew, she was at the police station right that minute. There was no way of knowing how much time he had before cars came screaming down the street.

"Dolores, Dolores, why'd you do this, baby?" He shook his head as he hurried to the back door. "You know when I catch up with you, I'm gonna have to kill you. . . ."

SEAN STEPPED THROUGH THE WIDE DOORS THAT opened into the small lobby of the Broeder Police Department and wondered for about the fiftieth time just what the builders had thought might someday be coming through that door that merited so large an opening into so small a room. Joyce was long gone, her place at the desk taken by the officer in charge that night. It was 9:35 P.M., what should have been the end of a long day, and he'd just dropped Amanda off at Greer's and seen her safely inside. There were two black and whites there, one out front, one parked in the back by the garage, keeping an eye on things from the rear of the property. His brother-in-law, newly returned from his trip, had found the whole thing oddly exciting.

To each his own. Personally, Sean couldn't wait till this whole thing was over and instead of playing bodyguard to Amanda Crosby, he could think about getting close to her in other ways. These days, it just never did seem to be the appropriate time or place to do much more than watch her back and focus on catching the son of a bitch who'd turned their lives upside down.

"Oh, Chief. I just tried to phone you," Kevin

Reilly, the duty officer, called to him. "You have a visitor. Said it's really important that she speak with you right away."

Sean closed his eyes. *Honest to God, Ramona, I don't have time for this. . . .*

"Later. See if you can get Chief Benson over at the Carleton P.D. on the line."

Sean leaned over the counter and took the phone when Reilly handed it to him.

"They're giving you his voice mail," Reilly told him. "They said he checks it every fifteen minutes or so at night."

Sean waited for the prompt, then said, "Bob, Sean Mercer. I need you to pick up Dolores Hall, Connie Paschall's partner in that hairdressing place. You need to talk to her about her boyfriend. Give me a call back on my cell and I'll give you the details."

Sean handed the phone back to Reilly, who looked up and said, "Chief, she's here."

"Who's here?"

"Dolores Hall."

"Jesus, Reilly, why didn't you say so? Where is she?"

"The little room just across from your office."

The conference room door stood open. Dolores Hall was seated in a chair facing the door, clutching a large gray cat in her arms.

They stared at each other for a moment, then Sean asked, "How are you feeling, Miss Hall?"

"Dolores. It's Dolores." Her voice was soft and shaky. "And I'm not feeling so good."

"I know this week has been hard on you. Losing your partner . . ."

Her eyes welled up. "Connie was more than my business partner. She was my best friend. Maybe the best friend I ever had."

"Funny you should stop in here today, Miss . . . Dolores. I just left a message for Chief Benson down there in Carleton to stop over and pay you a visit. I want to talk to you about Vince Giordano."

"Who?"

"Vince Giordano. We know he's been staying with you."

"You mean Vinnie." She frowned. "He said his name was Vinnie Daniels."

"Close enough. Whatever he's calling himself, it's the same guy."

He got up and went across the hall to his office and returned with a folder in his hands. He pulled out several pictures and handed the first one across the table to her.

"This was Vince Giordano on the day he was arrested for murder down in Lyndon."

"Who'd he kill?" she asked, her face paling.

"His wife and his two sons."

She went another shade whiter. "Why isn't he in prison?"

"Because he was convicted on tainted evidence, and his attorney got him off." Sean handed her the pictures that were taken at Connie's funeral. "And here he is, among the mourners at your friend's funeral."

Dolores sat and stared. She looked up at Sean with red-rimmed eyes and said softly, "I found her ring."

"Excuse me?"

"I found her ring. In the pocket of his jacket. The

jacket he wore the night she was killed." Her voice was flat, without emotion.

"Where is the ring now?"

She took it off her hand and placed it on the table.

"Are you sure, absolutely sure, that this was her ring?" Sean made no move to touch it.

She picked it up and turned it so that the inside of the band was facing him. "Those are her initials."

"You know that this ties him to her murder."

Dolores nodded, her jaw set with resolution even as her eyes were filled with fear.

"Dolores, why are you bringing this to me, in Broeder, instead of to Chief Benson in Carleton?"

"Because I was afraid he'd find me if I stayed there. I wanted to get away from Carleton so that he wouldn't find me. Besides, the newspaper said you were looking for this"—she started to rummage in her purse—"and that if anyone knew anything about it, to contact you right away."

She removed a piece of newspaper folded small, then held up a small box and handed it to him. Sean opened it, and his heart all but stopped beating.

The pendant from Marian's shop.

"Where did you get this?"

"He—Vinnie—gave it to me." She made a face as she spread open the newspaper article. "He said it had belonged to his grandmother."

"When? When did he give this to you?"

"About a week ago. On a Friday night."

Sean glanced at the calendar on the wall. That would have taken them back to the night after Marian had been killed.

"It's not exactly like the one in the paper, but it's

real close, don't you think?" Dolores appeared to study the pendant as if she hadn't seen it before, then covered her face with her hands.

Sean got up and went to her, sat down in the chair next to hers. "You are incredibly brave to come here, Dolores."

"He killed her. He killed her because he knew that she saw this"—she stabbed at the newspaper with an angry finger—"and he knew that sooner or later, she'd show me. He killed her because of me. I let this . . . this . . . animal into my life, and he killed my best friend. It's my fault she's dead."

"Dolores, it's Vince's fault that she's dead, not yours, you understand me? He killed her. He and he alone is responsible for her death, not you. You had no way of knowing who or what he was. Do you understand?"

She nodded but her eyes would not meet his.

"Where is he now, Dolores?"

She shook her head. "I'm not sure. He was at my house, but I don't know if he's still there. I'm guessing he's not going to hang around too long, after he figures out what I've done."

"What did you do?"

"He thought I was going to pick up Chinese for dinner." She smiled, a faint touch of pride tugging at her lips. "I already had stuff in the car 'cause I'd found the ring and, damn it, he was not going to get away with that."

The smile faded. "No way could I let him get away with that. So I packed the car and was just ready to leave when he came home from work, and I told him I was going to pick up some takeout while he was in the shower." She clutched the cat tighter. "God, I was so scared. I'm still so scared."

"You are one really smart woman." Sean shook his head in true admiration. "Brave and smart. I'll bet it made him crazy when he realized that you'd out-smarted him."

"You think so?"

"I know so. This is one smart, smart killer, Do-lores. And you outfoxed him." He shook his head in amazement. "You should be really proud of your-self."

"I'll be proud of myself when you catch him and I go into court and testify about how he took me to dinner that night—that night he killed Connie—at a restaurant right there in the shopping center where the Cut N Curl is. About how he pretended to get sick from the mussels so he could make believe he was in the men's room throwing up while he was really down at my shop putting a bullet through the head of my best friend."

"You can help me find him. You can help me bring him to trial, to put him back in prison."

"I will do whatever it takes." Even through tears, Dolores was pure steel. "He killed Connie. He didn't have to kill her."

"Let's talk about where he might have gone. You said he worked. You know where?"

"He said he owned his own construction com-pany."

"Know what it's called?"

"Daniels Construction. But I don't know where they were working."

"That's okay. We can check to see if he's applied for

any work permits lately. Know if he had any friends in the area, anyone he socialized with? Did he mention the name of anyone who worked for him?"

"No. He never mentioned no one."

"What is he driving, Dolores? What kind of car?"

"Lincoln town car. Black. Not real new. I don't remember the plate number."

"That's all right. We can get that. Now, how about Archer Lowell? Did you ever hear him mention the name Archer Lowell?"

"No."

"How about Channing? Curtis Channing?"

She shook her head. "Sorry. I'm sorry. . . ."

"Hey, it's okay. We'll find him. One way or another, we're going to find him."

"I just hope he doesn't find me first."

"He's not going to. We'll keep you safe, I promise you. For as long as it takes." Sean took one of Dolores's hands and said, "I know how frightened you must be, and I realize this is hard for you. . . ."

She looked up at him, one eyebrow raised. "Hard for me? He killed my best friend. I'll watch that bastard burn in hell and I will smile the whole time. Just what about this do you think is hard for me?"

Sean pulled out his wallet and took out the card with Evan Crosby's number on it. He punched in the numbers and when Evan picked up, he said, "I think you're going to want to head on back to Broeder. I have a surprise for you. And tell Anne Marie we're going to need her people a little sooner than we'd expected."

____ CHAPTER ____
TWENTY-EIGHT

"SHE JUST WALTZED AWAY FROM HIM"—ANNE MARIE
shook her head in disbelief—"and waltzed herself right
on in here. Incredible that she would do that. Do you
have any idea how rare this is?"

She closed the door behind the departing Dolores,
who, along with Cujo, would be housed in a motel in
the company of Officer Dana Burke until the FBI
could send an agent to protect her.

"She is one very scared and very angry woman,"
Sean told her, "but I think it's the anger that gave her
the strength she needed to do what she had to do. She
wants to see him burn in hell."

"Don't we all?" Evan said. "Any thoughts on how
you're going to find him?"

"So far, there's no sign of him. His car was found
abandoned in a parking lot behind a bar in Carleton
about an hour ago. The police down there have
searched the room he was renting, but of course he
hasn't been there. They're getting ready to put him on
the wires, put out an APB—"

"Don't," Anne Marie said.

"Don't what?" asked Sean.

"Don't put out the APB, not yet."

"Why not?"

"Because if he thinks everyone in creation is looking for him, he'll run, and it could take years to find him. Amanda will have to be looking over her shoulder every day of her life until we find him, or he finds her."

"And Mara, too," Evan noted.

"Once he's done what he thinks is his duty—killing Amanda—he'll most likely turn on my sister soon enough, yes. We need to outsmart him. Make him relax, make him think we're focused someplace else."

"Fine, but we have to get him now." Sean ran a hand through his hair, wondering how they were going to do that. "If he's ditched the car, he must still be in the area. He hasn't had time to go too far. My guess is that he's hiding out someplace close between Carleton and here."

"Then we're going to have to smoke him out." Anne Marie stated the obvious.

"Use the girlfriend, maybe?" Sean wondered aloud.

"He doesn't care about her." Anne Marie shook her head. "There's only one thing that will keep him around. Only one thing that he wants. Only one thing he'll come out of hiding to get."

"No." Evan and Sean both shook their heads simultaneously. "No."

"Sorry, guys." Anne Marie looked from Evan to Sean, then back again. "If you want him, you're going to have to put out the only bait that has a chance to draw him in."

"No. You are not going to use Amanda. I won't have it," Sean said. "We'll have to come up with something else."

"I'm with him," Evan told her.

"Then accept the fact that you will not get him. It's as simple as that." Anne Marie stood up. "When you decide you want him badly enough, you'll know what to do."

Sean rose to answer a sharp rap on the door. He opened it to find a tall, leggy woman with a mane of black hair that spread over her shoulders and ice blue eyes set in a gorgeous face.

"Sean Mercer?" She flashed white teeth. "I'm Miranda Cahill. Annie invited me to your party."

Anne Marie grinned. "Sean, I mentioned Special Agent Cahill earlier. She and Vince Giordano are acquainted."

"Livia Bach and I were in the neighborhood," Miranda explained as she took a seat across from Sean. "We flipped a coin to see who went where. Livvy won the toss so she's been sent to guard-dog your witness." She flashed a megawatt smile. "You lucky blokes got me. Good to see you again, Evan."

Annie tossed the photos from Connie Paschall's funeral onto the table. "See anyone you know?" she asked Miranda.

Miranda flipped through the stack. "Ha! My main man, Vince G." She shook her head slowly as she studied the pictures. "What happened to those fiery red locks of yours, Vince? And those glasses, my, my. But even those new tortoiseshell frames can't hide those cold dead eyes. . . ."

She looked through the other photos of Derek, Marian, and Connie.

"This all his work?" Miranda folded the photos together, as neatly as a deck of cards.

Sean nodded. "We believe it is."

340   MARIAH STEWART

"All right, then." She handed the stack to Sean. "What's the plan?"

Anne Marie brought Miranda up to date on the theories that had been tossed around and the discussion they'd been having on where to go from here.

"*Strangers on a Train,* eh?" Miranda sat back in her chair and ran the concept through her mind. "I can see that. And actually, it's the only thing that makes any sense. It would explain why Channing went after the judge and Vince's mother-in-law, why he was trying so hard to get to Mara. And then we have Vince going after people who had pissed off Lowell. So do we have three players, not two? Channing, Giordano, and Lowell?"

"It looks that way, doesn't it? But we haven't been able to figure out when and where they would have been alone together to have worked this out," Sean pointed out.

"Maybe we never will. I think the important thing right now is getting our hands on Vince." Miranda glanced at Evan. "Before he gets his hands on your sister. And guys, I hate to say it, but Annie is right on. The only way you are going to get this creep to crawl out from the rock he's hiding under is if he thinks he's going to get Amanda."

"I don't like this." Sean shook his head. "I don't like the idea of putting Amanda in harm's way."

Miranda studied his face, knew there was more there than a cop being worried about a potential victim.

She put her hand on Sean's arm. "We can do this in a way that appears that we're putting her out there, but of course she won't be alone for a minute."

"Won't he figure that out?" Evan asked the obvious.

"Not if we do this right," she told him.

"Maybe Amanda should be part of this conversation, then," Sean suggested. "If we're going to be using her as bait, she should at least have a say in this."

"I agree. Can we get her over here?" Anne Marie asked.

"I am not happy about this," Evan muttered.

"Neither am I." Sean's fingers played with a corner of the folder. "But I have to reluctantly agree with Anne Marie and Miranda. Unless we can come up with another way to get him to come to us, I don't think we have a choice. We're either going to get him now, or he's going to slip between our fingers. As much as I don't like the thought of him coming near Amanda, I like even less the thought of her living with that threat of him in the back of her mind. If we come up with a plan that's doable, and Amanda agrees to it, I say we go with it."

"Okay, then. We all agree." Miranda looked around the table. "Any ideas on exactly how we're going to do this?"

"How about this?" Sean was the first to speak up. "We get Bob Benson—he's the chief down in Carleton—to make a big deal out of having a suspect in the Connie Paschall murder. But he'll refer to him as Vinnie Daniels, not Vince Giordano, and say that he's a suspect in Derek England's murder as well, since the same gun was used. He'd expect us to figure that out. Anyone who watches enough cop shows on TV knows that bullets can be matched through a national database. We'll have a police sketch done, maybe one that only looks vaguely like him, so that maybe he feels a little more confident. We'll say he's been traced to another area—"

"Say the FBI has tracked him to New York or some damned place," Miranda suggested. "He'll expect us to be in on this."

"Won't he wonder why we don't know who he really is? He has to know there are fingerprints on file that will match with prints from his room and from Dolores's house," Anne Marie said.

"I think he's going to wait to see if that connection is made, and when it isn't, he's going to think that proves he's smarter than some small-town police department," Sean told them.

"He's not that stupid." Evan shook his head.

Anne Marie smiled. "But I think he is that arrogant."

"You might be right about that, Anne Marie." Sean sat back in his seat. "I handled my first homicide investigation when I was in West Virginia. A chimney sweep had murdered and robbed several of his customers. A veteran detective told me to give him a few days and we'd find him walking down a main street in broad daylight, because he really fancied himself to be so much smarter than the police that he thought they'd never catch him even if he was right under their nose."

"And of course he was picked up on a main street in broad daylight?" Evan asked.

"Sunday afternoon, strolling along through the town park. He was totally shocked when he was taken down."

"So maybe Giordano will believe that we're too stupid to figure out that he and Vinnie Daniels are the same person. Or at the very least that we haven't figured it out yet. I'm sure he thinks that eventually someone will make the connection," Miranda said.

"So we have to move fast, as fast as we think he's going to move." Sean contemplated the options. "How about this? We let Amanda move back into the house. Make it look as if she's alone . . ."

"But of course she won't be." Miranda nodded.

"Right. Now, he's been looking for her. He knows she hasn't been around. So it follows that he's going to be watching her house, waiting for her to come back. So we'll put her car right out there in the drive, we'll turn a lot of lights on. We'll have her coming and going in and out of the house . . ."

"So that if he is watching, he's going to be seeing a lot of her. He'll see her moving about the house at night. He won't be able to resist going for her," Anne Marie noted thoughtfully.

"How long do you think it'll take before he makes his move?" Evan asked.

"If he's watching her? No more than seventy-two hours," Anne Marie stated. "Maybe he'll only watch that first day, see what's going on. He's going to want to make sure no one is there with her and that the surveillance has been terminated. Miranda, you're going to have to be way under the radar, and Sean, we'll have to figure out how to get you in and out without being seen. Amanda's going to have to make it obvious that she's gone back to her old routine. My guess is he'll come after her on the third night. Definitely no later than the fourth," Anne Marie said.

"You're the expert on behavior," Evan said. "I hope he behaves the way you think he will."

"He will. This guy has a huge ego. He's going to believe that he has beaten you because he just *knows* he's smarter than you are. He's going to believe that you are convinced that he's left town, because that is what your common criminal would do. But a smart guy like Vince, well, he's not going to do what the average guy would do, which is to continue to lay low. Uh-uh. He won't be able to resist going after her in her own home. That's going to appeal to him bigtime. Like all the surveillance hasn't meant a damned thing—he can do what he wants with her. With the spotlight supposedly off him, he'll think he's outsmarted you again."

"Maybe we should let him see her move back in, but have a clear police presence around for a day or two," Miranda suggested. "You know, a cruiser in the driveway twenty-four/seven for the first thirty-six hours or so."

"To frustrate him." Annie nodded. "I like it. We flaunt her, make him itchy to get her."

"Then we pull the cars and the obvious surveillance . . ."

"And once he thinks no one is watching her anymore, he's not going to be able to wait any longer. He'll think she's a sitting duck."

"Except this little ducky will have a few surprises under its little wing." Miranda grinned.

Annie rolled her eyes and laughed.

"When do we start?" Sean asked, not in the mood for jokes.

"No time like the present," Miranda told him. "We start first thing in the morning."

"You know, I just thought of something." Anne

Marie's eyebrows knit together. "If Channing's victims were all people who had pissed off Giordano, and Giordano's victims have all had some connection to Lowell . . ."

She seemed to wrestle with a thought for a moment, before asking, "Doesn't it follow that once he's out of prison, Lowell is going to be going after someone connected to Curt Channing?"

The thought surged around them like a sudden gust of wind. Finally, Sean stacked his papers and stood up. "One step at a time. Let's get Vince Giordano first, then we'll worry about what Archer Lowell might be up to."

At two the following afternoon, Chief Robert Benson called a press conference, at which time he announced that they had identified one Vinnie Daniels as the killer of Connie Paschall. Further, he continued, the bullet used to kill Paschall was fired from the same gun used in the shooting of a Broeder antiques dealer. He displayed a hastily sketched drawing of the dark-haired Vinnie Daniels, then mentioned that the FBI had already tracked Daniels into upstate New York. It was believed that the suspect was heading toward Canada.

Vince laughed out loud and turned up the volume on the television in the living room of the late Derek England. He wasn't sure where Derek's friend Clark was, but it hardly mattered. Vince wasn't worried about him. He knew he could take him blindfolded and with one arm tied behind his back. He knew it could be risky, coming back to Broeder so soon, but he couldn't think of anyplace else to go. When he left for good, he didn't want to leave any unfinished business behind him, and that meant Amanda Crosby.

Damn, but it would annoy the hell out of him if he wasn't able to finish his task, as he now thought of it. Curtis had left a loose thread—he hadn't managed to take out Mara Douglas—but that was okay. Vince didn't hold it against Curtis, didn't see it as a failure on Curt's part. After all, he had rid the world of Vince's pain in the ass ex-mother-in-law and that bitch judge, hadn't he? Curtis had done just fine, and Vince would get Mara himself, sooner or later. He wasn't in any big hurry.

But he did want to take care of this last bit of business. He would do so with pleasure.

This one wasn't going to be a quickie with the old gun to the head. And it wasn't going to be a quick slash and slice, either.

He was going to savor his date with Amanda. She was young and beautiful and would put up one hell of a fight.

He liked a little fight in his women.

All along, he'd figured his best bet was taking her in her own home. He'd studied the house, knew how to get in and out without being seen, knew which of the stairs squeaked and how many steps there were between the top of the stairs and her bed. He'd had that all figured out. He knew just what he wanted to do to Amanda, and all along, he'd been determined to do it in her own bed.

He wondered where she'd been staying. He'd not seen hide nor hair of her, and God knew he'd been watching. Every day he set out ostensibly to go to work with his nonexistent construction crew on his made-up jobs and instead headed straight for Broeder. He'd seen the CLOSED UNTIL FURTHER NOTICE sign on her shop the time or two he'd stopped out there. He'd parked on the road that ran parallel to Amanda's street and strolled around the lake to the woods that backed up to her property. He knew the path that led directly to her back fence and which limb of which tree gave him the best view into her bedroom, but he hadn't caught a glimpse of her. He felt she would have stayed in the area, and he'd even walked around downtown Broeder a time or two, hoping to catch sight of her. But he hadn't seen her anywhere. He was starting to wonder if she'd left town.

Maybe now that the FBI had announced that he was on his way toward Canada, wouldn't she be coming back home, get her shop open again? Sure she would. She'd impressed him as the take-charge type. She wouldn't stay in hiding any longer than necessary.

He switched off the television and went into the kitchen, where he opened a can of soup and heated it on the stove. He ate it standing up, looking out the big picture window that opened onto a garden that was tidy and colorful, even this late in the season. He left the bowl on the table, then hesitated, thinking that if Clark were to return while he was gone, maybe he'd figure out that someone had been there and would most certainly call the police. Why take that chance?

Vince rinsed and dried everything he'd used, then put it all back where he'd found it. He stood in the doorway and looked around. No one would even know he'd been there. Which was just as well, since he might be back again later tonight.

He closed the door behind him and hopped down the back steps. Lucky for him that the property sat at the farthest point of the dead-end street, where no one would see the car he'd stolen on his way out of Carleton. He knew he'd have to dump it, and the sooner the better. If he needed to return here later, he'd pick up something else and hot-wire it, drive it to within a couple of blocks, ditch it, and walk back. He knew this neighborhood well enough, knew the house well, too. After all, it had served him well for a time while Derek and his friend were on vacation.

It was almost starting to feel like home.

CHAPTER TWENTY-NINE

"HOW ARE YOU HOLDING UP?" SEAN PEERED INTO THE living room where Amanda sat curled up on the sofa with a book in her lap.

"That's the third time you asked." She looked up and smiled. "I'm still fine."

"I'm amazed that you're so calm."

"Well, so far nothing's happened. It's easy to be calm when there's nothing going on. Besides, it's the end of the second day, and things have been really quiet. Makes me think that maybe old Vince really is headed toward Canada."

"Annie thinks we'll know before another forty-eight hours has passed." He walked into the room and stood near the end of the sofa but did not sit. Instead, he walked to the window and looked out as the sun faded on day two.

"You think he's out there," Amanda said. It was not a question.

"Yeah. Maybe not at this particular minute, but he's been out there, and he'll be back. I can almost feel the tension."

"I don't feel anything but chilled right about now."

"How about if I make a fire?" he turned and asked.

"I noticed some wood out near the garage. Want me to bring some in and get a little fire going?"

"That would be really nice, though I can do that myself, you know."

"No doubt." He grinned. "But you just sit. This one's on me."

It took Sean less than five minutes to gather some kindling from the yard and bring in a few logs. He stacked them on the hearth while he opened the flue and arranged the kindling.

"Did Miranda say what time she'd be back?" he asked without turning around.

"She made some comment about my pantry being more bare than Old Mother Hubbard's and she needed some junk food if she was expected to make it through the next few days, so she was going to stop at the supermarket. I think she said something about stopping to pick up a few things to read at the bookstore, too." She shifted in her seat. "You know, tomorrow you all are supposed to make a big deal about leaving me alone here. I think she wants to make certain that she has something to do while she waits for Vince to make his move."

"The idea is for him not to realize how many of us are in here now, so that he won't know how many are left behind when the cars are gone."

"Are you going to stay?" She closed the book she'd been reading. "Will you be here tomorrow night?"

"Yes." He stacked three logs on the grate, then turned around to look at her. "You don't really think I'm going to be leaving, do you?"

"I was just wondering. I mean, I know Miranda will be here. I was hoping you'd stay, too."

"You thinking about the logistics? How the whole thing is going to work?"

She nodded.

"I'll leave by that small side door early in the morning, while it's still dark, stick close to the hedge, walk up a few blocks, then Dana will pick me up. Miranda, of course, will stay here with you during the day." He rolled up a few pieces of newspaper and stuffed them under the logs. "Then after it gets dark tomorrow night, I'll come back in the same way."

"Can't he do the same thing?" Amanda frowned. "Sneak in through the hedges?"

"If he does, he'll never make it to the door." Sean lit the match and held it to the papers until the flame caught. "We'll have two officers there around the clock. We're hoping to get him inside the house, though."

"Why? What difference does it make where you get him, as long as you get him?"

"We want to show intent. Plus, if he's arrested in your house, it will help us when we have to state probable cause to bring charges against Lowell for conspiracy."

"You think you'll be able to make that case?"

"I'll do my damnedest. I don't want him back out on the street. I think we'd be putting three unsuspecting souls in danger." He used the bellows to fan the flame until the logs began to burn.

"Because of the conspiracy thing? Because he might be planning on killing someone for this Channing?"

Sean nodded.

"Remember how Archer reacted when he saw the photos of Derek and Marian and Connie Paschall?

He went absolutely gray," she reminded him. "I wonder if he is capable of killing anyone."

"You're kidding, right? This is the same guy who came after you, beat you up. . . ."

"Oh, I remember, all right." She nodded grimly. "But Archer attacking me was very personal. And for the record, if he'd wanted to, he could have killed me very easily. This other thing, though, I don't know. I just don't see him going to the trouble of killing people he doesn't even know."

"Well, it won't be easy convincing a judge, I know that much. Since we have no real evidence, it's all speculation."

"Guess there's no chance Archer would admit to being involved with Channing and Giordano?"

He snorted. "About as much chance as there is that Giordano will admit knowing Lowell and Channing. I don't see it happening."

She thought about it for a while, then said, "You wouldn't even know who to warn, would you? I mean, if Lowell got out of prison and really did intend to kill someone?"

"It would most likely be three someones." Sean replaced the fire screen and stood up, stretching the stiffness from his right knee. "So far, we've figured out three victims or potential victims for Channing and Giordano. If we're correct in our assumption that Lowell is tied into this, too, we could expect him to be going after three people. And no. We wouldn't know who to warn."

"Lowell will never do it." Amanda shook her head. "He's too cowardly."

"I hope you're right." Sean sat next to her on the sofa.

"You can't keep him in prison on supposition alone."

"Probably not. But filing charges would make him understand that we know what's going on and that we'll be watching him."

"How would you watch him? Would you ask the FBI to do that? What if he left the area?"

"I've already thought of that. The FBI will be put on alert, and we'd keep track of where he's gone and what he's doing through his probation officer."

"Assuming that you catch Giordano, what are the chances he'll confess and tell you about the conspiracy?"

"None." Sean shook his head. "I'd bet my life on it. If he's going to go down on someone else's behalf, you can damn well be sure that he's going to want the whole thing played out."

Amanda stared at the fire for a few minutes. When she looked away, she found that Sean was staring at her.

"What?" She prodded his ribs and he caught her hand in his.

"I was just wondering if you'd . . . well, if you'd been married before. Engaged, whatever."

"Never married. Came close once, though," she acknowledged. "And almost close one time before that."

"What happened?" he asked, mindful of the little stab of jealousy that poked at his ribs.

"Just didn't work out. Not to make light of it, but that's pretty much it. When it came right down to it, neither time felt completely right. Something just seemed to be missing. How 'bout you?"

"Not really. There was a girl I met while I was in the service—her sister was engaged to a friend of mine—and we spent a lot of time together. It almost worked out."

"But . . . ?"

"Well, as you said. It didn't feel completely right."

He put his arm around her and drew her closer. "This, however, feels right. Completely."

He leaned down and kissed her upturned face, tugged playfully at her bottom lip before getting down to the business of kissing her seriously. Her mouth was wet and warm and opened to his at just the right moment. His tongue traced her mouth before sliding inside, and she leaned back against the sofa, taking him with her. She twisted under his weight, and he eased himself alongside her, his lips never leaving hers. He felt like he was drowning, and he was loving every second of it.

"More," she whispered when she thought he was about to stop, and he covered her mouth again, assuring her that he had no intention of stopping.

His hands slid the length of her torso and back to her waist, once, twice, three times. She pulled her shirt out from the waistband of her jeans and began to unbutton it, bringing his hands to her flesh. His lips trailed from the curve of her mouth to her chin, to her throat, where they began a slow descent to her collarbone.

"He can't have you," Sean whispered as his hands claimed the soft flesh of her breasts. "He'll have to kill me to get to you, Amanda. He can't have you. . . ."

She leaned her head back as she undid the last button, urging his mouth lower. His lips made a hot trail across her skin, and she arched her back as the warmth spread through her with each passing second. She moved lower on the sofa, so that she was fully on her back. Sean's long body was just about to cover hers, when through a fog of tension and desire they heard the back door slam.

"Honeys, I'm home," Miranda sang from the kitchen, "and I have lots of goodies."

Paper bags rustled in the other room.

"Hey, Amanda, are you here? I could use some help with the grocery bags, if you have a minute."

"I'm here." Amanda made a face as she pushed Sean off, sat up, and began to hastily rebutton her blouse. "I'll be there in a minute."

Swearing gruffly, Sean gritted his teeth. "Damn feds . . ."

"Maybe it's too soon," Amanda whispered in the darkness. "Maybe he'll wait a few more days."

"He's already been held at bay for two days. Anne Marie thinks he won't be able to hold out past tonight."

Sean still didn't like the idea of Giordano coming into Amanda's house, contaminating it with his presence, but it was too late to think about that now. "The patrol car and the guards left this morning, just as we planned. If Anne Marie knows what she's talking about—and your brother seems to think she does—it should be tonight."

"I think if Anne Marie told Evan that Vince Giordano was the ghost of Christmas past, he'd believe her."

"He does seem to be smitten, doesn't he?"

"*Smitten* might be a bit mild. I can't remember the last time I saw that look on his face."

"What look is that?"

"The one he gets when he looks at her."

No doubt much like the one I get when I look at you. Sean smiled to himself. Aloud, he said, "It was hard for him to leave and go back to Virginia while all this is going on."

"Well, he didn't go quietly, that's for sure. But I didn't see any reason why he should miss out on that training. Besides, I think he understands that you're not going to let anything happen to me."

"I told him I'd guard you with my life, Amanda. I meant it."

She knew he would. Just knowing that made this whole thing so much easier.

"You okay, Amanda? You know that we can always—"

"I'm fine. Stop worrying about me."

"Scared?"

"A little."

"It'll be all over after tonight?"

"I think if it isn't, Miranda is going to go stir-crazy. She's been moving around this house like a ghost all day. And she made some comment earlier about feeling like the bride of Dracula."

"What was that?" Sean tilted his head in the direction of the hall, listening, then slowly stood.

"Pipes. They always do that soft little clink thing about this time."

"You sure?"

"Positive," she whispered. "Sit down, Sean. It's going to be a long night."

"I don't think so. If he's been watching the house, he'll be along any time now. We figured an hour or two from the time the lights went off. He's going to want to come in when he thinks you're asleep, so he's going to give you some time there. He wants you totally powerless. I think Anne Marie is right on the money with this guy."

"Can we talk about something else?"

"What would you like to talk about?"

"Ramona."

He groaned softly.

"Come on, Sean, you have to admit, she—"

"Shhhhhh."

There was an indistinct sound from the first floor.

"Showtime," Sean said softly. "Don't move . . ."

The footfalls on the stairs were barely audible, but in the silent house, unmistakable. In the dark, Amanda counted. When she reached number twelve, she held her breath. Twelve steps up, just seconds from the landing to her room.

The bedroom door opened so slowly that at first she was uncertain that it had moved at all. But bit by bit, the pale, pale halo from the night-light in the hall spread dimly across the floor. Not enough to see much more than shape and shadow, but that, of course, was the whole idea.

The form moved to the bed, then stood at the side for several minutes.

Then, in a soft, seductive voice, he said, "Wake up, dream girl."

He rested one knee on the side of the mattress. One hand reached for the end of the blanket and started to pull it back.

"Uncle Vince has something for you, baby."

"Baby has something for you, too, Uncle Vince."

The hard muzzle of Sean's gun pressed up against the back of Vince's head, dead center, and Vince froze.

The lights went on overhead as Miranda stepped into the room, her gun drawn.

Amanda stepped out of the closet.

"What the fuck . . ." Vince looked down at the shape on the bed.

Amanda pulled back the covers on the mannequin that lay facedown on her pillow. "Well, hey, would you look at that? Uncle Vince's dream girl is a real dummy."

CHAPTER
THIRTY

"You look as tired as I feel," Amanda told Sean as he parked the Jeep in front of Greer's house and got out. She'd arrived only moments earlier.

"You should be tired," he said, then amended that to, "We should both be tired. Up half the night waiting for Giordano, up the rest of the night and all day today writing reports."

"You were writing reports," she corrected him. "I was giving statements."

"Close enough. You sure you want to have dinner here? I'm sure Greer would understand if you wanted to go home and catch some sleep. I'm sure she has no idea what you've been through these past four days."

"I'm okay, except for the fatigue, and we all have that. Besides, I had to come by to pick up some things I left in the guest room. It was nice of Greer to invite me over for dinner, though."

"You know how she is. She's gotta be the momma-hen."

"After the past four days of no sleep and practically no real food, I'm thrilled at the prospect of a real meal. Lunch today consisted of half a bag of Cheetos—which I had to split with Miranda—and a package of peanut butter crackers from the vending machine in the lobby of the municipal building."

"Well, we know we'll do better than that here. Let's go on inside, have a great meal, and chat with Steven and Greer." He paused. "You sure you want to sleep in your house tonight? It still looks like a crime scene, with that tape and all."

"I'll be fine." She wasn't sure she would be able to get much sleep, all things considered, but she'd been thinking about it all afternoon and was trying to look on it as just one more challenge to be met.

Sean took Amanda's hand in his and walked with her up to the back of the house, their arms swinging between them, their hips hitting once or twice. When they got to the back door, Sean reached around Amanda to push it open, and she turned, looking up.

"I seem to remember being right here in this spot not too long ago," she said. "And you reached around me, just like that, to open the door. And then you—"

"Then I leaned down like this, and kissed you, like this. . . ." He did just that.

"No, I think it was more like this. . . ." Amanda put her arms around his neck and tugged his head down gently.

"I think you might be right." He nibbled at the corner of her mouth. "As a matter of fact, now that I think about it—"

Greer opened the door. "Sean, is that—" It was a toss-up between who was more startled.

"Oh. Well. Sorry . . ." she said, and promptly closed the door.

"Thanks, Greer." He laughed good-naturedly and

murmured into Amanda's ear, "Way to ruin the moment."

"Guess we might as well go in," Amanda told him.

"Might as well. Now that she knows we're here and what we were doing, she's going to be timing us." Sean pushed open the door and permitted Amanda to precede him into the warm house.

"Hey, Steven. How was the trip?" he called to Greer's husband, who was just walking into the kitchen.

"Good, good. Hey, way to go, Sean. Solving the crimes, putting that Giordano back in prison where he belongs, keeping the people of our little town safe." Greer's amiable husband spoke like the political animal he was. "You sure did make us proud."

"Thanks. I'm just glad it's over. It's been tough for everyone involved," Sean told him as he opened the oven door and peeked in, thinking that he had been right. Neither Greer nor her husband had a clue of what had really been at stake last night. "Something smells really good."

"Get out of there." Greer smacked him on the back with a dish towel as she came into the kitchen.

"What can I do to help?" Amanda asked.

"I was just about to set the table. Maybe you could take care of that while I finish up in here."

"Sean, hand me that stack of plates." Amanda reached for them as he passed them to her.

"It's already after seven," Greer noted as Amanda carried the plates into the dining room. "You both must be starving after the day you two had."

"I could eat." Sean grinned. "I guess Amanda could, too."

"I'm really proud of you, Sean." Greer turned the flame down under a pan at the back of the stove. "You did such a fine thing. I'm just . . . well, proud."

"Thank you, Greer. I appreciate that."

"I kept watching the coverage on the television this morning, and I kept thinking, 'That's my little Sean. He's a hero.' "

"If anyone's a hero, it's Amanda. She permitted herself to be used as the bait to catch Giordano," Sean said as he filled his arms with empty water glasses and headed toward the dining room. "She's the one you should save your praise for."

"Well, I am proud of her, too, of course I am." Greer turned her back to the door and began to shred lettuce for the salad. "I know having to stay away from her house, having to practically live with a stranger all week long, has been a terrible strain for Amanda."

"It never felt like living with a stranger, Greer," Amanda said.

Greer turned around. "Oh, I thought you were Sean."

"He sent me in for the flatware."

"You know where to find it." Greer pointed to the drawer next to the sink.

"It was good of you to take me in. I don't think I really thanked you for making me feel at home."

"It was my pleasure. I'm glad I was able to help."

"So am I." Amanda counted out the forks, knives, teaspoons.

"I can't imagine what it must have been like to know that someone like that terrible man was after you. You must have been very frightened."

"I'd be lying if I said I wasn't. But somehow I knew

that Sean would be smarter than Vince was."
Amanda took four napkins from the next drawer. "At
least I hoped he would be."

"Sean wouldn't have let anything happen to you.
He cares too much about you."

"It's his job, Greer. I don't think it mattered who I
was."

Greer looked about ready to say something else
when Sean came into the room.

"Greer, that chicken has to be about done by now,
because I'm about ready to pass out from hunger."

"Everything is ready," she told him. "Now, you
two go on in and sit down. Sean, you get Steve away
from that damned television and bring him to the
table, would you?"

At eight-ten, the doorbell rang.

"I'll get it." Steve placed his napkin on the table
next to his plate and pushed back his chair.

"Were you expecting anyone?" Greer asked.

"Beverly mentioned she'd drop off the minutes of
last night's council meeting for me to look over," he
said as he went into the hall.

"Beverly is the borough secretary," Greer explained
to Amanda.

Voices drifted in from the hall. As they moved
closer, Sean recognized the new voice as belonging to
Ramona. He rubbed a hand across his chin, wondering if Greer had set this up, mildly annoyed at the
thought that she might have. He looked over to meet
Amanda's eyes across the table, but she was looking
up, ready to greet the newcomer. He felt obligated to
do the same.

"Honey," Steve said as he led Ramona into the room, "you have a visitor."

"Well, Ramona." Greer put her fork down on her plate. "This is a surprise."

"I'm sorry, I'm interrupting your dinner." Ramona blushed scarlet. "I should have called first. It's just that . . ."

"Steve, pull that chair over for Ramona. Have you had dinner? I can make you a plate. . . ." Greer started to stand, and Ramona shook her head.

"No, no. I don't want to be a bother. And I've already eaten."

"Coffee, then?"

"Sure. That's nice of you. Thank you." Ramona sat on the edge of the chair Steven brought in for her. She brushed a long strand of red hair back from her face and looked at Sean. "I didn't know you'd be here. Sorry to intrude, Sean."

"Guess someone must have stolen my Jeep, then. I left it parked out front."

"I meant, I didn't know that you were here until I pulled up in front of the house. I had wanted to talk to Greer before I spoke with you. . . ."

"I can always leave."

"Sean, would you please sit back down and just stop it." Greer carried a pot of coffee in one hand and a cup and saucer in the other. She placed both in front of Ramona, then took her own seat.

"I saw you on television this morning," Ramona said to Sean. "It was amazing, what you did. And you." She turned to Amanda. "You were so brave."

"Not so very brave at all. I was hiding in my closet." Amanda smiled, trying to turn the conversation from Sean, who had made no attempt to hide his feelings at Ramona's arrival. "And Sean was in the room with a gun, and there was a well-armed FBI agent in the guest room across the hall."

"I wouldn't have even been there, if I'd thought that crazy man was going to come into my house with the intention of killing me." Ramona shivered.

"Okay. We all agree that Amanda is brave." Sean rested his fork and knife across the top of his dinner plate. "Now why don't you tell us why you're here."

"Sean, you're being rude," Greer admonished him.

"No, he's right." Ramona looked up at Sean with all the warmth he'd been giving her.

"You two look alike, you know that?" Steve said. "Except for her having red hair. You have the same eyes, the same nose—"

"Steven." Greer shot him a look that shut him up.

"Now, Ramona, if something's happened . . ."

"Oh, something's happened, all right." She took a deep breath. "I found Veronica."

"You found . . ." Greer's eyes widened.

"Yes. I found our mother." She looked from Greer to Sean, then back again. "Well, I found her grave, anyway."

"How did you find her?" Amanda asked.

Ramona turned to her. "Internet search."

"How did you manage to do that? I mean, I've been searching for months. . . ." Greer looked thunder-struck.

"When I couldn't find any match for a Veronica Mercer who could have been our mother, I started looking up Veronica Michaels, her maiden name. I finally found a match with Veronica Michaels Keenan."

"Keenan?" Sean asked.

"She apparently remarried about three years after she gave me up."

"Where . . . where is she buried?" Greer asked softly.

"She's in a small cemetery down in West Clearbrook."

"I don't want to know about this." Sean pushed back from the table.

"I want to know, Sean." Greer put her hand out to stop him from leaving. "I want to know everything."

"Why would you care, after all these years? The woman abandoned you, Greer. She abandoned us, walked away from us"—he glanced at Ramona—"from all three of us—and apparently never looked back."

"I guess I want to understand, Sean. I guess I want to know why she left us, and where she went after she did. Did she have another family, did she—"

"Leave me out of it, then," he said abruptly. "I don't want any part of it. The past is just that. Let's leave it there."

"I can't do that, sweetie," Greer told him softly, her eyes pleading with him to stay, to understand, to open his heart and his mind.

"You two are on your own, then." He headed for the door. "Amanda, I'll talk to you tomorrow. I'm going to need you to sign your statements."

His back stiff with what everyone recognized as a heavy burden of pain, Sean walked out the back door and closed it softly behind him.

* * *

It was close to eleven when Amanda parked her car across the street from Sean's house. She sat alone in the dark for several minutes, then got out and walked up to his front door and knocked.

"Amanda," he said when he opened the door. "What are you doing here?"

"I saw the lights on, so I figured you were still awake."

"I was just about to turn them off."

"May I come in?"

He stepped aside to let her enter.

She looked around for a minute, then said, "I'll take the ottoman, you can have the chair."

She moved a stack of newspapers from the ottoman to the floor, then patted the seat of the chair and said, "Come sit down, Sean, and talk to me."

"Did Greer send you over here?" He stood, hands on his hips, near the door, which still stood open.

"No. I came because I wanted to. I wanted your company. I wanted to talk. I was hoping you'd want to talk to me."

"What would you like to talk about?" He closed the door behind him.

"I know how you must feel about your mother—"

"No, you don't know, Amanda," he said flatly as he lowered his tall frame into the chair.

"I think you probably feel pretty much the same way about her as I feel about my mother." She paused. "Did I tell you about my mother, about her other family?"

"You told me she'd remarried and you had half siblings."

"My mother has four children with her second husband. When I talk to her, that's what she talks about. How beautiful her daughters are, how brilliant. What excellent athletes her sons are. What perfect grandchildren they've given her." She bit her bottom lip. "My mother can't remember my birth date and hasn't sent Evan a Christmas card in years. It's as if we don't exist."

"I'm sorry, Amanda, but it really isn't the same."

"In a way, it is," she insisted. "I have siblings that I don't know, don't want to know, because they have a place in her life that I will never have. Because she loves them in a way she will never love me."

"She didn't abandon you when you were a very young child, Amanda," he pointed out.

"No, she didn't. She waited until I was in my teens."

"Do you have good memories of her from your childhood?"

"I do." She tried to smile. "Oddly enough, at one time, we were a happy family."

"Maybe she wasn't as happy as you thought. Maybe she only really became happy when she divorced your father and married her second husband."

"Maybe." She crossed her legs and rested her elbow on a raised knee, cupped her chin in her hand. "Oh, I'm sure that was it. She just didn't have to make it so damned obvious that Evan and I were part of the bad baggage she was only too happy to leave behind."

"Did you live with your father then?"

"We did. Through his second and third marriages, then we both went to college."

"You still talk to your dad?"

"Sometimes. Not the way I wish I could talk to him, or the way I wish I could talk to my mother, though." She brushed away the tears. "I don't know why I'm telling you this. I hadn't planned on talking about me."

"I'm glad you did." He reached out and took her by the wrist, pulled her into his lap and just held her.

"Well, this is pretty pathetic, wouldn't you say?" she tried to joke. "Talk about your dysfunctional families. There's not one solid parent figure between the two of us."

"And yet we're both pretty solid, responsible people," he told her. "How do you suppose that happened?"

"Some people just have something inside. You just want to be better than what you could have been."

"That might be it." He held on to her, feeling her soft breath against his throat.

"Do you think it's possible to overcome all that, to move beyond it all and be truly happy, to fall in love?"

He didn't respond at first. Then finally his fingers tightened on hers, and he said, "I think it's not only possible, I think it's necessary. I think in the end, we all want to believe the future will be better than the past. You just have to be willing to take a chance, you know? Roll the dice and go with it."

They sat in silence for a very long time.

Finally, she pushed herself up wearily and said, "I'm falling asleep. I have to get home."

"I think you're too tired to drive," he said, his lips brushing the side of her face. "I think you should stay here."

"Oh, let me guess." She grinned, sitting up and making a point out of looking around the sparsely furnished house. "His and hers sleeping bags here at Camp Mercer?"

"Hey, I have a bed." He tried to look wounded.

"Right. One of those inflatable mattress things, I'll bet. Now, do you have the kind you blow up with a bicycle pump, or the kind that inflates itself?"

"Why don't you come on upstairs and find out?" With one motion, he picked her up, rose from the chair, and swung her over his shoulder.

"Looks like I'm about to do just that . . ." She laughed as he headed toward the steps.

Amanda closed her eyes and held on to the moment. Maybe, just maybe, Sean was right. Maybe the future could be better than the past.

She was more than willing to roll the dice.

Vince Giordano sat on the edge of the hard wooden seat, his hands cuffed behind him, and looked around the infirmary where he was about to have his intake physical. He had spent an hour with his lawyer that morning, then spent the rest of the day facing reality.

This time, there would be no reprieve.

No one was coming to step forward with proof that a member of the law enforcement team that brought him in had planted evidence or had lied in their report. After all, half the Broeder police department had been at Crosby's house—plus that hot FBI agent—when he'd been taken down.

Not even a chance of crying police brutality. He didn't have a mark on him. They'd barely touched him.

Well, that was that. He'd had a good run, hadn't he? And he'd come *this close* to his final target. He wondered if Channing had felt this same sense of letdown when he'd realized that that last target had eluded him.

And he wondered if Archer Lowell would do even as well, if he'd be equal to the task. He wondered if Archer Lowell would even try.

Well, shit, this was all his idea. He damn well better try. He damn well better succeed. He owes Curtis Channing. He owes me....

It occurred to Vince that Lowell should be getting out pretty soon. His sentence must be nearly up by now.

He damn well better keep the trust.

Vince grew agitated just thinking about all that Channing had done for Vince, all that Vince had done for Lowell.

Well, there was nothing he could do about it now. He was in High Meadow, and was going to stay in High Meadow for the rest of his natural life. Unless, of course, he got the death penalty. Pennsylvania was, after all, a death penalty state, wasn't it?

Soon Lowell would be out, and Vince would bet every last dollar he had stashed away in the wall of the old barn that Lowell was not going to give a second thought to him or to Channing once he walked out of here.

Sure. His dirty work had already been done for him. What did he care about honoring Channing's memory by taking care of his business? What did he care about keeping a sacred promise?

Damn, but Vince was really beginning to steam.

A shadow passed the door, then paused.

"Vince? That you? Vince Giordano?" A dark head poked through the doorway.

"Who's that?" Vince looked up and recognized the man who had at one time occupied the cell next to his. "Hey, Burt-man. How's it going, man?"

"Goin' good." The head bobbed up and down. "Couldn't be better. I'm on my way outta here. I am done with this place, man."

"Your time is up?"

"As of today. Honest to God, there were times I thought this day would never come."

"That's good, man. I'm glad for you. Got a whole life out there."

Burt laughed ruefully. "Yeah, well, some life. I been in here nearly thirteen years. My wife divorced me while I was in here, remarried, moved someplace, no one told me where. Took my kids. I got no job and a zilch-o chance of finding one, no education, no money. But at least I will be out there." He paused and looked past Vince. "Out there and outta here."

"So you got no plans . . . ?"

"Only plans I got are for a few cold beers and a few hot women." He shrugged. "After that, who knows."

"Burt," a voice from the hall called out. "Get back in here. You shouldn't be talking to him. He's going into isolation."

"What are you gonna do to me, Ralphie boy? Suspend my exercise privileges? I ain't hurting no one." He turned back to Vince. "Just waiting for the nurse to come back and sign my clearance, and then I'm hitting the first bar I come to. I been dreaming about that beer for weeks now."

He started to move back out the door. "Well, good seeing you, Vince. Maybe we'll run into each other one of these days, out there."

"There ain't gonna be no 'out there' for me." Vince shook his head.

"Not this time, eh?"

"I'm afraid my luck has run out."

"Yeah, well. Sorry to hear that, you know? You take care, Vince."

"Burt-man."

The man turned and looked back over his shoulder.

"You always impressed me as being a stand-up guy."

"Thanks, Vince. I appreciate that."

"You a guy who understands what honor among thieves means, Burt-man?"

"Hey, I been in here a long time, man. I know what it means to be able to trust someone to watch your back. That what you're talking about?"

"Yeah. That's what I meant." Vince had to think this through quickly. There was little time to make a decision. "Listen, I'm wondering if you'd do something for me when you get out there."

"What's that?" Burt-man's eyes narrowed.

Vince's voice dropped. "I'll make it worth your while."

"What do you mean?"

"I mean, I can tell you where I have cash—a whole lot of cash—stashed on the outside. Seems to me that a fellow like you, with no obvious means of support, might be able to use that cash. I'll never get to spend it." He laughed ruefully. "My lawyer has already told me that I don't have a snowball's chance in hell to get off this time, so I might as well fire him and get the court to appoint a lawyer for me. I'd rather see that money go to you than to have it found someday by some kids."

"What would I have to do?" Burt's sharp eyes sparked with interest.

"There's someone who has a job to do for me out there. I just want you to make sure he does it."

Burt came back into the room. "That's all I have to do? Make sure someone does a job for you?"

"That's all."

"Burt! Come on, man, get outta there. You're gonna get me in trouble," the guard called from the doorway.

"Get lost, Ralphie. I'll be along in a minute." Burt turned back to Giordano and lowered his voice. "And you'll tell me where this money is stashed if I just keep an eye on someone for you?"

"It's all for you, Burt-man. No one else knows it's out there. You just gotta keep this guy honest. Make sure he does what he's supposed to do. It's important to me, Burt-man. It's real important to me."

"In that case, I'm all ears, Vince." Burt-man knelt on one knee and leaned closer. "Tell me more. Tell me everything. . . ."

Read on for an exciting preview of

DEAD WRONG

by Mariah Stewart
Published by Ballantine Books
in June 2004.

OH, SURE, I HEARD THE LITTLE ONE CRYING. AND THE
*middle one, too. Only one I never heard was the
older one, the boy. They ain't lived here long—maybe
a month or so. I never saw much of them. Oh, once
in a while, I'd pass the boy on the steps. He never had
much to say. No, never saw the mother bring men
home. Never saw her much at all, though—don't
know when she came or went. Heard her sometimes,
though. God knows she was loud enough, screaming
at them kids the way she done. No, don't know what
she was doin' to 'em to make 'em cry like that. No,
never saw no social worker come around. Don't
know if the kids went to school.*

*Did I what? No, never called nobody about it.
Wasn't none of my business, what went on over there.
Hey, I got troubles of my own. . . .*

Mara Douglas rubbed her temples with the tips of
her fingers, an unconscious gesture she made when
steeped in thought or deeply upset. Reading through
the notes she'd taken while interviewing the elderly,
toothless, across-the-hall neighbor of the Feehan family,
she was at once immersed in the children's situation
and sick to her stomach. The refrain was all too familiar. The neighbors heard, the neighbors turned a

deaf ear rather than get involved. It was none of their business what a woman did to her children, none of their business if the kids had fallen through all the cracks. In neighborhoods as poor as this, all the tenants seemed to live in their own hell. Who could worry about someone else's?

Mara rested her elbow on the edge of the dining room table, her chin in the palm of her hand, and marveled how a child could survive such neglect and abuse and so often still defend the parent who had inflicted the physical and emotional pain.

Time after time, case after case, she'd seen the bond between parent and child tested, stretched to the very limit. Sometimes even years of the worst kind of abuse and neglect failed to fray that connection.

She turned her attention back to the case she was working on now. The mother's rights were being challenged by the paternal grandparents, who'd had custody of the three children—ages four, seven, and nine—for the past seven months. Mara was the court-appointed advocate for the children, the one who would speak on their behalf at all legal proceedings, the one whose primary interest—whose only interest—was the best interests of the children.

As their champion, Mara spent many hours reviewing the files provided by the social workers from the county Children and Youth Services department and medical reports from their physicians, and still more hours interviewing the social workers themselves, along with neighbors and teachers, emergency room personnel, family members, and family friends. All in an effort to determine what was best for the children, where their needs—all their needs—might best be met, and by whom.

Mara approached every case as a sacred trust, an opportunity to stand for that child as she would stand for her own. Tomorrow she would do exactly that, when she presented her report and her testimony to the judge who would determine whether Kelly Feehan's parental rights should be terminated and custody of her three children awarded to their deceased father's parents. It probably wouldn't be too tough a call.

Kelly, an admitted prostitute and heroin addict, had watched her world begin to close in on her after her fifth arrest for solicitation. Her nine-year-old had stayed home from school to take care of his siblings until Kelly could make bail. Unfortunately for Kelly, her former in-laws, who had been searching for the children for months while their mother had moved them from one low-rent dive to another, had finally tracked them down. The Feehans had called the police. Their next move had been to take temporary custody of the children, who were found bruised, battered, and badly malnourished.

Over time, it became apparent that Kelly wasn't doing much to rehabilitate herself. She'd shown up high on two of her last three visitation days, and the grandparents had promptly filed a petition to terminate Kelly's parental rights permanently. Total termination of parental rights was a drastic step, one never made lightly nor without a certain amount of angst and soul searching.

Mara knew all too well the torment of losing a child.

In the end, of course, the decision would rest in the hands of Judge McKettrick, whom Mara knew from experience was always reluctant to sever a parent's rights when the parent contested as vehemently as Kelly Feehan had. Much would depend on the information brought to the court in the morning. The responsibility to present everything fairly, without judgment or embellishment, was one that Mara took very seriously.

With the flick of her finger, the screen of Mara's laptop went blank, then filled with the image of a newborn snuggled up against a shoulder covered by a yellow and white hospital gown. The infant's hair was little more than pale fuzz, the eyes closed in slumber, the perfect rosebud mouth puckered just so.

Another flick of a finger, and the image was gone.

Mara's throat constricted with the pain of remembrance, the memories of the joy that had filled her every time she'd held that tiny body against her own. Abruptly she pushed back from the table and walked to the door.

"Spike," she called, and from the living room came the unmistakable sound of a little dog tail thumping on hard wood. "It's time to go for a walk."

Spike knew *walk,* but not *time,* which was just as well, since it was past one in the morning. But once the thorn of memory began to throb, Mara had to work it out of her system. Her conditioned response to emotional pain was physical. Any kind of sustained movement would do—a walk, a run, a bike ride, a trip to the gym. Anything that got her on her feet was acceptable, as long as it got her moving through the pain so that she could get past it for a while.

Mara pursued exhaustion where others might have chosen a bottle or a needle or a handful of pills, though there'd been times in the past when she'd considered those, too.

By day, Mara's neighborhood in a suburban Philadelphia college town was normally quiet, but at night, it was as silent as a tomb. She walked briskly, the soles of her walking shoes padding softly on the sidewalk, the occasional streetlamp lighting her way, Spike's little Jack Russell legs keeping pace. Four blocks down, four blocks over, and back again. That's what it usually took to clear her head. Tonight she made the loop in record time. She still had work to do, and an appointment in court at nine the next morning.

The evening's storm had passed through earlier, and now a full moon hung overhead and cast shadows behind her as she made her way back up the brick walk to her front door. She'd let Spike off the leash at the end of their drive and now stood watching as the dog sniffed at something in the grass.

"Spike," she whispered loudly, and the dog looked up, wagging his tail enthusiastically. "Come on, buddy. Time to go in."

With obvious reluctance, Spike left whatever it was he'd found on the lawn and followed his mistress to the front steps. Mara unlocked the front door, but did not go immediately inside. She crossed her arms and stared up at the night sky for a long moment, thinking of her own child, wondering once again where in this vast world she was at that exact moment, and who, if anyone, was standing up for her.

On the television screen, the earnest five o'clock news anchor droned on and on, his delivery as flat as his crew cut. Mara turned the volume down to answer the ringing phone.

"What's for dinner?" Mara's sister, Anne Marie, dispensed with a greeting and cut to the chase.

"I was just asking myself that very thing." Mara grinned, delighted to hear Annie's voice.

"How 'bout a little Chinese?"

"You buying?"

"And delivering."

"You're back?"

"I'm on my way."

"What time will you be here?"

"Thirty minutes, give or take. I'm just leaving the airport. If you call in an order at that little place on Dover Drive, I'll swing past and pick it up."

"Perfect. What do you want?"

"Surprise me."

"Okay. See you soon."

Pleased with the unexpected prospect of Annie's company, Mara found herself whistling while she hunted up the menu. She called in the order, then set about clearing the kitchen table of all the mail that had accumulated over the past several weeks while she had worked on the Feehan case. That case having been heard just that morning, Mara could pack up the materials she'd reviewed and return them to the courthouse in the morning. She wondered where Kelly Feehan had gone that night to drown her sorrows, her parental rights having been severed by Judge McKettrick until such time as Kelly successfully completed a rehabilitation program and obtained legitimate employment, at which time she could file for visitation rights. The odds that Kelly would follow through were slim to none, but the option was there. It had been the best the judge could do for all involved.

While the decision was clearly in the best interests of the children, it still gave Mara pause to have played a part, however small, in another mother being separated from her babies, even though she knew full well that Kelly had brought her troubles upon herself. Mara had wanted to shake the young mother, shake her good and hard, for having put herself and her children in such a situation.

You had a choice, Mara had wanted to shout at the sobbing woman as her children left the courtroom with their grandparents. *We don't all get a choice. . . .*

Mara scooped dry dog food into Spike's new Scooby-Doo dish, then gave him fresh water. She turned up the volume on the television, hoping to catch the weather forecast for the morning. She'd been looking forward to her early morning twice-weekly run with several friends and was hoping that the prediction of rain had changed.

". . . and in other news, we have a somewhat bizarre story of two women who have the same name, who lived in the same town, and who met with the same fate exactly one week apart." The anchorman spoke directly into the camera. "Jason Wrigley is standing by at the Avon County courthouse with the story."

Headlights flashing through the living room window announced Annie's arrival. Mara had just begun to head for the front door when the reporter's face appeared on the television.

"This is Mary Douglas," the reporter was saying as he displayed a picture of a white-haired woman in her early sixties.

Mara watched in fascination as he held up a second photograph of another woman years younger, with dark hair and an olive complexion, and said, "And this is Mary Douglas. What do these two women have in common besides their names?"

The reporter paused for effect, then faced the camera squarely, both photographs held in one hand, the microphone in the other.

"Both of these women lived in Lyndon. Both women were killed in their homes in that small community, in exactly the same manner, exactly one week apart. The body of the second victim was found earlier this afternoon. Local police have admitted that they are baffled as to motive."

Spike ran to the door and barked when he heard Annie's heels on the walk, but Mara's attention remained fixed on the television.

Video played of a prerecorded press conference. "Without divulging the manner in which the women were murdered, we're investigating the possibility that the first killing was an error. That the second victim may have been the intended target."

The police spokesman paused to listen to a question from the floor, then repeated the question for those who had not heard. "Do we feel it was a contract killing, was the question. I can only say at this point that anything is possible. It has been suggested that perhaps the killer had known only the name of his victim—no description, no address—and that after killing the first victim and perhaps seeing some news coverage or reading the obituary in the newspaper, he realized that he hadn't killed the right woman. According to friends and family of both victims, neither Mary Douglas had an enemy in the world. Both women were well liked, both lived somewhat quiet lives. So with no apparent motive, we can't rule out any scenario yet."

"Mara?" Annie called from the doorway.

The police spokesman's face was taut with concentration as he spoke of the murders. "Yes, we think he sought out the second Mary Douglas and killed her, though we do not know why either of these women would have been targeted, for that matter. . . ."

"Mara?"

"This is bizarre." Mara shook her head.

"What is?" Annie set the bag she carried on the coffee table.

"This news report . . ." She was still shaking her head slowly, side to side. "Two women named Mary Douglas were murdered one week apart. Killed in the same way, but the police aren't saying how they were killed."

Annie frowned.

"It's a little creepy—Mary Douglas—Mara Douglas," Mara admitted, "and what makes it worse is that there's a woman who works in the D.A.'s office named Mary Douglas."

"But she wasn't . . ." Annie pointed at the television.

"No, thank God. I was holding my breath there for a minute, though. She's such a nice person—a real ray-of-sunshine type. Friendly and a good sport. Not a day goes by when we don't get at least one piece of mail meant for the other."

"You don't work in the D.A.'s office."

"Yeah, but very often the mail room will mistake Mary for Mara or vice versa, and we get each other's mail. And if something is addressed to 'M. Douglas,' it's anyone's guess whose mailbox it ends up in." Mara watched the rest of the segment, then turned off the television. "I feel sorry for the families of the two victims, but I can't help but be relieved that the Mary Douglas I know wasn't one of them."

"Odd thing, though," Annie murmured as she pulled off her short-sleeved cardigan and tossed it onto a nearby chair. "Two victims with the same name. That can't be a coincidence. . . ."

"Intrigued?"

"Hell, yes."

"Itching to know more?"

"What do you think?" Annie carried the fragrant bags of egg foo young and chicken lo mein into the kitchen.

"Maybe you'll get a call."

"Well, it's early yet. Only two victims. Have they given out any personal information about them?"

"The first victim was a retired school librarian. Sixty-one years old, lived alone. No relatives. By all accounts a nice woman without an enemy in the world."

"And the other woman?"

"Attractive woman in her mid-fifties, two grown kids. Yoga instructor at the local YMCA. Husband died two years ago."

"Boyfriend?" Annie leaned against the door frame, her expression pensive.

"They didn't say. According to the news report, she was well-liked. Active in the community, spent a lot of time doing charity work. They haven't been able to come up with a motive for either of the killings."

"There's always a motive. Sometimes it's just harder to find. They need to do a profile on the victims."

"I was waiting for that." Mara watched her sister's face, knew just what she was thinking.

As a criminal profiler for the FBI, Anne Marie McCall's experience had taught her that the more information you knew about a victim, the more likely you were to find the perpetrator of the crime.

"Can't help it. It's my nature." Annie waved Mara toward the kitchen. "Come on, dinner's going to get cold. Do I have to be hostess in your house?"

Mara got plates from the cupboard while Annie removed the little white boxes from the bag and arranged them in a straight row along the counter.

"Buffet is good." Mara nodded approvingly and handed her sister a plate.

They chatted through dinner, but Mara could tell her sister's attention was wandering.

"Hey, I'm talking to you." Mara waved a hand in front of Annie's face.

"Sorry."

"You're thinking about those women. The Marys."

"Yeah. Sorry. Can't help it."

"You're wondering if the FBI will be called in."
Annie nodded.

"And if you'll be assigned to the case."

"Sure."

"You know where the phone is." Mara pointed to the wall.

"Maybe I should just—"

"Go."

"And actually, I have my own phone." Annie reached in her bag for her mobile phone, then paced the small kitchen while the number rang.

Somewhere deep in FBI headquarters, the call was answered.

"This is Dr. McCall. I'd like to speak with John Mancini. Is he available?"

Damn, but didn't that just beat all?

The man spread the newspaper across the desk so that he could read the article that continued below the fold.

He shook his head, bewildered.

Unbelievable. He'd screwed up not once but twice!

He ran long, thin fingers across the top of his closely cropped head, laughing softly in spite of himself.

Good thing I don't work in law enforcement. Sloppy investigative work like this would've gotten me canned. And better still that I wasn't getting paid for the job.

Not that he'd ever done work for hire, of course, but even so . . .

What was I thinking?

He picked at his teeth with a wooden toothpick and considered his next move. He really needed to make this right.

He folded the paper and set it to one side of the desk. He'd have to think about this a little more. And he would. He'd think about it all day. But right now he had to get dressed and get to work.

He'd been lucky to find a job on his second day here, even if it was only washing dishes in a small diner on the highway. It was working out just fine. He got his meals for free on the shifts he worked and he made enough to pay for a rented room in a big old twin house in a rundown but relatively safe neighborhood in a small town close enough to his targets that he could come and go as he pleased.

Of course, he'd had only three targets in mind when he arrived.

The fact that he'd missed the mark—not once, but twice, he reminded himself yet again—would prolong his stay a little longer than he'd intended. His real target was still out there somewhere, and he had to find her—do it right this time—before he could move on.

And he'd have to be a little more cautious this time around, he knew. Surely the other M. Douglases—there had been several more listed in the local telephone book—might understandably be a bit edgy right about now. It was his own fault, of course. He'd gotten uncharacteristically lazy, first in assuming that the only Mary Douglas listed by full name, the kindly woman who lived alone on Fourth Avenue in Lyndon, was the *right* Mary Douglas. Then, to his great chagrin, hadn't he gone and *repeated* the same damned mistake? He'd gone to the first M. Douglas listed, and in spite of his having confirmed that she was in fact a Mary, she was *still* not the right woman.

Not that he hadn't enjoyed himself with either of them—the second Mary had been especially feisty—but still, it wasn't like him to be so careless.

He was just going to have to do better, that was all. Take the remaining M. Douglases in order and see what's what. Check them out thoroughly until he was certain that he had the right one. The next victim would have to be the right victim, else he'd look like an even greater fool than he already did.

He shuddered to think what a panic a third mistake could set off among the *other* M. Douglases, and though that could be amusing in its own way, well, he didn't really need the publicity, what with the inevitable horde of reporters who would flock to the area. After all, this wasn't supposed to be about *him*. This was all about someone else's fantasy.

Oh, he'd fully understood that it had all been a lark as far as the others—he thought of them as his buddies, blood brothers of a sort—were concerned. It was supposed to have been just a game, just a means of whiling away a few hours on a stormy winter day, locked in a forgotten room with two other strangers. But then the idea had just taken hold of him and clung on for dear life, and damn, but it had caught his imagination. What if he went through with it? What if he played it out? What would be the reaction of his buddies? Would they, each in their turn, pick up the challenge and continue the game? Would they not feel obligated to reciprocate? To continue on with the game, whether they wanted to or not?

And wasn't it a matter of principle? Sort of a new twist on the old saying, "an eye for an eye."

His fingers stretched and flexed as he remembered his Marys.

He smiled to himself, trying to imagine what the reaction of his buddies would be when they realized what he'd done. Shock? Horror? Pleasure? Gratitude? Amusement?

It sure would be interesting to see how it all played out in the end.

As for him, well, Curtis Alan Channing wasn't about to strike out that third time.

He snapped off the light on the desk, tucked the little notebook into the pocket of his dark jacket, and headed off to work. He wanted to be early today to give himself extra time to go through the phone book and jot down a few addresses and numbers before clocking in for his shift. He needed to set up a little surveillance schedule so he could focus on the right target. This time, there would be no *uh-oh* when he turned on the TV or opened the newspaper. There simply would be the sheer satisfaction of having completed his task and completed it well, before he moved on to the next name on the list. Which he would most certainly do in short order.

After all, his honor was at stake.

She had a perfect life—until she was marked for death. . . .

THE PRESIDENT'S DAUGHTER

by Mariah Stewart

Dina McDermott is on top of the world. Attractive and independent at thirty, she runs her own business, funded by a generous inheritance. But an explosive chain of events will soon be set into motion—and her perfect life will spin out of control.

A journalist with a fearless instinct, Simon Keller believes he's struck gold when he unearths an unsettling story about former president Graham Hayward, one that started with a secret affair and ended in tragedy. The trail leads Simon to Dina McDermott's front door—and threatens to expose a parentage that would rock the political world. Shaken to her core by a shattering truth, Dina is suddenly thrust into the crosshairs of a cold-blooded killer—and on the run of her life.

Published by Ivy Books
Available wherever books are sold

*You can run from the past,
but you can't hide. . . .*

UNTIL DARK
by Mariah Stewart

A skilled compositor for the FBI, Kendra Smith has a way with witnesses, helping them to remember crucial details about their attackers they might otherwise have forgotten. She believes her work helps to provide closure—something that has eluded her for the eleven years since her brother was kidnapped, his body never found.

Determined to put her painful past behind her, Kendra throws herself into every case one hundred percent. Now she is called in to sketch the face of a man the press is calling the Soccer Mom Killer. It's a difficult investigation made even harder by the presence of Special Agent Adam Stark, a man with whom she once had a brief, passionate affair. As the ...mber of victims continues to rise, and with ...'ler always one step ahead, Kendra will ...lethal lesson.

...lished by Ballantine Books
...able wherever books are sold